MONARCH

THE RIFT BRIDE BOOK IV

ADA DART

PAINTED BLIND
PUBLISHING
LITERARY ALCHEMY

Monarch: Book IV of The Rift Bride
© 2025 Ada Dart
ISBN: 978-1-957469-15-7

Text: Ada Dart
Book & Cover Design: M. F. Sullivan

Ada Dart Online: adadartromance.com
Painted Blind Publishing: paintedblindpublishing.com

MONARCH

TAGS

*Inspired by Bluebeard, Beauty & The Beast,
and one or two others,
The Rift Bride is a reverse harem gothic romance
about a 26-year-old protagonist.
This volume is a much faster burn
featuring age gap romance,
homicidal MMCs, jealous/possessive love,
primal play, an HEA,
and just the right amount of angst
to balance out the very steamy scenes! 18+*

TRIGGERS

*This series is by and large about VILLAINS who will get
their happy ending, so be forewarned!
Plot content can be dark and triggers include
sadism, spanking, kidnapping,
reproductive elements, multi-partner activities,
bloodplay, and some shocking twists.
Reader discretion is encouraged.*

Malin, Eleison, Glenn:
the first three jewels in the crown of my love.

Yet while Glenn has stolen away into the night with Rosina, and Malin does battle for the soul of our nation, Eleison, sweet mate of mine, cannot be everywhere I am.

Only one lover is capable of that...

And, of all four, his is the most incomprehensible love of them all.

1

How I adore the Rift! It seems unfathomable, when I consider my origins, that I had been a child plagued by headaches and terrors every time the violet aura of the Rift descended upon the Earth. By the time I was closer to thirty than twenty-five—at least, in the typical terrestrial estimation of time—my relationship with the Events and the monsters they brought could not have been more unexpected. Almost as unexpected as my relationships with the men in my life.

Men like Eleison, whose bristling borro form pranced merrily as I patrolled the grounds of the Karris estate myself, my feet bare upon the soft, damp turf. The ventil inside me yearned to be released to dash and play with him, but I had of late resisted its pleas until the middle of or even the end of a Rift Event. That sweet doe, her antlers proudly decorated with alien flowers until just about this time of autumn, was a formidable warrior with keen reflexes and a speedy gallop; but I was never wholly in control of myself when I was within her. There was always some animal impulse that dragged me down below the human heights of consciousness and into earthier realms. Perhaps ironic, given the ventil was no more from Earth than I was truly human.

That was the key to finding freedom at the descent of the Events. The ventil had liberated me considerably; her emergence freed me of the agonies with which I have already acquainted my reader. Yet those animal instincts made her skittish and made me hyper-aware of every rustling leaf or cracking twig. Every moment of her existence was imbued with the inclination to flee. It was a cringing, reactive existence, the ventil's.

Not at all like the dharmine's.

Indeed, I was not human anymore. In many ways, I felt as if I had never been human; that the human Thecla, a simple terrestrial child, was a prefiguration for my true self. Malin had been apt in his description of my feelings toward that old shell: she was at once mother and victim to me, creatrix and prey. The question of whether I was literally the same woman would never be satisfactorily solved, but, during that first year of adapting to my new state, I decided the only thing that mattered was whether I *felt* myself to be the same woman. I had the same memories, the same inclinations. In that sense, there was continuity of consciousness enough that I still considered myself Thecla Farrow of Lescaut, Matrix of Gudrune, wife of Malin Farrow, and mate of Lord Eleison of Karris.

Yet was not the conscious being in a constant state of flux? Were not the threads of Time's tapestry forever weaving together, forming all the more clearly the image envisioned by that grand artist for whom Time is mere medium? And who could say with certainty that the raw threads destined to make up a given image were the same as they would be when in their more meaningful final form?

I often found myself pondering such heady topics during Rift Events, which was by far one of the sweetest things about such episodes of fluctuating reality. My triple-nature—altered, Riftborn, and dharmine—afforded me a peculiar perspective which was, I daresay, extremely unique in the world at that time. As an altered individual, the Rift was the home of my soul—a kind of imposing cosmic mother, a nefarious womb which produced terrors unceasingly on our hapless little earth. As a dharmine, the Rift felt like an extension of my body-mind, lighting up the neurons of my brain with a truly sublime set of connections that, in the absence of my husband, relieved and invigorated me almost as much as his blood.

And, as a Riftborn, the Rift was a window into something else: into the true nature of reality, insofar as it showed itself through the specialized lens of my mind. For the Rift Events now glittered in my eyes, and the world was brilliantly textured by the warp and weft of violet and silver threads which I by then beheld effortlessly every time the Rift opened in the sky.

What did these threads mean, really? What did they signify? Though I beheld them in all things—could even reach out and pluck them as the harpist plucks her harp—I could not help but take them as mere representations of a higher, more abstract truth. Symbols, in other words, which were filtered through my perception and reconciled into a form whose meaning I could comprehend.

Yet—if that were the case, why? Did that not bear the heady

implication that something (whatever lay behind the threads? whatever created them? the Rift itself?) wished to communicate information to me, or to, at the very least, engender my own search for that information? If so, what information was I meant to look for?

What strange thoughts these were to me! Even as I relished the psychedelic corkscrews in which my giddy mind twisted each time the Rift veiled the land, I wondered endlessly whence these thoughts came. They hounded me in some ways, invading moments of peace and interrogating me in a manner that was not accusatory but rather as inquisitive as a question posed by Arthur at Horizon Clean Energy Institute. I lived in a state of constant self-assessment, philosophizing and theologizing, but it was never more evident than when I wandered through the Rift, savoring the cool evening air and marveling at the gossamer shine of the metaphysical threads highlighting the dark.

His tail wagging, Eleison stopped with a grunt and drew me from my thoughts. As my attention refocused outward, I smiled. Though the targets were distant, my eyes—so vastly improved over my inferior, nearsighted human organs!—detected what had given him pause. A family of ventil, one doe and two little fauns, crossed along the boundary where the wild forest around the property gave way to manicured grounds. It seemed so rare to see young Rift beasts that I felt somehow honored. My brow furrowed as I admired the dutiful mother, her keen awareness turned toward Eleison and me just as we became aware of her. Her ears twitching, the mother turned her head to study us, tensing at the sight of the borro beside me. Yet Eleison, kindly even in the form of an animal, (at least when I was around), generously wagged his tail and rolled down into the grass, showing, along with his belly, his generous spirit of friendship toward creatures that were rightly his prey. Though still unnerved, the mother deemed it safe to walk on, and her babies stumbled after her into the violet night.

"How beautiful they are," I murmured to Eleison, smiling in fondness until the pain—the queer envy—settled in upon my soul.

Yes! How beautiful, children. How beautiful, two children, two little fawns.

By all rights, that happy ventil, this carefree matron, should have resembled me. Indeed, I ought to have been her, myself a ventil wandering in the dark with my own two children delighting in life alongside me. Instead of pure gladness, however, the doe sparked in my heart a bitter longing and endless lament.

It had been, quite shockingly, in excess of a year since I last held my sweet Rosina in my arms. My firstborn daughter was still off somewhere, taken by her father—oh, Glenn! For all the bitterness that filled my heart when I considered that name, it was all the bitterer to think of the love I'd held for him. The love I still held for him, unfortunately, in spite of what he had done. How could I avoid it? After all, he had not taken Rosina away to be cruel or to punish me. Far from it. I knew his character too well to ascribe to him such selfish ends. No doubt, the pain he caused me was, in his eyes, a necessary evil. His priority had been rescuing his daughter (and, of course, himself) from what he considered an evil house—or one that was run by an evil man, at any rate. The enmity Glenn held for Malin wounded me, yet I could not help but see in it the steadfast heart and heroic moral compass with which my third lover navigated life. I could not condemn him for it, as these were the very traits I most loved to see manifesting in him— particularly as I possessed an altogether different alignment. As the bird finds mystery in an unfamiliar object and feels compelled to investigate it, so I found great and admirable mystery in Glenn's principles: principles which, if lightly massaged, could be reshaped in a manner benefiting myself, my husband, and our territory.

The political turn of my thoughts bringing me back to the present, I drew my nightgown a little higher than my ankles and made my steady way toward the ventil and her fawns. They barely looked at me, either sensing the kinship they had with my heart or knowing me, as a dharmine, to be a fellow Rift beast far more likely to prey upon humans than upon a simple deer. As I watched, Eleison enjoyed the cool embrace of the grass and let his tails swish about in demonstration of his joy. I pursed my lips in a kiss-like expression, and through the rumpled ribbon of my mouth, I enticed at least one of the fawns to meet me. To my pleasure, one turned its head and, after studying me for a time, gamboled cautiously toward the hand I stretched out in front of me. The precious creature's black eyes shone with innocent intrigue, turning back toward its momentarily inattentive mother before focusing on me with greater intent.

On uneasy legs, the little creature came toward me, then abruptly stopped.

When its paralysis broke and it wheeled away in fright, galloping back to the safety of its mother, I turned to assess what had frightened it. I found that Eleison was not to blame.

Those who have had the dubious honor of watching a beast emerge from the Rift tend to report that such appearances happen suddenly, almost instantly. And those who are greatly attentive have only the lightest addendum: namely, that (much as when an altered individual gives way to their beast) the Rift radiation of a given spot tends to intensify, growing into a dense cloud that takes shape and quickly clears into the form of the animal emerging from it. Yet, with my augmented sight, I noted that and more: how the thickening radiation intensified the gleaming of the threads, which bowed and twisted and took on the shape of the creature that peeled itself from the background of its violet haze, as though the beast moved through a jungle of threads with which it was simultaneously united. As the figure associated with that general shape of threads—short black fur, four great arms, a strangely undersized cranium that jutted up from broad shoulders—took on detail, I found myself too amazed to react with the urgency Eleison showed by scrambling up to set himself between me and the giganturn. However, as the towering creature, larger even than the one that Dr. Gall had released upon me in his insidious 'experiment,' stumbled out of its native habitat and into the familiar lands of ours, my senses returned to me.

"Eleison," I called to my love, whose ears twitched and flattened even as he stared, growling, at the greater beast. "Stand—blast—"

Taking note of the borro snarling up at it, the giganturn bared its teeth and unleashed a howl of pure aggression. Two of its arms beat against its chest while the other pair tore at the earth, pulling up clots of grass and soil in a malicious display meant to ward us off. Its legs sprang up and down, and with a grunt of great effort, the beast hurled a small boulder like a shot put aimed straight for my beloved.

Instinct imbued my every molecule with effortless right action in those seconds. My speed of motion made time itself seem leisurely, and I moved with such haste as to surprise myself, darting past Eleison before his body had even managed to cringe down into the grass. Muscles tensed, I met the great rock with my bare fist. The sensation registered not as pain but as mere intensity devoid of connotation, either positive or negative. Indeed, what might have been pressure enough to crush a human's hand—and the human along with it—in that moment evoked only satisfaction. The strain of the rock against the greater force of my fist quickly gave way and its form yielded to mine, shattering into pieces that all but exploded before us. As a wild array of dust and pebbles filled the air, I twisted my face away—a mistake.

By the time I looked back, the bellowing giganturn rushed through that cloud of war toward me, one great forearm swinging across my midsection with such force I felt my feet lift from the ground as I was tossed into the air.

Again, time slowed for different reasons. My ears rang like the rest of my body at the impact of the Rift ape's massive blow, and while my nervous system absorbed the shock, I flew in an arc through the air and across the lawn. The momentum of the blow still controlling me, I grimaced as I skidded and rolled what felt like twenty yards, the rotations of my body provoking nausea and causing me to bite my tongue as I tried to shout. By the time I managed to sink my fingers into the dirt and skid to a halt, Eleison had ill-advisedly leapt into the fray, his jaws clamped around the ankle of the roaring monster. Once again beating its chest, the great ape turned to address its foe.

Just then, in a blur of motion so quick even my eyes struggled to parse it, a lithe figure darted before the beast and paused to draw its attention.

My very soul leaped into my throat, my worry for Eleison forgotten as I cried out the interloper's name.

"Telemachus! What are you doing?"

By way of response, my grinning son turned to meet the ape in its rage, the distance closing between them too fast for me to stop.

Dharmine or human—young boys are really all the same when it comes to showing off for Mama.

My Telemachus has never looked more like his father than in those moments calling for great action: for instance, in hunting or in battle—but also, I should qualify, when action of the mind and soul are called for. Then, his dark intensity matches his sire's, and leaves as little doubt of his parentage as there is of his maternity in those instances when, a carefree child tending toward leisurely books and mischievous pranks, he takes after me. Though I did not give birth to him by any conventional means and indeed did not set eye upon him until he was already twelve years old, I felt as great an affinity for him as I would have for any boy carried nine months in my womb—and all the more when, springing to catch the newly acquired log the giganturn swung for him, he entered the fray wearing the wicked delight that had engrossed his father when Eleison, unaware of the nature of dharmines, fell upon him in an ill-advised battle at our vineyard estate.

This particular skirmish was far less well-matched than that one had been. Indeed, as Telemachus twisted the unwieldy staff about and hammered it into the ribs of the raging animal, I felt guilty until I remembered the threat the creature had posed to Eleison. Then my only lingering protests related to the boy's wellbeing, but even these were feeble.

"Telemachus," I called as he used the log to pole-vault atop the beast's shoulders and beat it about the head, "come down from there at once—don't you realize what time it is?"

"You should be thanking me, Mama!" While the boy rang the giganturn's proverbial bell, the ape reached up and grabbed for its assailant. Telemachus laughed on. "What would you have done without me here? Eleison might have—ack!"

Now I obeyed my instinct to spring into motion, for the desperate monster managed to snag the back of the boy's nightshirt and snatch him from its shoulders like an unruly flea. As Telemachus twisted and kicked for freedom, the giganturn snarled in his face, winding back an arm to hurl him a far longer distance than it had me.

But Eleison, praise the Lord, was nearer, and released his hold on the animal's ankle to instead sink his massive fangs into its hindquarters.

Yelping in unexpected agony, the giganturn forgot all about Telemachus, who dropped onto the soft lawn with a boyish giggle. As my fearful attempts to comfort him went unrewarded with protests, ("I'm fine, Mama—really, I promise!"), Eleison released his hold and made another snap at a similar spot; but the giganturn, howling, dashed blindly into the trees. Thundering through them, it upended a young cedar in its desperation to escape.

"Good riddance," called Telemachus, cackling with delight. "That'll teach you to push my mother around—hey!"

"'Hey' is for horses," I told him, grabbing his collar and drawing us both to our feet. "Consider yourself lucky I'm the type of parent that grabs onto your collar and not your ear, you little brat. What are you doing up from bed?"

"Aw, Mama, come on! The Rift Event is about to end, and you never let me play in them! I just wanted to come out for a little while. I swear I was planning to go home when it ended."

Somewhat dubious of this claim, I eyed the child, then peered over at Eleison. "Are you all right, dear?"

The borro barked happily, his tails wagging behind him, and I nodded in satisfaction. "Very well...Telemachus is right, you know." Eyeing the beast expectantly, I said meaningfully, "Perhaps you'd ought to come in with me, darling. I'm sure you'll be ready to collapse into bed the moment this Event ends."

Taking my meaning with a smiling flash of white teeth, Eleison led the way to the house as Telemachus pleaded, "Come on, Uncle—talk some sense into her!"

With a noise that might have been a scoff or a chuckle, the borro of my mate led on, and Telemachus sighed as he was marched back toward the house.

"You mustn't keep up with this sneaking out," I told my son, letting him hear the annoyance in my voice. "I'm sure that, while it was just you and Papa, you felt inclined to run hither and thither over all creation at all hours, since you were strangers in a strange land. But now—"

This new sigh one of anticipation of a lecture he was coming to memorize, Telemachus recited, "'Now you're the heir of Gudrune and the most valuable child in the world.' Yes," the boy went on to tersely agree as I closed my mouth to find I had been so well forecasted, "I know. But can't you see I can take care of myself?"

Despite myself, I laughed and felt quite badly about it after seeing the somewhat stricken expression on his face. All the same, I went on to assure him, "I can't deny your talent for a good fight, but it's that talent that's so dangerous to you. If you look too eagerly for fights, eventually even you will find one you just can't win."

"I promise I'll be smarter than that," he said. "Don't you think I know what I'm doing?"

"I think you're thirteen, darling." And he was, indeed— encroaching on my height more all the time and bound to surpass it in a matter of months, a fact that lent a certain comical quality to the maternal leash by which I held fast his nightshirt. "Thirteen-year-olds are especially dangerous, you see, because they begin to emulate adult appearance and manner without understanding the contents of an adult's mind."

"I understand the contents of your mind," he challenged, balefully dragging his feet somewhat to slow me down as I marched him to the house behind Eleison's lead. "For instance, I know you don't think how other people think."

Somewhat amused by this claim, I arched a brow. "Oh, yes?"

"Yes," he said with a nod. "I know your brain works differently. Papa's, too. That's why he's so good at strategy, and why he'll have this war wrapped up by winter."

Biting back a smile to hear an exact quote from Malin regurgitated by the proud child, I worked my eyebrows in mock indignation. "Now, now, you know your father's mind quite well after twelve years of living alone with him, I'd wager. But what of my mind, which you claimed to see so clearly? What makes you think I'm any different from anyone else?"

To his credit, Telemachus did not tend to make such statements from a place of kneejerk defiance, and, as I had expected, he ruminated on the question a few long seconds before producing his answer. "Because," he said, "you pray, and weave, and sometimes you just sit at the window in your workroom and stare and stare, and I can see you thinking deeply. Miss Charlotte thinks, but only when her hands are busy; otherwise, she's occupied with looking around to make sure all's in order. And I don't think she's thinking quite like you."

This was likely a valid assessment. Loosened by its rebirth in the Rift, my mind was easily set down a great many strange byways—not only by atmospheric events, but by my solitude, as well. This was doubly true when I was alone, and my thoughts helped themselves to avenues that I would have preferred to shun. For existential questions were, in themselves, a delight to meditate upon; yet, so often, they led me to ponder an absence more mysterious than that of Glenn and Rosina. An absence that ached me more than I could understand—that I dared not ruminate upon in that instant, lest my mood be soured.

"You've still not explained the contents of my mind, which you claim to know so well."

Reflecting on my redirection of the conversation's burden, Telemachus pondered this for another handful of Eleison's heartbeats before suggesting, "You're thinking about why you exist."

What an odd thing to say! And still—wasn't that the only thing any conscious being really thought about? Wasn't he right, in some sense?

"Surely," I said, "all people must ponder that question from time to time, mustn't they, darling?"

But Telemachus shook his head. "No," he said. "Or we wouldn't be living like this."

"Like what?"

In lieu of an answer, the boy turned his gaze toward the country estate, which was surrendered by the dark purple of the velvet night. I understood at once just what he meant without a single word passing his lips. For indeed—if every man and woman whose life had graced the earth had really taken the time to critically analyze the implied meaning of their own existence (or even to accept the existence of the meaning in itself!) they surely never would have been capable of creating the institutions that permitted my family and me to live as we did. If every human being investigated his own meaning and rights and respected the meaning and rights of others, some solution would have been found aside from the style of living in which the entire continent was always busily engaged. The servant class that ran our home would instead find other means of subsistence, living for pleasure and creative expression rather than financial stability. How many painters, sculptors, musicians populated the halls of this house without my even knowing it? How many themselves did not even know it? It was the same as the trouble with war, like the war in which my husband was embroiled against the hunters. For those below the upper class into which I had been elevated, their war was a lifelong battle to stave off poverty and its many blights.

"Then I suppose," I told the boy as we mounted the stairs to the porch, "we should just count ourselves grateful that the staff is much too busy to think on such things. Perhaps asking yourself questions like that will keep you from escaping out your window every time there's a tinge of Rift radiation outside…pardon me—"

The servant struggling against a doze on the other side of the front door sprang to his feet, then paled substantially to note the boy in my grip. I pushed Telemachus toward him, saying, "The

Rift Event is ending, so don't worry about your post—just see to it that Telemachus here finds his way back to bed, and don't let him negotiate his way out of it."

At the man's acknowledgement of my command, I pinched Telemachus's cheek and didn't bother hiding the grin his theatrical scowl chanced to inspire. "Sleep well, my angel," I told him as he was led away in a sulk. "We'll discuss this more before your lessons tomorrow morning…perhaps, if we use up some of your leisure time on a lecture, you'll see the value in accepting what's allocated without trying to steal more."

While Telemachus, pouting quite admirably, followed his supervisor to the elevator, I smiled down at my still-animal mate. "Shall we retire, darling?"

His tails wagged; one fang appeared but a moment, then was gone as Eleison fell into stride with me.

Oh, my Eleison, my darling! There is no doubt that each man I love holds a deeply special place in my heart, each position being secured for a unique reason. Malin and I were partners in crime in quite a literal sense; his redemption of my poverty had formed the groundwork of intense admiration and loyalty that could never fade, no matter how sordid his past. Glenn, my would-be savior, wished to inspire my repentance as much as I wished to corrupt him. The lover whose name I hardly dared think, mystical Ba'al-Din, was a guide to me in lesser emanations, but during our single act of congress, he felt in the secret chambers of my soul like something, someone, far more elemental.

And then, before any of them, there stood my Eleison, my mate and my darling—like form and shadow, like moon and stars. Oh, my Eleison: like two friends! For that was what we were, above and beyond anything else—above and beyond even the intense love we shared in those early years of our romance. As I could speak to no one else, I confided in Eleison without fear. Whatever weary thoughts, whatever future anxieties or past regrets, no matter the shame or the heartache—I could speak of it to Eleison, baring to him the full truth of my heart, which so few could withstand. Together, we were easy: so absolutely natural that, even in the center of a busy estate, when Eleison and I were in each other's company it seemed as if the entire world was nothing but the two of us.

At the top of the staircase, his nose brushed my heel, and I giggled at the sensation. Then, his lips peeling back from his teeth, Eleison turned his head and gently nipped my ankle, inspiring a little shriek of amused shock. "You brute," I cried, laughing as he nipped at the other to make me skip down the hall toward his master's apartment. "I'll leave you to sleep at the foot of your own bed, beast—oh! Cad!"

A look of delight bright in his crimson eyes, the mongrel lunged and sent me, squealing with girlish delight, on a merry chase through the upper hall of the Karris estate. Giggling every step of the way, I dashed past doors where respectable guests slept (Aleister barely counting as respectful!) and rushed along to the waiting apartment, where I tried unseriously to bar Eleison's entry by shutting the door in his face. But as strong as he was in his human form, his borro form was all the stronger, and the beast threw himself at the gap to force the door wide and burst in after me. I laughed and screamed all the way through the salon as my pursuer toyed with me, bounding after me at a pace that could easily have overtaken my human speed. Before I could make good my escape into the bedroom, however, the borro overtook me, whipping around before the open doorway to face me down with an arched back and blazing eyes. Crying out, I fell back a step—only to be met by the predator's leap. I gasped, hitting the floor with an audible thud and another laugh.

A laugh that was quickly halted by the abrupt release of vibrant Rift radiation, and the shifting of Eleison's weight and scent and entire body, his animal form melting away and tightening—elongating—into the form of a man.

"I just love playing with you, baby," he remarked in a husky tone of voice that was still so much more animal than man.

His ruby eyes flicked down to my lips and then back up to meet my gaze. Eleison grinned in a way that made my chest and face and limbs all bloom with heat, a reactive flush of some adrenal chemical rather than the effect of circulation. "You're so fun to chase… but you know what I love most of all?"

His strong jaw and the heavy eyelids beneath that dark brow already tinged with the soft gaze of sex, I watched his mouth as I begged to know, "What's that, Love?" Yes, Love: for I had come to view him as a sort of living Eros—no, Adonis, as that old idol of the Rising-and-Dying One was once called—and thereafter couldn't help but compound all my pleasure and awe and hot, vibrant feelings for him into that singularly important title. And that was before I understood what a gift he was to me!

"My favorite part," he answered, his mouth lowering toward mine, "is that you always let me catch you in the end."

"This isn't the end, darling," I smiled, and then let my smile fade as I parted my lips to receive his kisses between the murmur of my answer. "This is only the beginning."

Eleison's lips tightened against mine in an irresistible smile, and I nipped his lower lip to make him sharply inhale. There was still, in him, a new tinge of fear whenever I teased him in this way—I, a dharmine, whose bite could bring about blood poisoning in a human who couldn't afford an emergency alteration procedure, or in an aged altered whose transformations had less pronounced physical effects on their ability to heal as they shifted between their forms.

But that tension melted into trust, and Eleison responded by plunging down against me. His tongue dove against mine; our desire was an overwhelming field in which we were encompassed. His desire to ravish me was obvious. For, having returned to his human form atop me, he wore no clothes and therefore had no means to preserve the mystery. And how glad I was...as I slid my hand along his taut belly and down the dark trail of pubic hair that led to his scepter, I grasped it, and he softly grunted his pleasure. Eleison let his kisses descend my throat and bring about a flutter of intoxicating heat in the very center of my womb. I moaned at the expertise of his lips upon the slope of my sensitive neck as I ran my leisurely hand up and down his admirable length, trying not to smile too widely.

"We should call Malin," I murmured.

Eleison kissed me feverishly for a few seconds before registering my words. Between kisses that now targeted my collarbone, he asked, "What's that?"

"Well—don't you miss him?" I smiled hazily down at my mate, my smile expanding as I murmured, "I know he misses us...and we should call him, anyway, just to make sure he's all right. Oh, I'm on tenterhooks."

"Don't be. I'm sure he's fine. But you're right...I do miss him."

With a significant look, Eleison climbed to his feet and offered me his hand. I laughed in delight as he swept me up into his arms, carrying me like a captive bride to bed. Then, with a lingering look of impassioned love, he turned away to fetch my pocket watch and bring it back. After lightly tossing the device upon the pillow beside mine, my gallant climbed atop me again, studying my face while pondering, "Now...where was I? Ah—right—"

As Eleison resumed his kisses at my cleavage, turning my soft giggling into sighs of pleasure, I opened the watch's main interface and placed a call to my husband's encrypted line. While it rang through, Eleison's mouth teased over one nipple through the light fabric of my nightgown, then along the other with a hint of tongue.

"Darling," Malin crowed, answering the call. "Ah, my pretty bird—you read a weary soldier's mind. I was just pining for you. How is my lovely wife this morning? Mm—or last night, I suppose that blasted time gap. I feel all three hours between us as though they were a thousand years."

Since reuniting with me after what, to him, was a twelve-year separation, Malin was more passionately devoted to me than ever—even considering all he had done to take care of me (and my ventil) during my pregnancy. I knew, therefore, that he truly meant those words, and I pressed my hand to my aching heart as Eleison's kisses tickled along my ribs and down my stomach, intent on lower regions.

"Malin," I murmured, "oh, husband, darling—I miss you, too. How are you keeping?"

"Aside from counting the days until I can come home to you, I'm quite well...and how's Eleison?"

The question came as Eleison's confident hand pushed my nightgown higher along my leg. I sighed with pleasure, shifting my thighs apart to invite the kisses that lowered over the fabric of my panties.

"Oh, hm—he's doing a good job." A bolt of pleasure rushed through me as his practiced tongue worked through the silken fabric of my underwear, tickling along the valley of my longing to make me moan and gasp. "Yes, oh, Malin…a very good job."

"Is he? Good man…I like to make sure my pretty wife is getting what she needs while I'm away. Is he fucking you yet?"

"Not yet…for now, oh—you know how good he is with his tongue—"

"Indeed, I certainly do. Spread your legs more for him…let me listen to you cum for him, Thecla."

Moaning, my pleasure increasing in a hot circuit that rushed from my toes to my head and back down to my sex, I consented, "Yes, sir," and did as I'd been told. My legs falling sluttishly apart, I opened myself to Eleison's kisses and made no effort to hide my moans as he pushed my panties aside to let his tongue play along my clit. "Malin! Oh, husband, fuck—Eleison is so good, darling…"

"I'm so glad you're enjoying one another. Ah…I miss you, angel."

It was easy to guess what Malin was doing on the other end of the line, judging by his low, somewhat breathless tone, and the thought of him stroking himself to listen to my moans for Eleison increased the intensity of my pleasure. All the same, I played coy, imitating as best I could a normal interaction between low groans of pleasure to feel Eleison's tongue probe into my soaking channel. "I miss you, too, Malin…oh, you know I pray for you every day."

"I know you do, darling…and I see you doing such a good job caring for Gudrune in my absence. You do everything I ask. Such a good wife."

Pleased, I meant to praise his guidance of me, but instead could only gasp as Eleison's flickering tongue once more traced up to that aching bud of absolute pleasure. "Oh—"

"He really must be doing a wonderful job tonight, eh…you dirty girl, I'm sure it makes you extra wet to tease me like this."

"Oh, I'm soaked, Husband…it's too bad you're not here to feel." With a sigh of intense craving, Eleison sat up to reveal his engorged erection, ready to deliver love to me. As my mate divested me entirely of my panties and I drew my nightgown higher around my belly, Malin lamented, "It's all right, it's all right…all things are temporary, even this. I'll be home before you know it. But…this call has me thinking you really ought to come for a visit, darling."

While Eleison's heavy cockhead first kissed, then pushed along the slick valley of my arousal, I bit my lip and asked, "Where—you mean, the front?"

"Of course…good for morale—the troops', and mine—and good for you, too, to see that I have it under control."

As the flared helmet of Eleison's big, bare length slowly stretched me open to the impalement that was to follow, I groaned softly. "Oh, mm—I'm quite sure you have it under control, Husband… but I'd love to see you. Oh! Fuck—"

"Now it sounds like his cock is in you…"

My breath was strangled by the knot of pleasure in my throat as, in one smooth, deep stroke, Eleison stabbed into me. As his hips rolled into motion, I moaned and confessed, "Yes, he—he's fucking me, darling, but…is it in my tone? How did you know?"

Eleison, paying just enough attention to chuckle at that, took me by the hips to jackhammer his cock roughly into my helpless cunt. "Who could know," he teased as I groaned, my voice reverberating with his strokes. "Who could possibly guess? It's a mystery…"

While my body tightened, winding up with intense pleasure, I arched my hips to meet his thrusts and tried to focus on Malin's words. "It's in your tone, yes…but you almost never use that word casually. Not unless you're getting your pussy pounded. Ah! My hot slut, oh, Thecla… yes, come see me, I can't live without you another day."

Moaning, I clenched my teeth and let my eyes fix on Eleison's point of entry into me. How I loved to watch him fuck me! Why, Malin was certainly right… I really did only use that word in a certain situation, didn't I?

"Poor Husband! Well, you'll have to wait at least another day or two for me, since I must tour the Horizon test facility and speak with—with Arthur, as you asked in your letter—"

"Let's talk about that in person," he said warmly. "When you're here with me, and I can kiss you, and give you the long, hard dicking you deserve. I know Eleison is quite talented…but I love fucking your adorable pussy for hours and hours myself, my Thecla. You are gorgeous…so responsive…such a perfect woman."

A furrow formed between my brows at the intensity with which Eleison fucked me. I braced my heels into the muscles of his ass to keep him hard at work no matter how he abruptly decided to tease me, which was always a threat with him. "Oh, Malin—of course, of course—oh, sweet fuck, darling, he's so thick, Eleison feels just delicious—"

His cock twitched inside me at my words, and I smiled at Eleison's visceral response, letting him see the tip of a fang that had slid free due to the inundation of pleasure. Seeing this, he redoubled his efforts, enslaving me to the mounting ecstasy within. I screamed and gripped the pillow behind my head.

"It must be Rift weather out there…you're sensitive tonight, angel."

"Fuck, oh—oh, yes, just passed—"

"Too bad. I love watching what an uncontrollable little bitch in heat you become when the weather turns. Maybe the Lord will reward me for being such a dutiful husband by giving us a nice, prolonged Rift Event when you come to visit. That would benefit us in so many ways."

"Oh, ah, Malin, fuck, I'm very close—"

"It sounds like you are. That cute whine in your voice when you're about to cum is always so precious. I'm glad Eleison is there to fill your pussy with his cum when I can't be. I know that's what you love…"

"Oh yes," I gasped. "Oh yes, oh yes, Malin—Malin—oh, fuck, I love it when Eleison cums in me! Fuck—"

My toes curled and my hips arched as a wave of pleasure immolated me. In those seconds, my pussy clenched to milk Eleison's cock, drawing out every drop of semen. Groaning, Eleison pounded into me roughly through the drenching waves of bliss, then emitted a low gasp and stiffened within me. Malin, meanwhile, exhaled, his voice a murmur in my ear. "Oh, that's it, darling, take it, take every inch, ah, Daddy knows what you need…"

A second, far smaller but quicker orgasm snuck up on me at that, the word Malin particularly loved to use at choice moments. He had been, after all, my stepfather before my birth: my mother died in childbirth, leaving me an orphan in my true father's care. Between that and the evocation that brought to mind his tenderness in the first moments of my new dharmine life, Malin had a way with rhetoric. He frequently left me quaking in ecstasy—helpless and desperate to savor every inch of him.

But cruel fate! He was so far from me, separated by the civil war into which the continent had plunged with the death of the

Overseer, Parvati. The battle he fought was not the simple matter of culling Rift beasts, nor was it response to any small rebellion. Rather, it was a battle for the fate of our territory, and for every other. In the midst of the power vacuum, the Hunter's Guild had taken militaristic control of the continent's capital city of Valquist. Left unchecked, they could have gotten any old idea into their heads and, indeed, had already attempted the enforcement of new laws to expel altered and Riftborn alike from the city. It was therefore vital that Malin take matters into his own hands and make his way through those territories poised to resist him. Last I'd been given a briefing on his position, Malin's forces had been closing in on a base of operations near Rheton, a large and well-supplied town some forty miles southwest of Valquist, in the forests of Elita; it therefore stood to reason that, if he could capture Rheton and use it as a hub from which to lay siege to the capital, he could have the whole mess straightened out by winter.

And we could control the whole continent.

As the waves of pleasure passed all three of us, they ebbed back from a newly conscious appreciation of my husband's glory, which shone before me so brightly I witnessed the resplendent twinkling of those fantastical threads in mere indoor illumination, with no Rift radiation about and no effort on my part.

"I adore you, Malin," I breathed softly, letting him hear the awe in my voice as I marveled on. "Oh, my Master, my conquering warlord...how hard you work for us!"

"As if you yourself don't spend every hour and more than I used to spend managing Gudrune...what a good wife you are, Thecla."

"Hm...I love you. We love you," I corrected, glancing up to panting Eleison, who slowly extricated himself from between my legs. "And we miss you."

"Then you'll come visit?"

The idea of taking a train all the way out to Rheton—across the continent, to the front lines of a war that had been raging for over nine months—was not appealing, but I knew my husband didn't relish being there either. He often spoke of how much he'd rather be home with me. And while he enjoyed exercising his talents as a military strategist, I knew he'd trade the grueling war for the comforts of home in an instant.

"For you, Malin," I said into the watch, my heart full of love, "I would go to Hell and back. Let's see if I can't be there by Monday."

"My darling! Ah, I can't wait to see you—you make me so happy. I wonder how quickly I can wrap things up in Rheton... there must be a hotel room we can enjoy for a brief respite before word gets out and I need a more discreet location. My Thecla...my pet. The thought of holding you in my arms again is enough to get me through this war. I can't wait to see you, Wife."

My soul fluttered at his words and my voice filled with affection. "And I'll count the minutes until we're together again, Husband. Now, rest. I know tomorrow will be another challenging day for you."

"Every day at war is a challenge, but it's worth it knowing I have you to come home to."

"Exactly...good night."

As I lowered the watch, Eleison chuckled and shook his head, settling onto an elbow beside me. "You're something else, baby."

"The least I can do, I think."

"I think most women in your position would be content with sending the occasional card or letter. Maybe a package every now and then."

As I laughed, Eleison grinned, rolling away to retrieve his cigarettes from the nightstand. I playfully swatted his rear, earning a grunt of surprise and a look that spoke of unspoken promises. "You mean to tell me," I teased, "that if our positions were reversed, you wouldn't miss me enough to write more often than that?"

"No, I said if I was a woman." Lighting one of the dark little cylinders with the book of matches in his palm, Eleison raised his head to let the smoke curl out from beneath his upper lip. "If you were off to fight in a war as yourself, Thecla, baby—you know I'd be right there beside you."

And that was one of many reasons why I loved him.

Though I don't have a distinct memory of making love another time that night, it's likely we did, given our customary vigor. Either way, we wound up heavily asleep, bundled together in the center of our bed—which seemed too large without Malin.

How sweet it would be to see him! I awoke before dawn, stirred by Eleison's turning over in his sleep. Instantly, my thoughts flew to my distant husband. My soul ached, not just from his absence, but at the thought of rushing into his arms for the first time in over two months. The last time he'd visited us in Gudrune, he'd stayed for a week—a relieving and sacred time after a period of aching absence. But no absence could be as painful as the void left by his human death. When he died, it felt like my soul had died with him, and I wondered if life would ever bring me joy again.

Therefore, I could bear this time of trial bravely, especially since my heart was already occupied with thoughts of my precious, absent family.

My mind, already active so early in the day, made me want to get up and get to work rather than laze in bed. There was so much to do, and only one thing I particularly wanted to do. Therefore, as was my custom in the early hours before my political duties called, I made my way to my workroom in the Karrisregion house. Behind its shut door, I sat down to study the weaving upon my loom.

How beautiful it should have been to me! These faces peering back at me were the faces of those whom I most cherished in the world—the faces of my true family, right down to our beloved Charlotte. But, in a year of weaving, I had somehow not managed to complete it. I had tapered off into other pieces, or turned my attention for months at a stretch to nursing Gudrune in Malin's absence, or otherwise frittered away time I could have been using to complete this homage to my beloveds and our children. Yet here it sat before me, still incomplete, even though by completing it, I had once hoped to invoke its like in the temporal world. Given all the parallels between my life and my previous tapestries, in my heart there lurked a superstition that hoped I might weave my life back together. That, if I finished this piece, Glenn and Rosina would arrive on my doorstep, ready at last to receive my devotion.

Yet that very superstition prevented me from concluding the piece; for what if I finished it, and there followed nothing of the sort? What if my magical thinking proved a vain effort at propping up my battered psyche until such time as real headway was made in the investigation into Glenn?

Or until he came back to me again?

My hands limp in my lap, I gazed at the figure on the far left side of the portrait, gathered with my family, yet only on its periphery. The base shades of his hair and eyes woven with brilliant silver thread that still paled in comparison to the weft of the Rift, Dinon's image stared back, the mysterious smile upon his lips but a poor emulation of that real expression that had been so erotic and infuriating to me.

Where was he? Oh, where? He had promised he would be back, yet I had neither seen nor heard from him in a year; and in that time, I had hardly felt his presence in my thoughts. How deeply I regretted not more consciously appreciating his symbiosis with me during the period when he served as my footman! I had considered him barely an animal, a demon to revile no matter how attractive I found him.

And he had, perhaps appropriately, been dogged in his patience. Any rational man would have long ago let his affection turn to hate, but Ba'al-Dinon was not rational, and perhaps not even a man in the conventional sense—though he was certainly gifted with the anatomy of a man, as I recalled from that fragment of time before (or during?) my death. On the other side of the Rift, he had made love to me in that strange platinum grass, and kissed me on the mouth, and looked at me with a tender love surpassing even the most heartfelt of Malin's admiring gazes.

How cruel I had been! How perverse I had been, when in truth Dinon was as devoted and gentle a lover as ever Fate had devised. The thought haunted me. As I grew fixated upon this simulacra of his beautiful visage, my hand raised to caress my throat as though shielding my voice box from the memory of petty human prejudice.

"You must despise me now," I murmured to his rendering.

Not you, Thecla—never.

My shoulders jerked with the all-body start that made me sit up from my ruminations. Excitement filling me, I whirled in my seat so rapidly that I didn't realize my environment had shifted: my loom was no longer in its customary space in the workroom, but had been transported back to the silver sands of that Rift beach where I had last seen Ba'al-Dinon.

And there he stood, just three feet behind me, his silver eyes glittering as they met mine, my soul soaring upward in a great and happy flight.

"Dinon," I gasped, flinging myself in like trajectory to throw my arms around his neck and kiss his receptive mouth. Indeed, sighing, Dinon fit his gentle hands to my waist and let his eyes fall closed. At the same time, his lips parted, and he well returned every avid caress of my tongue along his. Pleasure coursing through me, I went limp in his arms, urging him down to the beach so I could push him back and lie in his arms for the slowest, sweetest session of kisses I had by then ever experienced. One hand caressing the back of my neck so his fingers could tangle in my hair, Dinon stroked his other hand up along my waist, slipping it into my robe to do nothing more than sensually pet his way along my flesh.

"Oh, Thecla," he sighed at last, twisting his lips from mine to look at me through that gaze of feline intensity, "Thecla, my beloved...it's all right."

I hadn't even realized I was on the verge of tears before he said those words. At his premature consolation, they all came spilling out, racing down my cheeks one after another to entice the caress of his thumb along my face. My eyes sliding shut, I exhaled shakily and whispered, "But when will you really be here?"

"I'm always really here...I'm always with you, Thecla."

A kind of rage fluttered up in me, for that hardly seemed true, particularly not in that moment. "Perhaps in some manner of psychic connection you are always intruding in my mind in subtle ways of which I'm unaware," I allowed, opening my eyes to regard him sternly. "But I can attest that if you are near me, you are hiding yourself from me."

"I have to," he murmured, wiping his thumb across every tear before it could reach my jaw. "If I don't hide myself from you, Thecla, you become so afraid of me...even now, I'm hiding myself."

"But I see you perfectly."

My protest elicited a thin little smile from his beautiful mouth.

"Let's not talk about that now." His voice was a low purr, especially as I took the liberty of caressing his bare chest and stomach down to the button of his trousers. Yet Dinon caught my wrists and ignored my noise of incoherent protest. Rendered helpless by his strength, I had little choice but yield to the movement of his body and suffer myself to be rolled onto my back. He pressed himself to me through the torturous barrier of those same trousers I'd tried to undo. "Thecla...I just need to see you seeing me."

"What a strange thing to say..."

"Is it?" His silver hair flowed down to brush my cheek as he bent over my face. "Isn't that what everyone wants from their lover?"

"I suppose...but, why, it's more than that, isn't it?"

"You tell me."

Feeling as though I were being somehow tested, I squirmed in his grip and recalled, "For instance, when you lay me down in that lovely field of mithrae flowers and made love to me, why—that wasn't just a mechanical act, or an experience of you appreciating me appreciating you. That was—something sacred."

"And what made it sacred, Thecla?"

"All sex is sacred," I countered, gazing up into his softly smiling face, that pool of endless beauty. "You and Malin made me see that—it took dying to understand it."

"It took initiation," Dinon corrected, supping on a few slow kisses of my mouth before raising his head again. His gaze searched my face, his entire expression written in the longing of a dreamer for his dream. "Thecla," he said after a few aching seconds, "I need you to listen to the advice I'm about to give you."

My words a whisper, I asked, "What's that?"

His eyes drinking me in so deeply I felt exposed on a level beyond that of mere nudity, Ba'al-Dinon lowered his lips to my ear. As his damp mouth, cool against my hypersensitive ridge, brushed along my flesh to incite violent goosebumps in a rush along my throat, he whispered one simple word:

"Surrender."

Moaning softly, I begged to know, "Surrender to what? To you?" While my mind raced—especially as I felt him smiling against my ear, making light of my confusion—I could come to only one other possibility. "Surely you don't mean the war, do you? Why, that's Malin's business. And he would never—"

"I love you, Thecla," Ba'al-Dinon said simply, his lips pursing against the lobe of my ear.

As they lifted away, I awoke.

Yes, blast it. Awoke on my back amid the covers of our Karris bed, with no idea how I'd gotten back there (had I even left?) and nobody with me except for sleeping Eleison.

And oh, how I ached to my very soul!

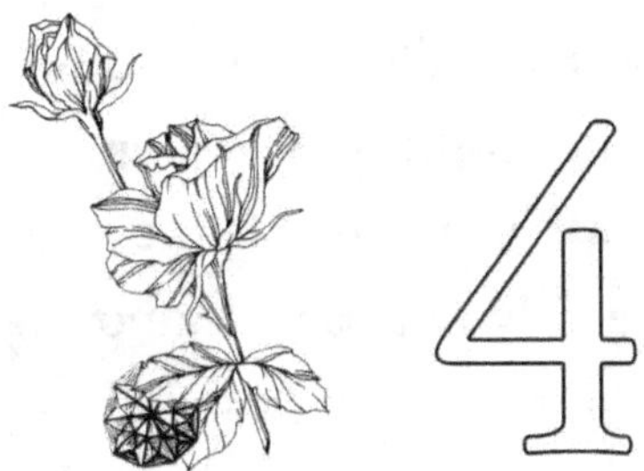

he pace with which Horizon Energy had expanded its energy program was impossible to comprehend, even for me—and I met with them or received a call from them at least once a week. In fact, their tests had reached a point necessitating the creation of another facility to complement the work of the one in Saalast. So, while my husband fought abroad, I had redirected precious funds to the construction of a new testing facility, where the research from the city could be safely implemented and iterated upon. Part of this facility's goal was to dissuade hounds from the media, especially during my visits—yet they always seemed to discover my schedule no matter what I did, and, like children disrespectful of their mother, had become increasingly impudent with Malin away at war. Though the papers were still careful to toe the line, the media had grown much less unified than in the first years of our marriage. Now, Gudrune's news was polarized; some media companies took the side of our involvement in the liberation of Valquist, while others criticized the war as an unnecessary and transparent power grab on the part of my bloodthirsty husband.

Of course, they were not wrong on that account, though the 'bloodthirsty' part was really somewhat on the nose—especially considering mine was the only blood he drank when we were at home together.

"Two completely opposing political factions," I marveled, peering out a gallery of windows through which Arthur and I could study the throng of reporters baying at the facility gates roughly half a mile down the road from the campus itself. "And still, there they both are, clamoring for our attention."

"It's a miracle they don't wind up getting into fights," Horizon's head researcher agreed with a light laugh, studying the distant crowd and then turning his curious eye upon me. "While we're on the topic, though—"

"Arthur." Smiling sweetly, I set my hand on the small of his back in a strategy plucked purely from Malin's textbook; and, as people so often did for Malin, Arthur turned automatically so our bodies were in alignment, and so I could discreetly shepherd him to the exit. "You know I would love to discuss politics with you, but surely you also know that I'm left somewhat in the dark. And whatever I do know of my husband's strategies, well—I really ought not to speak to them, even to his most trusted advisors. Not without his explicit permission."

"Of course." Somewhat embarrassed, his face faintly pinkened by a schoolboy's blush, Arthur adjusted his glasses and stammered, "Forgive me, Matrix, I didn't mean to be too forward."

"Not at all. Why, goodness knows I wouldn't mind getting

more familiar with you sometime, dear." The blood blooming in his cheeks made my mouth water, and I slipped my hand away from his back with a sighing glance toward the test chamber. "That's a topic for another day, however. For now—do you suppose there's time for a demonstration before I leave? I must confess, I'm burning with curiosity to see this thing in action."

"The new reactor is having its flagship test right now," he said, seeing my waiting expression and recognizing that I wouldn't readily accept a refusal. Deferent to his money source, he turned and nodded down the broad hall that had attracted my eye. At its end stood a tall, lead-lined door, sealed with a security panel that used the RMS network to permit entry via synced employee watches. All quite a fascinating and forward-thinking application of the RMS, I thought.

"It's already begun, but I timed it so we could probably sneak you in," said Arthur, leading me on down the hallway. "I had a feeling you'd want to see it... Right this way, Matrix."

Bless dear Arthur's heart. He was a prudent man whose apparently guileless surface yet belied a politician's soul. There was little doubt in my mind that he was the intellectual sort whose emphasis on mind left physical prowess lacking and who, no doubt, had gotten into some degree of trouble with peers who found his intellect threatening during childhood. As a result, he had learned that the best way to deal with those more physically powerful than he was to affect a light and agreeable touch. It was no small wonder that he was so well-liked by my husband. Surely, Malin saw in Arthur what I did: a shrewd man with innate wisdom and a successful future in matters of State.

Through the great metal door that yawned uneasily open before us lay the juncture of another corridor, extending left and right as well as forward. Guiding me to the right, Arthur explained, "We'll have goggles for you, but I must insist that you resist the impulse to look into the core of the operational reactor. One of my research assistants would have been permanently blind if he hadn't consented to alteration after an accident during a proof-of-concept test seven months ago."

"How frightful."

As we turned a corner, a pair of researchers hurrying down the stairs ahead of us reduced their eager conversation and ducked their heads with polite but nervous smiles. I smiled fondly back. By then, I'd grown used to the slight fear most citizens showed me. Immediately after my marriage to Malin and even after my promotion to Matrix in the wake of his temporary death, I'd still endured a vague sense of skeptical disrespect. Somehow, that had changed upon his public return. There was no telling exactly why that was the case, of course...but I had an idea or two.

At the top of the stairs was a locker room, which also consisted of a large number of showers and was ornamented by shapeless rubber suits hanging along the far wall. As I studied the tile floor, there sprang to mind vague childhood memories of a tour of a Lescaut slaughterhouse. Immediately after, there sprang memories of my father, who had comforted me in my upset, and whose image had to be pushed away. I refused to think of him. He was dead. Unaware of my internal resistance to my own mind, Arthur fetched a pair of silver-tinted goggles from a shelf above the eye wash station.

"Here you are," he said, affixing a pair of his own. "You know, Matrix—I really should apologize for not being able to offer you a demonstration sooner. You have a right to know where your money is going."

"Well, I'm so busy these days…and anyway, Arthur, dear, my husband trusts you. That's satisfactory to me. Personally, I loathe it when anyone comes to peer at my weaving over my shoulder before I've finished."

Chuckling dryly, Arthur led me on, and though I had anticipated another hallway, the doors here shot open to reveal an elevator with two buttons: up, and down. "I suppose it is somewhat similar. I remember reading that about you now, though—did you weave those tapestries in the foyer of Malin's Saalast apartment? Your Saalast apartment, I should say?"

"It's still Malin's before it's mine, but yes, I did."

While he hit the 'up' arrow and the doors slid shut again, Arthur's eyebrows worked in a manner I found vaguely theatrical. "You're being humble, Matrix… All of Gudrune is yours. Doesn't that mean you'd be capable of, oh, I don't know—walking into somebody's house and moving the furniture around?"

He laughed at his own joke after he said it, a little titter to encourage me to take his comment lightly. I laughed, too, and looked at him anew, and sighed in my heart after his charming demeanor and the way I knew he would shyly delight me if I took him.

"You know," I told him as the elevator glided to a quick stop, "I have a friend with whom I think you ought to speak. Do you have a wife?"

Arthur's blush darkened, and he stuttered, "Uh— well, you see, Matrix, my job— I—"

"So no, in other words." With a smile and a pat of his hand that had been fully internalized from the mannerisms of both Malin and our dear housekeeper, Charlotte, I told him, "I'll set you up. Just be yourself, and in a trice you'll be married to a woman happy enough to see you only on weekends."

His laughter slightly anxious, Arthur straightened his tie. "Interesting. And what is this lady's name?"

"'Kalypso.'" I assured him as we stepped out from the elevator into the observation gallery overlooking the chamber, "You'll love her—she's your exact opposite in all the right ways, and I suspect you might help settle her down somewhat. At least"—I slid on my protective glasses, though I didn't truly need them—"I would strongly advise that *someone* take that woman in hand."

"I met her at Malin's—er, at the, uh, the 'wake' at your home in Karrisregion. The Duke Montagne's sister? Seemed like a, er, uh—fascinating creature." I smiled on, withholding laughter lest he take it as being at his expense. Arthur himself took two steps forward before realizing his fluster had made him forget to put on those very goggles his earlier lecture had concerned. Clearing his throat, he slid them on over his glasses and said with a gesture forward, "I shall look forward to hearing more about this matter, Matrix. Thank you."

In the mind's eye, an observation gallery—as on, perhaps, the train trip that was looming ahead of me—typically consists of a long or even endless bank of windows designed to delight passengers with the experience of witnessing as much as possible. These windows, however, were narrowed to relative slits, accommodating two people abreast. They could be widened, but as Arthur explained while we stepped up to the most immediately obvious open window: "After the incident with the researcher I mentioned, and a few other learning experiences for our staff, we decided it was best to adopt a narrower field of vision."

And there it was, already in progress. Like a splendid little amethyst swathed in a gown of pink silk that waved and ebbed as if under the spell of some unfelt breeze.

What a strange anti-climax! To simply step up and see it, and realize there, on the glass's other side, was what my husband and I had created together: through the medium of Arthur and his team, and salvaged uranium mined from hidden deposits in Azstoria, and my dedicated defense of the dream he had nursed since his terrestrial youth, and all those many years of hard work and defense of his ambitions for the wellbeing of our society. Yet it stole my breath to know that this was the manifestation of our combined wills, and my intrigue was quite unfeigned. It pulsed and ebbed, its aura expanding to the metal edges of the circular frame in which it operated, often licking just past, like a flame. I wanted to see more, and to know more. Wanted, when I looked on this pulsating little ball of Rift radiation, to stare at it forever.

Indeed, it was a good thing that I was capable of staring at it with such impunity—I could not resist in that moment and found myself cursing the glasses I had consented to wear. "It's so small," I said, and Arthur smiled proudly.

"That's right. Exceedingly efficient. Our main bottleneck is uranium; you see, we have plenty of it, but the refining process requires something called heavy water, which is a labyrinth to acquire."

"You have a very difficult job, Arthur."

"It keeps me getting out of bed in the morning," he said with a chuckle, "and in the middle of the night. My point is that with even a small amount of enriched uranium during this testing phase, we're going to be generating power for, last I checked, seventy farms and vineyards located north and south of this site."

"Really! This little thing?"

"We're adding locations to our service all the time—complimentary, of course, as we continue through the next few phases of our research—but one of the biggest problems is electrical infrastructure. That's our second bottleneck."

"Well, Arthur, why didn't you say so? Money is tight, but if it's what you need, I can move some funds around and get some people to help you."

"Will there be men to hire?"

I gazed at the purple heart of that splendid orb, transfixed by its radiant light. Its glow was so intense after prolonged study that strange negative spaces were left in its absence, and I fancied one was in the shape of a human...or humanoid. Chiding myself for my own naïve longings for Ba'al-Dinon, I asked, "How do you mean?"

"Well, there's a bit of a labor shortage with the war, isn't there?"

I had been only half-listening, completely absorbed by the brilliant light as though I were a mere moth—no, not even a moth, but the thought of a moth. The mote of dust, returning to the fire that created it.

"Yes," I said belatedly, my attention snatched back to the conversation at hand. "Yes, I see what you're saying. Well, I'll... move some furniture around, as you said before."

What a splendid, intriguing little orb of light! What a strange longing it sparked in me. But it made sense, in a way; I was a creature of the Rift, through and through. What of me was terrestrial seemed limited to my form alone. Indeed, I felt drawn to the otherworldly light, my molecules called into the center of that vivid violet glow.

I miss you, too, Thecla.

Dinon's voice, crisp and clear in my mind, snapped me out of my reverie. What was the connection between Ba'al-Dinon and the alluring brilliance of the light?

Stepping back from the window, I flashed Arthur a winning smile. "Well," I told him, tucking a stray hair back instead of reaching for my goggles, "that is quite a fine sight. It's so good to know that even this test case is going to be put to positive use. Thank you, Arthur, dear."

"You're very welcome, Matrix. Thank *you* for visiting us today. I know your schedule is busy, but we truly appreciate your time and support."

I knew that my visits and the publicity they brought were likely just as important to them as the monetary support I could offer. Still, it was my pleasure to help. Seeing this manifestation of my husband's dream and its potential to help Gudrune filled me with joy and made me glad to be of service. And to imagine—this was what the Hunters had wanted to stop!

What they had wanted to use as an excuse, anyway, to depose my husband's line and expand the basis of the Overseer's power.

Oh, Parvati! I thought of you when, driven by Ignatius, I bade the carriage stop by the facility gates so I could address that throng of reporters. They eagerly rushed up, pushing and elbowing one another most uncivilly in an attempt to be among the lucky few to ask a question—but I ignored them all, raising my voice above their clamor to shout instead, "You may report in your papers that, aside from finding my visit to Horizon quite satisfactory, I will very shortly be visiting my husband in the front to raise troop morale and better acquaint myself with the current status of the war."

"How long will you be gone?"

"When will you be leaving?"

"Will Lord Eleison be coming with you?"

"As much as I would love to field your questions, I can reveal nothing that would bring potential threat to state welfare." That was to say, my own welfare. "Rest assured, just as soon as I am back safe and sound, you all will be among the first to know."

"Matrix Farrow, Matrix, wait—"

"Drive on," I told Ignatius, rocking with the carriage as it lurched into motion. With a hefty sigh as the reporters were quickly left behind, still uselessly shouting their unanswered queries after me, I patted my hair. "My word, they are tiresome. How does my husband keep his patience?"

"Years of practice," chuckled the guard, rolling up the window as he drove.

erhaps I was just jaded about journalists after my experience in Valquist. That abysmal city of hypocrites and liars! How I detested it—not for its own merits or lack thereof, but for the memories I held of the place. It had grown exceedingly hateful to me by the end of my visit, which the Overseer, Parvati, had orchestrated to measure me—and to try to bend me to her service by allowing the press of the Capital to publicly humiliate me with libel. By the end, when I had retreated to the sanctuary of Glenn's house, I had soured not only on the city but on Parvati...though it was not until after my husband's and my own resurrection that I considered killing her.

Perhaps I ought to have already been haunted by the Overseer's death! In truth, I was far more disturbed by that veteran who had taken a bullet from me in Valquist, and whose dharmine specter had given me a strange presentiment of the difficult season I was to endure due to Malin's deadly motorcade. Parvati's death, in my mind and in my soul, seemed resoundingly necessary. An ordained matter of natural selection. She had been weak, and I was strong, and therefore, my heart was in her hand by the end of the night of Malin's so-called wake. If I bore any guilt, it was in that I had permitted her to think me a friend until the final minute of her life.

Yet was that not a kindness in its own way, like showing a terminal animal great affection until the moment it was euthanized? Moreover, was that not a simple mirror of all Parvati had done to me in Valquist? Smiling at me from one angle and testing me from the other? I had first borne the bitterness of betrayal in our so-called friendship. All I did was return the favor.

It is easy to read these memoirs and think that every day, I became more like Malin; but the truth was that every day, I simply became more and more myself.

The transit home lasted until the afternoon, for the Horizon facility was in an isolated location, with concerns about security and the ramifications of possible accidents. Therefore, by the time I arrived home, I was drained from the trip and utterly famished. Arthur's nearness had been a trial of my will in my husband's absence, a constant wearing on my nerves. The promise of leaving in but a few days hence to see him felt like a dream. I craved him, his arms, his blood; for with his blood, I needed no other's. In my terrestrial year of dharmine existence, the pangs of hunger had lessened somewhat—at least, I was less feral with cravings than I had been in my first days of waking—yet the difference in my soul during Malin's absence was obvious.

No matter the generosity of my donor.

Before I could find him, however, I was arrested at the entrance of my home by a normally welcome sight: Charlotte, who in that instant looked almost bedraggled. Not just our housekeeper, but the former midwife who had ushered me into the world from the womb of my dying mother, beloved Charlotte was in every way a member of our family, and I had become well attuned to changes in her demeanor. In this instance, I was quite surprised to find my friend looking annoyed before I had so much as spoken a word. Usually, she endeavored to disguise her annoyance until after we had exchanged greetings.

"That boy of yours was such a nuisance this morning I confined him to his room so I could get a little work done. You must speak with him, Thecla—he won't listen to me."

Tutting, I reached forward in response to a rare sight—a stray hair just above Charlotte's ear, which I tucked back into her coiffure in echo of her maternal fussing over me. "Why, whatever's the matter with him? I know Telemachus can be a bit cheeky at times, but—"

"It's not that he's being cheeky. It's the badgering that tires me, especially when it's a matter over which I have no formal say. He's spent six straight hours begging to come with you to see his father." As my heart sank into a guilty mire at this news, Charlotte continued, "The boy did everything but threaten me to persuade you. He even offered me a bribe—a quarter of his allowance for a year if I could make it happen." I laughed despite myself, and Charlotte's mouth twitched, her eyes lowering to avoid giving into mirth. "Yes, well, I'm sure it's all very cute to hear about secondhand, but—"

"Of course, Charlotte, I understand. I'll speak with him, don't worry."

"Thank you." Her relief was palpable, her tone tinged with guilt. "Perhaps I wouldn't have been so cross if I didn't feel some sincere pity in the matter. After all, the boy spent twelve years seeing almost no one but his father. I'm sure it's hard to be separated from him now, even if it's necessary."

Indeed, it was, and for far more reasons than just the war. That thought had also crossed my mind, bringing with it grief for Telemachus, who, like all intelligent children, was deeply sensitive and introspective. It was also a valuable opportunity, as his attachment to his father might, if not tempered, prevent his development into a wholly independent young man. His time in isolation had left him wise in some ways but exceedingly innocent in others. It didn't help that he had no youths his age in Eleison's country estate. Those visiting courtiers with children formed a horseshoe around my son, either too old to come to court with their parents or too young to engage Telemachus in his transition from childish sports to the pseudo-intellectual broodings of a teenager. Even the charming daughter of the vineyard keeper, little Pauline—Telemachus's playmate while he lived in secret—was just slightly too young to relate to him now.

And even among hypothetical peers, who could truly understand him? His loneliness was real, and something that pierced my soul as, departing from Charlotte, I made my way up to the lad's room—that same suite that had begun as Eleison's abode, then been made the residence of Glenn, had now taken on new life as Telemachus's quarters. Even I, still a relatively new dharmine, could not fully appreciate what it was like to have been born into the condition: to have, from the cradle, been an apex predator in the most absolute sense of the term. Not an apex predator in the sense that mankind used to take itself to be before the advent of the Rift, but an apex predator *par excellence*, for whom no other predator—not even a giganturn—could pose true threat.

Pleased to find Charlotte had been capable of leaving the

external door unlocked—he was willing to be obedient today, if nothing else—I knocked as I entered, calling out for my son. When no answer came, I wondered if I had too quickly assessed his obedient mood, and half-expected to find his bedroom window hanging open with nary a boy to be seen. But instead, there he was, the picture of dejection, his back to me as I entered the suite's inner chamber.

"Are you napping, darling?" I asked this in an innocent tone, pretending naivety toward his mood. Turning over upon the bedspread where he lay gazing toward the window, Telemachus turned his eyes upon me with an artfully sullen expression.

"I'm sure you know I'm not—and I'm sure Charlotte's already spoken to you."

"So she did," I said, making my way to sit at his side. "Was it she who informed you of my trip?"

"I overheard her purchasing train tickets for you—must I really stay behind?"

With a tut, I opened my arms, and the boy regarded my hopeful expression quite dryly before yielding to my affection. He rolled listlessly toward me, laying his head upon my breast. Unable to maintain his despondence in the face of my affection, he released a quiet sigh of contentment as I folded him in my embrace. I rested my hand upon his head, my fingers tangling into the dark crown of his hair.

"I know you think you want to come on this trip, darling—"

"I know I do."

"—but the truth is that it will be terrifically boring and altogether too short to justify the time spent traveling. Why, your father is encamped not far from Valquist, and he plans to strike Rheton imminently. It may well be that, a mere day or two after my arrival, he'll send me home again—or be forced to by some unexpected hostile action on the part of the insurgents. Won't it cause you only more pain to see him for so brief a time, then to be parted from him again so soon?"

"That's better than not seeing him at all," Telemachus rightly observed. "And—well—Papa is the finest military strategist in the world, but—"

A pall cast over his features, Telemachus, who had raised his head to speak, rested his cheek once more upon my silent heart. "But something could still happen," the boy said, his tone soft, his consternation chastened to concern.

"Nothing bad will happen to your father." Perhaps I was too free in making this promise, given the circumstances, but the words felt true as I said them. "Anything is possible in this world. It's better to be prudent and a little concerned than to be brazen and set oneself up for disappointment. But, sweetheart, I promise you, your father is a wise man and, as you said, one of the most gifted military minds in history. He will overcome the Hunters, and he'll be home soon."

Yet Telemachus was not consoled by my predictions of the future. His present was bereft of the man we both admired, and I could only feel sympathy for the boy as he rightly pointed out, "If you truly believed that, you wouldn't feel the need to visit."

"Well..." My lips pursed as I considered how to respond. "It was he who asked me to come, not the other way around; and I suspect he has largely symbolic, political motives in mind for the trip and its utility."

"Then isn't that all the more reason I should go? What greater confidence-building measure than to let me, his heir, come to the front with him?"

There was no ambiguity about it: this was Malin's child, through and through. Telemachus had inherited from me a certain tenderness of heart, an inborn bent toward attachment and love—but from his father's lineage, he was well on his way to becoming a master statesman. The nagging and pleading of a child, in this Farrow mouth, could all too abruptly take a turn toward irrefutable rhetoric whose sudden appearance disarmed and disoriented whatever adult had unwisely let themselves be drawn into argument. Hence Charlotte's worn-down state of agitation on my arrival home: Telemachus had been at work on her, assailing her with reason, drawing back to recalculate at refusal, then battering her in a new wave of aggression. And while the circumstances of the past several years of my mid to late twenties had made me stronger—especially the circumstances surrounding the death of the Overseer and my own resurrection as dharmine—still I doubted that I was as psychologically equipped as Charlotte to withstand my son's logic.

"All the more reason for you to stay behind," I therefore said, edging with caution into this easily surrendered territory. "Can't you see how precious you are? Not only to your father and me as our beloved son, but as the continuation of your father's line?"

"Yes, I see that. But, Mama—"

Sitting up now, the lad looked down on me in an excitable way, and I knew already that I had lost the argument. The light in his eye seemed to signal a thought too excellent to deny.

"Why not let me kill a few men in one of my father's battles?"

"Good Lord in Heaven! You couldn't hold a rifle, you whelp! What on earth—"

"You know that's not true! Eleison takes me shooting all the time. And, anyway, you know I'm taller and stronger than most boys my age. I could do it. And think of the press!"

"Heavens, no. You're over-ambitious, Telemachus. Don't go courting danger, or you'll find it. You don't know what the front is like."

"And you do?" With an arch look, the boy leaned back and waved his hand toward the window. "I'm so tired of being alone. I know it's not your fault—I understand why things had to be the way they are. But I don't want to sit here any longer, reading books and hiding like some creature in a cave. I want to find out why life is worth living, Mama."

My heart ached for poor Telemachus, who had spent so long hiding with his father in the dark. How long precisely had they dwelled in the labyrinth beneath the vineyard house, accessible only through the hidden doorway in the rear of the bloody chamber kept locked at the bottom of the stairs? It had been commissioned by the dharmine of my husband and funded by the terrestrial iteration; that was to say, it had not been there when Telemachus was born. Did he retain even the haziest of memories of whatever time he must have spent as a baby in the apartments of this very Karrisregion manor? His mind was so sharp that I did not doubt it, yet I dared not ask in that moment when he was clearly on the cusp of anguish at his longing to be free and to experience what it was to exist in that freedom.

"I'm quite certain you do," I told him gently, trying to be compassionate. "But I am also certain that war is not one of the things that makes life worth living."

"If glory and valor don't make life worth living, then what does?"

"Love," I answered without hesitation.

And like that, the little spider had me in his blasted snare.

"Then let me go to him whom we both love," pleaded Telemachus, in a tone that was as much a request as a logical conclusion. "Surely you should let me go to him. I'll fight to be with someone I love, even if the only fighting I do is in my soul on seeing wounded men and listening to air raids from some bunker."

Expression grim, I rubbed my palm back and forth across my right temple, then stared at it as though hoping to find a solution written there. "You really are much too smart. When I think of who you might become by the time you reach my age, I feel a surge of fright."

"And how will I become that person without the requisite experience?"

With a frown, I asked, weaker by the sentence, "Doesn't it matter to you how worried I'll be with you out there, Telemachus? It's dangerous enough for me to go, especially given Eleison has to stay behind to run things in Gudrune."

"It doesn't seem to matter to you that *I'll* be worried." With an almost stern look, he let me sit with that weight for a sputtering second before he went on. "In fact, I think I should be more worried for you than the other way around. What about that giganturn the other night?"

Blinking rapidly, my face coloring in embarrassment, I protested, "That—I was—surprised."

"You could have really been hurt if I hadn't been there," he rightly observed, "and Eleison, too. I'm an excellent fighter, Mama; Papa has been teaching me for years, and now with shooting lessons from Eleison—I really think you'll be safer if I'm with you. Is Eleison really not coming?"

"No, we're taking Ignatius. Eleison needs to stay behind to obscure the timing of the visit."

"You just said 'we'," the scrupulous child enthused, making me groan with my own wretched failure. That slip of the lip signified a will too frail to maintain. "So you're considering it!"

"I'm—listening to your points," I confessed. "But I still don't know. I—"

"If Eleison isn't coming, then you *must* let me come with you."

"Dear, Ignatius is perfectly—"

"Please?" Telemachus's hand darted upon mine, his gaze earnest and unwavering. "I would feel so much safer," he said a little less firmly, a little more like a child in the wake of the politician's vivid emergence. Squeezing my fingers in his, he continued, "If we were all together, it would be so much better—and besides, aren't I more vulnerable when I'm left behind in Gudrune and everyone knows where to find me?"

"Well—that was part of the point of keeping the precise timeline of the trip a public secret, but—"

I ground my teeth lightly and at last relented with a hefty sigh. "Very well—but"—the boy knocked the wind out of me as he threw himself upon me for a hug—"if you sneak off—"

"I won't!"

"—or get into any trouble, you will be going with Ignatius on the first train back to Gudrune. I'll return at a leisurely pace in the company of some worthy man assigned by your father, and I will be very cross. You must promise to listen to me."

"I promise." Sitting up again, he grabbed my hands and looked into my eyes. "I promise, I swear, I'll be so good. You'll see! Oh, Mama, thank you—"

"Hm, you little scoundrel." Shaking my head, I pushed myself upright in the bed. "With a mind like yours—well. I shouldn't say."

"Say what?"

I had very nearly voiced aloud to him the thought—that, with his mind, he was bound to have either an exceedingly easy life or an exasperatingly difficult one, and each possibility made me deeply sad. Speaking such a thing aloud, however, seemed too like a curse: a burdensome opinion of which he had no need. I therefore kept it to myself and, caressing his cheek, simply said, "With a mind like yours," I told him, "I pity your future wife... and here I thought I had a difficult time winning debates with your father!"

Pleased, the boy grinned and preened and said in the manner of a dignified victor, "Don't worry, Mama...I can never win an argument with him, either. Not yet."

After six hours of travel, two hours of meetings and tours at Horizon, and a negotiation with our own young Cicero, I wandered into Eleison's apartments in the Karris house feeling like a shadow of myself. My body ached to my bones, and I found that when I got up from the boy's bedside, my joints were imbued with a fluish pain. It had been more than two days since I had consumed anything meaningful. The energy from plants such as those in our house and garden was meant to be a temporary substitute for dharmines, as my husband had observed when explaining the phenomenon to me. Indeed, their floral spirits had kept mine from wilting as utterly as theirs. But the fact remained: there was no substitute for blood, and, truthfully, there was no substitute for my husband's blood.

But, in a pinch, anyone's would do...so I was grateful when it was provided by the other man I loved most in the world.

In the master bedroom of the apartment, the room where he retreated to be at peace, I found Eleison settled back in an armchair with a book open on his knee and a lit cigarette held loosely in his right hand. The black paper made the cherry's orange glow all the more vivid, and though perhaps I should have protested his habit more strongly, I confess that the clove flavoring of his tobacco had a peculiar, sweetening effect on his blood. To my sensitive tongue, it tasted like mulled wine—albeit not as incongruous. All the more beautifully, my mate had stripped to his undershirt, a short-sleeved garment of white cotton that, owing to the slight crookedness of his neckline in that moment, gave the barest glance of the scar along his shoulder from my angle by the door.

Eleison! What a truly beautiful man. His crimson irises steadily scanned line after line, his eyelids gracefully lowered. A very statue, his sculpted lips were slightly parted, his mouth at perfect ease as though in sleep or arousal. A short shock of black hair, having disarrayed itself throughout the hours of the day, fell exquisitely upon his forehead.

How I wanted him in that instant! Yet I couldn't move; I could only stay still and look at him, absorbing him. His appearance was almost as nourishing to me as his rich, sweet blood.

It was when he turned the page that he at last noticed me. His head jerked up, and his eye leapt to the doorway. Then, his surprise relaxed, and he lowered the cigarette that had migrated into his mouth, a ring of smoke curling above him. "Thecla, baby, you're so quiet sometimes... how long were you standing there?"

"Only a moment," I told him, eyeing the book he shut and set aside. "I didn't want to interrupt."

"I'm almost done," he said with a wave of his hand, stubbing out the cigarette, too. "It's just the resolution now, really. The 'denouement', as they call it."

"That's always when I most hate to be interrupted," I reflected while sweeping to his side. I wrapped my arms around his neck and slid into his lap to enjoy a few slow, intense kisses, letting each one ease the tension of my body. "Oh... Eleison..."

"Your eyes are so silver today, baby," he murmured, his thumb massaging the purplish bruise that hunger had brought beneath my lower lid. "You'd better eat. Are you hungry?"

"Famished," I confessed, earning a frown from him.

"Why didn't you say so this morning? You can talk to me about anything, Thecla... ask me for anything."

"Oh, I know. But I don't want to—I don't know. It seems like so much to ask."

His hand, which had remained upon my face, slid down to the back of my neck and the tight arrangement of my hair. By this grip, he kept our eyes aligned as he said, "Nothing is too much to ask of me, Thecla. Not ever. I would do anything for you."

Excitement fluttered through me in a great erotic pulse of life. I whispered, "I love you, Eleison."

"I love you, Thecla," he said, gazing into my eyes as if he meant to kiss me. Instead, he gently released his dominant hold on me and let his eyes flick in the direction of the apartment's bar. "Go on, baby. Go get it."

The air around me crackling with the reverberations of a purr from deep within me, I pranced out of his lap and all but skipped across the floor in my eagerness for his donation. Eleison's chuckle followed me as he sauntered after. I hastened to the small kit that had developed for this very specific purpose—this tradition that had evolved in the absence of Malin's blood. From among the clean assortment of glasses at the bar, I removed a chalice that had come into exclusive utility for this matter. By the time I extricated it, Eleison had cornered me and within seconds had me pinned to the bar, the heat of his hard male body irresistible as he pressed into my back. I enjoyed the sensation of his growing desire pressing into my rear through the fabric of his trousers and my gown. With a shiver of pleasure as he lowered his head to kiss my neck, I reached back with my free hand, pawing at his thigh and down into his pocket in pursuit of the knife I knew he kept on his person. While rubbing his thigh—and something else—through the thinner fabric of his pocket, I enjoyed hearing my name on the low murmur of his desirous voice. I brushed something inorganic with the tip of my little finger. Soon the focus of my inquiry shifted to this handle, which I removed from his pocket while he nibbled my neck and nuzzled my ear.

"I really want to fuck you today, baby. I don't know what it is... then again, when do I not want to fuck you, if I'm being honest? Every time I look at your mouth, my cock gets hard." As he spoke, he folded me in his arms, raising one hand to cup and tease my breast through the bodice of my gown.

"Such obscenity," I playfully chided, taking his left wrist and extending his forearm so it rested over the mouth of the cup. "What a wicked tongue you have, Eleison...what would my husband say to hear you speak to me like that?"

"He'd agree," Eleison assured me with a confident grin, resting his cheek against the top of my head. "And he'd probably say something twice as crass until you were squirming, too embarrassed to admit you're aroused until at last we put our hands on you. Then, instead of the proper lady you pretend to be, you're just a cute little slut begging for our attention."

His sentence ended in a slight grunt as the blade pressed into his skin, dipping hard into his flesh and slicing it open beneath the incision of my increasingly skilled hands. "I guess I'd better watch what I say right now," he added with a husky chuckle, his lips nuzzling my hair to banish the stinging pain. "I don't want to antagonize you with that knife in your hand."

"Mind you don't, you wicked man..." While Eleison worked his fist, I lovingly caressed his inner elbow down to the edge of the wound, my eyes filled and my mouth salivating at the ensuing vision: at the beautiful ribbons of red blood that, flowing out from the slice across his forearm, splashed down into the silver chalice and stained its inner walls. Not much was required to sustain me a few days further, and the next Rift Event would likely mend him, leaving not even a trace of a scar as had been left along his deltoid by, as I understood it, the dharmine mother from whom he had defended his brother, Kyrie. This was when they were living as two penniless orphans in Karris proper, and was the means by which Eleison had found his way into Malin's service: without my husband's generosity, Kyrie certainly would have died of blood poisoning. More merciful than most would have credited, my husband had altered both brothers in exchange for their indentured servitude—a servitude ended by Malin's self-reflection while I wandered as a ventil, separated from him by my own mistakes and shame, and my own inability to forgive.

But there were no second chances when it came to blood poisoning. Once someone was altered—particularly once someone had been altered as long as Eleison had been—the effects of the dharmine's saliva in a terrestrial bloodstream could once again have disastrous consequences. Therefore, unwilling to test the limits of Eleison's healing, he and I had developed this slightly buffered method of donation…and all the same, watching his ruby blood trickle out, lapping upon itself in the open mouth of the cup like waves in the sea, I ached to affix my mouth to his wound and drink as deeply as my throat would allow. Indeed, my yearning was so intense that my fangs had extended behind my closed lips, as I felt when I accidentally pricked myself on one; shuddering at the sensation, for even pain had pleasurable notes in my form, I tore my eyes away from the lurid sight and fetched a bar towel to staunch the wound. While I applied pressure to the cut, Eleison bowed to graze his lips along the curve of my throat.

"You're getting to be a regular nurse, baby," he told me as I fished a roll of gauze from beneath the bar. "We just need to teach you how to give stitches…think of the photo op."

"And I suppose you'd be willing to let me practice on you?"

"Hell, no."

We laughed together until I turned my head to look at him. Then, the expression on his face stole the air from my lungs. When we first met, Eleison's every glance toward me had been tense with a poorly battled pain I didn't understand. How long ago it seemed by the time we stood at the bar of the Karris house together! It was almost unfathomable that Eleison and Malin should ever have been rivals, even if only tacitly. How my poor mate had struggled in those days, ached with longing for me—indeed, with a literal need for intimacy, as destabilized as he'd become by so many Rift exposures over the course of his service to Malin. But Eleison was such a good man, with a sense of honor and loyalty that was of truly rare substance. Even though it could have cost him his life, he resisted me and resisted me until at last his impulses won out. But he'd never been fully contented with our love. Not until the truth came out to Malin and Malin blessed it, seeing so much more clearly than either of us what a happy family we three could make.

Applying the bandage to Eleison's wound was a struggle of focus as the nerves along the right side of my neck grew hot and sensitive beneath the firm, sensual pressure of his tender kisses, his nibbling teeth. Even more distracting was that goblet of blood growing cold by the second, but I had become quite efficient in first aid, and by the time I had his injury bound, the contents of the goblet were still acceptably warm. Forgetting all decorum, I left the roll and the knife where they lay on the bar. My mate chuckled as I snatched up the goblet and took a greedy swig, gasping with relief as the flavor of life flooded my palate and rolled down my throat.

Oh! Ecstasy. The synapses of my brain sparked alive with a kind of music; my organs sighed and basked in it, like an arid field basking in the rain. "Careful, baby," Eleison said, his thumb sweeping a drop from my jaw, a caress that made me realize he was speaking. "Don't stain your pretty dress."

I couldn't have cared less about my dress, nor about anything but the blood and the man who had given it to me. I chugged down the entire donation, dizzy with the sense of taste and the sweetness of my lover's vital fluids. Only when the cup was empty did I tear it from my mouth, gasping, my tongue lashing across my lips as my knuckles raised to wipe away the excess that had crept between my lips and down my chin.

"There's got to be something wrong with me," Eleison said with a husky laugh. When I turned an arched brow upon him, he cupped my chin and ran his bloodstained thumb over my lip. As I gazed into his eyes, extending my tongue to lick the tip of his delicious digit, his nostrils flared.

"I shouldn't be so turned on by the sight of you covered in my blood," he explained, leaving me to laugh gently.

"Darling," I said, "it seems like a perfectly natural reaction."

His expression was dubious. "I don't know if I'd say that."

"I would." Beneath my bodice, my body warmed at the mere anticipation of the memory I was about to recount. Arms folding around Eleison's neck, my body pressing close to his strong torso, I gazed earnestly up into his features and murmured, "Why, when I tricked Malin into revealing his presence to me in the vineyard house—after his death, you know—I was frightfully excited to find myself his helpless victim, naked and defenseless, strapped to that table as an offering to his thirst."

As I spoke, my hand trailed down Eleison's stomach, then slid up his shirt to caress his flesh and tease along his belt line. Soon my hand drifted further, and he inhaled sharply as my palm fit along the rigid outline of his magnificent erection. Fondling him through his trousers, gazing into his eyes, I reminded him, "And even you… I spiral into erotic heat, sheer desperation, every time you exercise your power over me. I remember that first time you fucked me"—I clasped the zipper and drew it down while his hand slid along my back to cup and caress my ass through the fabric of my gown—"and how frightened and helpless I had been a moment before, when I thought I'd been kidnapped by some psychopathic stranger from off the streets of Saalast."

"Instead," he recalled, his fingers sinking all the more tightly against me as I guided the steel rod of his proud cock out for my admiration and our mutual pleasure, "you were kidnapped by your psychopathic mate."

"Yes…completely different, darling."

He chuckled, though the noise trailed off into a low groan

from the base of his throat as my fingers curled around his shaft. What a work of art he was... As much as I loved playing wicked spanking games with Malin, or letting Eleison fuck me while he watched, or dominating helpless Glenn, (a memory I could not avoid summoning as easily as I shunned the memory of that sweet lovemaking with Ba'al-Dinon), there was something about simply touching, admiring, and worshiping Eleison's cock that had a pure and irresistible impact on my arousal. It was a primitive, natural reaction: truly, sex as it was intended on a basic mechanical level, the hard heft of his desire making me keenly aware of all within me that was soft and empty and yearning to be not just filled, but claimed. As I savored the act of stroking his cock from tip to base, I stared into his eyes. "But you see, darling... arousal is a perfectly natural reaction to the presence of power."

"Hm...makes sense..."

"You sound so distracted." I tugged him firmly before lowering to my knees before him, giggling as I teased him. "Is something on your mind?"

"Absolutely not a thing," he assured me, his sigh ragged as I pressed my lips along his cockhead in lewdly innocent kisses I knew drove him to a state of madness. Gripping the shelves of glassware behind him, he groaned as I opened my mouth to give him a vivid view of my tongue. While I licked along the deliciously twitching shaft of his prick, he proved his focus on the present moment by seemingly forgetting all the ways he might have responded to our banter in favor of profaning my name. "Fuck, ah—Thecla—"

"Such a wicked mouth," I chided, tilting my head up to ensure he could see the tips of my fangs when I spoke. "When Malin is back, I'll see to it that he whips you...or maybe I will."

"As long as you promise to be nice to me again after," Eleison muttered, once again devolving into a low moan as I reverently guided his glans into my mouth between the treacherous peaks of my sharpened teeth. "Ah, sweetheart—"

"Better not move too much," I advised, removing my mouth from his erection long enough to speak. "I might make a mistake… before I know it, a space will have been made for your future self, and we'll have another dharmine in this house…"

Before I could engulf even his tip with my lips, however, he spoke words that thrilled my soul.

"Maybe I want that."

Joy rushed through me, though I knew better than to ascribe serious intent to what was expressed in sexual fantasy. Smiling all the same, I caressed and stroked the cock that pointed persistently toward my mouth, my eyes fixed up on his face. "Are you sure, darling? I know you have such complicated feelings on the subject."

"Yeah, well…" With a crooked sort of grin, he mugged roguishly at me while pointing out, "You and Malin make it look pretty appealing…and you said it yourself."

Though not as quick as a dharmine, Eleison had a dexterity that was to be truly admired: his hand, which had moved forward from the stabilizing shelf to stroke my brow and cheek, now roughly snatched a great palmful of my hair. I gasped, letting him drag me to my feet and push me against the bar, where he at once commenced tugging at my skirts. "I actually sort of fucking loved it when you were a little scared of me," he admitted, his voice raw as he bent forward to nip and kiss the shell of my ear. Groaning, I play-struggled in his grip, trying to squirm away from his efforts to expose me.

"Maybe I'm still a little scared of you," I moaned, my attempt to twist away from him ending as he caught me by the elbow and firmly turned my body to bend me over the bar. While one hand resumed working up my skirts and the petticoats beneath, his other hand kept tight control of my hair, forcing my upper half down against the surface of the bar.

"Nah," Eleison observed, at last reaching my knickers and slipping his hand beneath to caress my rear before tearing them away. "No, baby, you're too strong now…too confident…and that's a good thing. I love to see you confident. Your strength turns me on."

My squirming ceased when he pressed the hard, heated length of his weapon against my exposed sex.

"But"—I groaned to feel his hand brush my labia, now aware that he stroked himself against me—"I miss knowing that any time I like, I could wrestle you to the ground and fuck you senseless while I make you love every second. Yeah…that's what it is. I miss feeling you enjoying your own helplessness in comparison to me."

At last, he stabbed into me, his prick so thick and demanding that I cried out in sheer delight at the interfusion of pleasure and pain. As his proud weapon penetrated me completely, buried to the hilt within my eager cunt, I found myself too awash in pleasure to speak. He went on, one hand fitted to my hip to keep me still as he savagely worked himself within the core of my longing.

"Yeah, oh, fuck, Thecla—I miss being really rough with you, too. Baby, baby…I don't want to have to be careful with you, Thecla…oh, honey, I want to fuck you like an animal…I want to fuck you the way the borro wants to fuck you."

Groaning his name, my legs spreading and my hips arching up and back to allow him deeper penetration, I managed to gasp out the words, "Yes, yes, please—I need to be controlled by you, oh, Eleison. I need you to force me to behave—"

"I know, baby…poor Thecla…you can't help being a desperate little slut…with a body like this, you were made for it…it's natural that a woman like you should need as many cocks as she can get… but the only cock you really need is mine, isn't it…"

It was true—deeply, awe-inspiringly true. I needed Malin's love, and Glenn's forgiveness, and something from Dinon that went beyond words. But when it came to the actual mechanics of sex—to the mating act—I needed Eleison's cock on a profound physiological level. As soon as he was inside me, I was reduced to a primitive mess of animal impulses and immense longing, as though I were subject to some psychic itch that only he could scratch. It wasn't the size, though it was impressive and even intimidating. Rather, it was just—chemistry.

"Let me be the one to kill you, Eleison," I found myself saying, the words inspiring a shock of ecstasy that made him groan. "Yes, oh, please—let me ride your perfect cock and drain your blood to the last drop, and oh, when you come stumbling from the Rift to find me in pursuit of the memory of your death, I'll soothe you and give you everything you need…and as you remember yourself, as you come back to yourself, oh, Eleison—you can give me what I need, darling—"

"Thecla—"

"Let me mother you, Eleison…oh, darling, let me help you speak and think again…let me help you get your strength back, until you can treat me as roughly as I deserve…let me be the one to kill you, darling, so you can spend all eternity punishing me for it with your cock, oh— yes— yes—"

The glass bottles in the bar beneath us clinked and rattled with every hard thrust of Eleison's prick. Speech beginning to be strangled in my throat by the ecstasy, the pressure in me building,

I could utter no sound but a high set of cries that formed a sweet counterpoint to his panting: part of the thumping, rattling, slapping orchestra of bar and glass and flesh and us, the entirety of creation coordinated in the act of our lovemaking.

"When you're back," he barked gruffly in my ear, "when you're back—promise me you'll do it, Thecla."

"Oh, Eleison—"

"Promise me!"

"I'll do it! I swear, I swear—oh, darling, you'll die with your cock in me, and when you've risen again, I'll be the first person you see! Eleison! Eleison, oh, my love—"

"Thecla—"

As our pleasure reached its fulfillment, our souls and bodies bursting with mutual joy, he twisted my head to the side and kissed me—for the first time in a year, he kissed me without checking to see if my fangs were visible.

Nothing is sweeter than being trusted by someone you love.

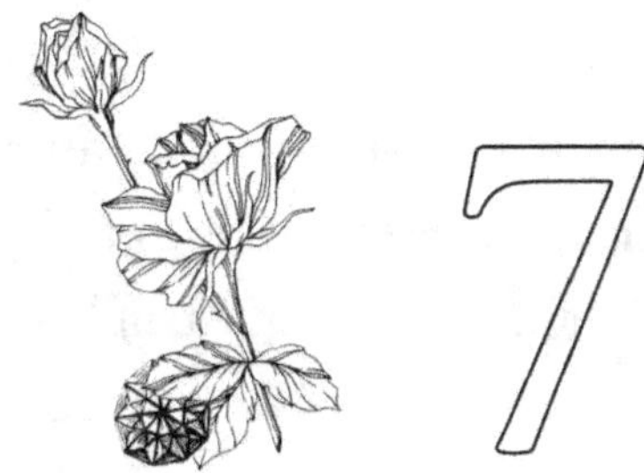

Two days later, my heart still full of love and now eagerly anticipating the love to come, we roused under cover of the early morning dark. Beneath this veil, we set out on our trip to the front. Eleison, bless him, came with us, though for him, it only meant a several-hour carriage ride to the nearest train station, a tearful goodbye, and then a long carriage ride back to the Karris house. The idea was exhausting to me, but Eleison bore it graciously; not a single complaint passed his lips as Charlotte woke us up. Not to say he didn't look quite a sight, with his eyes half-opened and his stubble unshaven…but I have always found the ruffled look quite attractive on him.

By comparison, Telemachus was evidently wide awake before Charlotte even set foot in his room. He had washed and dressed, and by the time we all at last met in the foyer, he seemed so energetic it might well have been noon on a summer's day instead of an autumn morning—and that, at the sedate hour of 3 AM. Who could blame him? I could empathize. Indeed, being freed from the fatigue and foibles of the human physiology, I found I had a much easier time waking from even the heaviest sleep, and that I needed less of it in addition. Yet—

Yet, there was a curious heaviness in my bosom as Ignatius drove Charlotte, Telemachus, Eleison, and me to the train station. Was there a Rift Event on the descent? No—I had grown increasingly sensitive to the weather, having been resurrected as a dharmine, and it seemed to me that the day would be clear, if rainy.

Perhaps it was simply the nature of the destination, I decided as my sensitive eyes made out the train station in the sluggish dawn. After all, it wasn't a light-hearted voyage to some resort town. Entering an active war zone was something I had never dreamed of, nor was it something I'd expected to do. The relative political stability of the continent during my lifetime had lulled me into a false sense of security.

Funny, in a way, considering my husband and I had been the cause of this dissolution into war!

That brought to mind the other suspected cause of my strange resistance to embarking on this journey. How much time would I really have with Malin once I arrived? A few nights of mutual comfort, perhaps a stolen hour in the middle of this day or that. And then it would be time to part again. Could the pleasure of our reunion really outweigh the grief of such immediate re-separation? I was quite skeptical… but, as I reminded myself, this visit was not ultimately for me, or even for Telemachus. It was for Malin, who was occupied by endless work and denied the comforts of home. His life was now in constant peril. The very least I could do was summon the courage to meet him as I was: to open my heart to the act of charity this visit represented.

So, as Telemachus leaped aboard the train—an arrival he marked with great astonishment, never having seen such a thing in person before—I held back just long enough to be kissed and caressed by Eleison.

"I sort of hate letting you go without me," he said, nodding to Ignatius to signal it was fine for him to enter the train car, "but at least I know you can take care of yourself...and if you can't, it seems like Telemachus can."

While I rolled my eyes at his wink, he laughed, and I kissed the corner of his mouth. "I doubt it will come to that...and hopefully any giganturns that do manifest will quickly be under Malin's sway."

That was one of the deepest comforts I had when I thought of Malin away at war: the notion that the very Rift could be leveraged to his purposes was something that I could never let myself forget. One well-timed incident of bad weather could turn the tide of battle completely against his opponents. Creatures of the Rift found Malin utterly irresistible, bowing to his will whenever he exercised it upon them, for it was in his nature as a Riftborn. As I could see those silver and violet threads of our reality, and as the old man who had heralded Eleison's existence to me could foretell true events, and as that wretched Vivian who had worked with Dr. Gall had been capable of converting altered individuals into feral states of madness in service to the Rift, so too could Malin extend his command to the minds of Rift beasts and make them tame to him and only him. The only question that remained for me was the matter of how many such animals he could possess at any given time; as a young man at war for the first time, it seemed the answer was already far more than one, for the Expansion had been largely won by these Rift-given talents of his. Now that he was a dharmine, and himself a creature of the Rift...who knew?

Eleison and I kept talking until, looking reluctant, a conductor arrived to inform me the train was momentarily to depart. While I pressed closely to him, my hands flat upon his chest, Eleison enfolded my face in his hands and pressed his mouth to mine. That deep love of his was a commanding love: one that did not just inspire submission but the immense desire to submit. I parted my lips and felt my eyes slide shut of their own behest as his tongue probed against mine, a sweet communion of possessive courtship that made me softly moan.

"I'll miss you," I murmured as he drew back, his crimson gaze heavy-lidded as he assessed my face.

"I'll miss you, too, baby," he said warmly. "But it'll only be a week or so, right?"

Nodding, I stepped back. "I'll call you every day we're on the train, but I suspect it would be unwise for me to call from the front—perhaps on Malin's encrypted line."

"We'll figure something out, Thecla. Don't miss the train now." With a chuckle and a glance over my shoulder as the locomotive vibrated to life with a great rumble and a warning whistle, Eleison raised his eyebrows. "Even the Matrix of Gudrune is no match for the punitive nature of the railway."

Laughing, I drank him in from head to toe in a brisk glance. "I'm quite sure," I said, then sprang forward, unable to resist, to kiss him once more before forcing myself away and hurrying onto the train. "I love you," I called, adding playfully, "Be good!"

"Me? Never." Eleison shot a wolfish grin, his teeth flashing with a brilliant, pleased little smile that was full of his wry humor despite our temporary parting. It was the last I saw of him then:

the conductor slid the door shut before me, leaving me standing on the stairs to the train car with a metal panel between myself and my mate.

Ugh! There was no winning. As soon as that door closed, my heart was twice as heavy. This blasted war wouldn't end quickly enough…I wanted my family together again so that my mate had no further need of Stabilify to keep himself from wildness in Rift Events, and so my husband was not forced to prey on humans for their blood, and so my daughter could be raised with mother and father both, and so that same father might learn what it was to forgive.

How morose I was! I tried to shake it off as I made my way to the same private compartment where Eleison and I spent the trip to Valquist in a haze of merriment and love. Now there was a boy awaiting me, his smile as glittering as the silver-tinted eyes that crinkled with glee to look upon me. Bouncing up from his perch on the edge of the bed, Telemachus threw himself upon me in a flurry of words, erupting so enthusiastically that I could hardly keep up.

"Thank you, thank you! Thank you for letting me come! This is amazing! Can we please see more of the train, please? I've always wanted to see one, but somehow it never occurred to me that I'd get to ride in one!"

My brow furrowed, and I momentarily forgot my own curiously negative state of mind, instead letting my son's delight soften the baleful edges of my heart. My Telly! So much of the life that I took for granted was, to him, a sublime and artful expression of human ingenuity—if not reality itself. Everything, seen through his eyes, was a detail of existence to be absorbed and made completely, deliciously conscious. It was deeply inspiring and moving in ways

I could not articulate by any means other than the sudden hug into which I drew him.

"I'm glad you're happy, darling," I told him, bending my head to kiss the top of his head. "You inspire me."

"Why?" Twisting his head up to regard me, Telemachus asked, "Aren't you happy, Mama?"

"I—"

To answer that question with too much truth was to lay an undue burden on the mind of a child, I always felt...especially when I myself could not fully articulate why I was so steeped in that joyless morass.

Thecla...you know why.

My soul stirred with excitement to feel Ba'al-Dinon's voice resonate through it so gently, so tenderly. Yet, afraid to hope for his meaningful return and still somewhat put out by the year he had spent in silence, I pushed the words aside and instead allowed their injection into my psyche to spur me into speech with Telly.

"I'm happy whenever I'm with you, and Papa, and all the rest of our family," I told him, smiling as I pinched his cheek amid his assessing frown. "My little prince, don't worry so much about your mother's feelings. She's just a bit sad to leave Uncle Eleison behind."

"So why are we?"

"Because someone close to us needs to look after Gudrune—and if Eleison isn't seen by someone somewhere during this time, everyone will know the exact period of my absence."

But his little moue of concern stubbornly lingered. "Perhaps we shouldn't tour the train, then," he said in a tone of fretful hesitation. "I don't want to cause problems for the country, or for you."

A click of my tongue against the roof of my mouth conveyed my disapproval as I ran my fingers fondly through his short locks. "Telemachus, darling, don't parent your parents. I've already told you it's quite all right to tour the train. And how could I miss the chance to experience that with you? Nothing is as sweet to me as your joy."

With only a little hesitation, Telly at last nodded. "Okay," he said, his eyes brightening with renewed hope. "May we go look around, please, if it's really not too much trouble?"

"It's perfectly fine. Come along, sweetheart." My hand upon his shoulder, I guided him back to the door of our compartment and assured him, "Let's find a conductor who can tell us lots of interesting facts about the mechanics...perhaps they'll even let you see the engine."

While Telemachus's expression all but glowed at that, I smiled and led him on, my mind turning to practical matters. Wasn't it funny how my thinking had changed? Once, all I could think of was my weaving. Now, bittersweetly enough, I hardly thought of it. My new priorities—political, social, ecological—encompassed too many aspects of my regular existence to focus easily on anything else. It was no small wonder that Malin, when I first met him, had spent so much time working. The duties of the territory stewards were duties related to maintaining life itself. If I failed to serve them, everyone on this train who hailed from Gudrune—along with their families and friends and all the properties they most treasured—would suffer needlessly. Depending on their economic condition, they might even die.

Yet, if I excelled in the task of maintaining the country, their lives could, on the other hand, be vastly improved. They might experience the kind of upward mobility that was impossible for me when I was a young girl in Lescaut—a weaver with no future but the factory loom someone else owned. All these people might flourish enough to find luxury in life and safety from Rift Events. Indeed, this very train—through which we were guided by a very kindly conductor, who was more than happy to inform Telemachus of the purpose of every nut and bolt—would someday soon be powered by the very Rift humanity so feared. With sufficient focus and dedication, Horizon and I could maintain my husband's momentum and hasten the progress that would allow us finally to harness the most reviled threat to humankind since the dawn of time. The territory could be changed.

The world could be changed.

Yet true change was never a simple matter. Metamorphosis was a painful ordeal. We had already experienced the pain of trying to develop this technology past the point of speculation and into utility. It was, arguably, among the foremost causes of the war in which we were now embroiled. Moreover, change often had a micro cost to accompany the great macroscopic price: and that change within the self was the hardest change to accomplish. Why was the heart so immovable? For instance, why was Glenn's heart (Glenn! Damn him—I had met him on this very train, met him on the way to Valquist, and he haunted my thoughts every step of the way on our tour, whether I wanted to admit it to myself or not) so stubbornly resistant to opening to Malin? Why did the hunter I adored so despise the husband who shared his home, his wealth, and his wife?

Then again—why was it that when we stepped into the dining car and I locked eyes with Josko, I found myself wondering with no small degree of seriousness how easy it would be to simply snap the man's neck?

That blasted former conductor. The one who had sold gossip garnered from Aleister to the Valquist papers. His moustache was unforgettable, as was his name—as was his betrayal against me, an indiscretion which, I suspected, was in part responsible for his sharp demotion to dining car waiter from the lofty position he had once held in the railway company. The anger passed through me in a pale wave that must have been visible in my face, for Josko, who had been smiling in his ingratiating way at a couple in a far booth, identified me with an almost comic double-take and, for his part, abruptly looked quite ashen. As he turned to flee, unaware that we were not there for breakfast, I plastered on a replica of my most winning smile and called out in enthusiastic surprise, "Why, Josko!"

Frozen on his heel, the man turned to reveal a ready-made smile of his own. "Matrix," he said in a polite but ultimately flat tone, "it's so good to see you again."

"Oh, it certainly is! You know"—I touched the elbow of the conductor giving us the tour, then smiled at my curious boy, who already knew my tone too well to mistake it for genuine friendliness—"I'm enjoying this insightful look into the mechanics of the train, but I would just love to speak with Josko over there! He did a very fine job of looking after me when I was on this train two years ago. Why don't you both go on ahead while I say hello?"

Not privy to the history of Josko's unprofessional duplicity, the conductor smiled warmly. "I forgot you used to be a conductor, Josko," he said as the now-waiter tried to disguise his reluctant stride with feigned eagerness. "Why did you ever let them transfer you here?"

"Who could say no to these tips?" he answered unflappably—a lie he had surely grown accustomed to telling, in variation, to soothe his ego and obscure the real reason for his demotion. Then, unhesitatingly offering his hand to take mine for a perfunctory kiss, he straightened up and worked his eyebrows as a substitute for actual pleased emotion.

"I'm so flattered you remember me, Matrix. I only have a moment, but why don't we catch up over here?" He gestured; the restaurant was on the upper floor of its car, with the lower devoted to the kitchen. As agreeable as ever, I nodded, waving off the conductor and my son at once.

"I'll be with you in a moment," I assured them as, reluctant, Telemachus nonetheless obediently followed his tour guide to their next stop.

And, for all intents and purposes alone with Josko, the atmosphere changed. The intensity of his smile faded ever so slightly. Josko nodded toward the stairs to which he had previously gestured—a discreet exit tucked between the fan-like leaves of a pair of potted ferns. I allowed him to lead me down the narrow stairway corridor, suitable for only one person at a time, and we paused on the landing where there was very nearly room for two.

Now, neither of us bothered smiling.

"You're probably here to—I don't know—threaten me, right? Tell me you're going to get me fired? Go on." While I quite marveled at this unexpected change in his demeanor, Josko's mustache contorted with a slight sneer. "You'd be doing me a favor. I've been in Hell ever since your husband had them transfer me to this restaurant."

Only a little taken aback to hear that, given Malin was the only person with the knowledge, motive, and power to bully the company's president into moving his own employees around, I straightened my shoulders and neck to emphasize the slight height advantage my transformation had earned me over the former conductor.

"I'm not here to threaten you, Josko."

"Then, with all due respect, *Matrix*, why are you here?"

"It seemed like a rare opportunity."

"Opportunity to what?"

A good question. I pondered it sincerely for a few seconds, shuffling through a stockpile of instinctively arising infinitives—"to harm," "to kill," "to ruin"—before finally managing to fend these off and produce a benign one.

"To understand, I suppose," I said, spreading my hands. "And to make you understand."

Beneath his mustache, his lips pressed into a thin, pale line. What I had just proposed was desperately futile; we both knew that. After all, how could Josko truly understand the humiliation he'd wrought—the damage he'd caused to me? Human nature inclined to gossip, and when his dalliance with Aleister during our last train trip had revealed some juicy pieces of gossip about my relationship with Eleison, Josko had simply done what humans do: he'd shared it. Where it crossed a line was when he decided to monetize that gossip by selling it to the Valquist tabloid that had publicly humiliated me during my visit to that pompous, self-righteous capital city of Parvati's. Yet if the city was self-righteous, Josko was self-interested. How could a self-interested person experience any meaningful degree of empathy, especially when asked to empathize with someone so far above his station that he undoubtedly felt—correctly—that I was not even human?

"I suppose that when I think of the last time on the train," I began at last, having turned the matter over for a few seconds of silent contemplation, "I'm just stung because...well, I had the impression that you were a kinder person."

Whatever Josko had expected me to say, it wasn't that. Indeed, he seemed more cut by that suggestion than he could have been by any sanctimonious lecture or tearful account. For a microsecond, his mustache twitched with the straining of his lips—the true mark of a self-interested individual. They might well—might gladly— defend themselves against insult and accusation of wrongdoing, but show them a reflection of their true selves, and they could not bear it.

Ask me how I knew, reader!

"Look," he began, but I raised a hand.

"I'm sure you'll have some fancy excuse, and I'm also sure it's not necessary. I understand greed, and impulsivity. I understand that I'm barely a real person to you, no matter how fondly you behaved toward me while you were our concierge. Trust me when I say that you aren't the only person who feels that way these days." After letting this settle upon him—and receiving no retort or denial in response—I lowered my hand and told him coldly, "But I *am* a real person, Josko. And the way you hurt me—it was very unkind."

"You're a fine one to talk of kindness," he said, backed into a corner by his conscience and lashing out in response. "Aren't you and your husband running a war nobody asked you to start?"

"The Guild started it, really."

"You mean the chapter of the Hunters' Guild located on the other side of the continent from Gudrune," Josko said, eyes blazing, his voice low but aggressive. "I'm sure your experience in Valquist has made you shy of newspapers, but you should try picking one up sometime. Most people are very unhappy that you chose to get involved in a conflict that doesn't concern you."

"Perhaps it doesn't concern us directly at this moment," I

observed, almost pleased that he had the temerity to speak his mind to me, "but with the greed and aggression of the Guild, it would doubtless be Gudrune's concern sometime over the next decade as Valquist's new rulers doggedly expanded their boundaries and overtook the continent with their hateful anti-altered, anti-Riftborn policies. But I didn't come here to defend policy decisions to you."

At this rejoinder, he shut his mouth, which had been opened to make some futile point in a useless argument. I was pleased by his silence and turned away, concluding, "I just came to tell you that, in spite of the character your actions revealed—I forgive you."

The color that enriched his face was so immediate and intense that I averted my eyes from his Adam's apple, an ornament upon his throat. Further adjusting my gaze to his starched white collar, I endeavored not to revel overlong in his humiliation. "That's all I really had to say, Josko," I assured him, making my way back up the stairs. "Thank you for taking the time to speak with me."

At a loss for any response, pithy or sincere, Josko remained behind, crushed beneath a mercy more embarrassing than justice, while I felt somehow free.

In itself, the train ride was no particularly noteworthy affair—at least not for me. Telemachus, on the other hand, might as well have been on an ancient rocket ship to the moon, he was so excited. The boy insisted on spending every second he could in the observation car, forcing Charlotte to work on her embroidery in the busy common area far longer than she would have surely otherwise preferred. When it became too crowded for her nerves and she finally succeeded in dragging him back to our compartment, I would then be regaled by reports of all the astonishing sights my Telemachus had taken in through the glass windows stretching the length of the upper deck. Why, one might have thought windmills to be sprung from God's finger, so moved was my child to behold them with his own eyes.

"My goodness, Telly—if I had known you would be so excited by things like that, I would have taken you to meet your relatives in Lescaut already. Your little cousin is still an infant and far too young to play, but I get the feeling you would love to learn about the mill where Aunt Sable lives…and perhaps Uncle Eleison could take you fishing. Wouldn't that be nice?"

That was a rather silly suggestion to make. Eleison was not, so far as I could see, a man given to any sport other than darts and billiards. Indeed, when the thought first formed in the back of my mind, it had been Telly's Uncle Glenn I imagined teaching him how to cast a line and wait patiently for the cherished tug. But, with a cold shock, I remembered that Telemachus had never met Glenn—had never even met his own sister!

Oh, Rosina. Rosina! My precious girl was nearing her third birthday. Surely, for all the time we had spent apart, I had been blotted from her memory already. To find myself on the same train where I met her father, my soul pined with profound agony. Didn't he understand a girl needed her mother, and that a mother needed her child? The same man that had been so defeated upon first discovering her—for her existence proved I could not, by hook or crook, be torn from the bosom of my household—had whisked her away in an act of desperation.

Yes. He was desperate. I had to remember that. It was why my meeting with Josko had been so important to me. I commanded myself to keep perspective; to practice forgiveness and compassion whenever I could, so that when I did eventually find Glenn, I would be prepared to offer more of that mercy. For the only alternative to mercy was justice: and to the mother who had her child wrested from her heart, the only justice suitable would have been an end to Glenn's life.

I didn't want that. Already, I was a killer twice over, and nearly a third time after my conflict with Winston Garland, which narrowly ended in his escape rather than his death in the Karrisregion house following Malin's funeral wake. But, more than any trouble of conscience, (which was, I should say, but mild), I wished to preserve Glenn's life because I still carefully nursed the hope that, someday, he might forgive me, too. Someday, his heart would soften toward me, and he would love me back not as he wished I was or as he pretended I was, but as I truly was.

Yet, looking back, I now realize I still did not comprehend my true nature. Indeed, I had no hope of that until it was revealed to me by something outside myself.

"Looking pensive this evening, Ma'am."

Stirred from my thoughts near the window in the parlor of our car, a comfortable nook of chairs and sofas arranged by a set of windows on the first floor, I lowered my book and smiled over at Ignatius while he checked in on me wellbeing. How truly fond I was of him! He was a kind man. Anyone could tell from the first conversation. Though he was tall and broad—so broad he had to turn slightly, I swear, to fit his frame through the narrow doorways of the train—and this scale contributed much to his prowess as a security guard, he was, in truth, a deeply gentle soul, witty and kind.

"Just pondering over matters in which I have dreadfully little control," I confessed with a laugh. "You never seem to brood the way my spouses and I do, Ignatius."

"What's the point?" With a spreading of his great hands and a pointed shrug, Ignatius took my gesture to the armchair across from my sofa with a smile and a nod. Hefting himself down into the cushions, then folding his hands—beautiful, broad hands, whose dark backs offset pink palms that did somewhat more to reveal his age than his frequently smiling face—my guard for the journey said, "If there's nothing you can do about a situation, then there's nothing you can do. You know what I mean?"

"I suppose I do." I sighed. "Though a person in my situation doesn't exactly care to admit when they don't have full control over their circumstances."

"If I may be casual, since we're talking like this, I think that's pride talking."

"I suppose it is...but pride is natural and good. It drives ambition."

"And breeds entitlement," Ignatius rightly pointed out, blanching my cheeks somewhat with this undeniable truth. Checking my features to ensure he had not overstepped with his advisement, he folded his hands between his knees and leaned forward, elbows on his thighs, eyes following the whipping scenery of the Azstorian desert rushing past the window in the deep golden dusk. "Pride is a dangerous thing," he reflected. "I can see the appeal. I can see it, and I'm not saying a person should put themselves down as an alternative. But pride gets in the way of some of the best, most important parts of life. It's like a pair of sunglasses"—he patted the pair in his pocket—"that you forget you're wearing. Pride keeps you from looking at yourself the way you really need to. It keeps a person from realizing they need to change. Sometimes, it even keeps people from asking for help—no matter how awful the circumstances or how easy help may be to attain."

My lips pursed as I was convicted by these words, and I had the strange impression that it was not just Ignatius who spoke to me then, but some deeper part of him. Some fundamental essence of his heart. "Pride is hateful, too," he observed. "Not just toward others, but toward the self. When the reality of who you are doesn't conform to the expectations of your proud heart—well, that can bring about a lot of ugliness. We hate ourselves when we experience that kind of dissonance, because we wonder why we can't measure up to our own basic expectations...but we don't realize that these expectations aren't our own, nor are they basic; they're the expectations of pride."

He was really so right. I was humiliated by the effortless way he held this mirror before me, and I subsequently realized that this sense of humiliation was itself rooted in the prideful nature I had cultivated since leaving Lescaut. For the briefest flash, I saw the humble girl I used to be: unused to wealth, uncomfortable with courters, feeling undeserving of the love and status I very quickly attained.

And, strangely, I envied her.

Tongue darting across my lips, I forced myself to ask, "Well— considering all this...how does one adopt a posture of humility, do you suppose?"

"Maybe you could start by remembering that all that exists is where we're at right now," he suggested, rubbing his jaw as he reflected. "I think that's what pride does, ultimately. It lets you lie to yourself about what is and isn't real, and that's what brings about that dissonance I mentioned before. Pride is always making plans, analyzing the past, concocting fantasy scenarios to flatter itself. It almost never looks at what it's doing right now." As I cast a reflexive glance at the book in my hand, he added, "But if you really want to adopt humility, Ma'am, I suppose I'd just say...it always helps to remember that nobody, not a person on Earth, is equipped to live life on their own. Even the hermit that runs away to the woods is doing that on the backs of centuries of human beings who made that decision a desirable possibility or equipped him with the knowledge to survive that situation. This train taking us to see your husband and all the people on it; your husband, himself; your son, Miss Charlotte, me." His hand flattening against his heart, Ignatius said, "Every second of life is a collaborative effort on the part of all mankind, living and dead and yet to be born."

"What a beautiful mind you have, Ignatius."

Chuckling as he rose, Ignatius lowered his head, saying as he did, "More collaboration, Ma'am. I do a lot of reading while I'm waiting in the carriage or standing outside your husband's meetings. Are you comfortable if I turn in for the night?"

"Yes, of course, that's just fine."

"All right, Ma'am. Have a good night, now... I hope that whatever is bothering you gets left behind here in Azstoria and doesn't follow you all the way to Rheton."

I smiled after him, amazed at the fullness of my heart even as the humiliation of my pride still stung. Yet was not the root of humiliation itself humility? Was this burning embarrassment not the first step in true chastening, just as the doctor's first step in healing was so often the stinging antiseptic that cleared the sullied wound? I reclined back in the sofa, ruminating on this, and suddenly felt altogether estranged from myself.

It occurred to me that, somewhere along the line, I had adopted a posture. Over the course of the last four years, a facade had steadily developed around me; and though I had not been fully conscious of it at any given time, it was the cumulative effect of a long series of small changes. Small steps away from myself as I had been, and into myself as I was. Though it was safe to say that all life was a state of flux, and nothing could ever stay the same—not even the dead in their vaults—I had perhaps changed more than I intended. It was not so much that Malin's love had changed me, as I had thought prior to my conversation with Ignatius; rather, I had changed myself to conform to Malin. In many ways, those changes were wonderful. My husband had opened my heart to pleasures and intimacies I had never imagined when I lived in my quaint little village in the Gudrune countryside. Because of him, I had traveled places and eaten foods I never otherwise would have experienced. I had Eleison, and my children—even if one was absent. Immortality was also mine, and of course, my husband's eternal devotion.

But in my enthusiasm to please him, and my desire to be loyal, I had compromised my own values. For what purpose had I served him in Parvati's death? Could Malin not have simply done the deed himself—in the darkness of night, his return from the unknown still unannounced—and made the task not just easier but cleaner for me and my soul? Instead, like a housecat proud to be her master's, I had killed a mouse and dropped it on his pillow as an unnecessary offering. Malin knew I was devoted to him, but in my pride, I'd wanted to prove it and receive his praise.

And now, my hands would forever be stained. There would be no untying those strings; no opportunity to revise that corner of spacetime's complicated tapestry. Overseer Parvati and I were linked forever in a union as intimate as that which linked a mother and her child. For it was that mother's work I finished when I held her hot heart in my palm: the trip from womb to grave, ended by me.

I still hesitated to admit—even in the silence of my mind— that I felt anything like guilt concerning the Overseer's death and all the disaster it caused...but I abruptly found myself wondering what might have happened had I not been so involved, even if the difference was apparent only to my Lord.

As I turned these thoughts over in my mind, my eyes slid shut, wearied by the early hour of our rising and by my lack of sustenance. I began to doze. Eleison's blood had been delicious and had given me the burst of energy I needed to make it to Rheton without incident of violence. Yet the contents of that small goblet had been a far cry from the amount of blood my body craved when I was not drinking from my husband. How much more I needed!

And then, I was thinking of another man I needed.

Another being, anyway.

The entrance of Ba'al-Dinon into my dreams has never been properly depicted in my efforts to write this memoir. One must call them 'dreams', because there is no other means by which to describe them; and whatever faculty of imagination it is that produces dreams in us is certainly their medium.

But Dinon's appearances were so much more than mere subconscious pieces of my mind, moving information from consciousness to unconsciousness and back again, as I have heard dreams more or less are. For when we are with a friend, we are synchronized together—us and them. All matter is made of energy; therefore, the energy they and we are made of is, if not shared, then at least somehow in resonance when we are in the same room. Imagined scenes and people may captivate and intrigue the mind, but are they not reflecting parts of us or, at the very least, forming a projection of the lover we wish to soothe our own innermost needs? Whereas an external friend, an 'other', leaves their energy with me by their speech and presence, and I frequently find myself spending days attuned to their manner of thought, taste, even posture. Moreover, there is just an indescribable feeling of presence that lingers on, either with the freshness of memory or with some harmonization of living souls.

So it was with Ba'al-Dinon's appearances to me in sleep. His presence was a shadow cast over the entire tableau—or perhaps I would be better off saying a light. When I responded to his presence in dreams, I was not responding to a dream. I was responding to him: to Dinon, the man.

To Dinon, whatever he was.

And how truly beautiful he was, my mysterious lover! How magnificent, a shining star of a humanoid, his alabaster flesh and enchanting silver eyes so utterly transfixing my gaze that I did not realize he stood before me naked. Not even that dark cloak with which he was so often adorned could be spotted. With his silvery white hair streaming down his back, every inch of his artfully sculpted body was on display to me. I yearned to touch him: to feel the strength of his arms as he held me to his heart and buried all his love deep within me.

"Don't be frightened, Thecla."

My mouth formed the words as he spoke, though I didn't understand this until I raised my arm to touch his chest and watched him complete the gesture I had willed.

"Just relax. I'm with you every step of the way."

Only when I tried to caress his throat instead, and his hand slid up his neck, did I realize what I was seeing: that my consciousness had been situated most intimately within his, fair Dinon's. I was not him, but I was somehow a part of him, or identified with him, or perhaps imminently within him in some incomprehensible way. A smile tugged at the corners of his lips as he regarded me through his own reflection, seeing deeply into me without needing the least trace of my bodily presence.

"I can't promise you it's going to be easy," he said. "There's much at stake for you."

One hand raised to caress his own cheek, as he might, with the edges of his knuckles, caress mine. I felt the sensation as though it were my own, as his left hand trail back down the planes of his chiseled stomach.

"But, Thecla, just remember...this is all for you."

His lips parted as his hand descended further, and I endured a shock of visceral pleasure. "I love you," he murmured. "This is how intimate we are, Thecla. And I know you don't yet understand... but that's all right. I'll help you."

Finally, he raised his hands, slowly pressing his palms to the looking glass before him. Gazing into me—himself—Dinon murmured to me the message he had imparted before.

"You just have to surrender," he said, his voice warm and tender with understanding. "Surrender, and let me take care of the rest."

How I longed to demand what he meant! How shocked I was at myself that my impulse was still to command him, as it had been while he was a willing servant to me. Though I did not then know all I know now—all that Ba'al-Dinon permits me to know now, at any rate—I had nevertheless become aware that Dinon's depths were fathomless, and his nature more powerful than he even permitted me to see. How strange he was. With his talents beyond explanation, as though he himself were blessed with every charism the Rift had to offer its Riftborn children, Dinon's nature may not have been evident to me, but it was obvious that his powers were great, and that I was privileged to experience his love. It was embarrassing, therefore, that I should still dare to command him. But he only smiled on, patient with me beyond all reason, and, in his heart—in a strange way that was itself not always congruent with the human anticipation of such an expression—kind.

"I love you," he said. "Remember, even if you can't feel me—I love you."

The grinding halt of the train was what awoke me from my rest; but there was his presence with me, as if he had just been by my side.

As though he was still there.

9

How I longed to bask in the knowledge that Dinon had been there with me, through whatever vehicle he moved when not bound by matter as you and I! Yet there was no time for such luxuries. The speakers built into discreet corners of the refined train's aesthetic design crackled with an ominous announcement.

"Ladies and gentlemen," the speaker commenced, "we regret to inform you that our train is being forced to stop due to reports of inclement weather. For passenger safety, shutters will be lowered now. We ask that you remain in your cars and do not attempt to cross between them at this time."

Rubbing my fingers back and forth along the conjunction of my brow and the bridge of my nose, I remonstrated with myself for falling asleep even as I nursed gratitude for Dinon's manifestation.

Then Ignatius's meditations on pride returned to me, and as I considered my displeasure with my exhaustion in that new light, I rose to my feet and made my somewhat unsteady, tired way to the second floor of the car.

And that was when the sight of Charlotte, emerging from my compartment with an ashen pallor, awoke me all too completely.

"Is something the matter?" I asked, earning a look of annoyance that was clearly directed inward.

"I was hoping against hope to find your son with you," Charlotte lamented. "It seems he's taken advantage of your time downstairs to further explore the train."

I tutted and shook my head fondly as I slipped past her into my compartment. "He's no doubt parked himself in the observation car again, or the library. Well, no matter...I'm sure a concierge can bring him back."

Sighing, I settled into the chair at the small table where, my first time on the train, Josko had served me champagne and an array of treats alongside fresh-cut flowers. This trip seemed so much less glamorous, especially with the turn in the weather! I pressed the call button built into the small silver panel on the wall, adjuring Charlotte at my elbow, "Let down my hair, would you, darling? I'm quite ready for bed."

"You look awfully pale this evening, Thecla."

"Mm, just a little fatigued. Traveling is difficult in my... condition." As Charlotte stood behind me, plucking pin after pin from my hair, I endeavored to turn my focus away from her scent and the radiant warmth of her body. "It would be much easier with Malin here...oh, Charlotte."

His name passing my lips snatched my soul entirely, an ache for my beloved husband grieving me even in my anticipation. "When will this blasted war be over?" I asked aloud. "My husband! I want him home. This visit will be like a cruel tease."

"I'm quite sure that Master Farrow never would have suggested your visit if he didn't think the situation was under control. Perhaps it signals a change."

"Perhaps. Yes, perhaps. One doesn't want to get one's hopes up, of course..."

I paused, listening for movement in the hall. Hearing none, I hit the button again, unsure if I had struck it successfully the first time.

"Hope is all we have, don't you suppose?"

For a woman who was normally so wry, Charlotte's comment caught me off-guard. In same second, however, I found myself considering that her vast inner life surely had to be stocked with an equally vast cellar of some kind of hope. Unmarried, with no family of her own except that of the estate to which she had cleaved as housekeeper, she nevertheless held her station with no outward trace of loneliness, boredom, or resentment. No doubt part of that was due to her practicality; but far more of it, I had to think, owed to some deep sense of faith in something better.

"Surely," I said all the same, "hope isn't all we have. What of action?"

"We *take* action, Matrix," reckoned Charlotte wisely, fluffing out a few locks of my hair and taking away the handful of pins to replace in a jewel box on the small vanity. "We don't have it. And, at any rate, why do we act if not in hopes that our actions will be worthwhile?"

"You and Ignatius are both in quite philosophical moods tonight, aren't you?"

"Or perhaps it's you, bringing it out of us without meaning to. And where is that blasted concierge?"

"I don't know! I've hit the button twice already. Is it being interfered with, I wonder?"

"By the storm, you mean?" Charlotte shook her head and, in pure muscle memory, unconsciously locked the door. "I suppose it's that, or everyone is tied up with other passengers at the moment. Here—let's take the chance to get you into your night clothes. If no one has shown up by then, I'll go send Ignatius to fetch someone."

That did indeed prove necessary. Fifteen minutes passed without a word, and by the time I was in my dressing gown and slippers, I was beginning to endure a keen but formless sense of anxiety. What, exactly, was worrying me? After all—the boy's point, that he could take care of himself during a Rift Event, was valid. He, like me, was a creature of the Rift, and really ought to thrive in it after living an entire lifetime as a dharmine.

But his absence gnawed at me all the same, and I returned to the small tea table while Charlotte assured me, "I'll be right back." There, alone, I sat, worrying the thumb and forefinger of my right hand while my eyes absorbed an unfocused space across from me. Once upon a time, I would have been frightened even before Charlotte stepped from the compartment to leave me alone. Now, I was just beleaguered and focused inordinately on the notion that perhaps a train powered by the Rift itself would be able to plow through the foul weather faster, instead of stopping because of some sort of electronic sensitivity.

Oh, the future was so grand! I was always waiting for it in those days, as though life were a house, and the future, a room adjacent to the one in which I lived. Walking into 'the future' was as neat and simple as crossing some threshold. Then, there I would be, uniquely positioned within some brave new world, having just come from the present that was now the past.

Yet wasn't it strange sometimes to become consciously aware that I and all my fellows, young and old and paired in age, lived within the same historical context! Did we not all advance forward in time at the same rate, the rich and the poor alike? Could even the most exorbitant use of resources hasten what could only be accomplished one day at a time? I knew, of course, that this was not the case, but some naive, child-like part of me felt that if we simply threw enough money at a problem, it would go away. With enough money, Horizon's research would be 'complete', and all lives would be universally improved overnight. With enough money, the war would end, and my conquering hero would return home.

With enough money, everyone would see the real me.

How right Ignatius was! How prideful and foolish I could be. Yet I couldn't cease my longing to be seen as I felt I really was, and not as other people saw me—or even as I saw myself. I liked to criticize Glenn for his perspective on a Thecla who wasn't really there, but even Malin and Eleison each had specific visions of me.

Yet there was one who saw all of me, loved all of me—even the parts of myself I couldn't see. Only Dinon had that sum total view of me. And when I thought of how he saw me, I felt as though he saw too much of me, exposing my soul completely, and the idea made me tremble in my seat.

"I can't seem to make up my mind," I murmured, leaning back in the chair and gazing reflexively toward the shuttered window. The metal panel that had slid into place over the window was well sealed, so remarkably flush with the structure of the train that I doubt even an alien bug from that other world could have managed to wiggle in. The train was about as safe as one could be while away from home during a Rift Event...so why was I, a being perfectly suited for this weather, still tight with anxiety? Indeed, anxiety that grew by the minute!

Something was wrong, though I couldn't put my finger on it. Charlotte had been gone too long; I had not heard her speaking to Ignatius in the hall outside the compartment. I frowned, concentrating, my ears straining with the intensity with which I listened to the silence. There had been no noise to indicate any kind of peril, of course...

...But that very thought made my blood run cold.

Sitting upright, I assessed the sill around the window and discovered the lever to control the emergency shutters. Owing to some precautionary mechanism to prevent passenger interference but for the direst of emergencies, it was stuck, but I was not to be deterred. Gritting my teeth, I braced my palm against the bottom edge of the lever and pushed up with the heel, marveling at the sensation of every muscle in my body coordinating to improve the efficiency of the motion. The pressure grew intense; the handle bit into my skin hard enough to bruise. Then, at last, with a feeling like the sudden loosening of a tooth and a little warning chime, the handle gave way beneath my dharmine strength and the shutter of my compartment rapidly withdrew.

And now I could see for certain what I had felt as I sat listening to the silence of the train car.

There was no Rift Event.

My flesh crawling with goosebumps at the sight of the clear night and its many stars, I leapt from my seat so quickly that I knocked over the chair. It lay there, an innocent victim of my urgency as, clad in my nightgown, I burst from the compartment and into the empty corridor.

Three steps away from my door, the tang of fresh blood

came upon me so strongly that my mouth watered and my fangs expanded before I even knew what I was sensing. At once overwhelmed by a bevy of conflicting intentions—hunger, longing, panic—I hurried in pursuit of the intoxicating aroma, my heart full of urgent prayers. Not Charlotte—I couldn't bear it if it was Charlotte—

Not that Ignatius was much better.

His body, dead in the corner of his somewhat more utilitarian sleeper compartment, was the first thing I saw even before I took stock of the men who appeared to be in the midst of an argument—even before I saw that one of them had Charlotte. Her mouth was stuffed with a rag, and her eyes, usually so full of spark and life, were ringed with uncharacteristic terror.

And still, no sign of the boy.

Rage filled my heart even as the men realized they had been interrupted. In those seconds, time seemed to slow, and I made quick calculations about these bloodstained brutes. In mere seconds, I had them pegged for what they were. One does not generally like to stereotype other sapient beings, whether based on ethnicity or social group or any other factor...but hunters always have a type: the disheveled look of men who are no more fit for society than the animals they cull. It was in their eyes, wild and untamed, and in the unkempt way they carried themselves.

It was in the way their faces twisted with hatred at the sight of me, and the hands that immediately went to the knives with which they had silently slaughtered one of my friends and now subdued the other.

I moved quickly, without thought or conscious intention. To my right was a heavy flower vase that lent cheer to Ignatius's quarters—now it lent me strength as I turned at the waist, snatching it from its pedestal and hurling it straight into the head of the man who had a hold on Charlotte. It shattered against his skull and he stumbled back into the wall before collapsing in a heap. His grip relaxed, and my housekeeper scrambled away while I advanced on the second aggressor. He made a wide arc with the knife, intending to plunge it into my throat, but I caught his wrist and tore the weapon from his hand.

"You're here for me," I demanded—a question that came out sounding more like an accusation. Even as I wrenched the man's arm hard enough to make him bare his teeth in pain, he scoffed in derision.

"What was your first clue?"

Without batting an eye, I bared my own teeth, then shoved his head aside and sank them into his filthy swine flesh.

But don't most humans love the taste of swine! So it is with me. The effect was immediate, and it made me realize how paltry was our solution of Eleison's donations. As the hunter's blood surged into my mouth, his struggles only speeding the pressure with which it pumped down my throat, I gripped him tighter and blithely knocked away the gun he tried to fumble from his belt. Every swallow I took of that great, gushing font made him weaker—made me stronger, more alive, my mind rushing with plans as my tired synapses refreshed their connections.

"Matrix," came Charlotte's urgent cry. This successfully diverted my attention for the seconds it required to take note of the concussed man, who had regained his hold of his knife and his senses. Without putting down the means by which I slaked my thirst, I drew back my foot and kicked this recovering fellow hard in the center of his diaphragm. While he wheezed, careening to the side, I gulped down the remainder of my meal and at last extricated myself. As the body crumpled at my feet and the world shone with new, vivid clarity, I turned on this wretch still propped against the wall and caught him by the collar of his shirt.

"How did you learn I was on this train?"

When he didn't look poised to answer, I pushed his head back and let him see my bloodstained fangs. A greater coward than his dead companion, he cried out and stammered, "A man on the inside—don't, don't, please—"

"Josko," I guessed darkly. "Now I see why he spoke so freely to the Valquist press…it had nothing to do with gossip or greed. It was deliberate sabotage."

And like the pitiful little fool I could be, I had thought I could instill in him a sense of shame! Indeed, pulling him aside to lord my apology over him was perhaps the inspiration he had required to connect with his companions and orchestrate this vile deed.

But wasn't that just pride? Glancing at Ignatius's corpse, his white shirt soaked in blood from the stab wound to his heart and perforated stomach, I realized I was so proud that I assigned myself some share in the decisions of my enemies.

No: there was nothing I could do to sway Josko, nor any of the hunters or their sympathizers. Their minds were made up about me, as they were about my husband. I was, to them, worse than any Rift beast they could encounter during an Event. They would rather suspend all their normal duties and turn their attention to overtaking Valquist and fending off my husband.

They would rather come here for me and my child than fulfill their oaths to protect the citizens of the continent.

After snapping the man's neck so quickly he didn't have time to cry out, I rose as Charlotte gasped—a breathless, short little noise that seemed perfectly suited to the pallid color of her features.

"Hide in my compartment," I urged her. "Lock the door; let no one in. Here." I handed her the gun, remembering that first time we met and the expert way she handled the rifle: picking off the wild borros until, at last, our carriage overturned. How helpless I had been then! As helpless as she looked now, absorbing the sight of the gun in her hand with a kind of uncomprehending fog in her eyes. Had she seen Ignatius killed, or had she only endured the misfortune of walking in on the conspirators in the seconds after the deed?

"Call Malin," I told her while snatching up the other man's gun belt to strap it and his knife around my waist. The evocation of my husband's name snapped her somewhat from her veil of trauma and, her expression sharpening, Charlotte nodded as I went on, "Eleison, too. Call everyone you can and tell them what's happening, and tell them—"

My lips pressed firmly together as I rapidly formulated my thought, then expressed it. "Tell them if you're not able to call them by the time the sun is up tomorrow, there's been a war crime."

At Charlotte's nod, I turned away and hurried to the compartment door, but she caught me by the elbow with a miraculously unflinching countenance as my bloodied face turned to her.

"Please, Thecla," she pleaded, "be careful."

How good of her to be concerned! How good Charlotte has always been to me. Yet, in that moment, caution was the last thing on my mind. I would have risked anything—anything at all—to see to the security of my son.

But, for her sake, I showed my bloodstained teeth in a fleeting smile.

"I promise, Charlotte," I told her as I left. "I'll do my very best."

10

The train's eerie quiet was an otherworldly, unnatural silence. As I stepped between cars, my keen ears alert for any sign of danger, I realized that the hush was a signature of deadly peril. The passengers, unaware of my nature and not privy to my sensitivities, thought themselves in the midst of a Rift Event. Perhaps they wondered why their watches hadn't rung out with an RMS alert. They waited out the night, braced and breath held, relying on the staff to keep them safe.

But I noted the staff's absence. By the third car, I recognized the signs, and by the fourth, my heart sank. I had hoped to find the conductors who were friendly to my family and who could help me locate Telemachus before any more blood was shed. However, it quickly became apparent that the hunters' operation had been coordinated before the train was forced to stop. They had secured the train and its staff before bringing it to a halt.

At the end of the fourth car, the train library—which lessened somewhat the sharp scent of the blood upon me by instead flooding my sinuses in the golden musk of old books—the rattling of the door urged me to action. Unwilling to risk myself when I had no way of knowing how many men I would be facing, I looked urgently around and took note, after what seemed like an eternity, of the access hatch built into the ornate molding of the ceiling. Before the library's door could slide open, I took hold of the handle and wrenched it violently. The adrenaline flowing through me was sufficient to snap the lever and twist the latch mechanism.

"Hey," said somebody on the other side as I threw the dismembered piece of metal away, then mounted one of the red leather chairs intended to give passengers a comfortable place to read.

While I am by no means a giant among women, my emergence from the Rift in this new form had given me an additional inch or two of height, and I blessed every one of those inches as, upon my toes, I managed to brush my fingers against the ridge of the hatch. Behind me, the door rattled more violently, and the conversation of men murmured through the car. Gradually, the rattling transitioned into slamming, and my palms grew slick with sweat as I urgently pawed at the edges of the hatch until, at last, my fingers hooked into a small niche that depressed upon my accidental touch. The hatch receded an inch, then rolled open, tucking itself neatly into the ceiling of the library car while the door groaned in protest against those who assailed it.

Bolstered by the black night and its glittering tapestry of stars above, I clenched my jaw and sprang up from the arm of the chair upon which I'd been treacherously balanced. As the seat upended with the force of my jump, my hands barely cleared the train and managed to catch hold of the hatch's edge. My stomach tightened along with every other muscle in my body as I mustered the power to pull myself up, first my arms, then my head, and then my torso bracing against the roof of the train in my persistent effort to emerge. When at last I collapsed upon that roof, grateful our accommodations were on the train's second floor, the door burst open and I knew I had no time to recover—nor could I afford to be seen. For, free of the train, I could hear many more voices than just those of the men who now swept the library carriage in search of me. Indeed, as I pushed myself up to take in the length of the train unfurling through the darkness before me, dread draped me in its cold veil. Like swarms of ants along the arid region in which we had been waylaid, (I believe it was Alberik), men gathered in clusters along each side of the train, evidently sweeping its cars in a systematic effort to find me.

And my son.

Ducking my head as flashlight's beam arced over me by accident, I committed myself to whatever was necessary, and I crawled.

This was, I must emphasize, not a small train, reader, and I had far to go. Each time I reached the end of a carriage, I was forced to wait for a break in attention, if necessary, before gathering myself in a feline posture from which I sprang over the gap to the next roof. But this was the duty of motherhood. I would have crawled through fire to find my son and rescue him from the evil intents of these hunters. Besides—what was crawling but horizontal climbing? Dharmines were fantastic climbers, as I had witnessed through that same son I sought. Therefore, I made my way steadily, forced often to stop and press down tightly to the top of the car whenever some errant noise—usually from my springing over the gap—caught the momentary attention of an adversary.

To my great relief, however, they hadn't caught on to the idea of searching the roof for me by the time I approached the electrical car. This was especially good because the length and speed of my crawl had been complicated by the need to, after a certain point, peer over the right edge of the cars and check for unhampered points of entry. At the slightest sound, a flashlight's beam might have arced up and exposed me, putting a premature end to my journey.

How insane it seems to me now that I did such a thing! In truth, I can't explain very well how I found the courage to do it. Strangely, I suppose it was a feeling of fatalism that drove me on. As I saw it, I was doomed either way: either I would be assassinated sitting in my private car, or I would be assassinated on my way to rescue my son, or we would both survive if I succeeded. When my options were laid out, I realized there was only one logical course of action: and that was, illogically, crawling along the top of the train in search of the electrical car.

But, as luck would have it, I found something better.

By the time I'd passed over what was doubtless thirteen carriages and even my preternaturally primed muscles had grown weary, the notion of a short break crossed my mind. However, in the name of hope, I took the chance to slide to the edge of the carriage and, gripping it with my bruised fingertips, lowered myself down to the window.

My eyes met the shocked gaze of a man who, after several seconds of mental exertion, was revealed to be the conductor who had so kindly given Telemachus his tour.

Once I decoded this image, I peered behind him and saw the

rest of the train staff, not always gagged but always bound, all of them pale or tearful or both.

And I remember thinking, My God! I only want to reach my son. Why are all these obstacles popping up?

Then, as if in answer to my plea—an answer that came with perfect clarity—it occurred to me that these weren't obstacles at all. They were human beings.

Moreover…they happened to be human beings who could help me very much.

While the man with whom I had locked eyes, heedless of my sudden and no doubt uncanny appearance as I bowed over the edge of the train, slightly jerked his head and guided my gaze toward the door of the bar car in which they had all been contained, I calculated the consequences of my possible actions as an engineer calculates the trajectory of a rocket. There were too many possibilities, and I rotated through them: transform into a ventil, shatter the glass of the window with my antler, then act as a distraction to lead at least a few of the hunters astray long enough for some of the hostages to escape—assuming some of the more haphazardly bound ones could wiggle to freedom through the train car window? Wrench open the surely locked door and free some of the hostages myself in the precious seconds we would have before the hunters responded to the noise?

Dinon surged in my mind like that same violet sea near which I had most recently seen him, eliciting memories of those other miracles he had worked for me: replacing Glenn's furniture, appearing as Eleison to help me escape the palace of the Overseer during my time in Valquist. Rearranging the roses, too—dressing me before the party where Glenn and I first kissed. Surely, it was a simple task for him to help here!

The lock in the window clicked open at the very second I realized whom I ought to have asked for help.

Endorphins flooded my body as I pressed my fingers to the glass and slid the window up with a little well-applied pressure. Then, clutching the edges of the sill and contorting down from the roof of the train, I performed what felt like the twist of a gymnast—a stunt I never could have accomplished as a human but which unfolded naturally from my dharmine limbs. With a silence eerie even to me, I pulled myself up into the window and drew my legs in after me, then found my footing, fixed my dress, and turned to softly close the window.

Wasting no more time, I turned and worked to free the first conductor, who didn't seem inclined to ask questions about my athletic abilities as I took the gag from his mouth and quickly released him from the cords that kept him restrained to his chair. "Thank God that window was unlocked," he said upon gasping for air, his brow furrowing with relief as I tore open the bindings with the knife I had taken off Ignatius's killers. "Are those robbers here because of you?"

"They're the Hunters' Guild," I explained shortly as I moved on to free his tablemate in a similar fashion. He, hurrying up from his seat, freed another by fumbling at the ropes with his bare fingers. "And, yes—it's safe to assume they're here for me."

As the second conductor sprang free and hurried to the next captive, I passed the knife to him with whom I conversed and exchanged a nod of gratitude. He worked far quicker now and had to concentrate less as I asked, "Have you seen my son?"

"I saw him heading toward the casino," the conductor admitted without thinking, adding only after a second, "I thought about stopping him, but I don't really know the etiquette for, er—"

For commanding the first son of Gudrune to do anything he didn't feel like doing. That was what sat on the tip of his tongue; I could tell.

Oh, my Telemachus! How I worried in those days about what such privilege would do to you—what the fierce reputation of your father would imprint upon your life in the way of too much ease. But there was so much more to worry about, I saw now—so much more, which was reflected in the peal of gunfire that drew my attention back toward the center of the train. Paling, I whipped in the direction of the sound, dropping the roped hands of the man to whose freedom I had just committed myself. The conductor looked with me and said with a jerk of his head, "We can take care of ourselves. Seems like you can, too." He glanced at the gun that still sat on my hip and I lowered my hand to it, at once feeling Eleison's spirit as closely with me as if he had come to my side in the flesh.

"We'll see about that," I said, setting off at a sprint for the door that adjoined the bar to the next car.

Quite a few worst-case scenarios rushed through my mind as, cursing my ineptitude, (as though I could have guessed which car my son was in while I was crawling along the roof to avoid our enemies!), I hurried back on foot in the direction of the casino, its bright lights and flashing colors having drawn my son in at an inopportune moment.

However—I should also say that, however inopportune, there come those moments that seem to define us, and I only say "seem" because the moment itself is but a byproduct of our actions. All our misdeeds, all our faults and our maladaptation, do not come upon us in the moment. They express themselves in the moment. It is simply that, in the moment, we experience ourselves acting on instinct. If we're left with no other choice—or no better one that we can see, at any rate—what is natural in man has a way of defying what is sensible or willful in man. We are still ourselves in those moments, but the change in how we perceive ourselves as a consequence of automatic, weak-willed actions can be sometimes overwhelming, and that is what happens 'in the moment.' The true nature of being 'in the moment' is really being alone in the eye of the hurricane—alone with yourself as you will be forever now, having acted thus. 'In the moment,' one's heart and mind become open to inevitable knowledge: that we are far stronger than we know ourselves to be.

And not always to the benefit of the soul.

As I reached that mangled room with its bloodied tables and shattered windows, the refuse of sawdust and human gore pungent in the air, and I looked past the late-arriving men standing in the wreckage—across the bodies of comrades left dead between bullet-ridden games—I realized that I had stepped into my son's moment.

My awareness leapt back to the hunters who were drawing arms on me, poised, it seemed, to shoot—

"Hold fire," barked a voice—a chill in the night, a voice that ought to have remained only memory yet now emerged with a nightmarish surreality.

A voice that explained why the hunters holding my son at gunpoint hadn't killed him on sight.

Still without having drawn his gun, the owner of that voice turned to face me.

As I beheld the face of my resurrected father, Dinon's voice came to me once more, in my mind and in my heart:

"Surrender."

Clarity of meaning at last.

It had been over a decade since his death, and as long since I had beheld his face, for I possessed no photographs of him that I'd brought with me to Malin's estate in the glorious springtime of our love. Yet, without hesitation, I recognized my father. There have been times I've seen Rigel in dreams since his passing, though neither very well, nor for very long. Indeed, even now I find that when I dream of my father, it is often from a child's perspective, and even with my old nearsighted human eyes so that his features are somewhat obscured.

All the same, there he was plainly before me, on the other side of the ruined gambling carriage where festivities had been interrupted by the hunters' hijacking.

And here were the hunters, along with their many injured or dead.

"No," I said. The word leaped from my mouth even before I was consciously aware of my son's change in posture—as though he were a millisecond from firing. Startled by my voice, he froze, his eyes flashing from object to object as though reorienting himself after a deep sleep. The confusion remained, however, when he looked at me and made full sense of my command. "Telemachus," I went on to tell him, keeping my voice as calm as possible, "don't move yet. Don't do anything if I don't tell you to. Do you understand me?"

"Y— well—"

"Say, 'Yes, Mother.'"

"Yes, Mother," replied the boy, the flow of killing broken by my intrusion and unlikely to continue without some very stupid action on the part of the hunters. As I exhaled, my father smirked beneath the bushy whiskers of his still mostly white beard.

"I'm impressed he's so obedient to you, Thecla."

"Not always," I assured coolly, my gun still raised, my mind somehow managing to gloss over the identity of the man at whom I pointed it. "But he's a very intelligent young man; intelligent children know when it's time to listen to their parents."

"Oh, yeah," agreed Rigel, his mouth still infuriatingly upturned, "this is definitely one of those times, sweetie."

"I am the Territory Matrix of Gudrune," I said, "and will be addressed as such."

While one of the hunters sneered, I tried not to let my face burn with shame at having addressed my father so—for, absurdly, my natural love and respect for him remained, even in these circumstances, even having known based on his mocking letter the year prior that he had strongarmed his way out of the Rift and into command of this war against my husband.

Rigel let his smirk fade. Folding his hands before him and straightening himself, he nodded.

"I suppose it has been quite a long time," he agreed, "with many changes between then and now. We can talk about it later."

"Assuming any of you are left alive when we're done here."

My father began, "Thecla," and took a step toward me, but I adjusted my aim, the gun steady at his heart.

"The same man who trained Telemachus in the art of shooting is the same man who trained me. Don't come any closer while we talk, Rigel."

Now he was angry—how absurd! "Don't call me that," he barked.

I thought about clicking the hammer of the pistol back, but didn't.

"I'll call you whatever I like until your men have lowered their guns. Telemachus has nothing to do with this."

"I'm afraid you and I both know that he does, Thecla...but that's why I insisted on coming. I know how things would have gone if these fellows had been left to their own devices."

"They all would have been killed."

"Exactly."

I had expected him to disagree, and I could see his men had, too. Glances were exchanged, then quickly averted. This was all absorbed in my periphery while my focus was firmly on my death-estranged father.

"How sad that you chose to reunite with me this way." I only then realized how tight my throat had become, and how the tremble Eleison's training had banished from my hand instead conspired to overwhelm my lips. "I always dreamed of seeing you again! In those early days, when you had just died, I liked to imagine there had been some mistake. Sitting at the big looms at Parsons' and singing along to myself, old songs you used to sing to me."

"Thecla—"

"I never realized seeing you would just cause me so much pain."

"It doesn't have to, Thecla," he told me, his palms open. "You've grown apart from me, but we don't have to stay that way."

"At a miserable trade, costing me my husband, my mate—"

"You don't understand how happy you could be if you would liberate yourself from these evil men."

"They are not evil," I said sharply, my eye darting over a corpse my son had made. "There are those who work against the Rift—"

"And those opposed to the better interests of humanity," the irritating man (had he always been thus?) rejoined me while my face burned. "You're deluding yourself, Thecla, if you think it's a good thing that the Earth is surrendering to a long-term alien invasion."

"Are you the maker of the world? For all we know, it's not an invasion, but a migration." At the annoyed contorting of his features, I told him, "Let the boy go with my maid, and I'll surrender."

"I can't do that."

Scoffing, I asked, "Do you want your men to die?"

"Do you want your son bearing that on his conscience? Even more death tonight? He looks like he was so young fifteen minutes ago."

While Telemachus's eyes narrowed, I regarded Rigel all the more frigidly. "I tell you, Telemachus has nothing to do with this, yet you drag him into it only more. Mind your own conscience, and let my son develop his based on the comportment of the men and women around him."

"Let's not fight like this now, Thecla."

"I'm not the one who hijacked a blasted train to—"

My eyes squeezed shut for an angry second before I opened them again, lest my foes take advantage of either my obscured vision or my unprocessed frustration.

"Very well," I said at last, doubly frustrated to find I inwardly agreed that too much killing tonight might prove, to the boy, too intense an initiation into applied combat mechanics. "Then compromise with me. Telemachus and I will surrender to—"

"Mother!"

I raised my voice over the balking boy. "—to you and your little militia without killing anyone else, under the following conditions: first, that my maidservant, Charlotte, is allowed to return home directly."

"Very well," agreed my father with a nod. He turned and tapped the man to his left, jerking his head. "Go radio up to the train right now and make sure the word gets out to let the woman alone."

"Thank you," I said, continuing on, "And Ignatius, my—"

"Who?"

Gritting my teeth at the interruption, I explained, "The security man your hunters killed. My security man."

A slight scoff raised on Rigel's tongue. "I thought I said no casualties."

"Yes, well, evidently your way was not the expedient solution. Not every child is obedient, Father."

"I know."

With a prim little sniff at being so rejoined, I demanded, "Ignatius wasn't married, but his mother is living, and he has a sister, too, I think. I must see that they're informed and compensated with expediency."

"I'd be happy to work with you to orchestrate reparations from Valquist's coffers," my father told me. "Anything else?"

"And my son and I are not to be separated during our time in your custody, which I hope will be abbreviated."

"Maybe you'll change your mind about that hope when we arrive, but all right. I will make sure you and Telemachus are confined together."

"Very good," I said automatically. The words were clipped and held no meaning beyond acceptance of whatever lay in store for me, even if it were a little prison cell the size of a tomb.

But perhaps that acceptance was not really so meaningless. It was, after all, an act of faith.

Ba'al-Dinon had urged me to surrender. I loved him immensely and already understood at a base level that he loved me with a love so vast it could not be apprehended without the assistance of the giver of that love. Therefore, it followed that if Dinon had told me to, in the face of all this, surrender myself completely, this advice had come to me from my lover's lips for a reason. I could not trust my father or the hunters; that was clear.

But I could trust Ba'al-Dinon: I could trust his earnest, infinite, thankless love and do what I never would have done on my own.

"Then I surrender," I said. "Telemachus—put down your gun."

"But Mama—"

"Put it down now."

Hearing, in my voice, a sharp edge he'd never before experienced, Telemachus obeyed with an uneasy look at the men around him. As he slowly genuflected to set the gun down at his feet, then rose with matching care, my stomach tied itself in knots. That natural, animal part of me that wanted to act on impulses 'in the moment' cried out in agony at the surrender, for it was an act that could not be taken back. And if I judged wrongly, and something happened to Telemachus, what kind of mother would I be? If I judged wrongly and something happened to me, what would become of my son? And poor Malin—poor Eleison! What would they do, knowing I was in captivity?

As soon as I asked myself the question, I knew the answer. They would fight for us—for the woman who had chosen to surrender.

"Remember our agreement," I told my father as I dropped the gun with far less care than my son had shown, half-hoping it would go off and misfire at one of the hunters. It didn't, sadly, and they swarmed Telemachus and me at once, clamoring to be the first to put us in handcuffs or hood us like birds. One man, I swear, was visibly thinking about taking a chance to pat me down for another weapon, as if the chemise I wore had any place to hide something nefarious. But, with a sidelong glance, my father could be seen carefully overseeing the proceedings, and the man thought better of it. Instead, he simply stuffed my mouth with gauze before the bag went over my head. I snapped at his fingers but didn't make it.

Then there came quite a lot of rapid talking. The incessant jingle of a radio rang endlessly in the compartment, so jarring that I had no trouble hearing it even amid the rapid conversation of the men in the disgraced casino. After one such alert noise, someone stepped up to my unguarded right side and bent to speak into my ear. My father: "We found your housekeeper confirmed alive. I'll make sure she stays that way."

Unable to thank him—and unwilling to, anyway—I kept silent.

The following time, like the time on the roof of the train, seemed an eternity, yet no time at all. I couldn't possibly fathom what on earth they were waiting for, given they had such high-value pairs of targets neatly in their custody. But gradually, my sensitive ears picked up the sound of the same sorts of utility vehicles that my husband had used on the Azstorian preserve where he kept sleepless watch over my ventil self. Oh, Rosina! A little fawn inside of me.

The child who had spent considerably less time developing inside me was sat roughly down beside me in the open auto-carriage into which we were thrust. While we were forced to crush against one another when a hunter evidently slid in at Telemachus's other side, the vehicle cruised off into the night, leaving behind the train, and Charlotte—and all comprehensible reality.

What was I to do now? Ba'al-Dinon hadn't told me that part, infuriatingly. I had done what he said: I surrendered. Surrendered to these hunters who despised my husband and wanted to use us as bargaining chips in, I was sure, some opportunity to kill him. Obedient, I had gone along with Dinon's commands even though I knew my son and I had the strength and skill to fight on and, at the very least, pass out of that room in which he'd been cornered. There was no question: we together posed a real threat—and I had instead listened to Dinon, this man who had not shown himself to me in a terrestrial sense in over a year, not knowing why he asked me to do what he did, or what would happen next.

I see everything you do, Thecla, his voice returned without hesitation, coiling around my diaphragm and sending a delicious shiver up my spine. *Especially the things you do out of love for me. I like those most of all.*

A strange feeling of serenity, so intense and sudden that there was something pleasurable about it, washed over me in that instant. While it was wrong to say I now had no control over the situation—for no one ever has full control over anything in life—I attained, through doing as Dinon had asked of me, an equilibrium of grace that seemed somehow to make my thinking clearer. I had not acted in a vacuum, but acted because, internally, my counselor's heart was known to me well enough that I could see its depths were not to be plumbed. I felt utterly helpless as Telemachus and I bounced around in our seats in the little jeep that sped who-knew-where, yet I tried to perceive myself as helpless in the way I was when in Dinon's hands. Helpless as in lovemaking, when one surrenders one's body to the beloved.

Trust me, Thecla, urged Ba'al-Dinon in my soul. *Trust in my love.*

When at last, after a lot of driving, we were tossed into an unrelated cargo train of some kind, the hoods were lifted from our heads, and we were permitted to look around the boxcar where we sat. "It's about nine more hours," said my father, who stood before me with a pair of blood bags stolen from some hospital. Tossing one into my lap and another at Telemachus's feet, my father went on, "If I were you, I'd try to get some sleep. Don't make me regret taking off those hoods, now…"

While he exited the boxcar unescorted, the trio of armed men I had been hoping would go with him stayed behind to gawk. While my son lunged upon his meal with fangs bared, his thirst no doubt exacerbated by all the killing, I glowered darkly at the hunters.

"I understand if you must stay, but must you stare?"

All three of them stared stupidly at me, and I was on the verge of repeating myself when, with a delayed look of dry mirth at his comrades, one obeyed, leaving the other two to roll their eyes and follow suit.

Unobserved and still as bound as my son, I let the bag in my lap slide to the ground before lunging upon it in emulation of him. The hair tumbled around my face, tendrils staining themselves and my cheeks with blood. Having gulped down the contents of the bag in eight or nine desperate, thirsty intakes, I sat up and felt my head sway like a treetop in the wind. Dizzy, I licked my lips, then bent and tilted my head forward to wipe my face as best I could along the fabric of my nightgown. Oh, propriety! I dare not leave you to die—there are days when you are the only thing that speaks reason to my heart, or to my husband's!

By the time I had recovered my senses, Telemachus had also finished, and slumped back with an exhausted and frankly curious look.

"That was wonderful," said my son after a moment.

Under the impression that he referred to the sustenance, I began to nod my agreement, taking advantage of the hunters' turned backs to work on my wrists. No give, sadly; very professional. The bindings were even capable of withstanding a dharmine's strength. I would have to really put my back into it to break free, and by then they would be upon me.

All those notions were silenced, though, when my son finished his thought, and I saw more clearly the contents and shape of his mind.

"Why did you make me stop?"

"You mean back there—in the casino."

Telemachus nodded, barely sparing more than a glance for the men who turned to face us again. "Yes, exactly. I wish you weren't so afraid for me all the time, Mama. I could have killed all the men we were with, and anyway—"

"That isn't the issue, dear."

Looking befuddled, Telly asked, "Then what is?"

While our guards exchanged glances and then were jerked slightly off-kilter by the lurching of our train into motion, I struggled to withhold an aggrieved sigh.

"Well, goodness, Telemachus, it's that I don't want you killing! Oh, my darling, you're so young. How many hunters did you kill back in the casino car?"

"Only six," he protested, his brow furrowing as he went on to ask, "But why are you so upset? They were trying to hurt us! Have I done something wrong?"

Nostrils flaring, I shut my eyes as the attention of these three impudent hunters fixed on me, openly listening to my conversation with my son. Keeping mental track of the heartbeats of the guards,

I was careful to say to Telemachus, "You haven't done anything wrong, but shooting men is different from shooting targets. Even if it doesn't mean much to you now, a day may come when you reflect on what you've done and feel horrified."

The continuing growth of the mountain of bodies behind me in my lifetime was a testament to that. I had gravely erred, and at times been forced by those grave errors into grim deeds. You already know, reader, that I pondered over the dead I had made. The recognition of oneself as a killer, even if only for defense, is a moment of reflection that should humble anyone. Eleison certainly seemed to regard his occasional assassinations on Malin's behalf—like the newspaper man in Valquist, when he was taking vengeance as much as he was doing his territory master's will— to be shameful deeds of which he wanted me to know no part. That served some social or emotional purpose; the shame had a function.

But Malin was unaccustomed to experiencing shame. He only seemed capable of conceiving it when his actions had a clearly negative impact on something that reflected upon him, such as my mood or the economics of Gudrune. And Telemachus had the possibility of becoming like his father in that regard, I then discerned—immune to the mortal ethics that constrained most reasonable beings.

It was only natural that the boy should be so immune, of course, for he was immortal by comparison to any unaltered human's lifespan, and perhaps even in comparison to an altered one's. No one knew when or if a dharmine could die of natural causes—which, for obvious reasons, one rarely got the chance to discover.

Though what did I know? With my condition and Malin's

hidden from the general public, perhaps there were more like us moving quietly through the world, having done as nature had intended and replaced their old mortal vessel seamlessly. Killing was in the dharmine nature, after all; so I tried not to be taken aback when my son, who had never been human, asked with sincere interest, "Why should I be horrified, Mama? Papa feeds me meat all the time, and it doesn't grow on trees!"

As the boy laughed, one of the guards tightened his hand around his rifle's grip.

"Yes, dear," I told him, pretending not to notice the guards' displeasure and opting to address my son, "well, that may be so, but the fact that the meat comes from…'somewhere'…is all the more reason for us to treat the act of killing with reverence. The onus is on us to be mindful."

For some reason, I was heavily assailed with visions of Glenn pursuing me through the wilderness while I was in the form of a doe; of Eleison's beast, which wanted at once to mate with me and devour me; Malin bending over my throat and swallowing down my blood until I revealed myself to him.

Dinon. Everything about him.

"There's a connection between the hunter and his prey," I told my son, glad to find he listened carefully to my words. "It's as intimate as the connection between the mother and the child she bears; the polar opposite of that connection, and as eternal as a marriage."

Frowning slightly, Telemachus lowered his head and let his gaze drift away from mine. "I see," he murmured.

"With all due respect, ma'am," said the first guard, who had been the one that first turned to let me drink unobserved, "killing just ain't all that serious. I mean, it's serious—but no need to get all mystical about it."

"If it happened to you, I think you'd take it rather poorly."

"Nah—what am I going to care! I'll be dead."

This one is already dead, Dinon told me, speaking clearly in my heart and opening my eyes to some strange secret.

"What this fellow here has said reminds me of something important, darling. Let me tell you a fact. There are the dead," I told Telemachus, accordingly, drawing his attention back to the matter at hand, "and the living. Strive ever to be among the living."

"Even if it means killing?"

"Yes; but don't take the act callously. A heart that's calloused is a dead heart, and little could be more horrible than to be among the living dead."

Perhaps you think I was being deliberately ironic! No, not at all; I considered myself fully alive, not just resurrected but improved in nearly every way. Already, I had corrected terrestrial misunderstandings about the nature of dharmines; and my son, for whom life had always been his growth into his dharmine nature, proved that our lives were not strictly dependent on the successful development of a human prototype.

So why was it, then, that I struggled to see my father as anything but a ghost? Yes! Some foul revenant, returning from the grave into which the man who would one day be my husband sent him—for what should have been forever. The long gap had made it so. My mind had become accustomed to thinking of my father as dead—for half my life, by then.

And that thought, during our long trip east, filled me with the bitterest anger.

hy had he not come earlier? Why had he arrived so late, and why had he taken sides against me? Did he detest Malin so much that he was giving aid to those who hunted him?

As Telemachus dozed against my shoulder, I pondered this and more. My mind had never fully recovered from my passage through death—from my increasing intimacy with Dinon and the Rift. It retained a strange openness, like a dish from which the cloche has been lifted and replaced askew, or left half-exposed. I was more sensitive, more prone to deep brooding. If you have experienced a sacred mystery firsthand—and I think few of my readers have—then perhaps you know this feeling. But I will avoid this digression: for now, it is enough to say that my mind had changed.

I suppose I ramble because it is difficult to describe the unpleasantly hot and uncomfortable circumstances in which my son and I traveled. We rattled about in that little boxcar, the guards looking as unhappy as we felt. When my son stirred, he regarded them with a mix of dehydration and wariness. They had reached a deadly point of boredom and fatigue. I felt Telemachus's gaze on me, wondering if I intended to act.

But I had surrendered. I intended to do as I was told.

And when at last, at the end of the train ride—after a full twenty-four hours, one rotation of guards, and the gradual bone-aching onset of sleep deprivation—we were transferred to a covered auto-carriage and driven off as quickly as the vehicle could go, I sensed we had to be close to our destination. Seated across from Telemachus and me, my father smirked while I peered out the window and recognized, somehow, the types of trees densely populating the dramatic landscape through which we drove.

"Are we going to Valquist?"

"Now that was impressive." Looking pleased, my father observed, "I thought you'd only been out here once. Do you know that through your deer?"

Ignoring his question and the level of knowledge it implied about my nature, I let him see the displeasure on my face. "You could have let us get a bit closer to Valquist before snatching us up and letting us rattle around in that tin can of a freight, you know."

"And give your husband time to dispatch an escort? We're smarter than that, Thecla."

"I wouldn't be so sure about that when it comes to your coworkers, Papa." Disgusted, I glanced out the window and informed him, "Most of the hunters I've ever met are bumpkins at best—bigots at worst."

"Ouch," he said with a dry chuckle. "I used to be a part of the Gudrune chapter, you know. Surely there must be a few good hunters in the bunch."

"One," I said, frowning out the window, and only belatedly covering my tracks with a carelessly added, "two, three—it doesn't matter. The whole organization is rotten to the core, and its intentions for the continent are deadly...evil."

"Do you think there's no hope for the organization to be reformed?"

A second or so passed before I realized my father was really asking for my opinion. Trying to comport myself like a grown territory matrix speaking to a terrorist rather than a child speaking to her father, I sat up a little straighter and raised my chin. "The Hunters' Guild is an organization founded on the premise that the Rift is an inherently evil and unnatural event—"

"And it is," he interrupted, "but go on."

Only just avoiding raising my voice to him at once, I bared my teeth, since my hands were still restrained behind me and I could not use them to suitably emphasize my points. "But don't you see what a deadly binary it is, Papa? That kind of ethos, given the reality of the world in which we live, is only going to be the root of destruction. If the Rift is inherently evil and unnatural, then its progeny—innocent Riftborn who have done nothing wrong, desperate altered individuals whose survival depended upon the procedure, you and me and Telemachus—are also inherently evil and unnatural. The hunters would like to see us destroyed like beasts."

"Yes," my father said, unwavering.

Quite shocked—and, somehow, strangely impressed by the fortification of his moral character, which had been strong during my childhood and somehow felt only stronger after his resurrection—I gestured with my shoulders as I asked, "And you're comfortable with that?"

"Thecla"—his hands folded between his knees as he leaned forward to look at me with that unflinching sincerity—"I want to make something clear, and I don't want you to take this the wrong way: I don't want to be here."

"Then go back to the Rift. I could help you, or—"

"I'm aware certain Riftborn have means by which we can travel through the Rift and into the world on its other side. But that's not what I want. I mean this, being here—still conscious and aware and alive after death. You know why I did this, Thecla? Why I'm here?"

"I didn't realize it was a choice," I said, trying to measure my tone. Nodding, my father sat back again.

"Everybody has the choice: whether they know it or not, whether they remember it or mean it. It's a choice you make every day of your life. No one is forcing the dharmine to leave the Rift and come here. They come because they think they want to, or because their will has gotten away from them.

"But not me, Thecla. I'm here for you."

Scoffing, I said, "For me?"

"That's right—for you. Because I recognized you weaving, and I realized what you were going to do, sooner or later. You'd choose to...'migrate'...and what would become of your soul? What would happen to my daughter, poisoned by the Rift? So—I felt compelled to go back. Even though I didn't want to and hardly understood what I was doing—even though it means somehow, someway, dying again—I came back to save you from yourself. No—to save you from the husband who's controlling you so well that you can't even see it."

"I'm beginning to find that presumption quite tiresome, Papa. Please, why not let's speak of pleasant things? Have you seen Sable's baby? What a cheeky little thing! She has a mischievous streak—"

"And mischief is too often perverted into evil," said my father, looking hard into my eye yet speaking also to my son, who listened closely. "There's nothing in the human heart your husband can't use as a tool—that includes love, Thecla."

"We all use love as a tool to a certain extent, don't we?"

A twinge of pain tightened my father's features. "I'm sorry to hear you think that."

"Well? Doesn't the infant elicit love so to be taken care of? Doesn't spousal love motivate guardianship? Isn't the love of brothers on the battlefield an important tool to keep combatants alive?"

"I suppose you're right," he said, studying the landscape. "At least, I'm sure you have good reason for thinking so."

How darkly I blushed at my father's remonstrations! How little he had to say! Based on the manner in which he had provided for myself and my son, it was safe to say he had found some symbiotic means of survival, receiving donations from the hunters in exchange for understanding of my husband's mind and military strategies.

Not that he needed this incentive to align himself in opposition to my husband, even when doing so was against his own best interest.

Rigel despised Malin; and perhaps, as regards the Malin Rigel once knew, he was justified. Still, given that it was Rigel who stole Malin's first wife and not the other way around, I sometimes wondered at my father's resentment. Perhaps that was one area where I was blind; for, to me and with me, Malin was a delight, and his faults were forgivable when he was contrite. Considering my mother's evident unhappiness, it seemed likely there was reason for that, but I also had no doubt that these feelings of dissatisfaction went both ways. I surely sound like an apologist...but aren't wives always apologizing for their husbands' bad behavior? Whatever Malin had done that my father so despised, I could not fathom it was worth holding on to here and now, so long beyond the grave.

And then I, numbed to death by my dharmine nature despite my best efforts, realized perhaps my father was not trying to rescue me as he claimed, but was more like a ghost avenging his own mortal destruction.

"Since Malin came into this world by killing you, Papa," I said, breaking the uncomfortable silence of the carriage with an even more uncomfortable question, "and you, therefore, could not replace yourself, who did you kill to regain some semblance of your faculties?"

"I don't really feel like talking about that right now."

"Then you shouldn't have kidnapped me. You should have come to visit and discourse with me in polite society." Though embarrassed to be so antagonistic toward my own father—especially given the nature of our reunion and the presence of my boy—I could not quite seem to stop myself. My tone a bit sharp, I said, "Until I'm treated like a sapient being capable of thought and granted basic rights, you shouldn't expect me to act like one."

"I thought setting an example would be important to you."

"It most certainly is. I blush with shame to think that this is how we're meeting after all this time—to think, this is how your grandson meets you! Assisting the side that's trying to kill his father, kidnapping us, forcing us both to kill to stay alive—you can pretend all you like that becoming a dharmine hasn't changed your standards of moral behavior, but it has, Papa. You've allowed it to."

Now it was his turn to look at least somewhat cowed. With a flash of his eyes in my direction, he resumed staring out the window, saying only, "You don't need to tell me that."

How tedious the rest of that trip was! Somehow, though Telemachus and I had spent an entire day and night as human cargo in a freight train, the worst part of it was that final set of hours to Valquist. Six hours, to be exact. By the time the city was in sight, dawn was rising, and Telemachus held his breath, though he did not speak his admiration aloud for fear of antagonizing me. Instead, he gazed upon Valquist in silent wonder; then, as the road dipped down, it flashed out of sight again, hidden behind the forested hills amid which it lay.

"You know why I picked you up when I did, Thecla?"

I deigned to look in his direction, the very act of moving my eyes revealing to me how exhausted my frayed nerves had become. Seeing I was in no mood to answer, my father said, "So you would have more time to think. A day or two before he discerns exactly where you are. There's a lot of countryside between here and where we picked you up; a lot of possible places we could be keeping you. A little smokescreen goes a long way."

"Here I thought you were simply using me as a bargaining chip. What, exactly, am I meant to think about?"

"Whether you really want to be the type of person you've become."

Soon, the cobblestone paths of Valquist were beneath the shoes of our artificial horses. Outside the carriage, Valquist seemed somehow different. Quieter; less glamorous. Like a vibrant young woman after the secret brute of a husband she's married lays a hand on her. It seemed, I think, a little dirtier and a bit less affluent, with shops having closed here and there without immediate replacement. "I can see the hunters are having an excellent impact on the local economy here in the heart of their resistance."

"Valquist is in such a sorry state because of Gudrune and its allies embargoing trade with anybody who's even thinking about providing aid or resources. If you want to blame somebody, blame Malin Farrow."

"I blame the uncontrolled militia that stepped into the power vacuum after the death of a beloved world leader."

"Yeah… I'm sure you and Malin were both disappointed you were too far away to act quickly in assuming control of Valquist."

"Look, damn you—" Turning to face him properly, I looked my father in the eye and told him, "From the very start of my acquaintance with Malin, he's been nothing but wonderful to me—lavishing me with gifts, listening to my thoughts, providing me the resources by which to refine myself. Moreover, I've seen him put everything he has behind helping his people: providing resources for important experimentation into the Rift, improving the infrastructure in rural communities, simply giving his life to Gudrune every day and long into the night. I love Malin. I am *going* to love Malin, and the last time someone tried to dissuade me of my love for him, Malin and I only loved one another more intensely in the end."

"You can love somebody and still know that the best thing is to be apart from them, Thecla. Just worth thinking about."

The carriage rolled to a stop in a very familiar location, a shudder rippling down my spine as the palace of the Overseer bore an uncanny resemblance to a courthouse in the dim, dreary light of morning in that humid place.

"That boy of yours is awfully quiet," said Rigel of Telemachus, who glanced back as the carriage rocked with the dismount of the hunters in its driver's seat.

"Papa always says there's no use in talking to somebody who's made up their mind," Telemachus explained while the carriage door was opened for us. "He says that once a thought is crystalized, we'll hurt ourselves smashing our heads into it."

With a dry sort of chuckle, Rigel stuck a key into the cuff of my restraints, snapping them open as he said, "Yeah, well—sometimes it's good to have a closed mind, son. You open it too wide, and somebody'll throw trash in it. After you, Thecla."

While I swallowed back my opinion of my father's choice of expression, (by Jove, was he like this before?), I ducked my head and half-hopped out of the carriage to the cobblestones below. Sighing, I rubbed my wrists and began to turn back, complaining to my father about those ridiculous restraints which he had just removed—and then, a little child's voice rang out with shrill delight: "Mama!"

And my heart changed.

Great art requires contrast, in my opinion. Without something fragile, one never recognizes what a brute one has become. Indeed, as I set my eyes upon Rosina, my soul illuminated with fireworks of joy. I opened wide my arms to her, only to find myself shocked by how much more nimble she had grown. How confident she had become! Almost like a different child—yet she was still my Rosina, still adorable beyond all compare, (perhaps even more adorable, if possible!), and she shyly paused in her darting toward me as though trying to gauge through the haziness of instinct and infancy whether I was also the same.

And I wasn't. But oh, my Rosina didn't care. That hesitation evaporated as I genuflected to her level; the girl hurried up the rest of the distance, throwing her arms around my neck while I gathered her up in my arms and cried, and cried, oh—reader! How I cried.

"Is this my sister?" asked Telemachus, his tone of strange astonishment making me laugh as I released the child who was technically my firstborn yet who still was not wholly of me. While the girl stumbled back a little to assess him, as if only just seeing him, I exhibited a similar blindness. So focused was I on wiping my eyes and answering my son's question and basking in the glow of reunion with my daughter that I was, at best, half-aware of the boots approaching from those same palace steps down which Rosina had launched herself.

"Yes," I said through desperate tears, hiccupping and gasping and even laughing at how small I was and at how much Ba'al-Dinon truly loved me to thus shepherd me. "Oh, yes, Telemachus, darling, this is Rosina. I—oh—"

"Oh," I vocalized, the surprise rising out of me like a bubble drifting away from my mouth on the breeze. For I had looked up: and he was more handsome than ever, his hair a little longer and a little less colorful from the stress of the last year.

But there Glenn was. Glenn—my hunter. My woodsman. My hero.

Unsteadily, I rose to my feet, no more able to take his offered handkerchief than I was able to accept his help. He grasped my wrist very gently instead, keeping me balanced, and frowned as he ran his thumb along the indentation the cuffs had left on my skin.

He had no time to comment on it before I wilted into his arms, melting against him with a new sob that I muted into his shoulder. He hushed me, stroking my hair, and after a few gasping breaths, Glenn gently fit his hands to my face and tilted back my head. "I'm so happy you're here," he said, looking me in the eye. "Come on, Thecla—come inside. We've got a room for you. The boy, too," he added, flicking a glance toward Telemachus in concert with a nod. "You look like you need to lie down—I've never seen you so unwell."

"I'm exhausted, yes—of course, I'm exhausted—but sleep is the furthest thing from my mind. Oh! Thank you for keeping our daughter safe."

"Of course."

"I should have known it was these blasted hunters who kidnapped you, darling. I knew you would never hurt me. You would never deprive me of Rosina, or of your company."

"Thecla"—he flicked a glance over my shoulder, (at Rigel, I assume), and then, focused back on me, lowered his voice—"how about we discuss this inside? I really think you should try to lie down."

"I've been sitting with my wrists bound for hours now—if it's all the same to you, I would much prefer to do something kinetic. Is that workout room still available, or have the hunters defiled it in their coup?"

"It's still in there…look, why don't you settle for some nervous pacing in your suite? That always used to pick me right up. I did some of my best thinking at Eleison's estate, walking in circles between the bedroom and the living room."

I frowned. "You could have walked in circles in the garden."

"Let's wait," said Glenn with a smile that was more like his old smile, before his time living in our home partially against his will.

"How about you show them to their rooms, Glenn." My father's voice was but a harbinger as he stepped into my periphery. "Since you're not in the mood to rest, Thecla, if you're still up at suppertime, you should join us."

"I'll consider it," I told him, my tone far colder for my father than for Glenn. How that fact broke my heart! I turned away from him and instead gestured for Telemachus to come along. He did, keeping in stride with me, his eyes roving wildly as we were ushered with urgency through the once opulent palace. The building looked like what it had become: a military installation. Now, instead of bearing the glamour and gravitas of the capital's crown jewel, its floors had dulled with neglect, and its halls smelled of the cigarettes of the soldiers who hovered here and there, either stationed at checkpoints to various parts of the vast building or making their businesslike way between them. The change in it made me quite sad, and I lowered my eyes as we were whisked by a small retinue of hunters to a guest suite far more luxurious than the one Parvati had afforded me. Telemachus and I, I was somewhat relieved to find, were to be consigned not to some claustrophobic cell but to a proper apartment with a living room, bedroom, and en suite. It even possessed a small dining nook, though no kitchen.

"We don't want to deal with any fires," said one guard as I complained, and Glenn sent them away. To my half-surprise, they obeyed. While Rosina and Telemachus hurried about in inspection of the new space, Glenn turned to me in a way that somehow telegraphed what he was going to say before he spoke.

"I did take Rosina away by choice, Thecla. Nobody compelled me to do it; I saw an opportunity to go, so I took it."

Pain stabbed straight through me. My mouth tightened as I averted my eyes from Glenn's and whispered hoarsely, "Yes, well—at least you're being honest about it, Glenn. I suppose you could have lied."

"I don't think your father would have let me, even if I'd wanted to." As he raised his hands to gently rest them upon my shoulders, he frowned when he studied my white hair. "The papers were right…you really had blood poisoning."

"Yes," I told him, emphasizing, "but I'm much better now. It doesn't matter anymore. Glenn—"

"I assume this was before you became a dharmine?"

Blast Rigel's loose lips. I ground my teeth, frightened that telling the truth would alienate me from Glenn's affections once and for all. But, unable to lie to him, I said all the same, "Of course."

"I'm so sorry that happened to you," was what he said, instead of the hateful thing I could have expected from any of the other men in that installation. "I'm sorry that I wasn't there to help you."

My darling. Here I was, a predator of men, and all he could think of was that he couldn't save me. Clearly, he had been turning that idea over for the better part of the year, beginning whenever Rigel appeared and shared with him the full context of my nature. Yet it was by his own choice that he had left! Taking him by the hands and drawing him down into the sofa, I looked into Glenn' eyes and begged, "Why did you leave? Malin had just—just been shot. If you had only waited, there would have been so much time for you and me to reconcile. You were just beginning to show signs of getting along with Eleison! Why did you leave?"

"Because, Thecla. The way things began—"

Glenn's lips pressed firmly together amid the fullness of his beard. He glanced away, sorting through his thoughts before looking back at me with a sorrowful plea for mercy softening his blue eyes. "I could never have been anything but a prisoner," he explained, looking sincerely back at me, his hands folding around mine to console me even as his words stabbed deep into my heart.

"The way I came to be there, a wanted criminal falsely accused, forced to hide my existence and make myself dependent on a man I don't trust—how could I ever have opened my heart to you, Thecla?"

"Come look at this view," exclaimed Telemachus, happily oblivious to adult woes while he and his sister enthusiastically admired the panorama of Valquist afforded by the palace's overlook of the river.

"I suppose I can understand why you couldn't trust me," I said, inhaling shakily and at last accepting the handkerchief he tried once again to offer me. "I know that I haven't seemed like the most reliable woman from your perspective. I'm sure—"

"What are you talking about?" Looking a little shocked, Glenn perceived I had no answer, and so he went on, "You're the most dedicated and driven person I've ever known, man or woman. The most passionate. I've never met anybody who sets me on fire the way you do, Thecla—you make me want to be with you."

"Then why aren't you?"

Nostrils flaring as I dabbed the edge of the handkerchief that smelled like him along my lower lash line, Glenn said, "Because—you're so driven and so passionate that I wasn't sure I could persuade you to see my side of the story. You remember some of the arguments we had in that house, don't you?"

"I'm so sorry I have a temper," I said weakly, grateful that the apology at least earned a gentle squeeze of his hand around mine.

"I do, too. It's all right…if I'm honest, it's one of the things I like about you."

I laughed a little, sniffling, and told him, while my vision at last cleared of the most blurring of my tears, "I was just thinking the same about you."

Glenn laughed along with me then, his eyes like pools of gold and his smile flashing, big and merry in his beard. How handsome he was! Even more handsome than my memory had fixed him as being. Our eyes locked in our laughter, and as that laughter cooled, the mutual joy and pleasure remained in our gazes.

"Can I kiss you," he suddenly said, so bold that my stomach tightened with desire and I found myself saying, "Please," without even realizing it.

More confident than I had ever seen him, Glenn slid one arm around my waist and fit his other hand to my cheek, tilting back my head to leave me vulnerable to his mouth. As his head lowered over mine and the warm, sweet substance of his tongue danced between my lips, I exhaled and submitted to him utterly. His breath mingling with mine in my happy lungs, he grew more forceful, drawing my face commandingly up toward his, his tongue driving deeper—

Until, aware of how stimulated we both already were, Glenn released me but let his gaze linger on my mouth.

"Thecla...look, I don't want to pressure you, but—if you come to dinner...if you feel like it...I'd love to talk to you more after."

How strangely happy I was! Oh, I was so happy. Relieved, too, that he knew already the change that had come over me. Rosina, I sensed, did not yet understand, and would not yet until some later phase of cognitive development. We had been together something short of twenty minutes, and in that time, I had been kneeling, collapsing into Glenn's arms, and then hurrying along with him and our entourage as we made our way to our rooms. I must also wonder if Rosina's changing proportions, her height growing steadily all the time, might not have tricked her eye, as I had last seen the child when she was but eighteen months old and very small. Now, at thirty months, she was positively mobile, scrambling across the gold-carpeted floor of the suite from one door to another out of a general disinterest in a room that had nothing fanciful to attract her attention. And I remember thinking, as her brother pursued her to the threshold and, discerning she was within our sight, headed back around to the en suite, that I was quite amazed Glenn had such trust in my son, even though he was Malin's and a dharmine.

Yet perhaps it was a matter of normalization. The other hunters with Rigel had known Telemachus and I were dharmine, and not just because of our fighting acuity; still, they had spoken to me as though I were a reasoning being. Surely it was experience with my father, who had retained—or regained—some memory of his time in that limbo before rebirth and had been able to correctly draw the conclusion that I was by now a dharmine just like him.

And how glad I was, for once, that this had been shared behind my back! It was one less lie that had to be told: one more way I could just be honest with Glenn. I delighted in the generosity of his spirit, and I took my daughter into my arms as, feeling less shy, she threw herself into the couch cushions between Glenn and me and snuggled into my embrace.

"I miss you," she said, my heart blossoming like a flower to feel the warmth of her powerful love condensed into a form so small she fit in my arms like a doll—yet not for much longer!

"I've missed you, too," I told her, kissing her forehead and sweeping back the soft brown curls that fell quite wildly upon her brow. "Goodness! Aren't we in want of a lady's maid—my poor angel has no one to do her hair!"

With a dry chuckle, Glenn said, "She's been allowed to run a little wild, I admit. And she's more spoiled than ever...a lot of the guys here are from outside of Valquist, and they miss their wives and kids. Rosina's a little ray of sunshine for a lot of people... especially for me."

A flame of anger rose up in me, but since Glenn was so forgiving, I tried not to ruminate on the notion that so many had been able to love my daughter while I, her mother, was deprived. Instead, I let it fade, saying with a smile, "Like in *La Fille du Regiment*. Now there's an opera you might like, Glenn."

"I do like a little opera," he allowed.

"Then perhaps, when all this is over, we'll see if we can't persuade the house in Saalast to put it on."

His smile looking a little wan at Malin's shadow passing over the conversation, Glenn leaned over and kissed my cheek. "I'm going to let you rest," he said, extending a hand to Rosina to help her hop down from the couch. "Because I know what you said... but you look pale, Thecla. It would do you some good to rest your eyes for a while."

"I'll try," I told him, smiling even as my heart seized in pain to see my daughter taken from me. "See you at supper, Glenn."

"See you then." The casual familiarity of his words, the glance over his shoulder; I felt how deeply he had missed me and knew with certainty that his love was true.

But I also couldn't help thinking with great sorrow about what he had said—that he was unable to open his heart to me as long as he remained in Eleison's country house under those circumstances. He had been a captured bird that escaped its cage but now landed upon the roof of the house from which it had fled, pondering which life was more fulfilling. I supposed, in that case, I had to trust in his love and hope he would choose to come back.

You don't have to trust in him, Dinon said, speaking so clearly in my heart that I knew it was neither fancy nor memory, but some form of distinct connection. *Trust in me. I'll give you everything you need.*

My chest warmed by my longing, I placed my hand upon my heart and stared into the middle distance. Yes—how many times had Dinon told me, in person and in my heart, that if he provided me Glenn against his will, Glenn would never truly be mine? I could think of several occasions where he had said such things or similar; and now, I had been rewarded not for pursuing Glenn and putting my hopes in myself and my men, but in waiting, surrendering, and acting as Dinon had told me.

"Please," I whispered into the empty room, gazing through the forms and associations of reality to catch the shimmers of those violet warp and silver weft threads, praying that by peering well enough between them, I could at least inwardly behold his face, "Dinon, oh, Love—won't you come to me?"

You have no idea how badly I want to, Thecla...but I can't yet. Trust the process...trust me.

How my heart longed to! But it was an undeniable struggle to trust the man I couldn't see—and why? After all, I could not see my husband at the present moment; all the same, I was certain that just as soon as he discovered my location, he would do whatever it took to get me back unharmed. I trusted him fully. I wanted to, anyway.

Yet when I pulled back from Ba'al-Dinon and took a serious, studied look at everything he did and said and was, I sensed that, based on some metaphysical scale I didn't understand, Dinon was truly a great being. The more I knew of him, the more terrifically small I felt before him. It frightened and delighted me, this power of his, this sublimity he represented. I was not afraid he would hurt me but instead I feared he might forget about me at any moment: might see my true unworthiness to be loved by one such as him.

I love you because *you're unworthy,* he urged me to understand as the shower in the bathroom at last ceased running, an absence of sound I barely heard as we spoke. *Thecla...you're my sexual fantasy. You're my queen. You're everything to me.*

And even though I could not behold him with my terrestrial eyes, I felt strangely in my soul as if I *were* beholding him: as if I might lean forward and kiss his beautiful face as he looked into my eyes and told me earnestly, *I could never, ever turn away from you. Not for a second.*

Perhaps this is embarrassing to admit, but between my exhaustion from the traumatic journey, and my fear and disappointment and longing, and the deep gravity of Ba'al-Dinon's gentle voice exuding so much love, I burst into tears as though I were a child. Feeling the nearness and attention of Dinon as I did, I half-expected him to appear and put his arms around me. But he didn't, and in my aloneness, I wept only harder, frightened and astonished by the power—the obsession—of the love this being had for me. My hand covering my eyes, I gasped pitifully, then remembered Glenn's handkerchief still balled up in my lap. I pressed it to my face, trying to will my tears away—but only love can distract the lover in mourning, even when that love comes in a different form.

The sofa cushion beside me compressed as my son sat down. I gasped, taking a deep breath and laughing, not having heard him exit the bathroom, let alone cross the floor. Yet there he was when I looked over, his expression stalwart, his hand resting upon my forearm.

"Don't worry," Telemachus told me, his sincere urging made with confidence beyond his years. "My father will help us. He won't let us down, Mama."

"I know he won't...oh, dear, how selfish I am! No young man

should have to comfort his mother; not until she's been reduced by infirmity to the dependence of old age." Laying my hand on his and looking him in the eyes, I asked, "How are you?"

He shook his head. "I have thoughts I dare not express. This room isn't very private, I think."

"I think not," I agreed, squeezing his hand gently. I intended to turn the conversation to the light and happy matter of his adorable sister. Oh, my! In all the whirlwind of reunion and the inertia of the transportation still disorienting me in spacetime, I hadn't taken the time to let my heart linger on the fulfillment of this special dream—this hope that I would someday see my children together.

Before I could in any way savor the peace of this experience, however, my son revealed his own thoughts to be more troubled.

"May I speak with you about personal things, Mama? Things that are not sensitive or political in nature?"

"Of course," I said, hastily adding, "and you don't need to be so formal with me, Telemachus. I know all of this is strange for you, but—I do hope that someday you'll feel more natural around me. Feel free to ask me anything."

"Is that man really your father? The bearded fellow, the dharmine?"

Ah! Like a sharp little dagger in my heart. In all the delirium of travel and the excitement of Glenn and Rosina's unexpected presence, the identity of my father and his resurrection had somehow faded from my consciousness. Now snapped from this dissociation by my son's question, I wet my lips and nodded. "Yes, he is. Rigel of Lescaut—my terrestrial father."

"Hm." With a glance of his tortoise shell eyes, as I had come to think of them, askance into some other dimension of thought—

his father likewise gazed sidelong into while solving some mental problem—Telemachus studied me anew after a few more seconds. "Why don't you like your father? I mean…aside from all this."

With a half laugh, I searched my child's expression for some explanation and, finding none, stuttered, "Why, I love my father, Telemachus."

"You don't really mean that," he said. "There's something in the way you speak to him. I don't know how to explain it. Maybe I'm wrong."

Exhaling slowly, my hands half-folded in my lap, I studied my slightly cupped palms while telling my son, "I do love my father, darling. Very, very much. I think what you sense is a combination of two things: my sorrow at the way we're reunited, and my own very childish—*immature* reaction to it, perhaps."

Remembering I was speaking to a thirteen-year-old child who had been sheltered, I cleared my throat before continuing. "What I mean is, when I was only a few years older than you, my father died unexpectedly, and my life became much harder. It felt as though he had abandoned my sister and me. But now—it's become quite complicated. Not nearly so open-and-shut as it once was."

I glanced away, thinking of Malin, who had eagerly awaited the chance to reunite with me after his resurrection. From my own imprisonment, my heart called to him to rescue me.

"Now that I know my father has been walking the earth as a dharmine for an undetermined period of time, and he never contacted his daughters or turned to us for any degree of help even when he made it to his senses still alive—that *does* feel like a betrayal."

And if the room was being monitored, I hoped he was the one listening, because it wasn't anything I wanted to have to say again.

16

Much to my surprise, when I stretched out upon the bed a few moments later—trying to have a few moments to quietly think—I right away fell heavily asleep. If I dreamed, it was not memorable; I felt as if a dense cloak had been pulled over my face, tucked warmly around my brain, and perfumed by sweet fragrances that eased my muscles so as to let my soul drift easily away. Now, of course, I suspect it was another of good Ba'al-Dinon's kind graces toward me, but as it happened, I awoke heavily displaced in time and confused by the quality of the light coming through the window shades. I rubbed my face, forced myself from the comfortable mattress, and emerged from the bedroom to find my son napping on the unfolded couch with a small and modest but reasonably tasteful rack of clothes waiting for me along the wall.

"Some lady wheeled that in a few hours ago," muttered Telemachus, turning his back toward me and pulling the covers of his bed more thoroughly around himself. "And some clothes for me, too... I don't have to go to dinner, do I?"

"No, darling, feel free to rest more. If I had a choice, I'd be staying in, too."

"But you want to see Glenn, huh?"

"Oh, yes, very much...but I don't think he and I will be able to do much real socializing." Hesitating, I rested my hand upon the cool metal of the mobile rack and asked Telemachus, "I know you didn't get to speak with him much—but what did you think of him?"

Rolling onto his back at last, Telemachus's hands emerged from the cocoon to fold thoughtfully upon his diaphragm. "He seemed like a sad person."

"He is, indeed," I agreed with a frown, glancing at the door through which Glenn had left. "I think he misses me quite terribly—but he has complicated feelings about certain aspects of my life, and your father's life. It makes it very difficult for Glenn give himself to me as he wishes to. So much of what love is about, Telemachus, is an opening of the heart. That's intimacy."

"I see. Do you think something has changed in him? Something that will enable him to open his heart to you now?"

"Only Glenn can tell me if that's the case. It doesn't matter what I hope or think. But I pray it is...because I do love him, and I hate to be apart from my daughter like this. I know Malin wishes to take care of them both."

"Some people really hate my father, don't they?"

"The average person just isn't built to understand your father," I confessed, rolling the rack into my bedroom while waving the boy back when he tried to get up and help. "Just rest now—anyway, you said it very plainly to my—to your grandfather. That business about people who have made up their minds…I'm still thinking about it. I suspect you'll make a great scholar or philosopher someday if you persevere in your studies, read widely, and think about the ways in which you and others live."

His gaze leveled toward the ceiling, as mine had been before I became anesthetized by sleep. "That sounds much better than being a soldier," Telemachus reflected.

"Yes," I agreed. "Much better."

Alone in my bedroom, I dressed myself, choosing a simple black dress that, with its long sleeves and ample skirt, was modest yet flattering. Its white collar and sleeve cuffs softened somewhat the otherwise funerary look. Remembering all the times during his window of service to me, (That *he* had served *me!* The shame!), in which Dinon had delighted in methodically braiding, nay, sculpting my hair, I pulled my mane back into a bun. Realizing with some annoyance that I had neither shoes nor stockings—a perhaps deliberate omission commanded by my father to keep me on the property—I made my way quietly through the living room of our comfortable little prison cell. Stupidly forgetting myself for a few seconds, I tried to use the doorknob. It was locked, of course, and I rolled my eyes at the undignified act of having to knock on my own door and ask for permission to leave my room; but I was spared, for the sound of the jiggling brass had attracted the attention of the hunter stationed in the hall outside.

"I was invited to dinner," I told him as politely as I could, even venturing to smile—a venture quickly abandoned when he didn't return it and instead raised his radio to his lips. A mutter I couldn't understand issued forth, as unintelligible as the static discharge that bandied back at him with a delay of five or six seconds. After nodding, he withdrew a pair of handcuffs from his belt and didn't flinch at my withering stare.

"Really?"

"Captain's orders," said the brute, snatching my forearm in his brown leather glove to snap one cuff heavily upon my wrist. I sneered as he applied the other cuff—binding me in the front, at least, I suppose—and, still gripping me, attempted to march me down the hall. Giving him a little taste of the strength that made it necessary to restrain me, I jerked my elbow roughly from his grasp.

"Don't touch me again," I told him. "Give the key to Glenn and let him uncuff me; I won't have a dog like you anywhere near me again."

With a snort, the man slung his rifle from his back. I tensed as the barrel nudged me. "Fine," he said. "Walk."

Gritting my teeth, I obeyed. He kept the gun on me all the way to the dining room, lowering it only when a man near the door— seeing us—radioed our arrival in. The man then opened the door for us.

Within the vast formal dining room where Parvati once hosted delegations and diplomats, the long table was now set for three. Both Glenn and my father rose from their places, with Glenn's expression sharpening at the sight of my condition—and then easing in mild befuddlement as the hunter walked up, silently placed the key in his hand, and walked back, passing me as though I were an armchair or a lamp. "Gentlemen," I said as he shut the door behind him.

"Was this necessary?" asked Glenn, hurrying over to take me more gently by the hand and insert the key into the lock. As soon as the cuff sprang open, his broad thumb rubbed gently up and down the vein of my wrist, soothing my ache and making me long to kiss him.

Yet, all the while, there was my father, speaking in the background: "Unfortunately, yes. Based on what we know about Thecla, it was very necessary…you're a bit of a hellcat these days, the way I hear it."

As his attention turned to me, I paused. "You're the captain that man was referring to, I take it?"

"I think it'd be better if we all just sat down and had a nice dinner before worrying about petty details like that."

"Why not do both," I told him, primly perching upon the chair across from Glenn's. Trying not to regard with total contempt the pot roast that sat before me, I picked up my fork and demanded, "Tell me, please, how did you wind up in charge of this—operation?"

Then, pausing once again and really piecing together what our surroundings implied about my father's authority, I narrowed my eyes at him. "Wait—are you in charge of this whole blasted *war?*"

"I delegate what I can," he said, plowing into his food with considerably more gusto. While I was relieved to see that my silver goblet contained a draft of blood rather than the beer that Glenn nursed, I took a swig and savored the feeling of actual sustenance entering my body. My father went on. "After you and your husband murdered Parvati, I decided it was time to renew my ties with the Hunters."

"Excuse me?"

Wearing an extremely dubious look, my father humored me by amending his words. "After Parvati mysteriously died during a visit to your territory, I approached the leader of the former

Gudrune chapter, who I thought might have some problems with you. Turns out he had even more problems than I'd anticipated."

Scoffing, glancing from Rigel to Glenn, I clarified, "You went to Winston? And he didn't try to kill you, given your nature?"

"I expect he would have if he'd been able to get up off the couch," my father said with a wry smirk, raising his eyebrows as he paused with his fork en route to his mouth. "Just so happened, though, that he was already fighting off a case of blood poisoning."

"I see." As I set my goblet down again and found it wasn't in me to even pretend to eat the contents of my plate, I wound up sitting with my forearms poised on the edge of the table, the knife and fork held uselessly in my hands. "In other words, you used his moment of weakness to shoulder your way into the role."

"You could say that. To me, it just seemed like providence— and proof that he needed my help. It didn't take very much work to get him to agree. I know you, I know Malin… I'm a very strong contender for the title of expert tactician when it comes to how to defend against both of you."

"And I can see it never once crossed your mind to fight *for* us, instead of against us."

"Oh no, Thecla," said my father with an earnestness that really rather disgusted me, "I'm most definitely fighting for you."

Seeing Rigel was a lost cause, I shifted my interrogation to Glenn. "And you?" I asked. "How, exactly, did you and Rosina wind up here?"

"We returned incognito to gather my resources and lay low with some people from the lower levels of the guild—men who knew I could never be guilty of killing all those hunters in my house during that Rift incident." Averting his eyes briefly from mine as he spoke of that time, Glenn availed himself of the meal's contents, saying only, "When Parvati died and Valquist went into a state of martial law, I sent a letter to Winston asking for his help in vindicating me with the Guild. And, as it happened, Winston was already on his way back here to Valquist…so we, uh, reconnected."

"And I'm sure it didn't hurt that your little ward is among the heirs of Gudrune's title."

He didn't look up from his food, but I could tell by his tone that he was displeased as he confessed, "You could say it has crossed my mind that I'm at least as much a prisoner now as I was in Gudrune."

"I wish you would stop with that nonsense, Glenn. You were never a prisoner. We were offering you asylum, blast it."

"In Eleison's mansion in the middle of nowhere, with servants around every corner and no real way off the property at my own leisure."

Rather blistered by his stubborn insistence, even all this time later, that we had somehow imposed on him by protecting him, I found myself wishing to argue. But as I opened my mouth, I felt a kind of embarrassment. For some reason, I thought of Ignatius and our last conversation in the belly of that train. Was this pride again, somehow obscuring my vision? If Glenn felt that he had been a prisoner all that time, did my intentions really matter?

Instead, I said, "I'm sorry," and the glance of his luptich-gold eyes was so astonished that I was almost hurt.

"Don't worry about it," he said, his gaze lowering again to his plate. "It's in the past."

"I was relieved when Winston introduced me to Glenn here," my father said, gesturing with his fork, "and explained to me that Rosina is my granddaughter. She's a sweet girl. Reminds me of you at that age."

"Yes, Rosina is a delight. I've been so worried about her, wandering the world with Glenn, missing her family."

"Isn't Glenn her family?"

"Well, yes, of course—but the entire household is her family, really. All the servants, the courtiers, and of course myself, Malin, and Eleison. The Karrisregion house was her world."

"It's healthy for worlds to expand," my father insisted. "And having a lot of family is all well and good, but if the members of that family are bad models, then the girl would be better off an orphan."

Balking, I insisted, "How can you say that Eleison is a bad model? You've never even met the man. And Malin, you might as *well* have never met—it's been nearly thirty years since you last spoke to him!"

"I won't sit here and pretend that people can't change," my father acknowledged, smoothing my bristling somewhat. Then, my temper flared back up as he continued, "But people show you who they are, Thecla. And based on Parvati's 'unsolved' assassination while she was your guest, I'd say your husband is doing a damn fine job of showing the world that his heart hasn't changed."

How difficult it is to maintain any sort of fiction. One has to hold two realities in one's head. Always aware of the truth, we become more defensive of our fictional alternative when it's put under fire. "I'm quite sure I don't know what Malin's heart has to do with any of this," I coldly informed my father. "It's true that neither he nor Parvati cared for one another; that doesn't make him responsible for her death."

With a long look, my father at last agreed, "No, I guess that's true. But, whoever was responsible for Parvati's death—is this really the kind of environment where you want to be raising a little girl?"

"She should be with her family," I said firmly. "And so should Glenn. Glenn, dear, you really should talk to Telemachus sometime. He's a good boy—bookish, a delight."

"Malin's son," observed Glenn. "But he's yours, too? There's all kinds of wild gossip about him. I couldn't get the math to work."

My father's expression turned bleak, the shadows in the pits of his cheekbones and sockets beneath his eyebrows turning dark. "Malin managed to exit the Rift earlier than was his due," he said. "I can't be sure how such a thing is possible; but is a man coming back in this—new and parasitic form before he's killed any less strange than returning after? Time isn't relevant to this form of depravity."

"Really, father." Feeling a strange and sorrowful tug at my center of gravity, as though something gripped my ribs and yanked them now and then, I felt nearly inclined to place my hand upon his in comfort; yet, still too bitter from his betrayals, I found I could not, and continued my rigid grip on the fork. "'Depravity' is a terribly strong word. You can't help your condition, and why, look! Now that you're within it, surely by now you know it's nothing bad."

"That's a lie you've told yourself, Thecla," my father said, his tone measured but firm. "It's the Rift in you, deceiving you, perverting your will to its interests. Look at the effects of your concupiscence on your family. The father of your first child is different from your husband, who ought to be dead but instead walks the Earth and brings about war and destruction and murder. Meanwhile, I've led to understand that you've...bonded...to this Eleison fellow you mentioned, and I don't even want to think about some of the rumors I've heard. With all these men and your political responsibilities, how can you possibly have time for one child, let alone two? How can you cite Rosina's welfare as a case for your own victimhood when the truth is that your daughter and her father are, strictly speaking, your prey?"

"They're your prey, too," I reminded him coldly, "and you don't seem to have any difficulty restraining yourself from acting like a bloodthirsty savage around them, do you? The entirety of the staff at all our Gudrune properties is perfectly safe from our appetites. I expect there are some things about dharmine physiology that you don't understand, so allow me to elucidate."

At last, pushing the untouched plate away entirely to sip from the chalice as I spoke, I explained to both my father and Glenn, "You see, fellows, near as I can tell, the human institution of marriage—the intimacy between husband and wife—is mere prefiguration for the matrimony experienced between a pair of dharmine. We feed from each other. That's how it's meant to be, you see, and how it hasn't been able to be since he went off to fight in this blasted war. Oh!" My eyes glossing, I blinked a bit and said in barely contained frustration, "I was so hoping to see him. I'm so glad to see you, Glenn, and—Father, Papa, how I wish this were a different occasion for our meeting. But I'm ached to my very soul, too, for the taste of my husband's blood— Ah—"

I sighed despite myself, my hand flying to my throat; and I found, much to my surprise as my vision drifted off to my right, that Glenn's expression was unexpectedly mesmerized by me. It reminded me of the night when he and I drank on the lawn of this very palace; when I kissed him, and he saved me from that breed of beast he did not then know he was due to become.

"I do not," I continued, "believe it is necessary that mankind become prey to the dharmine. A system could be simply arranged.

Given that cloned blood is used in medicine already, unmarried dharmine could—"

"You can't seriously suggest that dharmine be allowed to integrate into society," my father interrupted, as though he were not one of the beings under discussion. "We're not talking about natural human beings here, Thecla, or even altered ones who were born on Earth. We're talking about demons, born in the Rift and sent here to systematically replace human beings."

"Well—*good*." While both men made little sounds of astonishment to varying degrees of derision, I raised my eyebrows in defiance. "The human life is short and bleak in this world. Always worrying about death—that's what I remember from the point when you died, Papa, until Malin took me in. The entire human life is full of uncertainty, especially for the poor, and full of sorrow because they know it will end and they will take nothing with them. But how sweet it would be if we were all immortal! Wouldn't the urgency with which we lived dissolve? Wouldn't the hatred of man for his brother fade more quickly into meaninglessness? Wouldn't it be peaceful?"

"At what cost, Thecla? The entire human lineage would end if everyone became dharmine. There would be no new generations. What could we do to perpetuate history into the future if we had no new people?"

"Use our leisure to find scientific means of reproducing," I suggested, spreading my hands. "We will have all the time in the world...why not? But there will always be holdouts. Malin and I have discussed this before, theorizing over wine with Eleison."

Settling back into my chair, I summarized those discussions by simply saying, "We suspect there will always be holdouts—

always a certain strain of terrestrial humans who resist becoming dharmine, and who fight. There will be, as there are now, some who even successfully manage to murder their own future selves or the selves of their neighbors, thus dooming themselves or their friends. But as more individuals are replaced by their dharmine, you see, it will become easier to persuade the general populace to accept dharmines as individuals with equal dignity to the human beings from whom they came."

"Persuade," said my father darkly, "or force."

"Who knows what will happen behind closed doors, of course," I agreed with a thin smile. "But for the vast majority, I believe there will be an increase in willingness as time goes on. What's the harm? After the Rift is tamed, we can harness it for power for the expansion of life—"

"For the extinction of all species on Earth, to be replaced with the lesser variants from the Rift."

"Don't be ridiculous. How can you say with a straight face that the species with the finite lifespan is the superior one?"

"And how can you be sure," he returned firmly, "that our lifespans really are infinite? Nobody's ever seen a dharmine integrate successfully into society like you're describing."

"Nobody's admitted to being one, of course," I posited. "But now, knowing myself, my husband, and our Telemachus—if we're capable of disguising ourselves, surely there are many others. Most, I suspect, would be from the noble classes; dukes, counts. The initial dharmines who will have obtained footholds in this world would, it follows, be wealthy enough to live stable and discreet existences."

"That idea is terrifying," said Glenn in a moment of honesty, looking up from the middle-distance at which he had absorbed all of this talk between my father and myself. "Thecla—do you really believe that?"

"I truly couldn't say for certain, of course—but yes. I would say if you arranged each and every nobleperson all together in a room and gave them some foolproof test one by one, roughly one percent of them would already be dharmines. It only makes sense." I stared into my sweet hunter's eyes and let him feel the intensity of my message: that he was on the losing side, but that I could gladly protect him in this brave new world. "Think about it, dear. Where do you mostly see dharmines? In rural regions, in the outskirts of towns, where the slums are relegated. And how do we know these dharmines are spotted? The incidents are reported, and those hunters or officers, or other militiamen, or unlucky family members involved in the dispatch, give their witness testimony. These are unsuccessful dharmines.

"But how often do we hear of these incidents occurring among the well-to-do? In fact, when the Valquist newspapers were slandering me back in that hateful season I was last obliged to come here, it seemed already quite natural for them to suggest I was a secret dharmine. Tabloids are always suggesting that of aristocrats these days. Perhaps they're not all merely trying to push papers."

Having evidently lost his appetite, Glenn glanced down at my cup and lowered his fork back to his plate. Taking up his own flagon of some rich-smelling ale, he said, "I wish I could tell myself you were wrong."

"This is all the more reason why we need to do something now," my father pleaded, laying his hand flat on the table near me to return my attention his way. "Can't you see, Thecla? Humanity has struggled enough to maintain its way of life while simply dealing with the Rift. Now you want to hand the world to it!"

"The problem, Papa, is that we always should have been adapting to the Rift, rather than resisting it. What if the Rift is ultimately something natural? Something that would have happened eventually no matter what conditions were present in the system?"

My father looked poised to respond, but before he could form a sound with his lips, a sharp knock echoed upon the door. A hunter, different from the one who had accompanied me earlier, appeared, looking annoyed and somewhat cowed.

"I'm very sorry to interrupt, sir," he said to my father. Somehow, the way his eyes flicked toward me telegraphed exactly what he had come to say, and my soul soared with delight.

"Malin Farrow is calling for his wife, and he won't take 'no' for an answer."

17

ecause, thanks to Ba'al-Dinon's frequent penetration into my consciousness, I know what a truly psychic connection feels like, I hesitate to portray my connection with Malin as in any way willfully telepathic or psychical in nature. Our connection is not that sort of connection, nor is it owing to our shared nature as Riftborn. Yet perhaps my reader has experienced such instances of inexplicable psychic phenomena—these moments of synchronicity between oneself and one's loved one. Thinking the same thought, eating the same meal, sharing the same dream, all while miles or even time periods apart. It is something common to the experience of being conscious on Earth. And, as the astute scholars researching the history of my life are surely very interested to discover, later on I would learn that there may be reason for it.

At the time, though, it seemed like some evocation: some causal connection between the amount we had discussed Malin at that table and his subsequent interruption via the call. In truth, he'd been searching all day and night, engaging the services of every source to which his military operation had access. By the time I heard his voice, I was surrounded by my father and six other hunter militia men who operated various devices in an effort to trace and otherwise analyze the call. Malin had been awake at least as long as I had, and the sigh of relief he uttered when he heard me say, "Darling, oh, Husband, I love you," was the sound of a man collapsing from exhaustion.

"My angel—Thecla, Thecla, my jewel, are you all right?"

"Now that I'm speaking to you, I'm far better. It's been quite unpleasant getting here, but now that we're where we are—"

"Parvati's old palace, I understand."

While my father and a few of the men exchanged glances, I bit back a smile and said, "At any rate... now that we are where we are, they're treating Telemachus and me reasonably, all things considered."

"I assume they're there with you now?"

"Oh, yes, well—what can one do? I'm sure they'll realize soon enough what a mistake they've made."

"Just wait and see." Malin's voice sent shivers up my spine; I had never heard such a low, deadly note to his words, not even in our darkest sex play. I curled a loose strand of hair around my index finger, fidgeting as I smiled with pleasure. "If they don't respond to my demands that they release you," he continued, "I'll raze the city of Valquist and pluck you and our son from the smoldering ruins."

"I don't doubt that for a moment, Malin." My top teeth worried my bottom lip. "Oh, darling—I need you right now."

"And I need you," he said tenderly. "Keep your chin up, Thecla, don't worry. I promise, we'll have you home soon."

"I know that you will, sweetheart. Don't stay on the line, they're trying to trace your call—"

"Let them. I love you—oh, Thecla, my beauty, I love you with all my heart. Tell our son to trust in me."

"His faith in you is already unshakable, but I will. Be safe, my love. Good night."

When Malin was assured of my relative safety and we hung up, I was left alone with the hunters, who continued to exchange numbers, insights, and observations from the call: all of which meant nothing to me. Numb, I stared at the device in my hand, only half-aware of the male voice saying, "That sound in the background—was that a helicopter of some kind?"

Then my attention was arrested by Rigel, who took the watch from my grip and tossed it onto the nearby desk. "Let's go for a walk," he said, "just you and me, Thecla."

"I have no shoes," I demonstrated, growing all the more annoyed as he merely winked.

"Something tells me you'll survive...don't worry, we won't go far. Just around the grounds...I'd really like to talk to you one-on-one."

With a sigh, I folded my arms and nodded. "Very well," I said, still somewhat reluctant, even as the child in my soul longed to relive happier days with the Papa she remembered. "I suppose I could use the walk after being cooped up so long. And—"

Mouth tightening, I looked my father in the face and asked myself—was he even my father anymore? Was the Rift not my mother, and Malin my new father for having brought me out of it? Who, then, was this Rigel, also born of the Rift? My brother, now; not my father, not really.

"I think we should get to know each other better, as adults."

Outside, I was pleased to find the cool, damp lawn quite pleasant beneath my feet. The scent of the trees, the feel of the breeze—everything was a tender indulgence after that transportation in captivity to this despised place. Even supervised, I savored every second of this stroll and was amazed at how naturally and pleasantly I fell into conversation with my father all these years later—even with this new heartache for the man he had become.

"You'll never believe this," I told him. "Oh, it was grand—when I went to visit Sable last year, I happened to come to Lescaut on the same day that the circus came!"

"Did you, really?"

He sounded very pleased, and no small bit relieved to discover we could still have a pleasant interaction. I was, too, and let myself feel lost in time a moment as I told him, "Yes, it was wonderful—truly a boon from a good God."

My words drew a second look from Rigel, though I couldn't discern the source of his scrutiny until he asked, "You still believe in God, do you, Thecla?"

"Of course." Laughing at the absurdity of his question, I waved my hand between us. "One should think resurrection into these superior states would only reinforce the mortal belief in a deity."

"I'm not so sure this is the resurrection a loving God intended. Even if what you said about you and Malin is true—that's the exception. This condition is abominable and dependent on the deaths of mortals from the very second a dharmine comes into the world."

"All human existence, even the most benign and harmless, is dependent on the deaths of other beings. Do you think leather springs out of the dirt? That birds donate their feathers for our pillows or animals their furs for our warmth?"

"There's a difference between killing an animal and killing a human being."

"Yet you and I both know that from the internal perspective, there is no difference between the dharmine and the human being—not on the level of pure thought."

"Are you sure about that?" With a deeply skeptical look, my father observed, "My own mind feels very different after emerging from the Rift. I know something has changed. I feel like a black hole in the shape of a man."

"That just sounds like depression," I told him bluntly. "Depression you might not be feeling if you weren't full of self-loathing."

"This is more than depression, Thecla. It's the Rift, working within us." He ruminated on it while we passed a neglected row of rose bushes that now grew wild and untamed, their thorny branches missing buds for want of fertilization. I tarried, fondling a thorn that glittered in the sunlight, its long, cruel point calling to me. While I trailed my thumb and index finger back and forth along the needle, my father said, "I'm sure you feel it, too. A mind inside your own mind. A mind that's not your mind—thoughts that aren't yours. Thoughts that make you think that—"

My father, realizing I had stayed behind, stepped so he could turn to face me, and the motion of his frame drew my attention. I pricked myself on the thorn. Pain, no longer what it once was, now glittered pleasantly through me even as my father concluded:

"—maybe none of your thoughts are really yours. Ever. That you're not yourself, and never will be."

"Or that maybe you never have been yourself," I reflected, watching the blood bloom in the tip of my finger. "Maybe you're just a figment of God's imagination, no real purpose or meaning other than to fill in the spaces of creation around His own awareness of Himself. It could be we're all just ripples in the water when the rock's thrown in; an echo of someone or something else's movement, echoing out through time until we fade back into nothing."

My father looked at me grimly. "Yes," he said.

"But Papa"—I raised my eyes to his—"can't you see that was always the problem? Being human, you could forget about the existential dread, even if only sometimes. But now, as a dharmine, having lived through death, the question keeps spiraling: 'Am I real?' Yet what is 'real', after all? Am I the real me? If the real me is defined by who I was in the past, then am I only a developing zygote in my mother's womb? If the real me is defined by who I will be in the future, does anything matter besides who I am on my deathbed someday?"

"The real you is a continuum," my father said. I smiled simply at him, gesturing us onward through the grounds of the palace.

"My point exactly. And the truth is that it has always been a somewhat loosely connected continuum. We are happier by a significant margin when we learn to live with this fact. The only thing that has changed is us; and that's to be expected in life. Indeed, so long as we're alive, we must be changing; and when we run out of ways to change as human beings, we are invited into the opportunity to change as dharmines."

"That's a lot of lofty philosophizing, Thecla," my father said, irritating me even as he added, "and some worthy thoughts you've just inspired; but be practical. How can you really expect to raise Rosina?"

"God willing, she'll be a dharmine someday, once she's lived to her liking as a human."

"So you're comfortable with your daughter dying?"

I hesitated, feeling his snare tightening around me. "All mortal beings must die someday," I reminded him. "There's nothing exempt from this; even the most innocent cherub, a role with no contender but Rosina, must eventually see that fate hanging before her."

"And the thought of her personality being appropriated by something that might not be her—"

"I am myself," I told my father sharply. "And I know myself. Papa, I can assure you that I'm me. The same goes for you, for Malin, and for my Rosina."

"You are yourself," my father corrected, staring hard into my eyes, "and you are also the Rift. It's in us—it *is* us."

I recognized, somewhat belatedly, that we had stopped midway to the kennels from my first visit to this wretched palace. Rigel regarded me with a grim certainty.

"It's alive, Thecla," he told me. "The Rift is alive, and it's a mind. It's a person, with a will and knowledge beyond our own."

"And how would you know that?"

"Because I speak to it," my father went on. "All day. I catch it imitating me. Thinking in my voice; trying to persuade me to do and say and think things I would never—"

Rigel shuddered, stroking his beard while his eyes trailed somewhere past me and off into the dark. "Have you ever seen a convert? An altered who's been destabilized from a lack of Stabilify, or who has no mate?"

Eleison, his beautiful ruby eyes tainted with silver.

I had seen Eleison with those mercury eyes another time, too—shimmering like pools of toxic metal. And when was that?

"I've seen it," I said, remembering most especially that second time, even though it was the first instance that was most relevant. "And he wasn't himself."

"Who—Glenn? No—that Eleison fellow of yours."

"I'd prefer not to talk about that time," I said, suddenly struck through by the awful recognition that this truly was my father. With a sharp, pained laugh, I shielded my heart with my right hand and glanced down at the motion.

"I want you to think the best of Eleison," I told him softly, my soul far away with my beloved, my firm but merciful guardian. I was quite sure he was going insane with the instinctive demands of the Rift beast within that he find me.

Or perhaps that was just my selfish heart, calling impatiently for Eleison even though I knew my husband would have the situation well in hand. Even though I believed in Malin, I wanted things to unfold at my pace.

"Eleison would do anything for me, Papa. He's a good man, wise and shrewd and much too witty. I love him. I thought for a long time that I would have to choose between them; that I dreamed of running away with this man rather than marrying the territory master I adored. That I could speak of another man in such a way should tell you how Eleison moves my heart."

"Why didn't you wind up doing that, then?" My father looked at me with great curiosity, eager to hear about this man and that time—a time that was, even then, already so very far away.

"Because of you," was my answer. The puzzled contortions of his eyebrows were not nearly as amusing in that moment as they are now in my memory. "Because you and Mother showed Malin Farrow something important about the difference between love and ownership. He didn't love my mother; he only wished to control her. Out of pride," I added, reflecting on my dead friend and then, with hope, on Charlotte, who I was grateful to imagine safe. "But love should make us humble ourselves for the one we love and adore. We should open our hearts completely. And Malin's heart is a heart that is endless in its wanting. It wants and wants and wants. I think that might be one reason why we love each other so much—I have that kind of heart, too. That's why I'm always thinking about God these days, Papa...you see?"

While I turned toward the kennels, I assured him, "I've always been a black hole in the shape of a woman."

"Thecla—"

"Just where's that little ertiz?" My soul ached for something to hold since neither my husband nor my mate could be accessed. "Oh, he was just the cutest little—"

The words had not completely escaped my mouth before my body gave a sickening lurch. The breeze had kicked up many times, and I had smelled no animals—but I only now realized. Frightened, I hurried faster, half-jogging through the grass, and soon I looked with a heavy heart at row after row of these empty cages.

"They're hunters," my father said, coming to a stop behind me. He was aware of my distress without seeing my face. My shoulders quivered, shaking harder as he experimentally rested his hand upon one of the cages. As I burst into tears, Rigel—my father!—tutted, drawing me close and letting me rest my head upon his heart.

"Now," he said, his tone measured and gentle. "I imagine whoever kept the animals here let as many go free as they possibly could before the palace was overrun. My guess would be your ertiz is fine."

Empty words, perhaps. But in that second, everything

adversarial vanished. All the existential doubts of my father were proven null and void: less than nothing. For there was no doubt at all in that moment that this *was* my father, and I was his daughter. Death could not change that any more than could the Rift, or time, or space. I still wept with the hope that things might be okay; that once, it had not been thus, and perhaps someday it would once again not be so.

That is not often how time works, sad to say. Indeed, the greatest reunions, I have found, are often also the greatest heart-pains. There is a sudden ache of rekindled awareness, of entropy—we know that some things simply cannot be reverted to the way they were. Relationships will always bear scar tissue; knowledge of someone's inner character cannot be un-known.

Like the freshly crippled right hand of Winston Garland—all those bones and tendons never capable of returning to where they were before I crushed them, now permanently curved into a claw whose blue wrist vein was black from some blood clot—by which I recognized the man, these things would continue on, but in a changed state. The question was one of adaptation.

And, as my father and I re-entered the palace on nearly friendly terms only to run into the former leader of Gudrune's Hunters' Guild, Winston proved by his quickdraw that he was fully capable of adaptation.

18

The gun appeared so quickly that I barely had time to react, let alone to realize what was happening. I could not even process the sight of the hand that held it—and, thereafter, the hate-lined expression on Winston's face. Only in the next microsecond, as I was consciously piecing it all together, did my father's heavy arm raise roughly, sending me careening to the left with a bark of, "Winston—no!"

But there was blood in Winston's eyes; his teeth were bared beneath his unkempt mustache as he wheeled around and adjusted his aim. Now exceedingly grateful for my bare feet, I dashed along the edge of the otherwise inhospitable shooting gallery of the hallway by which we had entered, grimacing as I ducked and wove my way along the cool marble floor.

A sensation like an insect sting struck my cheek, but there was no time to attend to it. Bullets shot out wall plaster and already neglected plant fronds all around me. Each crack-whizz-shatter struck closer than the last! By the time my father had the man restrained, I'd made it to the end of the corridor and skidded to a halt with a yelp of surprise: I'd turned the corner in the rough direction of the stairs to my suite only to wind up nose-to-nose with one of the Hunters hurrying to investigate the gunfire.

What happened next is controversial. I've heard it said that I reached for his gun, but of course that's absurd. He was already pointing the blasted thing when I turned the corner and screamed, a screamed muted by his commands that I get on the floor as though I were some mongrel dog. I was startled, of course, as anyone would be, especially given the circumstances and my still pressing need for defense against the now far wilder discharges of Winston's pistol as my father wrested it away. Therefore, acting on instinct, as Eleison had drilled into me (pardon the imagery) many, many times over the past nearly four years, I simply disarmed him as I'd been taught. And in disarming him as I'd been taught, we wound up repositioned— my right hand around the gun, steering it down and pulling him forward along with it as my left hand raised in a fist aimed for his face. When this man therefore took in the spinal column the impact of a bullet that otherwise might have struck me, it was incidental… and, in so many ways, fortuitous. That it happened to be the same rude fellow who had held the gun on me all the way to the dining room was pure accident. I did not make the first move or antagonize him, as at least one witness wrote in some tawdry paperback tell-all interview recently published overseas, where such libel is legal; and I certainly didn't laugh, as it is sometimes claimed I did when the man was shot. Indeed, my heart broke to see this hunter dying for me by pure accident, even though he was a criminal brute. But there I stood with his gun all the same, and him dead at my feet as Glenn rounded the juncture at the far end of the hall.

"Thecla," he shouted, advancing toward me before falling back again at the presumed meaning of the tableau. Then, with another step forward. he, like me, took full stock of the several armed men around me, only one of whom knew to finally help my father put Winston under control.

"Be careful," I cried to them. "He vanishes—I think into the Rift!"

"He can't do it on camera," my father said through gritted teeth, jerking his head toward one of the chandeliers littering the ceiling of a palace—vindicating me, too, for I had sensed, from the start of my acquaintance with it, that the place was heavily bugged. "Or with sixteen eyeballs on him—stand down." He added this at a volume that made it impossible to tell whether he meant the angry bark for me or for the insurgents, or for both of us. And because of the insanity of the moment, I found myself laughing.

"What's so funny?" he demanded, causing me to at last lower the gun to the feet of the man before me, my eyes sidelong upon my father as I giggled on.

"Your tone just reminds me of that time when I snuck out to the circus, when there was that Rift Event—why, you were so outraged and relieved when you found me. When we were back home and the lecture began, you sounded just as you do right this minute."

"This does feel a little like that, somehow," said my father, passing a restrained Winston into the control of the man beside him. "Take him to the wine cellar and let him cool off for a while."

"Why do I suspect the wine cellar isn't exactly the party it sounds like...hello, Glenn, darling." I let shine a twinkling smile for my lover, who pushed through two of the hunters, heedless of the guns they were slow to lower as he rushed to my side. He fit an arm around me while using his other hand to turn my face and check for injuries—a bullet had indeed grazed my cheekbone, I now realized, that little stinging sensation I had perceived in my adrenaline-fueled haze earlier. I burned him with my eyes, gazing upon him while thinking of what I wanted him to do to me. For I have become aware, in my time on this Earth, that such thoughts have reverberations through the warp and weft with which the world shivers in such highly-charged emotional moments as this. "My knight," I whispered to Glenn, pressing closer to him while my father lumbered close enough to pull the gun from the last hunter still aiming at me.

"I said stand down, you maniacs. Champing at the bit to shoot a woman—and Malin's wife. You're convinced he has an atomic bomb, are you? You want to take away the one reason he shouldn't drop it on us?"

"This paranoid nonsense again." I couldn't help my snap even if my father had come to my aid; it was an old line, Parvati's excuse to restrain Malin's hand and keep him from mining some benefit out of the somber inevitability of the Rift. As Rigel looked over sharply, I forced filial associations from my mind and told him, as the adult daughter of a death-estranged father, "I've seen with my own two eyes how my husband's money is being spent in researching the Rift's energy applications. There are many elements involved, I admit, and some of those materials could be misused in the wrong hands—but Malin's hands are the right ones."

Looking amused but not in the mood to argue, Rigel nodded to Glenn. "Let's end this evening on a high note. Hey, Glenn—go ahead and walk my daughter home."

"She's been in that cramped little room all day. Did you spend much time in the library last time you were here, Thecla?" At the shake of my head, Glenn said to my father, "Let me take her there and talk to her for a while. I'll bring her straight back to her suite, don't worry."

"I'm sure you two have a lot to catch up on." After exchanging a nod with my guardian, my father managed a nearly cordial, "Good night, Thecla," and made his way up the corridor along which Winston, cursing me, was dragged.

"Good night," I said to him, the words tapering off strangely as I hesitated to add "Papa," or perhaps even "Father," before any addition became more unnatural than either one of those words had become in my heart after writing him off as truly dead. Instead, watching him go in this curious cloud of sudden silence that seemed to now brood palpably over me, I realized something so awful it might have driven me to tears were I not still arush with the thrill of the adrenal response.

Someday quite soon, I was going to have to watch him die again. At least, I would have to know about it. Someone would remark to me, as my stepmother once did, "Your father is dead," and that would be all there was to it. He would be obliterated—hopelessly this time—and I would be poised alone, a cliff jutted out at the edge of the sea. Worse, I knew I would have to hear it soon, because the only alternative would be that I would hear it a second time about my husband, instead—and I would never tolerate hearing that of Malin again.

Not ever.

"Thank you for hurrying to my aid," I told Glenn as he led me through the militarized halls, their once-proud gleam now scuffed from boots and smutty with the cloying veil of nicotine. "I wasn't sure that you would still feel so inclined to protect me. Not given my...condition."

"Well, getting to know your father has changed my stance on, uh…a lot of things. Here it is—here—"

We stopped by the broad double doors, arranged symmetrically to the ballroom on the building's other side. Thus, the library architecture was similar, with a vestibule permitting a second floor of books tucked neatly into inbuilt shelves that allowed a continuous flow of rococo elegance. While I marveled—the books so overwhelming in number and value that I could not fathom the knowledge contained therein—Glenn shut the door behind us and said, "I want to fully retire. Truly, formally. I've decided it."

"When did you decide that?"

"Seeing you," he told me, his eyes tastefully darting down my body and then back to my face. One hand in his pocket, the other stroking his beard, Glenn shrugged. "I was already planning on it, and then I was sort of obliged to take that 'sabbatical', you could call it, when Rosina was born. But…I guess I don't just mean retiring from the Hunter's guild. I mean—I want retire from killing."

Marveling, I said, "But you're such an asset. Even during Rift Events?"

"I can't anymore, Thecla." His voice was rough as he spoke my name, and as he stepped toward me, my stomach twisted into knots I hadn't felt since my youth. The color rose in my cheeks and I stood perfectly still, afraid that if I moved, he would startle and flee like some timid bird. Indeed, he hesitated just slightly before withdrawing his hand from his pocket and gently cupping my jaw with his thumb and forefinger. As he did, his thumb brushed a few stray locks from my healing cheek, and he was suddenly very close. I ached for his kiss, and he seemed to yearn for mine. "When the Rift comes, I—I'm among them. The beasts. I have to accept that. And I have to accept that I've never felt so alive. I feel compassion for them like I never felt before the alteration. I see now—now more than ever—that they're just animals, like our animals, truly just trying to survive. And, in you, Thecla…I see that every dharmine that's ever been eradicated was also a human being, a human mind, trying to live long enough to express itself."

Pained by the thought, I nodded, then found myself frozen again as Glenn rested his forehead against mine. "I see that in you," he emphasized. "I see that the dharmine aren't malicious. From the first moment I saw you, I wanted to be close to you—and seeing you this time, as you stepped off the train, I felt that again more intensely. Thecla…"

Unable to resist, I slid my arms around his neck and tipped my head back, offering my lips to him. He sighed and growled, his hands stroking up and down my waist as our lips met. "Maybe it's the mating bond from having Rosina together," he murmured between kisses, the grazing of our lips turning into a slow, deliberate interplay of love as we drank in one another's pleasure, "but I never want to be separated from you again."

"Then don't run away this time," I whispered, my eyes fixed on his as he let his hands slide lower. When I didn't stop him, he firmly cupped my backside, drawing me toward him, pressing my body to his. "You can have me whenever you want, Glenn…just stay with me and let me reward your chivalry."

"As long as you aren't busy with Malin," he growled jealously, his kisses growing more fervent.

"Au contraire," I teased, nipping his lower lip and pleased by his body's response as I whispered, "come have me while I'm busy with Malin…oh, Glenn, you're missing out on such delicious fun! My husband would love to watch you fuck me… without Eleison's help, or with it."

Glenn's breath hitched, the tent in his trousers prominent as he drew me back into the embrace of a leather armchair situated along the library's northern wall. I straddled him, letting him enjoy the nearness of my body as our kisses deepened; intensified. "Do they make love to you...together?"

He delighted me with his innocence, for the question was real and flustered.

"Mm, all the time...sometimes they take turns, or make love to one another while I watch... sometimes—oh, Glenn...that made you very hard just now..."

"It's just—ah—"

"Sh..." I reached down between us to caress the outline of his straining manhood, slowly unzipping his trousers while looking into his eyes. Anyone could have walked in on us, and so, as I reached into his fly to run my fingers along his cock through the silk of his boxers, I leaned in to whisper in his ear, "It's okay, Glenn...it's okay to feel good...it's okay if you want me to watch you taking a nice, deep fucking from my husband...or, is it—oh, Eleison...mm...that's what you want, isn't it, Glenn...well, I'm happy to oblige...and I'm sure he will be, too..."

While Glenn groaned from low in his throat, I slid my hand into his boxers and let his hips rock his prick up into my fist. He kissed and nipped my neck, making me moan with pleasure of my own as he admitted to me roughly, "I think I'd rather see you get fucked, Thecla—held down and pounded like you deserve, like it's a punishment..."

"Oh, my hero...don't be angry at me, please—ah!"

As animalistic as I'd ever seen him, Glenn gripped me by the hair and twisted my mouth toward his for a savage, almost frightening kiss. I succumbed, moaning against the tongue I'd tantalized as he dominated my unready mouth. My body relaxed into a natural response of pure submission and I let him catch me by the wrist to push me back down against the arm of the chair. Thus, legs akimbo, I marveled as he spread my limb to situate himself between them, "Oh, Glenn, you really are angry at me… mad because of all the times Malin and Eleison took turns fucking me without you there to watch…"

"I should have forced you to come with me when I left," he told me gruffly, tearing my underthings away with a rough cry of rending fabric and a sudden inundation of cold air against my exposed, soaking nethers. As I gasped, so did he, letting the fullness of his erection rest upon my cleft. His body covering me utterly, hands pressing my wrists down against the leather of the chair and leaving my body available even through my dress, Glenn sank his teeth into my lower lip while heeding only slightly my warning that he do so with caution. "Taken you someplace in the woods, kept you captive, gotten you pregnant again…that might have settled you down. You need to be tamed, Thecla."

After an absence of much too long, the tip of Glenn's bare cock pressed to the desperate center of my craving. I whimpered and nodded, my brow furrowed.

"Yes, please, oh, my hero—discipline me with your love. Educate me, Glenn, oh—fuck me until I'm a good girl again, darling—fuck!"

My mouth hung open in shock as, consumed by his desire too completely to tease me for very long, Glenn stabbed his thick cock deep into the velvet sheath that pulsed for him. I moaned, writhing with delight, my legs locking around him to encourage him deeper as I begged in a hot whisper, "That's it, that's it, yes, yes, oh, sweet fuck, Glenn, don't show me any mercy—yes, yes—!"

How wonderful lovemaking truly is! For I have no doubt that there were moments when Glenn thought of how I had transformed his life and, in those brief flashes, hated me. But sex is a medicant in so many ways. It takes these painful feelings, these sorrowful longings, this human loneliness of being alive, and transmutes it all into a celebration of unity and love. Those seconds in which Glenn hated me, that real desire he had to discipline me out of his frustration at my ways—all that became fuel for the fire of our libidos, this two-source blaze that raged between us with decreasing concern for being heard and increasing narrowing of vision into one another, until there was nothing but one another. And then 'another' flew away, leaving 'one' so that there was no sense of otherness between us. There was only this perfect harmony, the singular tension sustained between our bodies, rising and rising, cresting like music, until—

"Thecla!"

"Glenn! Oh, Glenn—I missed you—"

We kissed.

W hen the storm of love had watered the earth that formed the foundation of the love between Glenn and me, and, our clothes rearranged, I reclined in his lap with his arms folded around me and a fire dancing not far from the armchair, he suddenly said as if coming from out of some daze, "I never even asked you about all that with Winston."

"You mean, you didn't know?" When my lover shook his head, I laughed and suggested, "That's just like that cowardly fellow to hide information from you...I wonder if anyone knows but my father. Winston was trying to extort me—to bully me into doing as he pleased, reinstating the guild and the like. At first, he tried sweet-talking me, coming on very charming and friendly; but, when I didn't go for that, he started to wave Rosina's parentage under my nose, not knowing, as I did, about Telemachus."

"And," Glenn's brow worked as he at last was free to ask, "what is all this with Telemachus? He has to be yours—he looks like you. But—"

"Time doesn't matter insofar as the Rift's deposits of human consciousness are concerned." My tongue darting across my lower lip, I stared into the fire and explained, "I can't say I understand it, myself. But there are those who come later and those who come earlier. There may even be those dharmine who emerge from the Rift before they were born. Most, I suspect, will be after…but not all."

I considered my first episode of awareness, for lack of a better word—the death dream-vision-space of a new birth, that alien re-emergence out of some vague but essential self-awareness that was perhaps also the faculty which allowed the astute thinker to gain lucidity in dreams. Malin, taking me so roughly upon the indiscernible void-floor of that non-space, the footsteps of all those passing by us as they hurried through the barrier I had broken to re-enter Earth. As I ruminated on this, some energy center, some mystical spot in the middle of my diaphragm, glowed with golden light, and radiated warmth, and I felt the deep intimacy of that space and its experience in me—within my soul, perhaps.

"I've heard it said the Rift flows backward, in reverse entropy." I contemplated the vision, hardly seeing the man to whom I spoke. "Therefore, as there were a great many people hurrying to be among the first to come back to Earth, they passed me by while I stayed behind to finish my tapestry—"

"When was this?"

"Between this now and that then," I told him, reaching up to touch the crown of white seared forever into my locks. "After the blood poisoning Malin gave me when I enticed him to bite me without revealing who I was—for you see, Glenn, Malin was already living in in the world as a dharmine. As himself, along with my son. He remained behind in that middle-space to lay with me there a while, and then we found a baby there."

Comprehending at last that there was some connection between the word salad of my memories of that time and his initial question, Glenn observed, "Telemachus."

"That's right. The child that was in my womb when the hunters had me shot, or the child from our coupling there in that place, or both in some mysterious way." I pondered these and other possibilities for but a few of Glenn's heartbeats before saying, "Ultimately, however, I have thought it through and cannot make sense of it. There was a period of second darkness, which I felt I was in for quite some time, forgetting even myself; perhaps that was linear time again, or something else altogether. Perhaps that was the real moment I died, and my second life only began when I felt Earth's grass, and Malin's arms? Perhaps, perhaps, perhaps—"

I mused, feeling Glenn's eyes upon me as though I might a beloved pet's while I ruminated, but I conceded at last that, "It may be—perhaps even must be, if I think it through enough—that there really is a will behind the Rift's dispersion of creatures from storm to storm. That there is indeed a logic, but explicable only by a context beyond present terrestrial understanding."

"Like gravity," said Glenn, opening my soul to him with this evidence of how well he followed me even at a time like this.

"Yes, dear," I said, stroking his chest, "like gravity. Like love. Oh, Glenn..." Suddenly brought back to awareness of him by his speech and this caress, I smiled, tilting my forehead against his to whisper, "I missed you."

"I've missed you so much." Glenn's words came from deep in his heart as he murmured them into affectionate kisses I pecked along his mouth. "You've changed so much, yet you're still the same in some fundamental way I can't explain."

"Yes, darling, I've changed...you changed me when you abandoned me. The hunters changed me when they killed my husband, and my husband changed me when he returned from the dead. Then the Rift changed me when I followed him."

Ba'al-Dinon's beautiful visage imprinted itself upon my frontal lobe so clearly that I felt, once again, as if I looked upon him without looking. My heart swelled; I was drawn briefly from the moment with a great ardor, a longing to kiss him and lay my head upon his breast, and more. Why? The question dismissed the image and, suddenly plummeting back into the present moment with Glenn, I sat in a kind of delirium for another second before managing a laugh.

"I'm sorry," I told him, "I've become quite strange."

"Don't apologize, please—"

"It's when I talk about the Rift, and life, and death, and eternity; I have a very queer way of wandering off into this maze of thought."

"I find it beautiful," Glenn told me tenderly, his hand sliding into mine. As I tightened my grip on him and let my body go slack against his chest, his eyes softened as they had the first night I visited him in his Valquist home. I had seen the longing in his soul and knew he was mine.

"Thecla," he whispered after studying me for a few long thuds of his heart, "I'm sorry."

"No, you're not." I turned my face away so that I spoke against his shoulder and peered up at him from the corners of my eyes. "What a dreary thing to say, anyway."

"I truly am." His hand ran down my spine as Glenn murmured, "I shouldn't have left you."

"Then come back with me, Glenn. When all this is through, come back to Gudrune with me."

"I'm thinking about it." His hand stroked up and down my arm, his gaze pensively directed out toward the library books in one of the freestanding shelves filling up the vast space of the first floor. "I'm also still thinking of what I said earlier. About taking you away with me."

"You can't," I told him softly but unhesitatingly. "Telemachus."

"He's the only thing stopping me." Even through his brooding, Glenn allowed a small, lopsided smile to appear beneath his beard at his next thought. "He could come with us."

"The boy loves his father too much," I said with a soft laugh, a kind of curiously apologetic note to it. "He would never go for it, I'm afraid, even if I would."

"I guess not...so, another Malin fan, huh."

A kind of resignation had settled into Glenn's voice. It was not a full open-mindedness, but a vague acceptance—as when a husband comes to tolerate, or even grow somewhat amused by, his wife's propensity for horoscopes or other forms of idolatrous superstition. Accordingly, I smiled and nodded, a twinkle in my eye.

"And you know, while it's true that I experience myself as one being, and I know my husband does, too—perhaps this is an opportunity for you to see him as a new Malin. After all, the Rift deposited him some thirteen years in the past by now, and in all that time, he's been forced to raise our child on his own. Why, that's something you and Malin both have in common now, isn't it?" While Glenn looked quite stricken to realize this, his pupils shrinking as his gaze flicked askance, I mused, "Not just the love of me, but the experience of being, for longer or shorter stretches, the largely solitary caregiver to one of my offspring. How curious...perhaps you really will get along with him better now. Oh, Glenn—he's very different now."

"Yeah. Now he's got enough energy to assassinate Parvati and start a war."

Men! Oh, Husband, bless your even temperament before me. You brood, like Eleison. You hold mysteries, like Dinon. You express petulant instincts that cannot be given vent elsewhere, like Glenn. But all these things you do in the right amount, the perfect proportions, excellently balanced so as to keep me engaged as your emotional partner without overwhelming me in one way or another. For when I am thus overwhelmed, my mind rules me, and I misstep in my speech, as I did when I insisted with exasperation, "Glenn, Malin didn't assassinate Parvati."

"Do you seriously expect me to believe that, Thecla? With their history?"

"Yes," I said firmly, looking him in the eye, letting him see the Rift beast I was in the intensity of my stare. "I expect you to believe it because I was there. And I'm telling you, my husband did not kill the Overseer."

With but a few of his heartbeats having passed between us, I concluded, "It was not him."

Muscle by muscle, Glenn's face changed, slowly succumbing to the shock of understanding. "Thecla," he muttered, looking at me, his brow furrowed.

Somehow, his reaction was not as I had expected. I had anticipated that he would be angry—upset, at the very least—to conclude he had just made love to a murderess who happened to be the mother of his child. Having braced for a fight, I therefore was left stumbling when, instead of responding in anger, he looked at me as though his heart broke for my sake. It gave me new pathos for Telemachus upon the train, for Glenn studied my face as though something had been done to me—what, I did not know.

I only knew that, in that moment, I felt a shock of something I'd not yet experienced when reflecting on Parvati's death: real shame. I did not even identify the emotion as that at the time. I only knew that I had the sudden sense I had been living in some kind of bubble: some separate but coexistent world that had managed to go unchallenged until right that very second. Until someone whom I loved and respected looked at me, not with disgust for the murder or contempt on Parvati's behalf, but with anguish to know I had soiled myself in this way. With this blood that would never come off my hands.

'Forever' is the past, Madame, as much as it is the future... never forget.

Unable to look Glenn in the eyes, I looked somewhere to the right of his shoulder, far off in the left-hand corner of my periphery.

"So," I resumed at last, speaking in a somewhat automated fashion as the memory of Parvati's naked heart pulsed its dying rhythm in my clutching hand, "since I can assure you that my husband was not her killer, I hope you will open your mind to the idea of meeting Malin Farrow in friendship when next you cross paths."

"Thecla—"

"Will you take me to see him?" I laid my hand upon Glenn's heart and looking him in the eye as I clarified, "Winston, I mean?"

Nostrils flaring along with the expansion of his great chest, Glenn asked, "You're not going to try anything, are you?"

"Mm...you can hold a gun on me if it would make you more comfortable, my knight...I trust you."

Now it was Glenn whose heavy thoughts of amorous desire reverberated through the threads of reality. He looked me deeply in the eye, stroking my thigh as he confessed, "I don't carry a gun anymore."

With a chuckle, I bowed my head over his, relieved he still drank from my kisses just the same—perhaps even more avidly than he did before my confession. "That first night I really got to know you," I recalled, "at the party here in the palace, you showed me you didn't need a gun."

Almost despite himself, he grinned, and my soul sprang with pleasure to see the Glenn I loved—that innermost, perhaps sincerely saintly man trapped within the life of a hunter. "I also proved that I don't need to kill to get by in the world...no offense," he added awkwardly, clearing his throat a little. "I just mean, you know...with my retirement and all."

"I knew what you meant, dear," I said, pinching his cheek above his beard and leaning in to whisper in his ear.

"I love it when you get a little bashful," I murmured to Glenn. "It makes me want to do all sorts of wicked things to you...I'll describe them to you later, after you've taken me to visit Winston."

"You certain can negotiate."

While he spoke, Glenn chuckled and patted my knee. I took that as my cue to rise, and I made a move toward the door, but he had stood quickly after me and slipped his big hand around mine. As though I were some feral cat, I winced, used to men grabbing my son and me and restraining us these past forty-eight hours. Then, the feeling passed, and I realized with a kind of alien embarrassment that he was just holding my hand.

"You're not ashamed to be seen walking with me like this...in this place?"

"No," said Glenn very earnestly, looking me in the eye. "I'm not."

It was far from the first time that night he managed to make me blush.

The wine cellar of the Valquist palace was, in fact, the sub-basement—a strangely medical-looking corridor with a sequence of rooms. There actually was a wine cellar, which was how the floor acquired its name, but there were also, from what I could discern, a file room, some sort of private briefing room, one large exit that reminded me very much of the hallway at the Torea festival in that it was designed to accommodate vehicles, and a small set of cells. These bore the hallmarks of having always been built into that particular room of the sub-basement. While I very nearly made a smart observation that my husband had no such little jails in his domiciles, I reflected on the red room in the bottom of the vineyard villa and held my tongue.

A hunter with apparent respect for Glenn condescended to monitor a brief meeting between Winston and me: and Glenn absorbed information in that quiet manner of his, judging individual circumstances and people within them as though he were calculating justice and morality—taking the temperature of every interaction so as to take the most meritorious course. I loved him and wanted him to see that there were times when I was truly hated for reasons beyond my control…and I wanted to take advantage of the occasion to have a conversation with Winston about how we might learn to live on the continent together moving forward. It was such a vast place, after all!

But the vile hatred that seared from his eyes told me such a thing was not possible, and would never be.

And could I blame him? It had to have been by his crippled hand that I recognized him, for by the other damage I had done, his face was irrevocably altered. He was now a gaunt, shrunken man, his once handsomish features hollowed and sharpened by the long-term effects of his battle with blood poisoning. His hair and mustache were stark white, and regular contortions of his brow had, with alarming haste, deepened a set of furrows that had already begun to mark his forehead on a permanent basis. It was only by that hand and the hatred in his eyes that I *could* have recognized him. As I adjusted to the shock of his new appearance, still quite amazed the second time (or more, now that he wasn't shooting and I had time to appreciate these changes), Winston pushed himself up from his seat, barely glancing at me but taking a long, hard look at Glenn after spitting on the floor of his cell.

"Shouldn't be surprised to see you here with her," Winston said as Glenn met his gaze unflinchingly. "I knew you'd act predictably when she wound up in our custody. You've always been weak."

"Maybe you could have given me a little information about your, uh…pre-existing relationship with Thecla. You never identified the dharmine who got to you…I suppose I was the idiot for failing to compare your story to what Thecla's father explained I should expect about her new condition."

"You mean her corruption." Turning to gaze blackly at me, Winston gripped the bars of his cell and drew close against them to look me in the eye. "But it's going to take more than that to kill me. You hear me?"

I regarded him coldly, unimpressed and suddenly disinterested in extending the olive branch I had been willing to share. "I wanted to speak to you on companionable terms, but—"

His head jerked in a motion that strangely mirrored my flinch as a glob of phlegm rocketed from his mouth, barely missing my jaw and instead swiping past the lobe of my ear. My shock transfigured into a grimace of disgust, which Glenn mirrored as he hastened over to sweep his sleeve across me.

"If that's how you aim," I told Winston, "it's a miracle you've survived long enough to find yourself thus. What is it in me that you so detest, exactly? My husband was rumored to be a dharmine for decades, and your people have hated him, as you have. But I'd wager you've never harbored such hatred in your heart for him as you do for me."

"He's never—*ruined* me." Winston thrust his hand through the bars, his words rising from his lips in a snarl. Those eyes blazed with hatred as he showed me the withered claw that represented the loss of his livelihood and his whole identity. "Your husband may be a calculating, deceitful tyrant hell-bent on exploiting the— the—"

Winston's head jerked sharply to the right, and he began to wheeze and cough convulsively. Great gulps of air interspersed with choking and coughs, the occasional word—"proletariat," "fascist"—barely audible. To be frank, the weakness of his body had stolen my attention, and I looked at him with new eyes, recognizing how thin he had become.

"How much?" I asked, meeting his gaze again.

Recovering, he turned back to me, expecting some great argument. Thrown less off-guard than I'd hoped, Winston scoffed—a burst of incredulous breath that expanded his mouth into a sardonic flash of teeth beneath his now unkempt mustache.

"How much, what?"

"How much to ease your transition into retirement and make you forget this whole matter?"

His brows furrowed in dynamic incredulity, casting intense shadows in the hollows of his eye sockets. Once this offer had worked his way through his brain, however, Winston barked out a laugh. "You can't be serious. You think money will fix this? You ruined my life, you bitch."

"Who holds that responsibility is debatable. But if you must know, yes, I do think money could solve our disagreement if you'd let it. Think, Winston!"

Undeterred by his earlier outburst, I stepped closer to the bars, relishing the small surge of power as he recoiled. "You could live a life of sheer decadence, surpassed by few on this continent. My husband and I could provide for the rest of your days. No more medical bills eating away at your savings in a desperate attempt to treat your condition. Any theater, any restaurant, any transport, any home—all yours, if you put aside this petty grudge and go away quietly."

"A lot of words," Winston muttered, hate glinting in his eyes. "But it's easy for you to talk. You're not the one who has to live with the consequences—to live with the loss of a future."

"You think I don't have regrets?" The words tumbled from

my mouth before I could stop them, earning a sharp glance from Glenn. For a strange moment, it was as if the act of speaking was the very act of thinking, and I couldn't progress further in my mind—in Time itself—without releasing these feelings like a seedling bursting forth toward the light.

"Do you think for even a moment," I told him sharply, waving a hand, "that I have the least desire to find myself thus? Do you think I want the position of Matrix? That I desire to participate in a system of governance whose political machinations led to my husband, the love of my life, being shot in the throat while we greeted our own people? Don't you suppose that, if given a choice, we would retire happy in the country, safe and obscure, free to make love, eat rich foods, and raise a happy, healthy family of undisturbed children not subject to strange traumas or excessive privilege?"

The brutal intensity with which I suddenly realized I longed for this seemed to stab me in the heart. I felt awful pain for my son, yearning for my husband, and a bone-deep need for my mate—but I also knew I could never be satisfied without the man beside me, my gentle hero. I couldn't bear to lose him as a consequence of my unworthiness to love him.

For I was indeed unworthy of loving him. Parvati's blood had dried under my nails. I had been more changed by that murder, I suddenly realized, than by all the greatest trials of my adulthood to that point: not even coming into my destined second life as dharmine had changed me so much. It was tempting to presume that this was the change that had made the assassination possible— that some alteration of my morals had occurred during whatever transmigration was affected in that dark nether-space—but that seemed awfully convenient. I thought of Ignatius and our final conversation; I thought, also, of this new and ceaseless need to prove that I was still myself, no matter what my father claimed was influencing me. If I was truly the same Thecla then as now, then it did not matter whether some alteration of my nature had made it possible for my soul to compromise its dignity in this bloody way. There was no justification sufficient for what I had done to the woman who had been my honored guest, however she had treated me while I was staying in her jurisdiction.

And now here we were: at war, my family separated, my son and I held hostage explicitly—and my lover and our daughter, implicitly.

"Life is never what we want it to be," I told Winston, grateful I had the resolve to at least withhold my tears while I stared at him in his foolish animal face, uncertain my words were getting through. "It shocks us, it devastates us, and we must decide how we're going to respond. This is real life, Winston—not a fairy tale. But even if it were, do you want to know the truth?"

I drew closer, my voice low and my senses sharpened by the way his heartbeat leapt in my ears. He fell back a step, or tried, but I reached through the bars and caught hold of his shirt to keep him from escaping. I enjoyed the cold, white terror in his face even as I was alerted by the stir of Glenn's body in my periphery, keeping my focus on the man I could have easily killed before the shouting guards made it across the room.

"Even if it were a fairy tale, Winston—oh, fairy tales are ugly things. Eyes are gouged out; women have their hands amputated; human flesh is made a feast of by more than merely giants. The heroes and heroines don't stroll to their happy endings: they don't begin their stories as the head of the Gudrune chapter of the blasted Hunter's Guild and wind up as the Overseer of the

Continent without humbling themselves and giving in to a change of heart. But just remember…"

Glenn, having argued off the men for at least a few seconds, caught me by the arm and steered me back from the bars. I released my grip on Winston's collar, allowing him to fall free, allowing myself to be dragged away as I called out, "That meant they had a heart to change in the first place."

While my hunter shepherded me from the room before the guards could decide it was better to detain me, I pondered with a kind of shock the new question rising up inside me. It was a question that I had never fully thought to answer before; moreover, it was one whose answer alarmed me when I reflected on it in the cold light of day.

Did I like the person I was becoming? If the young girl I had been met the woman I was today and judged her harshly, was that because young Thecla was naive—or because young Thecla was right?

"What's gotten into you?" Glenn emerged with me in the upstairs hallway, in a wing that was blessedly quiet while still remaining plausibly on the path back to my own—one might argue 'padded'—cell. The firm notes of his voice betrayed not just his seriousness but also his love for me, and I let that love soothe a little the aching of my soul as he went on in that low, corrective tone that reminded me a bit of Eleison. "Don't you see they're looking for an excuse to put a bullet in your brain?"

"I've heard if you leave a dharmine's corpse in that condition long enough, the bullet will eventually be pushed out," I assured him with a morbid little smile. "Just stash me somewhere safe… perhaps loosely bury me a foot or two under the soil so no one will find me. I'm quite sure I won't mind. Whether I'm right or wrong, it'd be the right decision."

"Thecla."

"Sorry, dear." I stroked his arm, letting my smile fade. "Just a bit of gallows humor… I always used to jibe with the doctor when I had to visit, too. I get quite nervous sometimes."

"I wouldn't have guessed that." Though he relaxed somewhat, Glenn's tone remained strained from the effects of the wine cellar episode on his central nervous system. "You always seem calm and collected to me."

"To tell you the truth, dear," I smiled again, and even laughed a bit, unable to help it, "I feel as though I've been screaming since Charlotte collected me to bring me to Malin's estate, and I haven't stopped since."

A slight furrow formed between his brows—a mix of concern and amusement at my choice of imagery. He could only ask, "'Screaming?'"

"Yes, just that—not always in a bad way, necessarily. A scream can signal outrageous fun, after all… look at the circus."

That old man, Renard—the blind Riftborn seer who first showed me Eleison, then guided me back to my husband when I thought I'd lost him eternally. I that odd old man in my heart in a strange way; in the way one thinks of a friend not long before they call. I went on to Glenn, pushing the feeling away. "The truth is, I simply don't perceive myself the way other people do. When I look in the mirror, all I am is Thecla of Lescaut. I see a ten-year-old, or a fourteen-year-old. Sometimes, every once in a while, I see a twenty-two-year-old. I suppose when I'm thirty-five, I'll start to see a twenty-five-year-old. My perception of myself is very slow to adjust. In other words, I've opened myself to change in such a way that there are times I barely even know what's happening or what I'm doing or even quite why I'm doing it, other than for the inexplicable call I feel buried deep inside my heart. All I know is this urgent sense of the passage of time, and the fleeting nature of opportunities, and the truth that I used to believe—that I would only exist once, so could live without a care for consequence and take every opportunity set before me."

Eleison, pushing me into the bedroom of the Saalast house, on the cusp of making love to me before a well-timed crash from Charlotte interrupted our passion and alerted us to Malin's return; Malin not long after, watching Eleison roughly take me and patiently awaiting his turn.

"Sometimes, those opportunities yielded—continue to yield—wonderful fruit. Sacred fruit that fills my life with joy and security and unconditional love." Parvati's heart pulsing obscenely in my hand, her hot blood running down my arm, the metal taste edged with adrenal sweetness on my smiling mouth. "Sometimes, those taken opportunities are ones I might be tempted to undo if I had but understood the consequences at the time. But…"

Ba'al-Dinon, Ba-al-Dinon: oh, Ba'al-Dinon, whose presence filled my heart and loins and soul in a way I can only describe as profoundly erotic. I swooned somewhat dizzily, missing a step as I walked, and laughed as Glenn caught me; and I gasped slightly, too, to find how sensitively my body had been inflamed by even this internal evocation of that most mysterious of all my lovers.

I'm right here, Thecla, he said, *enveloping my body with heat.*

How I longed to interrogate the sentiment! To have the luxury of pondering his weird ways of communicating with the very center of my mind, or my soul, or both. Yet here I was, in Glenn's arms, his expression of concern only deepening until, with a graceful smile and recovery, I played it off as a simple catch of my heel while saying, "The truth is I've come to a somewhat different understanding—that the choices I make may well be eternal in nature and occurrence. There is no doubt in my mind that what I'm about to say is a little strange, but—"

"No," he said quickly. "I think about these things all the time too, Thecla. I understand."

I nodded once, saying only, "So I think the part of me that's screaming—that's some deep, deep part of me that is in touch with this deep ground truth of the eternal nature of Time. It's not unlike watching a moving picture at the cinema, you know—you can see it ten, sixteen, twenty thousand times, and it will always be the same. You can scream with delight or with fright or with outrage, but you'll never be able to influence what's unfolding on the screen. The soul, I think, is that part of ourselves that's held hostage to all our decisions in this way—or perhaps that's God, abiding in the soul. I can't really be sure."

"Do you think there's a difference?"

I tapped my chin in reflection as we rounded the corner and at last came within sight of the new guards flanking my door. "I think that when the war is over and I have the luxury of passing control of Gudrune back to my husband, I'll put in the time for a doctorate in Theology and give you my opinion once I'm educated."

"I'll hold you to it," said Glenn with a soft laugh, then pausing to look at me very sincerely. "Thecla—"

One hand, great and warm, raised to allow me a glimpse of the intricately bundled crios that twisted around his wrist beneath the edge of his sleeve, just near the luptich. "Please," he murmured, his voice grave as he looked into my eyes, head bent over mine, "please, be careful. Don't take any unnecessary risks."

As the guards approached to take me into custody before they risked opening the door to my rooms, acting as though Glenn were merely transferring me from his care to theirs, Glenn bent low over me and stroked my cheek with his broad thumb as I went still for him. His mouth was sweet and tender, each kiss soft and slow, conveying a deep longing for mutual forgiveness. I felt in that kiss every ounce of Glenn's longing to begin anew: to know me as I was, and not as either of us thought I should be.

And when he lifted his head, his gaze softening with pain, his caress was replaced by the clamp of a gloved hand around my bicep, then the bite of handcuffs around my wrist.

"I love you so much, Glenn," I told him with all my heart as they pulled me away. "Please, darling, give me a chance to learn to love you better."

"When this is all over," he said, "I swear to you, Thecla, I will."

My heart swelled with hope for the future, a much-needed balm during that complex period of my life. As my captors led me to my comfortable prison, and to the son who had surely also been inwardly transformed by these last days, I resigned myself to a continued stretch of deep unhappiness. But I grew determined to cling to that sliver of light Glenn had offered—a glimpse of his hopes for our future. If he still had hope, then so could I. If he saw joy in the future, then it was there.

But even in the midst of that darkness, there could be joy in the present: for the guards knocked sharply on the door, commanded all prisoners within (really only my Telemachus, of course) to step back, then snapped open the lock with one of their many keys.

And, to my bemusement, the door opened to the sound of my son's astonished laughter. As the door swung wide, I saw him standing in the far doorway to the bedroom on the other side of the suite's living area-cum-foyer, and I arched a brow at his delight, thinking at first it was mere relief to see me. But then the door kept swinging, and I saw the source of his amusement poised there like a mysterious altar in the spot where the living room's coffee table once stood.

The black loom from my visions awaited me, and I laughed.

We were interrogated separately for at least three hours, not just by my father but by a bevy of other men who exhibited varying degrees of hostility. Rigel was the only reasonable one, but even he seemed possessed of an unnatural, animal terror regarding the alien artifact that had suddenly appeared in the middle of the prison suite's living room.

"If neither you nor your son know how it got there," said my father, his tone somewhat strained, "then how did a multi-hundred-pound construction of wood and metal wind up in the middle of your—accommodations?"

"Honestly, Papa," I said, "you can say 'cell'. It doesn't bother me. It feels far worse when you try to lie to us both about it."

"Then how did it wind up in the middle of your cell, Thecla?"

Unable to help laughing at his agitated tone, I spread my hands. "How should I know? Haven't you enough cameras in this place? Parvati had them everywhere, I'm sure—oh, and don't check the ones in the library from this evening, by the by."

His nose wrinkled with disgust as he copped to my meaning. "*Thecla.*"

"What a tone with which to speak to a grown woman! I was just giving you fair warning, Father, dear. Since you're accusing me of—I don't know—being a magician, I suppose—you'd might as well be informed of my alibi."

"Somebody's got to know what the hell happened."

"Your men didn't hear anything?"

"No; and for your information"—Rigel shot an annoyed glance in my direction—"our microphones didn't pick up any sounds. They shorted out about six minutes before the guards opened the door to your cell."

"I'll assume that you're fixing them now," I said, leaning back in my chair and folding my hands in my lap. "At any rate, it's certainly a pity that the electronics aren't holding up. Perhaps that's just an indication of the poor maintenance your men have been doing since the hunters inherited the palace. As for the loom..."

I shook my head, smiling thinly. "I'm afraid I really can't tell you anything, Papa. So sorry."

Nostrils flaring, my father stared me down. He rose with a slap of his hand on the table and strode out, slamming the door heavily behind him. I waited, allowing myself a smile, and took advantage of the silence to rest. The lack of sustenance and overall stress, coupled with the exertion of lovemaking, had sapped my energy. All I wanted was to lie down, close my eyes, and rest for twenty minutes or so.

Yet when at last some officer, thrice as annoyed as my father, returned me to my chambers and my eye fell upon the loom they had not yet removed, the exhaustion left me. All I saw was evidence of the interference I had awaited since our train was hijacked by those blasted terrorists. With an unabashed smile of delight, I dashed to touch its strangely frictionless surface, marveling to behold it with my own two eyes for what I realized was the first actual time.

"Here I thought you fellows would have taken it away," I said as the guard who accompanied me cheerlessly shut the door.

"We tried," he replied, his tone pregnant with an untold story as the door clicked shut.

Left alone—alone as one could hope to be in such monitored circumstances—I bent forward against the loom and embraced it as though it were Dinon himself. With my lips pursing against its cool surface, my heart aflame, I let my soul bask in the presence of my beloved. I swore I could feel him reciprocate, his essence flowing into my dilated heart to overwhelm me with an almost bodily pleasure. My breath hitched to remember those times when, without resorting to the traditional methods of physical contact, he had brought me ecstasy as delicious as any given me by my husband or mate or lover. Submitting myself, I closed my eyes, murmuring, "Please," against the surface of the loom as I might between kisses I'd lay on Ba'al-Dinon's heart.

"How you torment me," I chastised the loom. My fingers glided along the smooth surface of the frame and occasionally caressed the soft fuligin fabric of the woven but not yet liberated textile. "You show me how near you are to me, yet you refuse to let me see you, touch you!"

You'll see me soon, he said; and these words, a balm as much as the primary instrument of all my sharpest torture, ached in my weakened spirit. *Sooner than you fear.*

As this pledge rolled through me, warmth strengthening my resolve, the door opened. I straightened and turned toward the sound as my son bounded into the room, guided back from his own interrogation. He cried out to see me, his expression serious. "Did they hurt you?"

"I'm fine, darling," I said as this next jailer left us alone, letting me caress Telemachus's cheek and gaze into those piercingly intelligent young eyes of his. Oh, those eyes! Something had changed in them. They were harder now. More like his father's all the time. "They didn't bully you, I hope," I told him as I released him and turned to hide the quick wipe of a tear.

"They didn't look like they wanted to," said Telemachus, unruffled as he threw himself down on the sofa arranged parallel to the brooding loom. "But your papa was there, and anyway—"

His grin widened devilishly, his eyes crinkling. "They didn't like my answer to where that thing came from."

Heart leaping with envy, I crossed to my son's side, knowing I didn't need to clarify as I asked at soft volume, "Did you see him?"

Telemachus nodded. "I've seen him before. He's visited Papa a few times. Papa calls him my godfather, but today was the first time he's spoken to me."

"What did he say?"

Here, my son's expression grew serious—so serious, in fact, that I grew somewhat afraid, a condition not at all abated when he responded, "I'm not sure I should tell you...you'll worry."

"Did he tell you that?"

"No," said Telly with a shrug. "But I know you will. He told me I can tell anybody anything I want...which"—my wise child chuckled wryly—"sounds like asking for trouble."

While the idea of my son keeping secrets from me, especially in the given circumstances, provoked in my heart no small amount of alarm, my instinct to demand he share the details with me warred with my sense that Ba'al-Dinon had phrased his answer to my son's query knowing that Telemachus was much too prudent to take up his invitation. Therefore, leaving the cherished loom, I sat at my son's side and took his hand. His eyes, which had briefly shut, now slid open to regard me with that same unnatural hardness: a new barrier of blood that had been raised between himself and the world. I pressed his palm between both of mine, seeking to plunge through that barrier.

"It is awful, isn't it?"

Knowing what I meant, my son's naturally pale features grew sickly; very nearly gray. "Yes," he said very quietly, his eyes dropping from mine to focus instead on somewhere just behind my shoulder. "It's terrible. More terrible than I thought at first, and worse every time I think of it. I...I keep—"

Though I had seen Telemachus respond with natural shyness to many people before, myself included, I had never seen him at a loss for words; and yet here he was, in our luxuriant prison, his mouth remaining silently open as his youthful brow furrowed beneath the weight of those horrors. It seemed there was nothing he could say; no way to complete his thought. And too well did I know why! I knew it because he surely underwent the same cycle of suffering I did each time I recalled the faces of my own victims. Even now, he saw them; felt the new, hard, inescapable reality that could never be changed. No doubt his heart traced their origins back, back to a root not completely dissimilar from his, and compared his own earliest memories to whatever he imagined he had taken from them. His eyes filled with tears and swept helplessly up to me.

"I didn't want to," he said in a small voice, the most childlike I had ever heard him use. When at least these words broke his silence, his mouth contorted in a grimace of pain and shock, and I, soul aching for him, drew him into my arms to press him close to my heart.

Oh, how pitifully my poor son cried that day! I had never seen him cry before, and I daresay I have not seen him weep since; at least not so copiously. But, in retrospect, I suspect he wept for more than his bloodied hands. Instead, he wept for a past not lived and a future that would never be free of sin. He wept to fully realize that the world was not what he dreamed it could be, but simply itself: mysterious, beautiful, gravely flawed.

Unending.

When at last his tears quelled, I held him until he became submersed in sleep, quite exhausted. Gently lowering him back upon the cushions of the couch from which I withdrew a comforter, I tucked him in and remained there, humming softly to ease any slight disturbance caused by his repositioning.

Then, no longer able to resist, I turned my admiring gaze back upon the loom.

What a queer thing to see in reality! Perhaps it sounds mad to say, but each time my eye fell upon it, my heart insisted in response, 'This object should not exist.' Indeed, though in form and function it was like any other loom, its material defied light in a way that made it seem not an object, but an anti-object: an allotment of spatial dimension from which the shape of a loom and its textile had been cut. Viewing it this way and reflecting on the party where it had appeared to me as a half-real vision—a consequence of the mithrae flowers in which I had indulged—I found myself wandering down all numbers of strange avenues of thought. The strangest avenue of all being: perhaps the anomaly was not the object itself, but our collective ability to see it. Not unlike those threads of reality that showed themselves to me at strange times, when I met a certain threshold of consciousness: in trance, exhaustion, deep meditation, or now, as a consequence of studying the loom. For indeed, after a few moments of absent contemplation, my eye followed a glinting thread that ran the length of the beam, and following this thread revealed others, which called out still others, until, with belated awareness, I looked around myself to find the entirety of the room—the entirety of being!—contoured by these gleaming warps and wefts.

How funny! The novelty of such a sight has never worn off, and it is not just the inherent strangeness of the experience at work but the presence of divinity which blossoms like a flower in my soul as I ease into such visions. The mysterious threads carry a depth of metaphysical meaning that is unexplainably powerful; even the sight of them evokes mysteries beyond measure. For instance, as I adapted to the sight that particular time, I looked down and found a great number of the threads flowing from my lap were woven into my son's being, as well. This joy filled my heart with deep love, and it occurred to me that no matter how far apart we were, we were always interconnected by these infinite threads: indeed, even before I knew of his existence, or the existence of the threads themselves, we had been connected by them. Moved, I caressed his hair as he slept. Then I stood, determined to find comfort enough in this sentiment to sleep, myself...until it occurred to me:

If such a thing were true of Telemachus, it was surely also true of my spouse.

Frozen in motion, the force of this revelation bore down on me. I studied my hands, my arms, my waist. Of those threads that plunged from me into my son, a great number seemed to carry on, surging out of him and off into the furniture and ephemera of the suite. Though I was afraid to wake him, I extended my fingers to the row of threads above his head and, one at a time, leafed through them as one might the pages of a book or the strings of a harp. They responded with apt vibrations, ringing with non-corporeal tension at my touch.

And, amazingly, as I focused on the soft thrum of this vibration as I never had before, I discovered that the sound, in some strange way, bore with it information that bloomed naturally into my mind. It was so subtle that I did not understand the connection at first: intrusive thoughts flowed naturally into my head—notions from old novels and the scents of flowers and imagery from the Karrisregion house emerging as naturally as they might in a state of unfocused meditation. Only after a time did I realize these were not my associations—they came from books I hadn't read, flowers for which I had no special memory, perspectives drawn from heights that did not quite match the scale at which I saw the world. Incredulous, a kind of euphoria flowing through me as I was made unexpectedly privy to the secrets of some subtle form of clairvoyance, I felt through these untouchable threads, my mind awash in thoughts not of my own: thoughts of me, of Eleison.

And many, many thoughts of Malin.

It was these thought-strings on which I focused my investigation. Further matching them to the strings that extended through me, I found a chord that met my requirements. Drawing from it note by note of thought, I opened my mind to what seemed an increasingly tangible presence—my husband's presence, as unmistakable as though he sat in the room with me—though in reality, I knew he was far off in some broad tent of a Rheton war room, brooding before a fire, his expression bleak while that ceaseless mind of his rotated through every contingency he could possibly imagine. Yes, every possible measure and counter-measure he could utilize to liberate us was sorted in his head, passed over again and again as he interrogated the possibilities to find the most assured means of acquiring our release. Quite astonished by the clarity of this vision which I took at first to be imaginal, I soon acquired the sense that what I beheld was no construction of my imagination but instead some remote perspective of my husband carried forth to me by the contact with these threads. My soul ached with an excitement and longing I daresay I have not experienced since: I very nearly cried aloud, but instead, so as not to disturb our weary son, formed the words as a thought.

I miss you, I told him, thinking to him and finding, with no small amount of amazement, that his head in this projection upon my heart turned a few degrees as if in response to verbal speech.

Thecla, came my next thought, emerging within me in the voice of my yearning husband. *I'll find you.*

Exhilarated to feel his thoughts as though they were my own— though that impression is still not quite an adequate depiction of the phenomenon, as, at such a time, those thoughts I would attribute to my husband often feel foreign somehow, as if deriving from another part of my brain, or slipping in from some means I could only imagine are linked to those mysterious threads—I stroked those happy strands. As if, in touching them, I could also touch directly the far-ranging mind I held so sacred.

I know you will, I consoled him, endeavoring to send all my love and devotion, imagining it as some fluid that could be poured out through space and time directly into his soul. As though sensing it, his hand clenched into a fist, and I swore I could feel it so well I had to look at my own palm to persuade myself I still had control over my own body.

Then there came something else—an anguish so black and terrible that it seemed alien, a demon. Something foreign and out of sync with my own nature, which clearly did not belong to me.

Oh, my husband! I had never known before that moment what despair truly was, nor that you were made to suffer it so cruelly. That the man I so adored had the capacity for such great grief struck me through, and I wished for little more than to plunge into his heart and console him. Yet, I was helpless! Even if I could make him understand that the thoughts and feelings I sent into his soul were a sign of our intimate connection, it seemed to me that I would only cause him greater pain by making some direct contact. The idea that we were so close and yet so far apart caused me pain, and after feeling the depths of my husband's urgent concern, I dared not worsen it. Instead, I was on the cusp of forcing myself to lift my hand away of my own volition, thus hopefully severing the connection until it could be of some comfort or advantage for us.

However, before I could, two things happened to disrupt the connection, each on one end of the proverbial line. Firstly, a footfall drew my husband's attention away from the reverie that had made sinking into his consciousness so simple. Secondly—I say 'secondly', though it was as close to concurrent as could be imagined when two events occur at such a distance—the urgent barking of male voices carried down the hall not far from our room, soon loud enough for me to recognize Rigel's among them. By the time I was on my feet and facing the door, it burst open. The bustle was as inconceivable as the gun that was thrust at me—a gun that my father no more commanded be taken away than he commanded the men who fetched my struggling son away before he could even stumble out of sleep and find his balance. As I cried out and lunged toward him, another gun, thrust in my face, kept me still so a woman (the first I had seen since arriving at that wretched palace) could manipulate, pose, and grope me in a search for weapons.

"How did you contact him?" my father demanded, looking at me coldly. Baffled, I stood with my hands up and let myself be pawed. Pulled as I had been from that sweet communion with my husband, I thought for just a second that they meant Malin, and wondered how they could know what had transpired in the depths of my mind. Then, thinking better of it and realizing they had perhaps salvaged the footage of Ba'al-Dinon speaking to my son, I raised my eyebrows to indicate confusion.

"I'm not sure who you mean," I told him, allowing myself to look as unimpressed as I felt. My father's lip curled past his teeth.

"Don't play dumb, Thecla. We both know you're not a stupid girl."

"Indeed, those days are long gone, Papa…I'm a stupid *woman* now." When no one laughed at my joke, I rolled my eyes and barely restrained an audible tut. "I'm quite sure I would love to answer your question and get these blasted guns out of my face, but I've no way of knowing what you mean. Who are you talking about? I've had contact with you, Winston, Glenn—"

"Eleison," snapped my father, his eyes blazing with fury. Though the huntress patting me down stepped back from me with a shake of her head, my mate's name inspired such a rush of awful vertigo that I grabbed her for support, keeping upright with a grip on her shoulder that made her jump. "I just had some men bring him in for interrogation," my father went on, "after finding him mid-reconnaissance around the palace property."

"Don't you dare hurt him," I said, the words leaping from my mouth with a violent, nearly animal tone I had never heard myself use. "If you lay a hand on him, I'll personally turn every one of your contemptible hunters inside out—starting with this one."

The fellows pointing guns at me looked just about ready to fire, but my father's mirthless laugh stayed all our hands.

"You're too late for that," said this cruel stranger I used to call my father, the title of another lifetime. "If anything, you should be thanking me. We've got him in the medical wing right now, treating his injuries."

Feeling myself grow as pale as my son, who looked urgently worried to hear his uncle was in their custody, I demanded, "What injuries are those?"

How ugly Rigel looked then! The malice in his smile, the pleasure in his eyes: it was no small wonder he thought all dharmine to be innately evil when he had become so himself.

"The shrapnel from a flash grenade caught him in the eyes," my father told me, taking pleasure in relaying the news. "I'm afraid your boy toy's gone blind."

I have already discoursed on those moments in life where we are stricken by irrevocable change, but there is no way to truly express how incomprehensible such a moment can be. The mind attempts to continue down its normally chartered course, plunging through the same pathways it always has, only to find itself at a sudden roadblock. Consciousness, with a shock, encounters this wall, this difference in a greatly accustomed chain of logic that, at a loss, it attempts and re-attempts to navigate in the same ways it always did before.

That 'Eleison' and 'blindness' should now be linked seemed just such an unnatural wall. As I hurried to the medical wing under the supervision of my father and his chosen hunters, I felt as if some thread leading into an otherwise very clear future had been cut. What did it mean that my mate was blind? Could he be healed? Would rebirth as a dharmine be the only solution? Would such a suggestion offend him, as though to imply I could not love him if he could not see? He could not see—oh, God, Eleison could not see!

As soon as the cloying, pseudo-sweet scent of antiseptic struck my sinuses, I darted forward, shooting past my guards and shoving by the pair flanking a door I nearly knocked off its hinges. For all the rotations of my mind—for all that I had done to prepare myself in that too-long, too-short crossing from one wing of the palace to the other—I was still unready to see my darling at all, let alone there on his back, handcuffed to a cot, a layer of gauze and bandages concealing the damage to his precious eyes while some volunteer nurse made a show of checking his vitals. Seeing the wild look on my face and the haste of my movement, she released her grip on the blood pressure monitor and stumbled back from the bed; in that same second, Eleison's head jerked upright, his voice raising in urgent concern and desperate relief to cry, "Thecla!"

"Eleison, oh—darling, my darling, what have they done to you—"

The horror was too much. Exploding into tears like a child, I stumbled to his side and draped myself over him, pressing my face to his chest so my weeping might go somewhat unobserved.

"Thecla," he repeated, his voice hoarse as his unencumbered hand raised to thread his fingers through my hair. "I'm so glad you're here, baby."

"Why on Earth have you come to this wretched place? Oh, Eleison, you should have waited for some larger operation, or—"

"I couldn't wait," he told me simply, his hand sliding around to caress my jaw and cheek with a familiarity he had shown a thousand times over in the dark. As his thumb pressed beneath my eye to wipe away my tears, his lips parted. Eleison murmured,

"I couldn't just sit there while you and Telemachus were trapped in this place."

"So you got yourself trapped with us, you—oh, you beautiful imbecile. Eleison!"

My soul ached, and I was momentarily imbued with the strange compulsion to tear away those bandages, as though they were at fault for the condition of his eyes. I became furious at them, and then, by extension, at the people who had applied them, and at those who had done the damage, and even at Eleison himself, who had done something as foolhardy as trying to find me in territory that was unquestionably the possession of the enemy. All this boiled over until, at the sound of my father's bootstep just behind me, I whirled around and struck him across the face with the back of my hand. My knuckle caught on the edge of his tooth, sending a sting of pain through me. But when Rigel looked back at me, a combination of befuddlement and rage on his face, he now had a nastily split lip. I reveled in his suffering and unhesitatingly snarled, "Are you satisfied, Papa? Does it please you to have done this to my family?"

"Your family is in Lescaut," he told me, wiping his mouth on the back of his hand. "Sable, and your stepmother—I'm fighting the criminals who stole you away from them and corrupted you so deeply that you don't even have a conscience anymore."

Nearly mute with the inundation of outrage that grew ever denser in my heart, I exclaimed, "Me, no conscience! You're gloating that you've blinded a man—!"

"An enemy combatant," he interrupted.

"—who I love," I went on, my teeth bared and my eyes shining with tears, "and you're telling me that I'm the one with no conscience! You disgust me, you—!"

"Thecla," he said sharply.

Eleison's free hand caught me by the arm with such an uncanny precision that, wound up with my indignation, I nearly leapt out of my skin. It was only the gentle stroking of his thumb over the vein of my wrist, as though I were the one injured and in need of comfort, that could have put me at any degree of ease. Indeed, I was so awash in grief and terror that I couldn't even take refuge in the proximity of my mate! Beneath all my anxiety and heartbreak, in fact, I didn't feel the ease of our mating bond at all; the situation was too urgent, I supposed—and the surroundings too objectively populated with hostile forces—for my nervous system to reap the benefits of our great intimacy.

"Don't make it worse for yourself," urged my beloved, always thinking of me before himself, even in an awful situation like this. As I eased into his touch and, using my free hand, tenderly smoothed the sweat-drenched hair from his brow, he squeezed my forearm tighter. "It'll be okay—I'll be okay. Don't give them an excuse to mistreat you."

Grinding my teeth in frustration at my own impotence, I told him, "In mistreating you, they've mistreated me terrifically. They might as well deny me sustenance. It might as well have been *my* eyes they blasted out, the animals! Oh, Eleison, my love!"

Sobbing, I folded his upper half into my arms, pressing his wounded eyes to my bosom and remembering that time early on when my love had reversed the damage done to his psyche by the conversion which occurred when an altered person was too long in the Rift without Stabilify. If only I could kiss those lovely eyes of his! I might heal them to their original state of sharpness, bright and shining with mirth, those red borro-irises of his like brilliant rubies in the perfect setting of his face—

But before I could place my hand on his bandage long enough to try, my father caught me by the arm and dragged me away. His strength was only slightly in excess of my own, but just sufficiently so that I was helpless to refuse.

"There'll be no comfort for him, Thecla—nor for you. I think I've been too kind since your arrival—it's my mistake for letting my heart soften when I look at your face and think about the girl you used to be."

"And when I think of the man you used to be," I spat, furious, baring my teeth between my words, "I begin to feel as though he was little more than a child's dream. A fictional image I concocted based on my glimpses of you through the dim light of adolescence. This ugly wretch, this beast you've become, surely points not to the nature of dharmine individuals as a whole but to some kernel of wickedness originating from within you."

"Can't you see I'm trying to save you?"

"Oh, yes, you and Glenn, both—always so nobly trying to save me from myself, from the men I love, as though I were still a child and needed protection. As if I can't make my own decisions! You know who can't? Rosina can't! My daughter, who was taken from her home in her father's misguided attempt to protect her— she cannot make her own decisions. She is not even old enough to understand what is really going on! She only knows that one day, her father took her on a very long trip, and this week is the first time she has seen her mother in months: it's been so long for someone her age that she hardly remembers what it is to have a mother."

Rigel relaxed his grip on me somewhat, but did not release me entirely. "I know it seems insulting. But, Thecla—"

"Here comes some nonsense justification as to why I can't

make my own decisions. How exhausting you are! Do you know, Papa, why I love Malin and Eleison so deeply? Indeed, one is my spouse and the other my mate, but our intimacy surpasses those titles and instead comes from the way they treat me! They trust me. Neither one of them attempts to control me, or manipulate me, or instruct me as though I were in some way morally deficient. They see me for who I am—they see my heart. My actual heart. Not some false motivation or naivete they're projecting onto me."

Tears welled in my eyes as I looked upon Eleison, his head tilted toward me to listen with greater acuity than ever. "I don't want anything other than to be with my family," I lamented, now turning a desperate eye on my father as I pleaded for his understanding. "This war and its violence, this awful tribulation, Glenn's exile, even the blasted energy project my husband cherishes—do you think I want any of it? I don't. I want nothing but to live quietly with my family. I want to live in peace, as though we were common people, albeit the blessed sort who needn't struggle. I only want—"

Lips trembling, I found myself saying pathetically, "I just want an end to suffering and an entry into a time of peace."

"That's what I want, too, Thecla," said my father solemnly. "But sometimes to get to peace, you must first endure war."

"Why must that ever be the case? Why can we not simply reason things out like sensible adults? I understand my husband is shrewd, but he's not above negotiation."

"What I want is something Malin will never give away."

I couldn't fathom what he meant for a few seconds, and my mind leapt through embarrassingly pedestrian possibilities— wealth, land, investments, titles—before I realized what he meant. Paled, I leaned away from him, no more able to extricate myself from his grip than I was to tolerate his proximity.

"You mean you'll stop at nothing until you've claimed his life, don't you?"

The silence in which my father assessed my features spoke such volumes. I saw in it far more than the intention to kill my husband; I saw in it, also, the question of whether or not he would be forced to kill me. It dashed across his stony features for what I suspect was the first time before, for a quarter of a second, his eyes opened wider in faint shock. Then, that astonishment closed down into determination, and I knew in a way beyond knowing— perhaps by some invisible thread connecting my heart to my father's—that he had achieved whatever justification he required to do what he felt needed doing. By some set of esoteric mental gymnastics, he was able to write me off as an expendable casualty of Malin's demise, like the price of entry to a carnival funhouse. Perhaps it was because, being now dharmine in nature, I was not the daughter I used to be; or perhaps he had always thought less of me than I'd realized.

Surely that latter possibility wasn't the case! Even touching on it evoked so many times he had worried for myself and Sable, had patrolled during the dangerous nights of ghastly Rift Events to keep us and our neighbors safe from harm. It evoked his face during that one particular night when I had crept out of my room and found myself caught in that treacherous storm. Yet, in the same way, he dehumanized me to justify his own ill intentions; and I also found myself dehumanizing him—dissociating myself from him by saying in my heart, 'this is not the man who raised me', lest that memory be forever destroyed.

There is a strangeness to men that I suspect I shall never fully understand, which is no doubt part of what keeps them so interesting to me. One can often set eyes on them and have—

for instance—a general sense of the exorbitant and multilayered calculations going on in the mind of Malin, or an idea of the steady recycling of Eleison through the same old thoughts of sorrow to further boost the luxuries of the happier present, or a perception of Glenn completely absorbed in the sensory experiences of watching Rosina draw a picture or smelling a bouquet I've cut for his rooms. Yet, there is always some layer of strategy or mystery I perceive at work within their minds as they, in their turn, study what they believe they know of the world around them and do the same with me. I suppose it is Ba'al-Dinon who, for reasons far too appropriate to elaborate upon now, exemplifies that quality in an archetypal way, in that I look upon him and feel I know everything and nothing of his thoughts in a sublime superposition beggaring all description.

My point, I suppose, is this. The men who have known me in the sexual sense *do* know me, and look at me like they do. They look at me in a manner signaling, on some primordial level, that they know me better than I know myself—not in a manner that is condescending, but in the simple way that I, too, see very clearly those things about themselves that they tend to keep in blind spots. That is the intimacy of the lover and the beloved, and there is nothing that can replace that truly open-hearted understanding when it is rightly manifested. When it emerges from a place of truly wishing to know one's partner—the true depths of that self and not the external projections produced by a lifetime of learned defense mechanisms in one or both individuals—it is truly an experience of connection that seems a foretaste of Heaven.

And so it is apt that the corollary—when someone looks at me as if they know me, as if their cleverness is so advanced that they might know parts of me I have never even revealed to myself, when they are only seeing their own worst traits reflected upon me so they may smugly blame the mirror for the spots upon their face—has always been a kind of Hell for me. Perhaps it is only another sign of pride, as Ignatius warned; perhaps it is how I justify myself, knowing I am capable of much and therefore having an acute sense of my own moral failings and strengths. Whatever the case, nothing has ever quite boiled my blood like a flawed assessment of my personal character. Those papers in Valquist sprang to mind.

But no such thing had ever outraged me as that almost mocking expression upon Rigel's face, his eyes a-twinkle with infuriating paternal mirth as he said, his grip still tight around my wrist, "Don't worry too much about my private business with your husband, sweetheart…I'm sure God and the continent will understand someday that all the things you did, even your marriage, were under duress. And maybe you will, too."

I couldn't take it anymore. Truly, I did not know who this man was, and even as I raised my free hand in a fist—feeling as though I watched it fly from somewhere out of my body—I wondered once again if this was not truly who my father had always been. Had he hidden himself from me? Perhaps this was how I would always have come to find him anyway, had he not posthumously been given an otherworldly air of untouchability shared by my mother. That figment of myth and legend who seemed more and more like a simple conceit for a fairy tale; the unconscious matter-goddess in the creation story of my soul. Death had given me a reverence for both my parents when it had collected them while I was young, instilling also a feeling of abandonment that could never be resolved into the anger a grieving person needed to fully experience.

And it was that anger exploding out of me as my fist cracked so hard into the bridge of my father's nose that I felt the bone snap inward. I was too furious to even marvel at the sensation, the shock of my swiftly bruising knuckles, the gush of purplish black blood streaming from his nostrils and mouth like a glorious fountain. I thought of the Rift beasts being slain at the Torea festival and laughed for some strange reason, drunk on incredulity at my own actions, delighted when the pain caused him to release me and reel back, doubled over in pain, his blood pouring down over his open hands. The men around us stumbled away from us, exchanging glances of horror at the lethal contagion spurting from Rigel's face to puddle on the floor and his boots. They were in such a stupor I very nearly had a chance to reach Eleison, but one fast-recovering fellow who had obviously seen his share of combat in recent days raised his rifle too fast for me. As my hands jolted into the air on either side of my head, my father, eyes blazing in rage, lifted his head to bare his teeth at me in an appropriate show of animal ire.

"I think she's too unstable to be trusted," he said, pressing one hand over his nose while gesturing to the nearest hunters with the other. "Remove the boy."

"No!"

Eleison and I shouted the word simultaneously, though I daresay my intonation was shriller in my urgent horror. "If you separate my son from me," I roared, staring him dead in the eyes, "the second time you die will be by my hand."

The air took on a strange, hyper-real quality—one of those turning points in the course of a human life. Rigel and I stared each other down, a battle of wills that became increasingly difficult for either side to win without collapsing the waveform into a physical state—a tangible experience of violence that would leave one dead and the other changed forever.

"I'd like to see you try," he said, turning his back to hide his wince from the rest of the room as he snapped his own nose into place. Then, his words an even more outraged snarl as the pain resonated through his facial nerves, the sort of pain too visceral for even a dharmine to enjoy, he advanced on the fellows who recovered from their paralysis enough to spring into action before he neared them. "Go on! Bring him to me—and while you're at it, check the suite again for any hidden device that could be used to contact Malin. I don't like her paramour showing up uninvited."

There was so much more I wanted to say and do, especially upon imagining the men sent ahead of us detaining my son as though he were some common criminal. Yet, I found I could say nothing; I could not speak at all. Almost lost in the chaos of the moment, the footsteps of another hunter echoed up the hall and to the door of our ward with an urgency that, in some moment of foreknowledge, made me strangely sick. The fellow burst in, panting: too wild to be startled, as I had initially interpreted him to be. In fact, it was quite the opposite. With an incomprehensibly jovial tone, he shouted, "We've struck their encampment near Rheton! It's destroyed—there's no trace of any survivors!"

And it seemed in that instant as if the whole world fell apart.

24

It was that blasted phone call. Malin's insistence that we speak so he might reassure himself of my wellbeing was his undoing (for I wished, somehow, to blame him, as if otherwise there was a chance for the responsibility to be with me). By, I believe, a means of triangulation involving the projected distance from the highway heard in the background of the call, the hunters had managed to airstrike the projected location of my husband's encampment. Yet, for all the world, they might as well have dropped their armaments upon my soul, for I could hardly feel or think after I received word of this obliteration.

It was all so much at once: Eleison, blinded; Malin, perhaps dead again, this time irrecoverably; Telemachus, already taken from the suite to which I was returned by an altogether much too jocular pair of hunters.

Suddenly, all I had was the black loom, which stilled their patter into the silence of religious terror.

The door shut behind me, but I did not hear it. Slowly, slowly, not yet moving from the doorway, I sank to the floor but did not weep. I sat, completely silent and still, my face numb, my fingers tingling in a curious manner.

I had nothing. Nothing, nothing. No—I had Glenn and Rosina somewhere in the sprawling, much-too-populated complex of the palace. I had blinded Eleison. I had no proof that Malin was dead. Indeed, I did not have 'nothing', per se.

Yet, with my suite totally empty, now devoid of even my brooding son's happy but strained greeting, I felt as if I had less than nothing. It was impossible to think of what I did have when what I did not have—certainty, security, peace—was so substantial in my eyes. Indeed, I've heard it said that the needs of mankind could be thought of as pyramidal, with those three objects I was denied forming a pivotal foundation. Without the least surety that I would even survive the night myself, let alone that my husband, mate, or son would, I could think of nothing else but the same recycled fears, the same old traumas, the same bad news, over and over. The bombing of Malin's encampment recalled Malin's assassination; Eleison's blinding was some emulation of the night he'd almost sacrificed himself to save Malin and me; Telemachus's removal from my suite seemed in so many ways a symbolic reinterpretation of his removal from my womb when that bullet had caused his miscarriage and ensured his only life would be his eternal one. Even the placement of Glenn and Rosina in some unknown spot in the sprawling palace seemed a microcosmic recreation of their macrocosmic flight. A thousand daggers from which I had almost begun to recover were re-inserted, all their old wounds gouging open beneath this newest twist of the blades.

But somehow, bafflingly, it was the sight of the black loom and the absence it implied—the absence of Dinon, who had sworn himself to me and served me as loyally as an adoring slave—that cut the deepest. He, who could but snap his fingers and rectify every tragedy of my life, was nowhere to be found. Where was he? When I needed him, when my life was amounting to sudden and insurmountable loss, where was the one who claimed to love me the most?

I'm right here, Thecla, he swore to me, words that rang out so clearly in my soul that I burst into tears, weeping at what seemed like cruel mockery.

"No, you're not, you bastard," I shouted aloud, surely sounding like a madwoman. "If you were truly here, you'd hold me."

Always, Thecla. He was earnest and unruffled by the hurt, even had I lobbed such an epithet in a moment of pain. *I'm always holding you. You're always in my arms; always safe with me.*

"What useless platitudes! I won't be consoled by your intolerable ambiguity today. Whatever you say, on a terrestrial level, I'm objectively alone."

What do you mean by 'terrestrial'?

More annoyed than ever, I wiped my fingertips beneath my eyes, then followed up with the heel of my palm, dismissing his Socratic ignorance with a wave of my free hand at the same time. "You know what I mean. Don't play stupid. It's unbecoming. *Physical,* I mean. Tangible, concrete, objectively verifiable."

And 'objectivity'?

As I rolled my eyes in disgust, Dinon emitted a laugh that was somehow more casual than any emotion I'd heard him produce before.

"I'm glad these semantic games amuse you," I told him, "but the fact remains that you know exactly what I mean. Objectivity is opposed to subjectivity. From my subjective perspective, I am in the midst of a dreadfully annoying conversation with you; from an objective viewpoint I am a woman sitting alone in my cushy prison cell, maintaining a conversation with a—with a loom." I appended this when I realized that my eyes were fixed upon that new center of gravity within the room, that eerie object that locked my attention every time I mentally approached its event horizon. Indeed, it seemed somehow as though my attention on this object improved the crispness with which I experienced Dinon's voice in my soul, as a radio antenna improves the fidelity of a broadcast. And so, I had no trouble detecting the entertainment he took in asking his next question.

And you would know what it's like to have an objective viewpoint, would you, Thecla?

Slowly cajoled out of my tears by the sheer level of frustration I endured whenever these pseudo-philosophical debates reared their heads, I looked at the loom as though it had eyes with which to behold my incredulity. "If I did," I told him through it, "then my experience wouldn't be subjective."

But everyone else's experience is subjective; so where is the objective experience coming from?

With a slight stutter, I rejoined, "Well—I suppose a subjective consciousness like mine can't fully answer that without defaulting to the assumption that such a perspective belongs to God."

In other words, my absent lover mused, *there is no real way to prove anything is objective. Mankind's only evidence for anything arises from a collection of subjective viewpoints. Therefore, it's impossible to say what's happening objectively when you're talking to me in this room. There's only your perspective, the perspective of the men listening from outside the room, and your father's perspective as he eavesdrops on the recording.*

"Perhaps that's so, but if that is the case, group consensus is the only factor that matters; and in that, I am outvoted."

Mm, I see… so what you mean is not objectivity, but the difference between a consensus reality and a private one.

"I suppose so; and if that's so, then I'm discussing the difference between sanity and madness."

Or the difference between conformity and creativity.

With a slight laugh, I brushed a loose eyelash from my cheek, examined my hand, and said as I dusted it away, "I suppose that, if it wasn't a matter of life and death, that would be the case…you do rather have a way of distracting one, haven't you?"

I've had a lot of practice. His voice carried a chuckle and something about it soothed me with a kind of familiarity that was sorely needed. Despite myself, I was comforted, though the notion that I was giving in to that comfort prevented me from dwelling in that state too long.

"Would you tell me, Dinon—when you spoke with my son before, was it this absence of his that you advised him about? He's growing as cryptic as his father."

We discussed that, answered Dinon, *among other things.*

"Cryptic as his godfather," I corrected in a mutter, brooding now, frustrated to be kept so completely out of the loop. I glowered at the loom and told its master, "You know, if this doesn't have some kind of happy ending, I'm going to be very disappointed in you."

Thecla.

All his mirth evaporated, and Dinon spoke to me with such

sincerity that I could practically see him through his loom; his face seemed to form from the spectral mists in the center of my imagination. The words themselves filled my heart, gentle and true.

I promise, Thecla—I'm going to give you everything you want. Try not to worry... I'm here for you, I promise. Oh...poor Thecla.

The love imbuing his words caused my tears to bubble up again. I covered my eyes with my right hand, my shoulders shaking violently as I wept. "When," I sobbed, "when, when will all this be over? I don't know how much more I can take of it—all of it. It's intolerable: politics, sociability, warfare. I never asked for any of this. I just want to be with the people I love. I just want to live in peace, Ba'al-Dinon."

How sorry I felt for myself! Yet the truth was I hadn't let myself accept the misery of my circumstances. I had not felt the influx of emotions that came upon me when I was absolutely alone.

You're not alone, said a voice, soft and low, from the doorway.

I felt alone, anyway, and that was what counted in that moment of entitlement. Sobbing like an inconsolable child, I discounted Dinon's companionship altogether, not understanding, furious and sad. "I feel like you've abandoned me," I exclaimed, my chest heaving as I wept on the floor, doubled over, nearing the point of collapse. "I'm just here, trapped, with no way out. Everything and everyone I love has been taken from me. Oh! I feel like I'm in Hell."

It must feel a little like being a murder victim, my interlocutor observed wryly.

Again, my tears stilled: not from distraction but from sudden shame that I should weep at all. Damn him—damn that contemptible Eldritch thing in the skin of a beautiful man who loved me to a point of cosmic obsession! Damn him, but he was always right. Ba'al-Dinon did not need to condemn me; rather, he made the observation, the sly comparison, and gave me an opportunity to convict myself in my heart—that pang of guilt that was the curse and gift of self-awareness.

Perhaps it is absurd to you by now, reader, who have followed me through infidelity and treachery—through callousness, lies, and murder—when I say that I no longer deal well with such a feeling as shame. Before the time I recount to you now, I certainly felt guilt; but it was a meaningless thing that could be easily reasoned with—rationalized—when, for instance, the rewards were submission to the pleasure brought by Eleison's body behind Malin's back. That was far too sweet an experience to deny; and, in the end, I can hardly say I regret the way things turned out.

But what I didn't understand in those early years of my mid to late twenties—not until after that conversation with Ignatius had time and trauma enough to really sink deep into the substrate of my heart—was that guilt was not like a thermometer, or an RMS readout, or any simple measurement. Rather, it was the sign of something happening within me. Like the slipping of an ice shelf, more and more, until at last it slides into the sea with what only seems sudden to the untrained eye. That ice shelf has, for years, felt the shift, the shift, the shifting away, the weakening of its structure from the glacier that bore it; and only as one slips into the sea does it realize that perhaps things could have been different.

I have decided since the time chronicled in these memoirs that the change signified by guilt is not acceptable to me, and now I avoid behaviors that trigger the feeling at all costs. It is my proposal that this hard recognition began at that moment, when Ba'al-Dinon, in his absence, nevertheless held up a mirror to my crimes and revealed to me how I was indeed to blame for the bombing of Malin's encampment…and far more. Every single moment, everything that had gone wrong, was inarguably my fault: at the very least, it had all flowed out of my wrongdoing—by pulling out Parvati's heart. There it was again, beating in my wet, red hand. There was everything since.

What a foul, evil woman I was! How had I let myself become this? My God. My father wanted to blame Malin, or the Rift—anything but me. But wasn't it all my own doing? Could I blame this on anyone else when, if I hadn't killed that woman, I wouldn't have been alone, my future in ruins?

My face burning, I thanked the floor for keeping me steady as I sat there, humiliated and dizzy. Rubbing my brow, I murmured, "I can't possibly sink lower than this without being killed, can I?"

Dinon's silence was conspicuous.

Feeling pained, I let the matter drop. I understood that Dinon had insights beyond my own, and that I was better off being patient than pressuring him to respond to my whims, however desperate they seemed.

Yet I could not accept the impression of his absence, however false that impression truly was. My head swam; I longed for his nearness, for him to drape himself around me.

I think it was that imagery that at last made me recognize the object I had woven upon the loom. There are those epiphanies that rush upon us, but there are others that simply appear in a strangely natural way. An extraordinary act snaps into its place in the grand scheme of ordinary reality with such a logical connection that the very epiphany itself seems unextraordinary: it becomes only the simple organic unfolding of a thought within the confines of material spacetime. Thus it was that I recognized the fuligin threads I had been compelled to weave upon this alien loom belonged to that very fine brocaded cape that had, from the first time I met him, draped from Dinon's shoulders to swirl about his feet with a frightful, regal air. Somehow more amazed that I had not recognized it before this moment than I was to find I recognized it now, I cautiously approached and examined the style of its heddles.

My soul throbbed with longing. With that same mysteriously intrinsic drive to act on what I knew needed doing, though I couldn't explain why I felt so compelled. Newly driven all the same, I began at one end of the bottom of the weaving and, thread by thread, reverently plucked the warp from the notches which maintained the tension of the textile. It eased, sagging within the frame of the loom, the cloak somehow losing some of its otherworldly quality. As it grew beholden to the commands of gravity, it seemed newly manifested into reality: fully realized in this three-dimensional form almost suitable for physical existence.

In a kind of daze, gathering the material into my arms, I sank back into the sofa and regarded it in numb silence. My body worked in mechanical, unthinking automation, the oft-repeated movements of tying the fringes of a weaving coming back to me in meaningless cause and effect. I worked without speech or song, using my teeth to cut the loops, before tying them off in careful, even knots. My work only paused when I realized something was missing; on the hunt, following some deep instinct, I rifled through the closet of the suite's bedroom. From its dusty back, I extricated a sewing kit stashed there years ago, forgotten after a long parade of guests and uninvested servants. I returned to the sitting area and, using excess warp, sewed down the threads, dissolving into the work—everything suspended in this task that held my focus—this ribbon and button pilfered from some pillow to serve as the clasp—

Until Glenn's urgent knock and call of my name broke me from my fugue state, and I dropped my work to leap up from the couch with a cry.

"Oh Glenn, darling!"

"Keep back from the door," one of the guards barked. I obeyed, but as soon as Glenn was through that door, I threw myself upon him, hiding in his embrace with a wretched little sob. "Glenn," I cried. Exchanging a glance, the hunters shut the door behind us to blot out the sound of our reunion. "Oh darling, I just don't know what I'll do, you must help me—"

"Thecla," he said, brow furrowed. "What's happened?"

"They've taken my Telemachus away," I lamented, "and, worse still, Eleison—"

But Glenn was no longer listening. His hands tightened on my arms, his eyes glued to the room somewhere past my head.

"I've dreamed about that loom before," was all he could say, somewhat dazed.

Eagle-eyed readers with memories as sharp as my fastidious husband's will perhaps recall a dream I mentioned earlier in these volumes—wherein I saw Glenn on the other side of the mirror in that strange middle-place the black loom seemed to call its home. I often wonder if he was not having the same dream at the same time, or the other side of it, at any rate: like two people meeting in the center of a dark tunnel, having entered from opposite ends. Having no measurable proof of this, I can't say for certain; however, given the way these metaphysical things tend to work, I wouldn't be at all surprised if that were the case…though it's all irrelevant in the end.

However alarming it was to re-experience the memory upon setting eyes anywhere near that solemn device, Glenn was at least able to compartmentalize well enough to refocus his attention on me and sit with me beside the suite's empty hearth. It was as I found myself overcome by a new flood of tears that his attention became completely diverted, and the loom was altogether forgotten. I related the circumstances surrounding Eleison's abrupt arrival, Telemachus's relocation, and the abject horror I experienced at being denied the right to see to the wellbeing of my beloved mate.

"I don't know if my presence would do any good for his injuries," I lamented, briskly wiping the heel of my palm beneath my eyes to banish my tears—a dangerously common automatic response, of late. "The last time he needed my presence to stabilize his condition, he still required a trip to the hospital for an infusion of Stabilify. For the case of physical damage done to an organ like his eyes—" Dizzy, I doubled over toward my knees and tried my best to steer my thoughts away from that abyss. Glenn, bless his good soul, knew what I needed was not advice but patient listening, and he sat in silence as I squeezed my eyes shut to more cautiously express my thoughts—and perhaps, on an unconscious level, to align myself more sympathetically with my mate.

"Eleison could be crippled, maimed, made too abjectly wicked to merit compassion from the common man, and I would still love him, Glenn! But it's that very love that makes me—that makes me so pained"—I beat my fist against my breast, my teeth bared—"to think of him suffering this way! Oh, darling, I know you've never got on well with him—"

"That's not true," Glenn assured me softly, the sudden, warm weight of his firm hand soothing upon my back through the fabric of my dress. As his caress put an abrupt end to my tears and left me gasping softly for the air I needed to settle my mood, he stroked between my shoulder blades. "To tell you the truth, I feel like Eleison and I get along pretty well. We could, anyway. I can see us being friends, especially if we had met under different circumstances—"

"You mean, without Malin's relation to him," I supposed, feeling bratty and resentful even of my heart's closest helper in that moment. Lucky for me, Glenn took the comment in stride, his hand gliding up to the base of my neck, his thumb aligning with the divot of my spine at the base of my skull.

"No," said Glenn, "I mean without you."

Scoffing, I looked over at him, genuinely quite amazed that he had the candor to say such a thing to me at all; and in this moment, of all moments. "Are you blaming me for your inability to get along with my mate, Glenn?"

What a mood I was in! Yet how clearly Glenn revealed his heart to me by laughing instead of taking offense. His eyes crinkled slightly, the electric hue of his irises shining even as he tried to maintain a somber expression so as not to antagonize me. "You know, Thecla," he observed, his hand now shifting from the back of my neck to the curve of my cheek to smear away the remaining tear tracks, "it's interesting to me how you don't see these things. You live in your own little world; or, maybe it's just that you see the world in a way that's so totally foreign to me. I can't explain why, but it's sexy to me—maybe because I feel like I'm observing…I don't know. Some exotic creature. Some alien being." With hesitation that gave me time to color under his words, Glenn added, "I guess now I am…or maybe I always have been, in some way I can't explain."

Suddenly, more commanding than ever I had known him to be, Glenn tipped my head back and bent down to pour his kisses into me. His tongue penetrated my soul by way of my lips as I gasped and melted fully into the unexpected pleasure. The warm, wet throb of his tongue spiked my appetite, but before I could worry about the emergence of those hunting teeth of mine, he drew back and gazed intensely into my very essence.

"Don't you understand I'm jealous, Thecla?"

I laughed a little, blushing more sharply at the introduction of that word into my happy little hedonistic family life. Then, with some astonishment, I realized I had shunned the concept so utterly after adapting to Malin's ways that I had all but eradicated it from my mind—or tried to. What use did any of us have for such a notion when my husband took special delight in witnessing the exact moment my mate's cock first split me open for the night (or morning, or afternoon), or when my heart thrilled to see them love one another with a savage kiss that reminded one of two great beasts playing at games of dominance, or when I knew that our hearts were all so deeply embedded in one another that no other woman could hold any worth to them in a romantic sense? There was no way in which jealousy served us anymore. Even Eleison had released it quite quickly, adapting to this new way of life with greater ease as he himself submitted to falling in love with Malin. Thus, we had been perfectly happy—and I had not been able to figure out why Glenn couldn't, wouldn't, fit into that happiness the way I thought he ought to!

"I—I—" With a bit more embarrassed blustering, I confessed after a second, "Perhaps I hadn't considered that quite as clearly as I should have."

Nostrils flaring, Glenn gave a short, repressed laugh. He gazed at me intently, swallowing me up in a stare that contained not just all of me, but me as experienced and evoked in his fantasies. "That's what I mean," he murmured, his eyes focusing down on my mouth for a few seconds. "I used to take it the wrong way. I thought you were arrogant, or oblivious, or maybe that you just didn't love me enough to see why I was hurt."

While his words shot me through with awful pain—that he had ever thought such a thing!—Glenn went on, "But then, while we were apart, I started to think about things…especially when you were promoted to Matrix of Gudrune. For some reason, reading tabloid stories about you over the past year made me realize…you're not doing all this maliciously. Your focus is just elsewhere. You're an artist…you have different priorities, maybe even different expectations, than the rest of us. There's something beautiful about that. Something innocent."

Biting my lip to contain a strange admixture of sadness and excitement—for it was erotic to think I had the power to make a sensitive man, whom I loved and who loved me, so jealous that he would run from the pain this jealousy caused him—I stroked Glenn's chest through his shirt, trying to decide whether the desire I saw in his eyes was only a projection of my own lustful hopes. "I wouldn't call myself 'innocent', darling."

"You're right…that's probably the wrong word. But—maybe it's not. What's the alternative—'naïve?' You're definitely not that. And you've done your fair share of conniving, I think it's safe for me to say. But…I don't know. The intent is different. The attitude. You live in a way that shows me you don't fully realize the effect you have on men…on me. You don't know what it does inside of me when I think about Eleison or—or your husband bending you over the bedside and fucking you."

The surge of arousal that rushed through my body was so intense I swooned. It seemed as if this previously taboo subject of sexual jealousy released a hidden side of Glenn: I could tell he took pleasure from the thought whether he wanted to or not, and his very inclination to experience pleasure from it drove him utterly mad. Experimentally, I slid my hands up to his neck and let my wrists hook behind his nape, my body fitting closely to his as his pupils dilated. "I wish you would have been straight with me about this sooner," I chided, pouting. "How didn't I see it? It's not Malin you hate at all, is it...not anymore, anyway. No..."

Letting my lips graze Glenn's as I spoke, I murmured, "It's the thought of his big, bare cock filling me...and being worshiped by my mouth."

Inhaling as I slid into his lap, my legs splaying slightly to accommodate the fit, Glenn let his thumb sink into the flesh of my cheek a little more as he confessed, "It has occurred to me that might be the root of these difficult feelings of mine."

"Poor Glenn! Poor, jealous Glenn. You have no reason to be jealous, darling...in fact, I think you're confused about the real reason why you're jealous."

"Oh?"

"Mmhm." My tongue ghosting out along his lower lip, which moved to invite an entry I resisted, I told my heroic hunter, "You're jealous of their freedom, Glenn...you're so jealous because they let themselves love one another and love me, too. They live in such freedom that they take joy in sharing me, in seeing me shared. In fact, I wonder if that isn't what the trouble is. If you would but give yourself permission to watch and enjoy the sight of my ecstasy at the hands of another man, you might feel far more satisfied... certainly more included."

Unable to argue with the effect my words were having, Glenn's eyes lidded as if to shade his intense thoughts. He confessed in a soft animal growl, "I think maybe what worries me is what I feel inside myself when I think of that happening. It's the things I want to do to you in those moments. The urges I have...they make me think of myself in a way I don't want to think of myself. They make me feel things about you, Thecla, that I don't want to feel."

Flush with increasingly intense desire, the adrenaline of my fear for Eleison and his condition heightening my arousal, I furrowed my brow and nibbled my underlip. In other words, I did my best to visually amplify the qualities Glenn had a moment before interpreted as innocence. "If you feel the need to punish me, Glenn," I murmured, looking into his eyes, "I understand. My lovers know what's good for me. If you'd let yourself enjoy us all at once, you'd know I always defer to a man who thinks I need discipline...especially if he intends to give me his cock and make me feel better afterward."

With a long, intense stare, Glenn's expression grew haunted by the enormity of his desire. He worried his thumb back and forth along the curve of my cheek, then allowed that same hand to slide to the back of my neck. He pushed me forward, guiding me until I was draped over his lap, my ass in the air and quickly exposed by the dress he yanked high.

My pussy was already soaked, the bud of my clitoris aching to be touched. No doubt, all this showed as I gazed back at him with pleading eyes. But my hero took his time, letting the cool air kiss the wet heat of my labia. His fingers explored my sex slowly, rubbing and massaging the outer lips, sliding around and around my opening without going in.

"What if I fucked your throat?" he murmured, his voice husky. "Would you like that, Thecla? What if I decide you need to choke on my dick for a little while?"

I felt my face flame. Glenn hardly ever spoke this way— something in him had begun to rage with new intensity, and I loved it. "Yes," I said, my breath catching. "I'd love to have your cock deep inside me, oh, Glenn! Every part of me, even my mouth. Maybe especially."

Glenn gave me a wicked grin, a smile I had never seen on his face before. I saw, at last, how wicked he could be if he would only be at ease, and my desire for him increased tenfold. "Maybe I'll make you suck it first, then fuck you the way I know you want." He began to push a finger inside my pussy, just a little bit, but all too quickly he pulled it out, leaving me wanting more. His brief presence just barely inside me made me all the more cognizant of my ache, my emptiness. My need to be filled.

"Yes!" I let my legs splay slightly apart, amazed at how quickly he had gotten my body responding with total abandon. As the flower of my sex shamelessly flowed for him, I arched my back and presented myself to him as I begged, "I'm desperate, oh, Glenn—I need you now more than I ever have. More than I could possibly say, my love...let me show you I can be yours just as much as I can be theirs."

For a few seconds, his expression turned serious. I feared I had lost him again—until, to my relief, one hand slid into the thick of my hair, his fingers tangling there. Exhaling, I shut my eyes.

It therefore came as a total surprise when his other hand swatted the swell of my ass with enough force that I yelped. Glenn, my beloved Glenn—meek, mild, somehow innocent Glenn—was spanking me, and the sharp sting of his open palm made me gasp.

"Oh! Oh, Glenn, I..."

"I'll fuck you," he assured me. "I'll make love to you and give you everything I have to offer. But don't forget, sweetheart, you're not the boss."

His voice was rough with desire.

"When you're mine, you're *mine*. Do we understand each other?"

The words rocketed through me, racing through every part of my body and inspiring a pleasure even Malin's claim over me hadn't provoked. Perhaps it was because, unlike Malin or Eleison, there was no admixture of fear involved in being loved by Glenn. There was only devotion: the complete devotion of a serious, good, and loyal man. I was Glenn's, and I belonged to him. My body, my mind, my heart, my soul, and my flesh were his, and I surrendered them gladly.

"Yes, yes," I agreed, gasping as he smacked me again. "I'm yours, oh, Glenn—oh, put me in my place, darling. Yes, oh, don't you see—every time you feel jealous, all you need to do is discipline me. You'll remember you're in charge...you'll feel so much better, darling. Oh! Oh—"

My toes curled and my body writhed as his swats lowered, following the nates of my stinging ass to strike my thighs. While I bit back noises that might have reached the ears of the guards outside, Glenn's voice was firm, his breath hot against my ear.

"Don't tell me how to discipline you."

"Oh!" My eyes were tearing and my hips jerked with every sharp slap of my increasingly sensitive flesh, but I couldn't keep from moaning. "Oh, please, Glenn—please, just fuck me."

"I will," he promised. "I will, and you'll love it." His breath was hot and fast on my ear. "You'll feel so guilty, baby."

"Darling," I whispered, gasping as he struck me again, "oh, Glenn, I could never feel guilty about fucking you—"

"That's not what I mean," he breathed. "I mean you're going feel guilty about the other ones. Malin and Eleison—anyone you ever even kissed back in Lescaut. You'll know you should have always been with me and me alone."

"Oh! But—but who would be around to make you jealous? Who would make you this eager to fuck me into obedience?"

He smacked me again and I couldn't help but let out a squeal of pain, arching my back and writhing.

"You're so sexy when you're helpless," he told me in a tone of enchantment, his spanking slowing down and his hand focusing in on the apex of my thoughts for his steady, affectionate swats. "I don't think I've ever seen you like this."

"Yes, yes," I gasped, "I want to show you how much I can belong to you, how happy I am to belong to you. Glenn! Oh, please—"

"You're so beautiful when you beg. When you're helpless and can't think about anything except how badly you need to get fucked. You really are mine, aren't you, Thecla?"

"Yes!" I insisted. "Yes, oh, I'm all yours, darling—oh, I'm so sorry, I'm yours forever—"

"And you'll make up for all this, won't you? For driving me away. You'll take a little while to think about how you could have treated me better; how you could have waited for me to come to you, rather than trying to catch me and keep me tucked away." He stroked my sex, gently spreading my lips apart and sliding his fingertips over the soft, slickening flesh. "Won't you?"

"Yes! Oh, please, darling, please, yes, I will, I'll do anything you say—"

"Good," he purred, leaning in close, "good, good girl, my love. You're doing such a good job. I'm going to let you come, sweetheart. And I'm going to give you what you need."

I was practically sobbing—not from the pain of the spanking, but from the intensity of my desire for this new, bold side of my heroic hunter. I wanted him so much I couldn't stand it, and he wouldn't give himself to me. Where by now neither Malin nor Eleison would have been capable of resisting my pleas, Glenn stood torturously strong.

"Glenn," I pleaded, "please, please, oh, I want you to take me. You're so perfect, you're so good to me, Glenn, oh, please, I'm yours forever." With a low moan, I rocked my hips, each brush of my clit against his fingertips sending another spark of wild pleasure pulsing through my body. The intensity was too great, and I could barely catch my breath; I felt I would go mad. I didn't care—all I wanted was to feel him inside of me, fucking me. To feel his hands on my body and his gaze fixed on mine.

"Please," I begged.

"Not yet," he whispered, leaning forward. "Beg me a little more, Thecla. Tell me what you want."

Something strange happened then, in that moment. The sexual frustration from his teasing spilled over into a kind of real frustration—all the heartache and pain of his disappearance mushrooming up within me like the fallout of a bomb. "I want you to come home," I cried out, twisting as much as I could to look him in the eyes. "Glenn—I want you to come home, and I want you to make love to me every day. I want you to be a family with me again—with Rosina and Malin and Eleison, and now Telemachus, all of us together! Please, oh, darling—"

Unexpectedly—overwrought with all I had experienced, and perhaps with this new invocation of Eleison and my stolen son—I burst into tears so overwhelming I couldn't make out his expression. "You have no idea how much I've needed you. How many times I've needed you while you weren't there for me. Please, please—just come home with me, and you can have me whenever you want. Glenn. I'll do anything."

He kissed me suddenly, passionately. A few seconds later he drew back, panting, a look of amazement filling his face. My hunter gazed down at me for several heftily thudded heartbeats, his heart pounding in his chest. A whimper rose from my throat as he slid his hand from me; the aching void of my body was more apparent to me in that moment than ever before. Amazing that no matter how many times I made love with the men I adored, I wanted them more and more every time. There was no bottom to the ocean of love into which they plunged me: no limit to the vulnerability and sensitivity of my heart in their hands. Hence, as he seemed intent to slide me aside and rise, I sat up instead, catching his bicep and gazing into his eyes. "Where are you going?" I begged, frightened of being alone just then, flush with the arousal of unfulfilled lovemaking. "Glenn, darling, don't leave. I need you."

"You're coming with me," he said determinedly, his voice soft but his words firm. Struck by his tone, I relaxed my grip on him, mystified as his hands cradled either side of my face to keep me still for the thrilling eye contact with which he drilled down into my soul.

"Where are we going?"

"To get Eleison," he said, "and the kids. And then, I'm going to do whatever it takes to get us all home."

Home. How sweet the word sounded upon his lips!

26

Only now do I realize how much blasted sneaking there is in this contemptible volume of my life! It seems an appropriate metaphor, in a way. When I consider the arc of my life, I spent much of the first portion of it shielded by this kind of inborn guile I now identify as something of my father's—some disease that was passed to me without my realizing, but which had such apparent lineage in him in a notion with which I was forced to reckon during that time where I was his prisoner in Valquist. I can be critical of myself now in a way I wasn't then—in a way I couldn't afford to then because I was in the thick of it all. But now I cannot help seeing myself as having been somewhat selfish and wicked and spoiled from the start. Oh, yes… I was a nervous girl, an inexperienced young fledgling thrust from her nest and into the purview of some looming harpros, a bird of prey; but it was only by this means that I realized I was like him, a harpros as much, a brilliant predator made to soar through otherworldly skies and feast on flesh not made for mortal lips. From my relationship with Eleison to that dark and hateful heart I shielded from Parvati—until at last I held hers in my grasp—I recognized what I thought was a severe desynchronization between my inner and outer selves.

Now, I see it was worse than that, for the truth is there is no difference between that which is inside of us and that which is outside of us. It is all the same, and we are kidding ourselves if we think that we can quarantine the people we are within.

All that is a very belabored way of apologizing to my poor readers for more sneaking, this time tiptoeing through hallways and darting past opulent stairs in favor of more austere ones intended for servants. Yet, at the time, I was so preoccupied that I was hardly aware of it all while it was happening. Here, I thought I had dissociated when in pursuit of Telemachus on that train. Now, on a similar mission to find him, as well as to obtain Rosina and Eleison, I was completely absent from my body. My thoughts were miles away, whole territories apart from my actions, when the unexpected afterglow of Glenn's emotion-inspiring attention too abruptly cleared to be appreciated yet somehow also responsible for the sense of surrealness with which I found myself standing alone in the room, listening as Glenn stepped out under the supervision of the guards and let them shut the door after him. In childlike pursuit of comfort, I draped the newly finished cloak around myself, fastening it around my neck and thinking with longing of happier times.

"How long do you think she's going to be under arrest here?" His voice carried to my sensitized ears without strain, perhaps due in part to my familiarity with the low umber notes of his tone. I had to focus to parse the first hunter's speech from his laughter.

"Why," I eventually decided I heard him ask, "it's not like you have to bring her anywhere to get her to put out. Hope you were safe, by the way...I hear that's how she got Winston."

"He wishes," Glenn said, without humor.

The sound of a scuffle began. Behind the locked door, I waited in anguish, my thumb worrying the fuligin fabric's edge. I was frightened and frustrated to think of Glenn risking his life when my intercession could have helped were it not for this lock. Yet, I feared that in that moment I would have proven beyond useless even if given access. A thousand worries occupied my mind: my thoughts ever rushed back to my husband, to the cold terror of not knowing his whereabouts—along with the terror that came with knowing Eleison's too well. Then there was my son—where would he be? And Rosina—how could we keep her from crying? And what of my father—

"Open the door," Glenn commanded in a tone so hard that the very room seemed eager to open of its own accord. I stepped out, never before so glad to find him standing with a gun to a man's head.

"Thecla," he said in a somewhat more measured but still urgent tone, his eyes darting to the rifle on the floor between us. I stooped to pick it up, examining the object in my hand with a vague sense of indifference. The unarmed man beside me, like the one whom Glenn held fast with what no doubt had once been that man's own gun, regarded me with the cold certainty of his own impending death.

Far be it from me at that moment of all moments to kill anyone at all! My soul in complete disarray yet, by Glenn's willingness to escape with me, pacified into this state of sick self-reflection, I recoiled even from the gun in my hand—though it was a necessary evil by which I was to accomplish the task of my family's salvation. I could not waver now or appear weak as I internally felt; therefore, adopting the dead air learned from witnessing, with a sadistic little thrill, my husband's most fearsome moments of remonstration toward some hapless fool like Parvati's pet ambassador, I pointed the gun at the man by the door and nodded toward the room. "Give me your radio," I instructed, "and get in. They'll notice you on the feed soon enough, I'm sure."

With this and the other man quickly sequestered in my former prison, Glenn placed his hand upon the small of my back. It was a small gesture, but it smoothly hurried me along, guided me, and assured him of my safety all at once. That most dire of circumstances only increased my need for even a microsecond of love, which steadied my resolve and lit the fire I needed to move forward. Because, while it was possible my husband was once again dead and my mate was permanently blind, and these thoughts compounded with all else such that I wished little more than to dissolve into nonexistence and forget all this horror, I could not indulge in the luxury of abandoning everything as I might have preferred. Rosina and Telemachus needed me too much for that. They needed their mother; and as each had been denied that for a greater or shorter duration of time, I was all the more dedicated to this mission of rescue, whatever it cost us.

"Stay behind me," Glenn urged, relaxing the contact of his hand and instead nodding in the direction of the corridor unfurling at our backs. "Make sure nobody's coming up on us from the other direction."

Mouth dry, I nodded. How grim I must have looked in that moment! Strangely, as I write it now, I picture myself in a manner I usually don't—my own face, haunted, gaunt with hunger and stress, circles under eyes that dart from Glenn's before locking forward with the same determined nod that causes a wisp of disheveled hair to flutter about my brow. Perhaps I see it so clearly because I was forced to imagine it then by way of the sympathetic look he shot me—piteous and kind. After squeezing my hand in encouragement, he set his own gaze forward and led the way, and I was his only security.

Poor Glenn! Eleison had trained me, and the inarguably predatory nature of my new being made the pressure somewhat more intense than anticipated, but I fear I was wholly inadequate cover for my beloved as we made our way across the palace to the quarters where oblivious Rosina awaited freedom. Luckily, though my stomach was tight and my adrenaline high—and I was always ready for the sounds of boots to come rushing around some corner—violence didn't prove necessary. The most treacherous part was the area near the stairs. These were broadly open and designed for glamorous photo opportunities as dignitaries descended mid-conversation with the Overseer or partygoers from the latest fête made their way up to pretend to be in pursuit of a glimpse of one of the palace's more obscure works of art. If we tried simply to walk along the hall to our destination, we would be seen right away. Therefore, at the edge of the mezzanine that provided a vantage from which we could see to the far side of the vast entry space, Glenn and I crouched behind a few plants and took stock of the hunters milling about at an intersection not far from our destination. With a few seconds of contemplation, he picked up the comm device confiscated from my former guards; as I watched, he lowered his voice somewhat, interrupting their conversation by radioing in.

"Anyone hear that crash from the ballroom's first floor? Over."

With a glance triangulating the three of them and speaking of too much concern to think overmuch about whose voice they were hearing, the fellow to the left of this small group plucked up his radio. "What'd it sound like?"

"Like a crash," said Glenn in annoyance. "How am I supposed to know? I'm by myself here; do you have backup right now to go check it out? We don't want it to be a stray luptich."

"Or another spy," agreed the hunter. "We'll check it out and report back if we find anything."

Nodding to his comrades, the first man put away his radio, and the other two followed him as, looking unhurried, they made their way to the ballroom. All the same, as they rounded the corner, one of them rested his hand on his gun.

"This way," whispered Glenn, breaking me from my awareness. I hurried after him, reality narrowing to that experience of pure momentum. Elsewhere was trauma: here was duty. I had to keep pushing, had to keep going. I had to surrender to maternal love, not grief and despair.

At last, with a well-timed dash past an archway and a friendly glass door, we circumvented several busy halls by following an external colonnade. The arcade framed the face of the moon in a rather ominous manner, but we ducked back into the palace and slipped into Glenn's nearby apartment, hurrying to shut the door. The radio burst with static and the ominous words, "You sure that was the first floor?"

"We don't have much time," he said, handing me his gun and hurrying into the suite. His apartment, far more lived-in than mine, was filled with books and various odds and ends. Only one object caught my attention: a small thing sitting on an end table. As Glenn opened a door out of sight, I made my way to it.

Amazing that this small dragonfly trapped in amber could bring a new wave of grief. I clasped the cool stone, pressing it to my heart with mingled joy and agony. It might as well have been my own gift from Malin, I was so touched to see it! But, before my thoughts could fly off into these torrents of pain, my daughter's voice crying out for me in excitement—"Mama!"—drew me from useless ruminations and into my hurry to embrace her.

"Rosina," I gasped, cradling her to my bosom and burying my face in her curls. My body collapsed into the peace and stillness of two magnets snapping together after time apart. "Oh, my darling, my little fawn—"

"Let's go," Glenn urged, taking advantage of the child's distraction to somewhat obscure, by the angle of his body, the gun he picked up from where he had left it on the table near the door.

"Where we going," asked my daughter, the naturalness of her question and the simplicity with which she spoke it breaking my heart for the cognitive leaps I had missed her undergo.

"Your father has decided it's time for you two to come home," I told her, tapping the tip of her nose with my finger, then setting the amber in her hands before gathering her into my arms to rise with her in my embrace. "Why don't you close your eyes, angel? Sleep on the way. We'll fetch a carriage, and you'll wake up already on the way home. Won't that be nice?"

Her eyes lighting a little in eager regard for memories I was surprised she was able to summon, Rosina asked, "Home? With Papa and Unky?"

Even as my heart seized by more kinds of pain than I could have parsed in that moment, I forced my mouth into a smile. "Yes, sweetheart," I told her, stroking the dark curls of her hair before urging her little head delicately down into the nook of my neck and shoulder, "yes, just so—close your eyes, now. You'll be overtired if you don't get a bit of sleep on the way."

Sensing nothing, obedient and trusting, the girl did as she was told, letting out a sigh of relief to be in my arms. Glenn and I locked eyes, and, looking more determined than ever, he turned away while murmuring, "I say we look for Telemachus first...let's check the cellar."

Under normal circumstances, the suddenly so much more concrete idea of my son held captive in a literal prison would have been enough to boil my blood past the point of rage and into something approaching mental cataclysm. Yet, there was not time for even that: for, hastening forward, Glenn caught hold of the doorknob.

As it went on barring our entry amid the ominous silence of resistance, the RMS panel on the wall sparked alive, and I realized we'd been had.

"I'm insulted you thought I was going to let you walk out of here," my father mocked, his voice filling the line. His derision palpably seeped into the room, further shaping my perception of how he had been changed by time and death. "You seemed plenty aware of the cameras before…did you think we weren't going to be watching you two playing espionage games around this place?"

"It had occurred to me," I mused in exhausted response, my hand, which had rested upon the back of my daughter's head, now sliding rather discreetly over her ear so as to blot out this conversation in which she merited no part. "Once I stopped thinking of you as my father and began thinking of you as some stranger wearing him as a disguise, your behavior became much more predictable…but I will not be separated from my children. Surely, you can empathize with that."

"Mama," Telemachus called urgently through the speaker of the RMS panel, making my spine sharpen with fury as Rigel's revenant barked to someone, "Keep him quiet."

"I'm coming for you, sweetheart," I told my son, adding by way of some compulsion that made me feel, as I spoke, the truth of what I initially thought to be a confabulation, "and your father is, too."

Why did it feel like such absolute certainty? The notion sat in my brain and even my mouth like the truth, the confident and fully known truth, as when one introduces oneself at a party to the long-missed friend not seen since childhood and now belatedly recognized. Even as Rigel scoffed, "I don't believe it's wise to lie to the boy," I slid into pensive thought patterns so immediately that I did not even realize I was looking at the weft strand of that thought, gleaming softly into the distance. While awareness of that strand and the vast length of it increased my firm consciousness of that confident notion, I raised a finger toward it, tuning my father out even as he railed on. "The invading Gudrune camp has been obliterated. Valquist has more armaments than those, and bigger, too; but I don't think they'll be necessary with Malin Farrow dead. I would expect an imminent surrender from the remaining troops."

Glenn watched me, an admixture of curiosity and fascination on his face, like a butterfly collector who had stumbled across some rare and fabulous specimen from the Rift. Indeed, it was that very Rift I was suddenly aware of, the atmosphere of a gathering Event rising around and within my body. Perhaps the weather was taking a turn.

"No," I answered my father in a tone of distraction, my finger crooking to pluck that string that only my eyes could see, "no... my husband is alive."

These words, this ever-firming knowledge, filled my breast to the very brim, as though the soul were a tangible organ that could be perceived and affected—and do the saints not assure us this is so? So it was that, bodily, I felt a part of myself wracked with immense physical longing, yet closeness: inextricable closeness, as of a magnet seeking its partner, careening rapidly into the sweet snapping-together of reunion. Somehow, by some means too strange to illumine here, I seemed to feel my husband's soul throbbing within and against mine, even from this distance—especially with that thread still vibrating from the pluck of my fingertip. Exhaling, swaying, holding my present child closer, I stared hatefully into the RMS panel that was my father's surrogate and warned it, "And once he has rescued his son and his wife, he'll put you in the blasted ground all over again, Rigel…assuming there's anything left of you to bury."

"If you really think he's alive, why run? Why not wait here with Glenn and Rosina?"

"I was amenable to that approach before you blinded my mate and took my son from me," I assured him. "But since you won't let me provide basic restorative benefits to Eleison by even so much as sitting with him, I have to take matters into my own hands… and if I'm going to go that far, I'd might as well leave Valquist altogether, mightn't I?"

"Guess I should admire your ambitions."

"Yes, well…you know I've never liked being told 'no.'"

With an indelicate snort of joyless mirth, my not-father muttered, "Now *that* is the truth."

While Glenn stretched an arm above the intercom to lean against the wall, he asked, "So you've decided Rosina and I are also your prisoners? Is that it?"

"That would seem to be the case," Rigel mused. "But let's be honest…wasn't that always sort of how it was? At the very least, you haven't been entitled to change residences without a lot of oversight and something resembling house arrest so we can keep tabs on you."

Glenn shot me a bleak look. "I've certainly gotten that impression recently."

"It's not that I don't like you," my father's replacement—no, unfortunately, truly my father—said amiably, "Matter of fact, I like you quite a lot. You've got an honest heart, and that's a rare thing in this world. It's also an exploitable thing...and, as I expected, you've been exploited, too. A victim of exploitation, perpetuating it on someone like Glenn—don't you know what it is to be used, Thecla? To be commodified and manipulated like you're a tool? Some kind of chattel?"

"I'm certainly not using Glenn," I told the brute, my tone as bitter as the loving childhood memories that had reached a kind of expiration and now begun to spoil. "Glenn and Rosina are my family, just as Telemachus, Eleison, and Malin are." My soul ached to say 'and Dinon', but for some reason, I could not bring myself to it and said instead, "Just like Charlotte and my footman." Even as some strange consolation bloomed in my mind—as if Dinon were right then by my side, stroking my hair and assuring me that downplaying somewhat my love for him had been no slight in his eyes—my face burned with shame to have reduced the role to which he was quickly ascending. Yet there was no time to dwell on my sin against my mysterious lover, and I went on in a prickly tone. "I love Glenn and Rosina, and I can see what you yourself have admitted is obvious—they are prisoners just as I am. It's only natural to wish to free them with me."

"So he can be free to play third fiddle in your little chamber orchestra, huh?"

My face burned with rage, and if I had not been holding my daughter at that moment, I might have punched a hole through the fragile glass forecast screen on the RMS panel. "What a disgraceful thing to say," I remonstrated. "You have no idea what my life is like, nor of the inexhaustible source from which my love runs. A source which I had thought you yourself had been responsible for showing me; but perhaps I was incorrect in thinking so."

The abrupt silence on the line was thick and satisfying. When he still said nothing after three long seconds—and three seconds are indeed very long when they come in the middle of a tense conversation—I showed him the mercy of moving our discussion along and alleviating somewhat the pain of the same wound I had just inflicted. "If I believed my husband was dead," I told him, my words icy, my hand still upon Rosina's ear while I prayed that she be spared any memory of this night, "then it would be far more prudent to remain here and try to make friends. I flee because I believe my husband is alive, you see...and if you don't look the other way, you and your men will face dire consequences."

"That's bold talk coming from a princess," mocked my father half a second before an unknown voice shouted half-coherently on the line.

"Ah! Fuck! You little shit!"

The tone changed at once, a shift so abrupt I couldn't process what had happened until, in a panicked tone, one of the hunters in the background said, "He's got my wrist!" and Rigel snarled, "Grab him, you idiots! Don't lose track of him now—no!"

With a peal of gunfire that left me pale with fear even as my soul sparked high with righteous flames, the RMS panel's speaker system snapped off, and the room we were in went silent.

"Mama," asked Rosina, her faint doze interrupted by the outburst from the panel and my sudden tension, "what is it?"

"It's nothing, dear," I whispered, stroking her hair and glancing urgently around the suite for an exit. Windows, but no doors. Always the same. "Just go back to sleep, it's only a show on the RMS."

Content with this, Rosina grunted softly and nestled her head back against my shoulder.

"We have to figure out where he's going to go," Glenn said hurriedly, giving the door handle another, harder rattle. "There's got to be a screwdriver around here somewhere."

Perhaps, yes. I cast my gaze about in search of one such item—or anything else that could be of use, for that matter. In my heightened state of anxiety, all I seemed capable of truly observing were those blasted threads. An accursed distraction, or so I initially perceived. My son's life was threatened. If I delayed in finding him, it might make him nearly impossible to discover. We would only wind up with more hunters between us as more and more of them searched the palace for their unaccounted-for hostages. Therefore, the longer it took us to get out of this room, the harder everything would become.

But I could not help my eyes from fixing on the threads! I, still prone to a kind of hyperfixation owing to the novelty of their phantasmic appearance, found myself lightly sorting through them whether I wanted to or not—and the first of them belonged to Telemachus. The day of our meeting, when he rose, nervous and shy, from the sofa in the vineyard's villa. This first thread of love yielded others, and still others, and still others, each observation drawing so many more into relief. And for all these which I touched, I thought of someone, or multiple someones, an event, a dream, a trauma: my sister, Sable, and the man destined to be her husband, getting into a tremendous row over the time he hid outside our house to throw flour on her new dress. Malin, old Malin (oh, my husband had been old! I only now saw clearly that the Rift had made him sleek and young) pausing in our walk so he could acquire me a flower, and how the unseen thorn punctured my thumb, and he kissed it. Eleison on a picnic with his brother and me, content and at ease for just a moment. Rosina, a tiny baby, glued to her father's heart, swaddled in cozy blankets. Telemachus, patiently permitting me to read to him as though he were a child four to eight years younger, as filled with the yearning to make up for the long-missed sound of my voice as I was to make up for the unknown sound of his.

My father.

Blast him, my father, my wonderful father, disfigured by time and death and sin into this man I did not recognize—my father, who held me on his shoulders to help me see the borro-taming show, who let me ride in a wagon to pick apples in the fall, who watched proudly as I helped my sister learn to walk, who told me Torea Festivals were wrong and saved me from danger and loved me. My father had loved me. He showed me what it was to be a good man, with a good heart, and a great devotion to his own legacy and that of his dead wife.

That was my father.

This was my father.

That was what I wanted to say. But somehow, just thinking about those memories as I plucked through the strands in search of those I wanted caused a strange correction to stiffen my spine. No, this new conviction seemed to say to me: if I am still myself, even after all I've been through, then surely my father is also still himself. It was simply that the pressure—and this new, perceived lack of consequences, the urgency that swelled upon becoming fully cognizant of having passed through death—forced us to reveal ourselves. There was no point in hiding anymore.

And in that moment, as Glenn negotiated with him, it occurred to me quite distinctly that Rigel had not just deceived me but, in fact, everyone. It was a matter of course with my father: part of the fabric of his existence. He and my mother had deceived Malin, then gone on the run and hide for such a span that I was conceived while they lived out their sham marriage in Lescaut—a mockery of the kind of life I dreamed of living peacefully with my own larger family. While in Lescaut, he had roped townspeople into a lie about me, a conspiracy to keep me oblivious to Malin's claim on me, and had done this so religiously that he even induced, or persuaded, my stepmother to continue that lie after his death. His death: which was, I now regarded with bleak appreciation, the moment my husband's dharmine and my infant son entered the world together. There was the substance of my father's lifetime of lies. That its punctuation should serve as the entry to a new sentence of repentance, of my once-lying husband who had since grown into the truth with me, suited me very well.

So my exercise in plucking at these strings did help me surrender to that notion, but they did not yield the result I wanted: namely, even a single thread that might connect me to Dinon. For, as I felt the throb and pulse of my husband's life through those threads that brought us together, so perhaps Ba'al-Dinon's threads, I thought, might evoke in him some awareness of my hope for help.

Yet—no matter where I touched, no thoughts of Dinon came to mind. When they did, they seemed to reverberate only insofar as he was party to another, more pressing episode: whisking me to the location where Malin was hostage, repairing Glenn's living room back in Valquist, taking rather obvious delight in

Eleison thrusting the gun against his head (an action I am quite sure my mate would have taken even if there were not a common misunderstanding pertaining to the avenues by which one may be infected by a dharmine). It was as though Dinon hid even the memory of himself from me...or as though his presence were somewhat dispersed across my conscious perception.

How that absence infuriated me! How troublesome that even in these threads—in what of my mind was somehow woven into the fundamental fabric of my reality—Dinon obscured himself! The anger nagged at me such that I gave an especially sharp tug to a strand that happened to also relate to the time Malin was kidnapped. That night, to bypass Ignatius and the rest of the household staff, I stayed awake until the early morning hours, fastidiously braiding threads into a rope with an efficiency that seemed otherworldly.

And by this memory, a curious idea came to me; one so strange and fantastic that it made a certain, absurd kind of sense.

"Would you hold Rosina for a moment?"

My whisper interrupted Glenn's rifling through the end table. In that automated manner of which only a distracted human is capable, he accepted the girl in his arms and, his eye still upon the end table drawer, only seemed to realize he had received her a few seconds later. He turned, a word half-formed on his lips.

But whatever he intended to say was lost forever. Indeed, I paid him hardly any mind at all, for I was focused on another dimension in the most literal sense possible. Now free of the child, I plunged my entire attention into those strands. In the same way that lying under the stars for more than a few seconds brings entire galaxies into relief from the tapestry in which they've been hiding, a plethora of threads began to emerge from the environment. So many, in fact, that I was first stunned, then somewhat frightened. They were overwhelming, and not just in number. The more intently I studied these threads, the more completely I drew my consciousness into them, and the more the environment disappeared in favor of that which constituted it. In the same way that, when one is close enough to a weaving, one may lose track entirely of the subject and craftsmanship in favor of careful study of those threads constituting this face or that flower, I became inundated with the sudden, dizzying sense that there was no reality—no chair, no end table, no Glenn or Rosina or perhaps even Thecla—but only these threads making up something we interpreted as reality. This idea of universal instability was unnerving to such an extent that when Glenn at last spoke the words, "Are you all right?" I was startled by them.

"Wait," I told him softly. "Just a moment—"

As my hand extended before me, his tone became a bit firmer. "We can't wait around, Thecla. We have to figure a way out of here. What if they find Telemachus and take him to another location in the city—or out of it?"

Uncertainly, my fingers pinched a section of thread that was the center of my focus. At first gingerly, soon with vigor, I pulled. It sagged out of place enough for me to hook a finger beneath and tug it more completely out of place. While I bent to apply my teeth to it and sever it, Glenn was somewhere, saying something else, and I'm sure I must have seemed quite a sight biting the open air! But my fingers had already worked free another thread, and then another, and then another.

"Thecla—"

"Sh," I bade him, unraveling this tapestry that was invisible and yet visibility itself. "Fetch something, anything—make a sling for Rosina."

"But what are you—"

"Hurry," I commanded him. This second iteration of his voice snapped my attention back to the fullness of reality—my perception of the threads distorting in favor of the man, the room, the child that they made; yet those threads I had loosed were still evident in the air before me, at least to my eyes. Looking over at him, I pulled what I had freed of the warp and began to weave, my fingers flying at a fully unnatural pace permitted by my dharmine reflexes and by whatever Riftborn nature ran through my soul. His gaze diverted to my hands, which he watched with befuddlement for but a few seconds before his face began to pale against the darker color of his beard.

He looked at me like I was a stranger.

s much sympathy as I have for Glenn, his frightened expression tears at my heart even now. That someone I so loved should be so afraid of me was painful, but I understood. There is a certain magic trick, a stereotypical act, that involves, oh, pulling a long rope or a chain of handkerchiefs out of a space that seems too small to contain so much fabric. To watch that upon a stage as a form of entertainment is one thing. To witness the inexorable appearance of these shimmering strands appearing from out of thin air—which seemed to materialize on contact with my fingertips and leave my hands as a coil of thin but sturdy rope—was an entirely different matter. His eyes flashed between this sight and my face; his countenance paled, and his eyes slightly bugged at the strangeness of it all.

"When they decide that they can't find the boy, they'll be here in a trice," I told him, shaking Glenn out of his stupor as I gathered the threads into a single weaving. "Intending to use us, or me, or Rosina to draw Telly out of hiding. There's no time."

Those words jolted him into action. While Glenn hurried off to ransack his bedroom in search of something suitable, I was free to focus. As quickly as I had managed to work the earthly threads of my weaving room into a rope capable of bearing my weight that fateful night of Malin's rescue, it had still taken me all night: yet now I worked so rapidly I may as well have been one of the machines that had been installed by the new owner of Parsons' Weaving at home in Lescaut. As reality once more faded into its component threads, this shimmering rope of otherworldly substance expelling from my palms amid the deft work of my fingers seemed to grow at a rate of a quarter inch every second, or more. In short order, it gathered at my feet, developing into an admirable coil of Rift violet and Dinon silver.

And, as the rope wove, the threads liberated from the tapestry left behind a gash that expanded, and expanded, and expanded, until this great hole in the work became a window to some other world.

I realized I was looking at it only gradually, and in a strange way that seemed so self-evident that what normally would have caused me some great inrush of mystical knowledge instead seemed simply natural. The violet warp threads framed a fantastic, expansive sky of similar vibrance that went on endlessly and seemed to me to be the same sky I had seen in some brilliant dream; the uncanny grass of silver and copper curled in a wind I could not feel, coaxing me like fingers to entice me into this other world. At last, as a comet like a streak of mercury flashed through the sky and blipped off into the atmosphere, I became fully aware of what I watched and found my weaving had somewhat slowed. Yes, I had in fact seen this place before: I had seen it in dreams, in fancies, and in my death; or, more precisely, in that vision before my death.

"Okay," puffed Glenn, having found a solution—a bed sheet he tore and used to affix our daughter to his chest. She was now wide awake and increasingly curious to see her mother hard at work on something she couldn't fully understand. Given that Glenn made no comment on the shimmering void through which one could clearly see a geographically impossible space, I assumed his only evidence of what was happening lay in the rope that became visibly embodied as it passed through my hands and into reality. But my daughter, her glittering eyes wide with childish amazement, spoke over him. "Pretty," she exclaimed with delight. "Beautiful sky!"

"Isn't it?" I smiled indulgently at the child, who, like her mother, had been born in Rift weather and was therefore sensitive to all its ways. "Perhaps someday you'll go there. It's so pretty that Mama is thinking of going there right now."

Glenn's expression shifted from mystified to worried. "Go where? What is she talking about?"

Before either my daughter or I could speak, however, chaos erupted in the hall. A clamor of footsteps drew urgent looks from the adults in the room. We both sprang into action: Glenn hurried over to push the nearest piece of furniture, a sofa, back across the door to buy us time, while I set to work detaching the rope. By the time I'd torn it fully free with my fingers and teeth, the door handle produced an ominous click—a key snapping in the tumbler of a lock. Heart seizing with fear, I hurried with Glenn to the nearest window. While he pushed it open, I hastened to tie the frayed, unwoven end of the rope to the sturdy leg of a desk overlooking the city of Valquist. As I cast the rope through the window, it seemed to fall short. I clenched my jaw and cursed under my breath, but Glenn caught my hand. "It's fine—let's go. We can jump from the end; it isn't that far of a drop."

It wasn't—perhaps ten feet at most, painful but bearable with the right landing—but that, of course, wasn't the trouble. Nostrils flaring, I squeezed his hand, my fingers tightening around his before I extricated myself. "I have to find Telemachus," I told him. "I can't leave without him, no more than I can leave without Eleison. Go on. Flee Valquist."

"But—"

I caught his face in both hands and drew his mouth to mine, collapsing his protests while, behind us, the couch groaned beneath the pressure of the beaten-open door. As its legs snapped, I pushed him away from me; my hand swept from his shoulder and down across Rosina's burnished curls. "I love you," I told them both. "Be safe—be careful. Oh! Ba'al-Dinon, shield them."

As though they were you, he said in my heart, *I swear, I will.*

That was all the assurance I needed of their safety. Turning away to face the men who began to barge in, I unslung the gun from my shoulders and wondered how I could possibly bear to use it; but Rosina's bright voice drew my attention back to her father as, reluctant but left with no choice, he stooped to catch hold of the rope.

"Mama," cried Rosina, her outstretched hands flinging the smooth stone of amber into my unready but reflexively closing grasp, "careful!"

"Just where the hell do you think you're going?" Rigel's gruff shout echoed through the room as, at last, the couch gave way enough for our captors to rush in. "Don't you know we own this city? You won't even make it to the gates; we'll find you."

Swiftly dropping the smooth stone into the pocket hidden in the folds of my dress, I snapped, "I'm not going anywhere. Some of us believe in loyalty to our family. My son and mate both need me."

"You're damn right they do. The only thing keeping them alive is you, Thecla. The boy is a bargaining chip with or without you, but if you want to see your mate after today, you'd better come with us quietly."

While a few gunmen peeled off from the group a futile attempt to meet Glenn at the base of the palace, I leveled the muzzle of the gun with my father's head.

"If you want me," my finger slid along the trigger, "come and get me."

In truth, I aimed a little high. After all I had been through, the last thing I wished was another death on my conscience. My intention, therefore, was only to provide suppressive fire—enough that Glenn and Rosina could flee. Even so, as I shot just above the heads of ducking men, my soul cringed. With the least wrong move, I could kill or maim or paralyze someone, and it was not a prospect I relished.

Not for any of the men present, save perhaps one.

"I see somebody's taught you how to shoot." Rigel's voice filled the gap between bursts of gunfire; his smug tone rose above the resultant ringing in my ears only because of some deep instinct remaining from childhood. "I'm surprised you can stand the recoil."

Smoke rose from the barrel of the gun, dust and plaster pouring from new holes punched through the wall and that same door through which the other men had rushed. Only Rigel remained, half-crouched behind the sofa, a pistol in his hand as he once more rose to his feet. Vaguely, I recognized the one he had been buried with, and realized why he had not been inclined to speak about his homecoming to the world: for he must have dug up his own rotten corpse and ghoulishly gnawed upon the bones until he came enough to his senses to go elsewhere. "Surprised you would shoot at your father, too," he added, his lip curled in a slight sneer.

My hands trembled with adrenaline. All the steadiness that was there as I braced myself against the bucking gun now resolved into the weakness of overexertion. "You've changed," I told him. "We've changed, our relationship has changed—let's not be too surprised by anything the other does."

"That's fair."

His pistol cracked with its discharge, and my hand erupted in sparks of pain. Blood gushed darkly from the wound and ran along my fingers, which convulsed from the damage to the delicate tendons beneath. As I dropped my weapon, new sympathy for Winston blooming in my chest, a cry escaped my lips. I barely managed to spring out of the way of another bullet, this one aimed at my feet.

There was so little time to respond. My options were few. Behind me was one exit: the rope, which would give me freedom from the palace but at the cost of Telemachus and Eleison. It would also allow the insurgents to focus on acquiring Glenn, Rosina, and me all at once, making things far too simple for them. Next was the door, barred by my father on this side and a slew of hunters waiting on the other, all armed and ready.

But third, and most enticing, was that exit only I could see: the vibrant void into the pulsating Rift. Its frayed edges shimmered, beckoning me closer.

I wished to stay; I couldn't bear the thought of leaving Valquist for even a second, knowing my family was in peril and about to be left behind. Yet, as my father raised his gun again, his thumb slamming down the hammer, I realized I had no options. Springing into motion, urged on by the fiery pain in my hand—made worse as my dharmine flesh began the stinging process of extruding the bullet—I flung the rifle's strap from my shoulder and, giving it the momentum of a hammer toss, hurled it at my father's head. He ducked, giving me exactly as long as I needed. While he cringed down behind the sofa, I dashed forward, springing through that private window to the Rift, my heart intent on making a hasty return to the palace as soon as I was free to leave without drawing excessive fire.

And then, as if the crisis vanished into nonexistence, the report of the guns fell silent.

If only I had known what I would find, or how long a diversion it would seem! At the time, when momentum had me rolling through the soft tendrils of grass before I caught myself, all I could think was how relieved I was to be alone. Having not even been sure that I could access that other world seen through the snag in those threads, I even laughed. Raising my head, I looked around to ensure I had evaded danger.

My laughter faded when I looked back the way I had come.

There was no window back to the world from which I had come: only the unbroken violet sky of the world on the other side of the Rift.

29

The emotions that surged within me as I realized my situation were beyond words. They flooded me so fast that, for a second, I couldn't think. Then, as the confusion cleared, I fully comprehended the absence of the portal by which I had come to this alien world of silver hills and an indigo sun. As confusion turned to cold, clear reality, fear washed over me.

What an awful mistake I had made! How foolish. It occurred to me then that I had been like someone who leaped headfirst into a lake without stopping first to check if the end they entered was the shallow side. Stumbling to my feet, panic overwhelming me, I whirled around in search of some trace of the portal that had brought me here, but to no avail. As all manner of stress hormones flooded my brain anew, intensifying the already overwhelming adrenaline coursing through my muscles, I even took pains to walk forward from the direction in which I'd been propelled, my arms outstretched, my fingers groping for some phantom sensation that might indicate the presence of the anomalous doorway.

Yet, nothing. Only open air and the grass under my feet, and the gradual dawning of a consciousness of what I had done to my family.

Who would help Eleison now? My darling, blind and unable to be healed but by me! And poor Telemachus—no doubt afraid for his life as he hid under a bed or in some bureau, in one of the seemingly infinite rooms of the Overseer's palace. Glenn and Rosina, attempting to escape that hateful city, and my husband, missing. Indeed, I was so preoccupied with the state of my family that I could hardly stop to reflect on my own dreadful exile, which alighted upon me last of all, a great hand landing nefariously on my shoulder.

What if I could never get home? What if I was trapped in this place, subject to the wild beasts of this alien world on the other side of the Rift, for all eternity? Perhaps I could learn to survive: yes, of course I could—especially in my condition as a dharmine, a creature whose physiology was primed for this very environment. But, alone in this hateful and surreal landscape, I would surely go mad. Without another conscious human being, surely, one day at a time, I would lose all sense of myself until, at last, I was hardly more than a beast, sublingual and beyond all comprehension of the events around me, just as I had been when I first awoke in the dark void to the love of my husband.

Still…that very notion drew my attention to another point. It shattered the fear I felt and turned it into a kind of mystery. For, in my panic, I had lowered myself to the ground and pressed a hand to my chest, trying to breathe and get my disordered thoughts into bearable shape. As my mind whirled, my eyes darted rapidly from sky to horizon, over my shoulder, and into each periphery. I anticipated a harpros would descend upon me or a borro would come charging from the grass, fangs bared.

Yet—there was nothing. Nothing at all. The longer I sat, the more I realized with a strange, surreal shock that the landscape was silent. Not even a beetle crawled upon my hand or nibbled at my gown.

I was alone.

The silence pressed in around me, thick and heavy, and I marveled at the realization that a world of dangerous predators was preferable to this uncanny emptiness. This cosmic silence was so absolute that I might have thought myself deaf if not for the breeze and my own rapid breathing. How was this possible? If there were no Rift beasts here, then was this truly the world beyond the Rift, or had I landed in some intermediary plane similar to the empty black space where I first encountered the loom? I couldn't say why, but my senses insisted that this was, indeed, the Rift-world. Without proof, however, I couldn't explain this insistence. I found myself wishing for someone to ask.

Then, for a fleeting second—there was hope. A spark in the darkness.

"Dinon?"

I sat up, crying out as I looked around, reaching into myself for the substance of my soul: that mysterious force that connected me to my uncanny lover.

The wind blew, whistling through the silence, then easing to a stop before picking up again.

"Ba'al-Dinon?"

I called out again, my voice thunder in the stillness.

"Ba'al-Dinon," I screamed a third time, louder, my eyes filling with tears as I remembered all the times he had sworn he would always be with me. "Dinon, please!"

My scream faded into silence—into the nothingness that I felt myself to be when, small and unobserved by any living thing, I could not even be fully sure I existed in a meaningful, typically accepted sense. New fright and betrayal overwhelmed me. Hadn't he told me he would always be with me? Had he lied, or had I perhaps misunderstood? The idea that I had been deceived by Ba'al-Dinon sickened me even more than I had been sickened by the discovery of Malin's deception regarding his old relationship with my mother—and I could no more articulate the feelings accompanying that betrayal than I could articulate the intense love that flooded me at the thought of Dinon, even in his apparent absence. That love and its very intensity weakened my soul such that I burst into new, more overwhelming tears, a torrent of sorrows flooding my face as though I were a helpless child.

I will freely admit that, at many points in my young life, I was given to swells of self-pity that gave me a perverse sort of satisfaction, as though abiding in my sense of my own helplessness justified in some way my moral failings. I was a helpless and sad girl, practically still a child in the very center of my heart; therefore, as with children, anything I got away with was permitted in the name of abating that sorrow. Here, though, I became aware of the bitter uselessness of such a position. There was no one to help me; no one to feel sorry for me. No one might walk past the shut room of my soul and, like Charlotte, remonstrate me, advise me, comfort me. There was no one to cheer and distract and love me as in the case of Malin or Eleison or even Glenn.

There was only this empty landscape, myself, and the hole in my heart that was left in the absence of Dinon.

Choking a bit, breathless with sorrow, I listed to my left and rested upon the ground, my body curled in a small ball, my head tucked toward my knees. My frame shivered and jerked with my hiccupping sobs, and with each spasm, some rock pushed awkwardly into my hip, stirring discomfort. In great annoyance, I sat up again to find it and toss it away. Only then did I realize it was within the pocket of my dress. Frowning, I reached inside to do away with it.

Of course—Rosina's bug.

Looking upon that dragonfly had a quite curious effect on me. Though one might well have expected my tears to double at the memory of my unreachable daughter, instead, they quelled. With a shuddering breath, I wiped my cheeks with my fist, examining the amber-enclosed creature as the wind played gently in my hair.

My children needed me. If there had been a way into this place, there was surely a way out. More than that, though there were no Rift beasts present, they did indeed have to come through the Rift somehow. Therefore, there had to be some means of escape.

And it occurred to me belatedly that perhaps those same threads that had provided the way in would also prove the way out.

I was so overwhelmed with emotion that I had not thought of it immediately and felt very silly when I did indeed remember them. But the state of my mind was such that even once I remembered, a great deal of concentration was required for me to see them. Finally, I was able to bring them into relief by following the line of the billowing grass up and up, until my eye was no longer among the silver blades but instead the silver weft. At the sight, my soul throbbed with ecstasy. Yes, yes! Surely, very surely, this would be the way out. As I created the last doorway into this place, so I would create a new one home again. It would be so very simple!

Except that I witnessed immediately two very strange things: one of them alarming, the other intriguing.

All the violet threads which swiftly leapt into my consciousness after I finally caught a hint of their silver counterparts converged on me, a number so thick and brilliant as they plunged into me that they seemed like the infinite points of a brilliant indigo star of which I was the very center. As the shock of this wore off enough for me to see through the wild aura of brilliant color to a hint of simpler, more straightforward silver, I recognized that the silver threads, also, seemed to be running to some point in convergence, far off in the distance.

And I just had to know.

Perhaps I should have experienced more disappointment or frustration to realize there was nothing to unweave, no tapestry in which to pluck a happy hole: but my sudden awareness of this mystery was too compelling. Quite astonished, I stepped forward, taking one step after the other in a state of half-awareness. All those threads radiating from my heart followed me, and I hesitated, realizing how difficult it would be for me to keep continuous track of them along this foreign landscape as I tried to trace the silver through this glittering purple radiance. Instead, like a child playing a game of hot-and-cold with the man who had once been my father, I advanced as far as my confidence could carry me. Then, once more bringing into relief the threads, I would assess what I could discern of the silver strands and correct course.

The journey was long, yet I felt no anxiety. I questioned this over and over. I do suppose I felt a kind of obligatory, superficial nervousness at times. More than once, I reminded myself that it was the understanding of most learned researchers that the universe on the other side of the Rift was one of reverse entropy, and that the foul weather of Rift Events was due to that universe abutting against our own. If indeed I was in that universe, did not that mean time was flowing backwards with respect to my world's terrestrial state? I shuddered to think of what that meant for my arrival back on Earth, if I returned; but with the threads here already disparate, I could not fathom how it was that I was to pluck the weaving open and return home, and, anyway, I could not spare the time to worry about it when I was so arrested by this peculiar sight coaxing me onward. Something in my heart promised me that pursuing this mystery would help me resolve the question of coming home, but I could not articulate why or how I knew that any more than I had been able to fully fathom why I was so certain Malin remained alive after the bombing of his outpost near Rheton.

I think I should be embarrassed to say how little Malin crossed my mind on that journey, and Eleison and Glenn, too; but the reader will soon see that they were not all that escaped my mind during that mysterious time. I can make no real excuse for the events that followed, nor for how completely I permitted myself to forget all the people I most cherished…yet that place produced a strange alteration in my consciousness. Perhaps it was the isolation, the alien quality of the place, or the trauma and stress that would soon give way to something completely different. Whatever the case, I felt a strange buoyancy as I beat a long path through brilliant, luminescent fields of flowers, whose pollen, wafting on the air, perhaps had some mild psychoactive effect and was the real culprit. As the hills on the horizon grew nearer and the sky darkened, the point of convergence no closer, I felt tempted to go on. Yet there was something lurid and beautiful about the idea of sleeping in an open field in total safety, where no men or wild animals could come upon me. Therefore, I did, unable to proceed further. And though I had many stressful dreams about, of all people, Aleister, his sister, and Arthur, when I awoke in the embrace of a luscious pink dawn, I felt deeply rested, and at an inappropriately deep ease.

In a way—and this will sound perhaps foolish or cruel of me to say—that time was a powerful grace for me. A gift. Dinon had told me over and over that I needed to surrender, and I had *been* surrendering...so I thought. But only in following those silver threads did I understand what true surrender was, for I had to surrender absolutely every fear and doubt and question that was in my heart. All agency flew out of my hands. I submitted wholly to this mystery, putting inexplicable trust in what I could neither see nor understand; and in this state, even my anxiety was surrendered, dissolving ever deeper into that quality of supernatural, unjustifiable peace.

I journeyed for two nights; only during the second night did I stop to ponder the stars, their layout totally unknown to me. Though they existed there amid the rich texture of the velvet night, I recognized not a single constellation. Nor could I be sure east and west and north and south meant the same things positionally in this place as they did on Earth. It didn't really matter, because the threads were my compass; but as I passed out of the valley where I'd found myself and into hilly countryside that turned, through an impressive forest, into a mountainous hike I was forced to undergo in my barefoot condition, the disorienting nature of the geography and astronomy of the place made me feel all the stranger. That second night, I slept at the base of a fantastical sapphire tree whose viridian leaves waved like streamers in the breeze, and I awoke in the early hours just before sunrise, pleased to find the silver showed up well in the pre-dawn.

It was worth noting, however, that the streaks of silver were beginning to withstand the inundation of purple threads surrounding me quite well, because they were beginning to increase in density. Indeed, as the sun rose that day and I reached a high overlook from which I could assess the terrain ahead of me, I felt as though I stared into a thickening cloud of silver. Gradually, descending down the mountain's other side, I became enveloped in this mist, and I kept the threads at the focus of my vision more often than not now, especially when the breeze now brought with it the sweet, cool aroma of a briny sea. I sighed in pleasure, my lips parting to afford me a taste of this fresh sweetness in the air. And, at the next scenic embankment, I found myself overlooking the moon-silver shore of that brilliant purple sea I remembered from two sweet, sweet dreams.

My heart seized with joy, bursting into a field of flowers in my breast. Following this little cliffside down and sinking my toes into the sand, I looked about me, delighting to find I had also been plunged into the thickness of those fine silver threads. I knew; I knew. I knew, but I dared not presume. I dared not breathe, either, as I hurried along the surf, allowing the violet brilliance of my own glittering haze to become wholly submerged in the silver starburst toward which I was ran. Excitement overwhelmed me with the strange sense of coming home, as I felt when Eleison and I visited Lescaut.

Yet, when at last I reached the most brilliant and overwhelming density of silver threads, that feeling of homecoming made perfect sense.

The point at which those silver threads converged was, amid the rocky edge of that particular section of platinum coast, at the mouth of a deep violet sea cave; and, splayed upon the soft, wet sand before that cave—inert, unconscious, beautiful, absolutely naked—lay the man I had known in my heart I would find.

Ba'al-Dinon

very inch of him sent a fire raging through my body. After two nights of seeing no other living being, the male form was a particularly alien and alluring thing—made all the more alluring by the man in question, who reclined upon the sand as if asleep or dead, his eyes closed, his lips parted, his silver-white hair flowing out behind him like bedclothes covering the mattress of the shore where he slept.

"Dinon," I gasped, rushing to his side. "Oh, darling, my darling! You're here!"

Despite the upsurge of wonder in my voice, he did not stir; fright seized me, especially as I took note of the tide crashing up across his face to swallow his nose and mouth. How long had he been out here? I had seen him accomplish such strange things that it seemed impossible to find him in a state of any vulnerability at all—yet I feared with a kind of incredulity that he was well and truly dead, in which case, I would have no advocate in this world or any other.

This notion, though, was less horrible than the simple idea of Ba'al-Dinon being departed from me: of Dinon not existing before he and I had had an opportunity to bask in the fullness of love, as I so often had with Malin and Eleison, and as I had even enjoyed with Glenn. While it was true Dinon had given me a kind of supernatural pleasure, had touched me and kissed me and, in a dream-like state that I now knew was a real occasion in some mysterious manner of the soul, made love to me, we had never had the opportunity to be at ease together. I had not had the chance to fully express my love for him, and I could not stand the thought of him dying without him knowing that from me.

Acting with great urgency, then, I stooped to grasp him by the shoulders and roughly shake him. When that did not rouse him, my fear only deepening, I slipped my hands under his arms and pulled him back up the shore before the greedy tide could defile him a third time.

As strong as I was since assuming my dharmine nature, Dinon was so dense with muscle that it was rather like trying to drag a sedated borro up a sandy hill. The action was unwieldy, and I had to bend to pull his torso more fully into my arms, his broad, hard chest pressing into my body and his head slumping against my shoulder. As I did, the proximity of his cock stirred something feral within me. It stiffened upon brushing my thigh; I exhaled, my center pulsing with warmth. Flushing hotly, I kept my eyes resolutely forward and hauled him along until, at the edge of the grass, I reclined him in this new, drier bed and assessed his condition.

How pale sweet Dinon was! He always had been pale, of course, but now his skin had taken on a bluish tint: a consequence of exposure to the waters for an unknown period. Yet—surely he could no more die of drowning than could a dharmine. Without thinking, I removed my fuligin cloak and used it to briskly dry his body, trying not to look overlong at that equine tumescence resting along his adonis belt—a consequence of our friendly brushing and nudging as I'd carried him to safety. My hands itched; my body ached! Still, I resisted, draping the fabric over him and frowning at his placid expression.

As ours was a village with a river and a watering hole near the town's edge, the boys and girls of Lescaut were educated by responsible parents on what to do in instances of near-drowning. Should one of their cohort—or their own eventual progeny—be carried to a deep point and inhale too much water, one must push down on the chest, applying pressure to the ribs to get their lungs moving. Then, one would catch the face in their hands, push open the mouth, and apply their lips to theirs, filling the lungs with air. Though unsure if such an act were possible or useful in the rescue of a being such as Dinon, I nevertheless pushed down upon his chest, applying a few bursts of pressure against his ribs to get his lungs moving before I caught his face in my hands, pushed open his mouth, and applied my lips to his. With the great breath of air I had gathered beforehand, I filled him, life billowing into his mouth in one mighty gust as mentally I prepared to perform the action all over again beginning with the chest compressions.

Yet once was all that was required; for, beneath the pressure of my lips and the air I gave him, Dinon gasped, stirred, and emitted a sensual, somehow sweet groan into the cavern of my mouth. As though I had touched a switch on an RMS panel, he animated, his lips brushing back against mine—indeed, pursuing mine as I attempted to lean back. He leaned with me, sitting up as I raised my upper half on my haunches. With a sigh of my own pleasure, I plunged my tongue into the sweetness of his mouth. With another pleasurable rumble of sound, his tongue sprang to life, too, slowly trailing up along mine and pursuing it to its root. I submitted, letting him explore as he sat up enough to let the cloth fall away from the upper half of his torso so that it obscured yet somehow altogether emphasized the shape and proportions of his growing erection. With slight delay, he raised uncertain hands to my face and pawed at me.

It's a funny way to describe the caress, I know, but that was what it was. It was clumsy, like a blind man feeling for the first time the features of a new lover. As he feasted on my mouth, Dinon's hands interrogated every part of me, gripping my hair until I squeaked, then releasing to slowly fondle their way down the column of my neck and caressing into relief from the atmosphere the curves of my shoulders. He clutched the fabric of my gown, examining it and only now releasing me from his kiss to regard with some befuddlement just what the substance was. A question grew in his silver eyes—one that deepened as that gaze raised from the fabric to my love-warmed face.

His pupils dilated.

"Oh," he said, his eyes dropping again, now to my pale knees beneath the slightly hiked hem of my dress, "oh—oh—"

Looking deeply curious, he caught hold of the hem of my gown and pushed it up while I stuttered and laughed.

"Ba'al-Dinon," I gaily remonstrated, my blush deepening as my body was overwhelmed with eagerness in a feeling I felt the need to at least somewhat temper. "My goodness, don't I even get a 'hello'?"

He looked up at me muggily, like a man hearing himself addressed through the veil of a dream. "Hello," he murmured as his hand raised again to my cheek, broad his thumb brushing over and then, more experimentally, between my lips. "Hello, hello... hello, Beauty."

"Thecla," I reminded him as his digit glided back out, having received a graze from my tongue. "You remember me, don't you, darling? I'm your Thecla."

"My Thecla," he repeated from his state of delirium. "Mine... what makes you mine?"

I thought about that for a second. It was a good question—a fair one. What did make me his, aside from the devotion he showed me?

"My desire to give myself to you, I suppose," I said as his thumb trailed down from my mouth along the line of my jaw. While his eyes trailed down to my bosom, he lowered his hand and cupped my breast through my dress. I softly gasped. "Oh—Dinon—"

"Why," he asked in a murmur, exploring me, his thumb rubbing along the increasingly stiff peak of my nipple through the soft fabric of my dress.

"Why would I want to give myself to you? Well—well, I—"

Panting at the intensity of the pleasure that rushed through me as he touched me with such intimate yet strangely innocent curiosity, I caressed his cheek and gazed earnestly into his eyes. "Because I love you," I told him, meaning it from the fullness of my soul, with every single part of me, without any hesitation or conflict. That conflict had with the other men acted as an aphrodisiac when I loved Malin despite his age, Eleison despite Malin's courtship, Glenn despite Malin's marriage. With Dinon, the aphrodisiac came from the crystalline quality of my freedom to love him. There was an unfettered purity to my love for him that I had not recognized or perhaps had not been capable of experiencing until that very moment; for it was only in that moment that we finally seemed, however briefly, on the level of peers. Whatever had happened to him had dragged him down to a level of simplicity and approachability, a kind of amnesiac naivete that made him fully accessible to me. And I, a dharmine with many strange powers of my own, had no cause to be frightened of him—or, I thought with what seemed to be clarity, ever. His was a consequence-free love that, divorced from causal reality and all its rules in the same way he could come and go through spacetime on a whim, could be enjoyed along with my terrestrial loves without quarrel in my soul. Especially now, in this strange innocence after his sleep.

"Love," repeated Dinon, enchanted by the word, intoning it in a reverent whisper as his eyes trailed over my body. "Love, I love. I love you, Thecla...oh..."

My hand trailed down his alabaster chest and tickled now along his stomach. As I dipped into the fabric of his cloak and enclosed his rock-hard shaft in my fist, he gasped in a way that was so utterly astonished it was as though he had never been touched before—had never even touched himself, having had, before that very second, no conscious awareness of his own bodily existence. As he gazed urgently into my eyes, his thick cock leaping aggressively in my hand, I caressed him in a few long, luxurious strokes, and the movement of my hand beneath the ultra-soft fabric of that cloak brought to mind—to the edges of my mind, anyway—the mysterious nature of that cloak itself.

"Dinon," I whispered, "do you remember me at all?"

"N-no," he gasped as he eagerly thrust into my hand, bucking reflexively in a way that made my body throb to receive him. "This is—the first time we've met...o—oh, ah!"

His brow furrowed, and his entire expression formed into a

mask of beautiful fright at the same instant that his cock abruptly throbbed and leaped in my hand. With a gasp of pleasure, I drew the fabric back in time to watch the lust-reddened tip of his beautiful prick burst with a thick ribbon of white semen that consequently splattered along the pretty abdominal muscles of his pale stomach. While he gasped helplessly, I caught his face in my free hand and tenderly kissed him, milking his cock steadily through his orgasm. "My Thecla," he gasped, "I love you—I love this, oh, oh—"

"How sweet you are!" Captivated by him as he was in this surreally unpracticed state, I drew his head to my breast, cradling him to me as he emptied his balls and whimpered at the feeling rushing through him. As the storm passed, he remained hard, his hips thrusting needily up into my hand as he instinctively fucked my fist. My entire body pulsed with pleasure, especially as those adorably clumsy but desperately passionate hands of his slid up my thighs, plunging beneath the fabric of my dress to grope through the fabric of my underwear.

"Where's yours?" Dinon twisted his mouth up toward mine to plead for more kisses as I laughed. "I want you to feel this, my Thecla—I want you to feel my pleasure."

"I'm there," I whispered, opening my legs for him a little, offering myself to him for his exploration. "Right in the same place, darling…just different, that's all."

"Please," he murmured hoarsely, his silver eyes fixing again upon mine, desperate yet shy as if with the fear that I might refuse him. "Please, let me see—show me, let me see you."

I chuckled, releasing my hold on that scepter of delights, drawing back upon my rear with my legs akimbo as I drew up the hem of my dress. There was something in him, in that encounter, that made me sink into a state of immediate abandon.

Yet as my release of his cock made him sigh, it also signaled a clarity that had a chance to emerge from his orgasm.

"You love me," he recalled, staying my hands and looking at them with great interest. He compared his hands with mine and reflected in silence until his eyes turned up toward mine, boring into me. "Why?"

I didn't really know what to say. Why did I love Dinon? Why did I have such a deep and special love that had gathered in my heart like a mist, drawing itself thick until it grew into a fog that enveloped all other things in the world?

"Because you're kind to me," I reflected, raising my free hand from my hem to touch his cheek again and brush a few wet strands of hair from his beautiful, high cheekbone. "Because you always help me when I need it most. Because you're always there, and you're always so patient and consoling to me. Always ready to do incredible, impossible things for me."

"Impossible things?" His tone was rightly mystified, and I laughed guiltily. The sound made him smile—not that wry, somewhat wickedly knowing smile, but a bright-toothed, shiny, boyish smile that made my heart burst into flowers. I rested my forehead against his.

"Yes, well, not impossible for you, dear." My fingers combed along his scalp to produce a low sigh from his still-pale lips. His eyes fluttered shut, but now his hand slipped from its place overlain atop mine and resumed the work of pushing up my dress as I murmured, "You're incredibly powerful, Dinon."

"Powerful," he echoed; the word hung softly in the air, a murmur drifting like the plume of a single feather. His eyes opened. "Yes. I am."

Shuddering, I nodded, adding somewhat coyly, "You frighten me."

"That's wise," he agreed. "You show wisdom. Why does my frightening you make you love me?"

"I don't know," I admitted with a laugh, gasping as his thumb pushed gently under the edge of my panties and glided gently along the crease of my sex. As the heat in my womb grew more intense and bloomed up into my bosom, I whispered, "I think perhaps I like being frightened of someone who chooses instead to be kind to me. The way I used to feel about Malin, before I came to consider him my peer—that's how I feel about you always, somehow, Dinon."

"Ba'al isn't a word from the language you're using," he observed, adding as an afterthought while his thumb glided gently between my labia, "you're very soft, Thecla."

"And you're quite hard," I whispered. As my hand trailed along his groin and tucked gently down against the silken sac of his balls, Dinon sucked in a breath and made me cry out in delight as he tore my underthings down my thighs. "Oh! Dinon—"

"Beautiful," he whispered, glancing at the patch of flowers amid which we were arranged, then pushing my legs open wider to trail his fingers along the petals of my femininity. "Yes—yes, I love you. Oh, Thecla...I'm so happy you're here. You don't need to be frightened of me. I want to be kind to you. Who is Malin?"

Moaning as his fingers gently, tenderly petted along the stiffened nub of my clitoris, I explained, "Malin's my...he's my... my husband. I love him, too!"

"Husband," Dinon pondered, rolling the word through his mouth. "I'm your husband," he announced, and before I could correct him, he bent his head and kissed me deeply. I cried out into that supple, commanding mouth, gasping softly as his thumb worked in circles over a spot he rightly noted to be very sensitive.

As his tongue slid into the back of my throat—unnaturally long and deliciously sensual—I moaned his name and melted into the pleasure.

While my fingers trailed along the underside of his shaft, I found myself baffled to find my protests about his title melting away. Yes—somehow, on some deep level, I felt a profound acceptance of the fact that Ba'al-Dinon was my husband. I wasn't sure at all how or why that could be the case when we had never married and I was already wed to Malin; yet, it was such a plain and simple fact accepted in the innermost core of my heart, and as his thumb glided down, following along the trail of a riverbed to its thundering source, I felt an indescribable intimacy enveloping us like the violet light of the morning. Perhaps Dinon was not my present husband, but a husband of my eternity-future-past: my bridegroom from outside the bounds of ordinary spacetime. As his thumb sank into the tight channel that positively wept for his attention, a low growl rumbled up from his throat.

"You are mine," he marveled, observing this, feeling it deeply. "'Lord', you call me."

Gasping as his eyes fixed on the sight of his thumb probing into me, I savored every inch he gave me while letting my fingers sink into the grass. "Yes," I managed, "I believe that's what 'Ba'al' means."

"Say again that you're mine."

"I'm yours, Dinon," I gasped, tugging his cock toward my center, my eyes locking with his. With full understanding, he glanced up at me, then removed his thumb and pushed me down upon my back with such force I couldn't help but scream in giddy delight. "Oh! Yes, Lord, yes! I am all yours, Ba'al-Dinon—for all eternity!"

"Eternity," he whispered; and his sharp eyes darted askance, dropping, focusing deeply into some vast inner region of spacetime as if he bored into the infinite complexity of the molecular and information structure of the very blades of grass and flowers and flecks of soil beneath us. Only when I touched him did his gaze dart back to me, and, feeling my hand upon his cheek, he reanimated with a new, deeper ferocity in his eyes. He sprang upon me, his hands enclosing my face as he thrust himself down against my sex. I groaned and laughed and bade him to be patient. Gently squeezing that finely veined, steel-sharp dagger of his, I made his Adam's apple bob with a shocked little noise of pleasure by guiding the firm head of his cock up and down the valley of my sex. Then, my eyes upon his, I nestled his tip against my pleading entrance and whispered, "Be gentle, at first, please, Lord, my Lord—you're so big—"

His breath hitched between his parted lips, his eyes fixed in amazement upon mine as gradually, carefully, Ba'al-Dinon pushed himself inch by inch into the saturated depths of my being.

As I cried out his name, he murmured mine, and his mouth plunged against my lips before kissing fiercely along my cheek, then bruising and rippling down my throat. All the while, being as gentle as he could possibly stand to be, Dinon plunged that thick, overwhelmingly hard cock as deep inside me as he could go. His manhood was so large he could not fit all the way the first time, so he drew back a little as if to try again, then made another strained sound of comprehending pleasure at the sensation. Glancing down to watch himself disappear ever deeper inside me, Dinon clutched my thighs with an expression of astonishment written across his face—a look that surely matched my own!

Oh, there had been something very vivid and undeniably real

about the so-called dream that had taken place in this space on the special night of my human death. Still, that interaction had lacked the complete sense of visceral presence one acquires when experiencing an event in full consciousness.

This moment had no ambiguity. This was really, presently, unquestionably happening to me. Ba'al-Dinon was inside me, upon me, covering me and filling me with all of himself, his mouth draping across mine with kisses that were an ecstasy all their own. I clung to him, helpless in his arms, absolutely his, and more—for that same sensation of soul-awareness I had begun to enjoy was more palpable and absolute than ever, and that metaphysical organ was a sweeter, secret sex into which Dinon poured an unending inundation of love. This is one of those things that seems like metaphor when described, but I cannot emphasize enough how literal the sensation truly was—truly is, whenever my Lord comes upon me at any time of day or night. It is as though my heart is dilated, my soul gently fondled and kissed and coaxed open by his mirrored actions upon my body; and then comes the sensation of this inrush, this great all-body flood of powerful adoration and infinite love that is more perfect and complete than any human affection. That is not to say that Malin and Eleison and Glenn have small loves for me; our loves are vast and rich, more intimate and tender romances than I'd ever known to be possible with terrestrial men.

Yet with Dinon, I had the sense of something in greater excess. That word, 'eternity', had stricken him, and now it struck me as his fingers sank into my hip before slipping around to grip my rear. Dinon drilled himself into me with a kind of power and instinct that made my legs tremble. I gasped, clenching around him as my fingers tangled in his hair, crying out, "Oh yes, oh yes, oh, my Lord, my Love! It makes me so happy to be yours. Protect me, Ba'al-Dinon—protect me, take me, stay with me forever! Oh, darling!"

My climax came on urgent and intense, shattering through me and proving so powerful I felt an almost literal break in the chain of my cognition: as if I had truly died for a fraction of a second when that great cock of his hammered into me with such force that my entire body responded to his might. As my fingers sank into his back, I leaned up to kiss him. The need I showed by pleading for his mouth like this pleased him so that, with a few more savage downstrokes of his cock deep into my center, he released inside me, coming so deep inside me that I whimpered to feel the way his perfect prick bucked and jumped dangerously against my cervix. As a little melody of fright arose from me, my heels dug into his glutes. He kissed me deeper, then drew back to nuzzle his lips along mine.

"Don't worry, Thecla," Dinon murmured, shamelessly reading my mind. He did not know what shame was, and we had no need of it in that sacred place. "I'll make it all better. I'll never let you stay in pain for long, I promise. Look at me—"

As his great hands framed my face again, I gazed into his eyes and found deep in them a sincerity that was truly otherworldly.

"Trust in me," he bade me. "I promise, Thecla—you're mine forever."

A shiver of surreal understanding rushed through me. I slid my arms around his neck, pressing my body closely against his.

"Yes," I agreed, "I think I want that most of all."

We must not have moved more than fifteen feet from that soft grass where Dinon and I made our first bed; not for the first twelve hours, anyway. When at last I persuaded him to take a break from our mutual exertions, it was only so we could make our way down to the tide and wash the sweat from our bodies—and even there, we enjoyed hardly more than a few minutes of frolicking before our kisses grew fonder, our caresses more avid. He tangled me in his embrace, taking me in the water, then hounding me to shore for more and more and more.

There were things I wanted to ask him. Things I needed his help with, but—somehow I couldn't remember quite what they were. My clothes and his cloak lay abandoned: not far from us, but as thoroughly forgotten as whatever it was that had brought me to this place.

Yet hadn't I always been here? Again and again, I had the uncanny sense that I had indeed been in this place my entire life, or longer. That I would always be in this place: always be fully with him. That thought filled me with supreme ecstasy and a deep relief, for there were moments when something passed through my head—some echo of necessity that informed me in a furtive whisper it would not always seem so, even though it would always be so. At such times, more eager to inundate myself in my awareness of his love, I threw myself as completely as I could into the present moment. In so doing, I formed a barrier between myself and all cares and responsibilities.

Surely, though, it was not all by my choice, nor by some selfish working of my mind, however much I wish to blame myself for it now. There were immediate signs that something was strange about that place—beyond, I mean, that brilliant amethyst sky. My first morning of awakening with Dinon was just as beautiful a storm of pleasure as had been the night before. But this time, in the placid quiet of the aftermath, while I reclined in his arms and he, positioned upon his hip, scrutinized me with the kind of gentle fascination of a researcher watching an unknown animal (or, perhaps, of the wild thing watching the researcher), it occurred to me that I had experienced no hint of appetite in the entirety of the past three days. Yet here I was, fit and strong, showing a vigor as though I had been feasting on the most wholesome foods...or the richest living blood, I suppose. As at last my synapses formed this connection and I lay there, puzzling over its meaning, Ba'al-Dinon caressed a lock of loose hair from my eyes.

"What is eating?" He looked at me in soft but definite interest. I laughed a little; though, as I explained, not at his question.

"You've always been fairly flagrant about reading my mind," I told him, adding after a moment's reflection, "or you will be, anyway—whatever 'will be' means in this place outside of terrestrial time… But, *you* know, dear. Eating—consumption. It's how most bodies ingest energy so they can use it to move around, or think, or make love."

"Oh," he said in a slightly chastened way, as though I had spoken to him of something quite obvious. And, of course, I had; but as his gaze lowered from my face and he turned inward to some ageless ocean of thought, pity stirred in my heart. Poor darling! He had really and truly been alone in this place before I came to him. He had been so alone that he had not even been conscious until I awoke him. At the touch of my hand upon his cheek, he raised his eyes, and I found him so suddenly shy that I had to violently restrain the impulse to push him down and make love to him that very instant.

"How is it"—I could see the sudden sharpening of his gaze and the expansion of those great pupils as he experienced my experience of that impulse—"that you can speak my language, but you don't know what simple concepts like eating are?"

"I do know what eating is; you just told me."

"Well, yes, but—" I tried not to roll my eyes as I waved a dismissive hand. "Before, I mean. And there have been other rudimentary things you've had to ask me, too. However, you can speak just fine. It seems very odd for a man to speak and not know what he's saying."

"Yet I sense they do it all the time now that you've said that to me," he said, searching my face as if gleaning information from each muscle. "I suppose you could say that you are—drawing my attention to these things. When you explain these things, I realize they exist. When you spoke to me, I realized speech exists, and I knew it; then I realized you exist, and that you're different from me. And then I realized love exists, because I don't want you to be different from me. I want to understand you so well that you become me, and that I become you. That makes me realize other things exist; because, in order to understand you, I have to understand these other things. You are making me aware of this world by teaching me, but that world already exists for you. So that is how I know about speech; because it already exists, and you exposed me to it."

"I see," I said, though in truth I barely did until my mind made the connection that, "so it's rather like deriving a concept in mathematics. Not a question of invention, but of discovery."

"Yes," murmured Dinon, his expression taking on that mysterious, distant quality of inward consultation as he agreed. "Like mathematics."

My Lord in Heaven, but how intense and beautiful it would be to witness that moment and so many other moments from within Ba'al-Dinon's consciousness! If indeed he derived the component pieces of reality as they were spoken to him and thus drawn into his vast awareness, then my simple speaking of the word 'mathematics' before him very likely contained, for his understanding, the sum total of all mathematical concepts. From basic arithmetic to trigonometry to entire branches of mathematics that had yet to be formalized and named in my time. Accordingly, he looked a little dizzy, his vision unfocusing as though he were hypnotized by his own thoughts—not, however, in an unenjoyable way, but in some profound, ecstatic way that seemed to have the effect of a sweet daydream. His expression became unspeakably peaceful, enchanted beyond all measure of joy.

And, I'm ashamed to admit, it made me very jealous.

Jealous of what? Of the entire concept of mathematics? No… of the idea that Ba'al-Dinon could take pleasure in anything but me. This thought settled upon my soul like a moth upon a garment, nibbling away at the fabric until startled by the man who noticed it upon me well enough to be drawn somewhat from his thoughts.

"Jealousy. Hm."

Embarrassed to hear him bear witness to this most pitiable inclination of my heart, I averted my eyes and patted his chest. "Yes, jealousy," I told him. "And if you could truly appreciate how beautiful you are, you wouldn't blame me...come, darling, we've been horizontal for hours now. Let's walk and talk a bit, shall we?"

"I'd rather watch you think," he commented, and I laughed at first, thinking he jested. All the same, as we stood naked side by side and his alabaster hand slid around mine, he kissed it with a look that made my laughter fade into a nervous titter. He wanted to kill me with his cock and resurrect me so he could do it all again. I understood that he was serious about unfolding the contents of my mind for nothing more than his own pleasure, and my hand quivered slightly as he lowered it, his thumb rubbing consolingly in the well of my palm.

"I would never, Thecla," Dinon said, and his tone made my heart quiver. "This is the self-expression that will never hurt you."

What on earth did that mean? I wasn't entirely certain I wanted to know.

"Not yet," he told me in a way so gentle it only frightened me more, sending my body into motion—some kind of automated panic response my body gave to a deep metaphysical truth for which my mind, and perhaps even my soul, was still quite unprepared to grasp.

"It's very strange to get used to a man just—being in one's mind." I chuckled as the thought occurred to me that Malin would love that—indeed, fancied he already had access to it and sometimes very well seemed to.

As I had the thought, Dinon smiled.

"Try not to think of it," he said.

A blush of shame colored my cheeks as I saw how evenly his words were both a jest at my speech and a response to the private comments of his mind...and rightly so. Was I not here with him, Ba'al-Dinon, now? Were we not someplace far away, where time was not congruent with our own, and where it was only him and I, and that cool, sweet breeze, and the flowers, and the lovely violet sky? It was all so very good, most especially him: and I longed to abide in that goodness, to let it envelope me like a cloud. Like an awesome wave that—powerful, warm—rushed me back up to the shore and left me lying there, half-drowned as he had been, fully undisturbed in unconsciousness where I'd found him. How beautiful that must have been...how beautiful he was, inside and out.

Yes. I saw that now. It was funny to think that I hadn't seen it before. In his omniscient and alien nature, I'd seen something mocking and malicious. I was, after all, a mortal girl, living in a mortal mind, consigned to die and blow away like ashes from a blaze. But then I became not ash, but part of that fire: a being capable of raging forever in perfect environmental conditions. Perhaps not quite so long, for only *he* could live so long, I suspected; yet perhaps that was not true, either, for he could surely keep me alive as he desired. I had seen him produce furniture and weave a gown from Rift radiation, and even walk through walls. All those things that had been terrific and frightening had certainly not lost their awesome edge, but they became something quite different when I saw that they constituted works of love, not works of power. How shocking to discover how pure and beautiful and inwardly gentle this strange creature of a man truly was! I began to wonder if I had not been projecting my own desire for control upon this being whose love I had been unable to comprehend because I had not yet uncovered its full context—the deepest source and realization.

And, in truth, I still wasn't entirely sure of the cause of it. He was so great—so unfathomably great that his greatness overwhelmed me. I could not yet perceive why, finite as I was, a being with Dinon's bottomless intellectual capabilities could ever experience love, let alone for me.

Then, well, it occurred to me that perhaps I was too petty and human—still too terrestrial—to comprehend it. My love, for all its worth, remained an imperfect thing, fleeting by comparison to however it was Dinon experienced time. And I had a great many questions about that, (how did, after all, this Dinon relate exactly to the fully cognizant and somehow more worldly Ba'al-Dinon, who had been to me a happy slave even as he could have crushed me with a thought?), but, like whatever idea was then already creeping up on me in some vague presentiment, I could not dare think overlong on this notion lest I should come upon some thought I could never unthink. It was already overwhelming enough to think that meditation on a thing could unpack for him an eternity of meaning about a thing: an infinite depth of understanding, a fractal of contemplation that could, by his infinite mind, be mined infinitely until another concept became the source of that infinite plunge in a strange paradox of time and space and understanding.

He was so beautiful—so beautiful to me. Yet how cruel I had been to him! How distorted my love had been toward him. Unwise, uncharitable, and untrusting. There was nothing loving in the way I had treated him. Even when I began to realize I had deeper feelings for him, there was something so impossibly pitiful—self-serving—about it. Had I not been crying out to him very largely out of fear that I literally could not live without him in a practical sense, rather than a romantic one? There was so little in me that had loved him out of the kind of purity and passion with which I loved, for instance, Eleison. How revolting, how spoiled I had been! And how mistrustful... I had lacked all comprehension of Ba'al-Dinon's motivations, and because of that, I had lashed out.

And now here I was, walking hand in hand with him, thinking all these thoughts in front of him while the Rift flowers surrounding us had their sway upon my consciousness and made me forget his deep presence within my mind until that very moment.

When he laughed in my ear in response to my thoughts, my face burned for as humiliated as I was—no matter how much I loved the sound of his mirth!

"It's okay, Thecla," Dinon said very gently, stroking my hand with his free one, then raising a hand to my chin and turning my face toward his until I finished the realignment myself. Only then did he look into my eyes, his own soft and crinkled and smiling, his voice almost casual—always infinitely understanding.

"I forgive you. Don't worry about it, okay?"

"Okay," I said softly, glancing down as he fit a hand to the back of my neck while he kissed me. A fantastic reassurance and peace washed over me, and I returned his kiss, my tongue's explorations of his mouth becoming far familiar, yet more reverent. The thought that he permitted me such a privilege as tasting him was overwhelming to me, and there were some moments where I found myself growing shy in yielding to him. Yet that pure and infinitely self-giving love of his also incited me to predatory impulses I could only barely resist, and he smiled at the thought.

"You are teaching me a lot about myself, Thecla," he said in a way that was as pure-hearted as it was terrifying, given all I had thought. "Thank you."

When, dizzy, I swayed in his arms, Dinon tightened his grip to help me stay upright, his expression calm and devoid of concern: instead, soft with tender love.

"Ba'al-Dinon," I whispered, looking at him with a mixture of confusion and terror, "am I... creating you?"

"No," he chuckled, sensing that I had steadied myself, "but you're helping me derive myself."

"Like mathematics," I whispered.

Dinon smiled at this.

"Yes, Thecla," he whispered back, "like mathematics."

32

The next day, I had the sense of having made a mistake for the first time; or, I should say, that night and into the following morning. We remained awake beneath the stars, the wind cooling the sweat upon our bodies, when Ba'al-Dinon suddenly spoke, breaking the silence as if he could no longer bear an unanswered question.

"You thought something about predators before," he recalled, his gaze flickering briefly away before fixing on me again through the indigo veil of night. "They have something to do with eating, don't they? They eat prey."

"Yes," I said, then added, "I see—so you're deriving these thoughts in binaries, in sets of corollary principles that imply others. How beautiful, Dinon." Truly mystified by this excellent quality of his mind, I said, "I love you."

"I love you, too." The words were distracted, though, and he went on very quickly but in a way that somehow by no means dampened his sincerity. "But I'm missing an axis, as they might describe it in mathematics. What are predators and prey?"

"Well—beings," I elaborated with a shrug. "Types of beings."

"Beings," Dinon repeated.

"Yes, dear."

"Like you and me."

Blushing darkly, a reflexive thought of Eleison (blind!) like a shooting star that was quickly dwarfed by the meteorite of terror that came upon me to think of Dinon as not just a being but a *predatory* being, I agreed, "Yes, Ba'al-Dinon...we are beings."

"Am I supposed to eat you, then?" He asked this in a kind of casual clarification that made me sputter and blush despite myself.

"Well, there are some people who might say that, but they only mean it as a figure of speech...you are much more powerful than I am, but I don't think we're inherently predator and prey, particularly since we needn't eat."

"Mm." Considering this with one of those far-off looks, Dinon more quickly returned this time from his innermost depths and agreed, "This makes sense. So there must be other beings, then, who do need to eat. And so, some beings consume other beings?"

"Yes, well, it's hard to get around. In a certain sense, even these grasses, flowers, and mushrooms are all forms of being. Not sentient like animals, perhaps, or at least not in the same demonstrable way; but it still means that even the herbivores, peaceful creatures that consume such matter, are destroying something alive in order to sustain themselves."

For the first time in not just my visitation but the entirety of my conscious awareness of Dinon, I found him looking troubled.

Perhaps "quizzical" was the word, in truth; but whatever the case, this notion arrested him, and after what seemed a long time, he defaulted again to that question he loved.

"But why?"

That was a difficult question. I frowned a bit, then suggested, "Well—it's a matter of sustaining increasing degrees of complexity. This grass…well, I shouldn't speak of the ecology of this world, as I'm not sure it's the same as where I'm from, but terrestrial plants usually absorb energy from the sun. They're very simple beings; and mushrooms absorb nutrients from where they grow. Then there are very small beings like worms. They're simple things, and—"

"They eat the dead."

"Among other such matter."

"But there's no better way yet found?"

I started to say that there wasn't; then, I thought about my husband and how we harmlessly quenched each other's thirst. "Not one that is widely accepted or understood," I answered after reflecting on this. "But—how can I explain it?—because the self I am now is not the self I was when I was a babe on Earth, or at least because by some strange translation I have inhabited and assumed the being-ness of the woman who was that babe on Earth, I am no longer subject to Earthly rules, but instead subject to the rules of…wherever I came from."

"And it wasn't here?"

Spreading my hands, I explained, a bit lost for words, "I—I don't think so, Dinon. No. It was a dark place, very strange, with many people passing by me. And, well…"

I tilted my head back and studied the stars above us, Dinon's knuckles brushing my cheek as if he couldn't help himself while I thought.

"I now understand that time here in this world runs opposite to Earth's. Need I explain the concept of time to you, dear?"

"It's how we're able to be together," he observed. I paused and laughed, a little embarrassed.

"What a silly thing for me to ask…I should be the one begging you to explain time to me."

"No," he whispered, unable to stop caressing me now, his thumb trailing over my lips and down my jaw. "No, please. I love hearing your thoughts, even the ones I already know. I want you to tell me everything. Go on."

"Well—the only point I was trying to make was that, in whatever that dark place was, time seemed to flow with Earth's; because, when I emerged as I am now, time had passed from the moment of my simpler human life's transformation."

"I see…and you don't remember where you were before that dark place?"

Though I almost said 'on Earth', I sensed this wasn't true in some fashion, and shook my head while meeting his intent silver gaze. "No, I don't."

"But you don't think it was here?"

I felt almost as though he were trying to lead me down a specific train of thought to engender in me some understanding, and I grew nervous about it. Sensing this, Ba'al-Dinon's great hand slid to the nape of my neck and stilled me for his kiss. I received it as a balm for my soul, drinking him in so deeply that I forgot every anxiety and trusted whatever it was he wished to show me.

"I think," I told him as our lips parted so that he could once more survey my expression, "what makes me reluctant to assume I've ever had anything to do with this place is that—aside from brief visitations prior to this one and not necessarily as objectively incarnate in my own body as I am now—there is nothing here but you and me, Ba'al-Dinon."

"There are flowers," he pointed out, "and mountains, and the firmament, and the sea—"

"That's not quite what I mean."

"Ah—you mean 'complex beings', to paraphrase your words earlier."

"Yes, I suppose I do."

Ba'al-Dinon saw something new in me then. He tilted his head like Malin constructing a thought in the middle of writing a speech. "That bothers you."

"In the sense of a puzzle unsolved," I said, knowing it was at best a half-truth as it wafted from my mouth.

"You just lied to me," he said.

Though the observation chilled me, he said these words not in an accusatory way but in a manner of interested observation, for he had just in that very second discovered lying was possible. He mulled the concept over before asking with genuine, open-hearted interest, "Why did you give me false information?"

"I—I—I suppose I didn't want to hurt you." My face was deep red, I'm sure, and I was glad for the darkness. "You're so gentle, Ba'al-Dinon, and so kind to me. I love you."

"I love you," he said, and, with a soft smile, he lowered his head to kiss his way down the line of my throat. "Doesn't love mean telling the truth?"

"That's intimacy," I explained, "and related to diplomacy, and tact, and wisdom…none of which are natural to love, which is really quite insane."

"These are all fascinating words." As his mouth radiated electrical energy, waves of delicious pleasure that warmed my skin beneath his tongue and teeth and lips, Dinon urged me, his hand upon my breast, "Go on, Thecla. Go on, my love."

Barely remembering what I had just been saying as his thumb trailed in teasing circles around my areola, I stuttered and babbled my way back to some semblance of the place I'd been coming from before. "Uh—well—well, um, you see, Dinon, darling, love is like a little wild animal. An ertiz, darting about and yipping, mad, yet irresistible; and intimacy is like taming that animal. Like domesticating it so as to acclimate it to a deeper and more intellectual kind of life."

"That's what I want. I want to domesticate you, Thecla." Ba'al-Dinon raised his head to stare into my eyes. "I love everything about you. Every last single thing. Even the fact that you lied to me, though it seems to bother you."

Quite amazed, I asked, "Doesn't it bother *you*?"

"I think it's beautiful how free you are," he whispered. His kisses poured hotly into my mouth, staunching further speech.

How good he was! How patient, even though my understanding of the world was so limited compared to his ever-growing perception of an infinite variety of constellations into which it could be parsed. I routinely embarrassed myself before him, too often with new faux pas, but mostly with reflection on my old crimes against him. Yet he bore it all so patiently. I could see this interaction, however, remained with him in a particular way; because, after we made love again, he was deep in thought. Exhausted from our exertions, I fell asleep very peacefully the moment my cheek landed on his chest, and I was unable to pry.

And the next morning, as I awoke for the first time alone, panic came upon me in a fit of childish insecurity.

My every urgent thought was of finding Dinon and making up with him for whatever it had been that rightly pushed him from me at last. I flung myself upright, propped on the heel of my palm, looking quite frantically around—(as if a being of infinite love would ever abandon me…but I simply did not then understand, and confess I still seldom can)—

And then the sleek little ertiz came dashing up, its tails wagging and four ears twitching, producing a few happy, high-pitched cries as it danced around me, rolled through the flowers that were my bed, and at last leaned up to set its front paws upon my sternum in its efforts to reach my face for a curious sniff.

"My goodness," I managed to cry, laughing with delight as I recovered from my stunned state and cupped its adorable face. "Hello, hello, my dear! Oh, aren't you cute!"

"I'm glad you like him." Glancing toward the sound of Dinon's pleased voice, I found him seated upon a nearby rock. He looked every bit like a statue of a man as he smiled at me. "I wasn't sure it would be the same one," he confessed—or perhaps, now having adapted to the concept, fibbed in a humble way. "But I can see that he is."

"The same one," I repeated, trying to determine just what he meant by that. In that small handful of seconds, I was assailed by images of that dear domestic ertiz of Parvati, and the hateful news that the Hunters had exterminated all the Rift beasts on taking over the palace, and—

"Why…it is the same one!" Clasping the ertiz to my breast with happy surprise, I kissed its dear little head until it wiggled away to sprint in a figure-8 around Dinon and me with its tongue lolling joyously in its open mouth. Eyes aglow, I gazed up at Dinon and asked, "How did you do that?"

"I experienced the information about him when you mentioned ertices last night. Then I was thinking about beings, and about you and me, and it occurred to me that there must be another type of ertiz; and sure enough, there's a second one running around here, too." With a small grin and a knowing look at our own love-nest, he suggested, "I get the sense that she's making some sort of den someplace private."

Amazed and delighted but nonetheless a little concerned—not just for the welfare of the happy little ertiz gamboling about and pausing to nibble away at its excitement upon its own haunch but for the introduction of change into our happy little stasis of lovemaking—I blinked a few times until managing to note, "There's nothing around here for them to eat, Dinon!"

"That is the world where they need to eat," he said, nodding his head in an orthogonal direction but also vaguely toward me, indicating the world from which I came. "This is the place where it is not necessary to eat. After all—we do not need to consume to survive in this place, so why would they have to?"

It was a valid point, though uncanny and awesome. Yet that awe was only the veil for a more powerful and sincerely fear-inducing realization.

That, on the blank slate of this place, Ba'al-Dinon had created life.

And he had done it by witnessing me.

33

After all I had seen of him, was it really so extraordinary that Dinon should create life? Was it all that alarming? After all—he had manifested so many objects and accomplished so many amazing feats in the time that I had known him. Why, then, should it frighten me that he had drawn from out of a kind of non-existence not just an ertiz but this specific little ertiz who regarded me with friendly familiarity intermingled with the high-energy wariness of a small, frenetic animal? Was producing this adorable creature really all that different from refurnishing Glenn's home during the handful of seconds in which I passed from one room to the next?

The answer, of course, was that yes, it was jolly well different. To produce a living thing—not just a living thing, but a specifically identified individual derivation of that thing—was a depth of power that had far broader implications, and I found myself preoccupied by them all. We spent the day together very comfortably, but now it was my turn, in so many ways, to be as deeply plunged in thought as he had been the night before. What I found myself revisiting was the question of why it was so preoccupying; why it was so deeply different.

"Because it's more intimate," Dinon decided after I had experienced this thought two or three times. "Deriving is the most intimate experience one being could have with another."

"Yes, of course. I can certainly see that. But—what troubles me is the how of it." Since he had dropped the pretense of my abolished mental privacy to address this matter that troubled me, I availed myself of the opportunity to be very frank with him. Sitting up slightly, my knees drawn toward my chest, I observed, "I've never understood how you do the things you do, Dinon. There was once—no, in the future of yours—or in a future that I might have experienced with you—" At a loss on how to specify, I hedged, "I'm trying to say, I have a memory of you doing things for me. Creating a dress out of thin air, manifesting a piece of jewelry, and so on and so forth. But how are you doing those things? How, in a practical sense, do you draw these things into existence? Moreover, how do you call into existence a specific living creature like that ertiz?"

His hand on his chin as he considered how best to describe it, he finally shrugged, at a loss for words. "I just think of them. I think of them with us, and there they are."

No more comforted by that than I was satisfied, I balked. "Surely that doesn't make sense, darling, if you'll forgive my impudence. After all—I think of things all the time: imagine or remember things. And it's not as if they appear before me."

"There's an act of the will involved, too," he clarified, leaving me no better informed than I had been a few seconds ago. Unable to help looking at him in wry annoyance, especially as I perceived that impudent streak of my soul, I pinched his lower lip between my thumb and forefinger, tugging lightly and earning another flash of that wonderful, boyish smile.

"That still doesn't make any sense, my love."

"It does if we're in my imagination." This observation was so casually delivered that it had a moment to settle deep into my core before it had an impact. While I looked at him in befuddlement, he smiled on. "Do you think that's unlikely?"

"Well—well, I just don't understand how it could be possible. Wouldn't that make me a figment of your imagination, too, Dinon?"

How his face changed! A tidal wave of pain softened his eyes, wiping across his entire being so that he was stilled but for the slight furrowing of his brow. "Not a figment. No, but—I don't want to talk about things like that right now. Please, Thecla. Can we talk about something else?"

Feeling a little dizzy at his response, I sank my teeth into my lip, nodding. "All right."

"Thank you." There was real relief in his voice, and I found myself thinking that, whatever it was he was shielding me from, the rate at which his deep cognizance grew was overwhelming to us both. We had been together three days, and in that time, he had gone from a vague comprehension of pleasure and language to an understanding of consciousness, spacetime, and reality that was surely already far beyond my comprehension even from within my dharmine perspective. How mystifying it was—how mystifying he was! And how deeply I craved to know him, even still. He smiled at me so tenderly as I had that thought, his forehead coming to rest against mine so I could look nowhere but his eyes.

"I want to know you, too, Thecla."

"Don't you already?"

"But there are parts of your heart I want you to want to reveal to me. I want that intimacy with you...my domesticated Thecla. Open yourself to me, my flower."

"Haven't I already?"

With that deep fondness only growing in his eyes at the vulnerability of my question, Ba'al-Dinon kissed me on the mouth, then tilted his head to plant a few more highly stimulating kisses along my ear.

"Tell me about other animals you think belong here," he pleaded, his hand stroking along my thigh. "I want to know them all."

I lay awake with him long into that night, telling him about the many Rift creatures with which I and most other terrestrials were extensively versed. When I awoke from our postcoital doze that afternoon, the most peaceful harpros I had ever witnessed glided mellowly through the violet sky, at perfect ease and not even dreaming of descending upon the small ertiz couple chasing each other about not far from where Dinon watched me awaken. Seeing him, my hand raising to stroke along his chest, I asked, "Don't you ever sleep?"

"I slept before. I don't need it now that you're here. Sleep... it's a kind of practice for death." His hand raised to fit over mine, pressing my palm flat against his heart as he told me with deep sincerity, "There is no death here, Thecla. Not for you."

"Then why do I sleep when I'm exhausted by all your...vigor?"

"Because I love to watch you sleep," he murmured, his great body covering mine as his kisses trailed heavily along my mouth. "The same reason you cum for me here, Thecla...I want you to. Want you to have the contrast to increase the pleasure of it all."

Shuddering, delight racing through me as his hand slipped between my thighs to appreciate his favorite valley in all that alien world, I took a breath to try and hold back my whimpers of erotic ecstasy. "Then perhaps," I murmured, my entire body drowning in pleasure as he discovered how wet I still was from all the lovemaking earlier that day, and from the simple act of waking up beside him, "I should be wearing clothes, at least from time to time...so you can enjoy the contrast, and the experience of taking them off."

That strangeness again passed through his eyes: that urgent longing he had to protect me from something. "Don't do that," he bade me. "Just be as you are with me. You don't need clothes with me."

"All right," I said, somewhat uncertain beneath a nagging sense that there was, in fact, something I needed clothes for. But... for what? Why had I ever worn clothes, and why did I place any value on them? Dinon didn't wear them, after all; and neither did the animals he had created for us to live alongside. It made me laugh when I thought about it. I set my hand upon my smiling mouth, then shook my head.

"What a silly thing to say—why did that come to mind?"

"Why did what come to mind?"

"Who knows," I murmured, moving my hand to lean into a tender kiss with him. "Who knows, my love, my darling? Oh, Dinon...keep touching me, yes, please, beloved—oh! Keep touching me there..."

Those hands of his were skilled—wonderful—but once the orgasm passed, there was no more distracting me from the nagging sense that I'd forgotten something of grave import.

What could it possibly have been, though? I couldn't seem

to remember anything of relevance to my life outside of Dinon, whose existence was a kind of oasis to me. In his presence, I was filled with a peace so incomprehensible that I never wanted to be separated from him for even for a handful of moments. Yet those brief instances of separation were so very sweet, for they afforded me the chance to set my eyes on him again as though for the first time. My heart and body ached for him, desperate for the fullness of his attention.

Yet was there not something else for which my heart yearned? Was there not another set of thoughts that ached me, dismaying my senses and giving me the feeling that I had somehow gotten lost? Of course, getting lost implied a destination and an origin. I was therefore deeply uncertain as to what it was I lacked, because something deep within my soul told me the destination and origin were in this case the same: that I was endeavoring to return somewhere.

But where? Hadn't I come *from* someplace? Why would I want to go back, when here with Dinon I was so enmeshed in the sweet warmth of eternal love?

What had I spent all my time doing in that other place, at any rate? I fumbled through the slippery dark of my consciousness to find some explanation for that, and I once more had the queer sense—which my soul insisted with certainty to be truth—that I had never not been with Dinon, even in that separate world. But surely, I must have had things to do other than be with him. How was it that I had ever spent my time in that other place where mankind had to eat and sleep and die and wear unnatural garments for reasons that hardly made sense to me now?

Aha! But that was it, wasn't it? The thought of garments caused the concept of weaving to spring into my mind, and I sat up slightly at this unexpected recollection. Yes, yes! Weaving—threads on great looms, warps and wefts, the steady rocking of the heddles of a great machine so like the hush-hush of our nearby tide as my feet worked the pedals and my hands threw the shuttle back and forth, back and forth, back-and-forth. I had spent my time on Earth, in that strange other place that now felt so unnatural, on a strange and unnatural activity that was nonetheless somehow glorious and beautiful, for it was an act of creation particular to the style of mind into which I had been born—the conscious mind. How many things I had woven! Towels and shirts and tapestries: most especially tapestries. I had, hadn't I? Endless tapestries, or so it had seemed. Yet they, too, must have had an end, since I was now here.

All this begged the question—what was the last thing I could remember weaving? Struggling through the desultory haze of my otherwise too peaceful mind, I groped around in my memories to discern the specific nature of my weavings.

"Would that make you happy, Thecla?"

Before I could advance upon the general form and shape of whatever piece I had left off, Dinon spoke up, sincerity in his voice despite a certain quietude that had settled upon him as I swirled into thoughts he witnessed intently. "I want you to be happy. If it would make you happy, I would gladly give you something to do—weaving."

"Perhaps it would," I idly confessed, hastening to add with my hand upon the firm surface of his delicious chest, "But I am already happy. It's only—why, I know I could never do all that you do, Dinon. Yet when I awaken every morning and see all you're calling into existence along with us, it appears to me as if I while away the hours doing nothing at all."

"Is living to worship me really nothing?"

Those words! They sent a ripple of the most intense arousal through me, and I couldn't stop myself from letting my hand glide down the well-defined pathways of his abdominal muscles to fondle the broad, proud scepter of his cock as he looked on so tenderly.

"It's not nothing at all," I told him, leaning up to swallow down a few of his deepest, sweetest kisses and deliver some of my own. Like a great luptich humoring its smaller mate, Dinon rolled onto his back to give me total access to him. I rolled with him, continuing to nibble his lip and suckle his tongue as I stroked that insatiable prick ever-harder in my hand. "I love to live for your pleasure, Lord of my heart…and it's not so much that one wishes to work. But…"

Feeling a little pitiful, a little helpless, somehow small before this man—I swore I'd dreamed I'd discovered him wholly inert and unconscious once!—I bit my own lip now and gazed into his eyes as I begged him to understand. "I want to do so much more for you. You do so much for me—more than I suspect I even know." His eyes crinkled slightly at the edges upon hearing this, exuding something sly and catlike that made me wonder all manner of things I resisted the urge to ask. "I wish to somehow express and remember all these things you do for me," I went on, "and to—emulate it, in some way. Oh, Dinon…"

A low sigh rolled from my lips as his great arms folded around me, drawing me completely upon him so that I straddled his hips. As I settled my body upon his to barrage him with more kisses, the needy flesh of my sex fit to his with such perfection that I cried out in unexpected pleasure. His hands massaged the flesh of my rump as I squirmed a little and let that sweet bud of my pleasure grind against the crown of his own. Meanwhile, Dinon gazed into my eyes with an expression of fathomless mercy and compassionate understanding.

"I love you." His eyelids lowered to contain the pleasure flowing freely between us as, with a whimper, I guided the head of his sacred cock just so into the happy hug of my core. "Oh, Thecla…you can have anything you want, anytime you want. I'll give it to you…you said before that out of love, you don't wish to hurt me…but it hurts me when you doubt my love enough that you make excuses for what you want or even need. Don't be afraid to tell me what you want from me. Okay?"

As he asked this, his hand raised to my cheek, his thumb trailing over the temple of my forehead. Flushing deeply, I nodded.

"Okay," I whispered, my mouth opening in shock as I took him to the very root of his cock and cried out as I did. "O-oh, Dinon! Oh, Dinon, my darling—"

While my toes curled, he arched his back and slid those broad hands along my body to fit to my hips. "Thecla," he groaned, his tongue stabbing into my mouth with those intense, addictive kisses. "My Thecla, my life…my bride, and my queen."

Then, I did not see how those four sides of myself with respect to Dinon's love were literal ways of seeing me: the facets of a prism through which the light of my soul was divided and by which he witnessed me in ways no other being could.

Now, I see it all so clearly…and even still, not clearly as he.

34

The next day, smilingly asking me to keep my eyes closed tight, Ba'al-Dinon took my hands and guided me along a path our feet were beginning to wear in the grass toward the shore. We walked there almost every day to wash ourselves and play in the water, and each time we did, I looked with deep fondness upon a certain sea-cave which seemed to be the place of our meeting, if any place could be called that. By now, I had lost all track of time and all ability to remember anything outside of Dinon. Even the conversation of the day before was somewhat muddy, so that when instead of drawing me into the shore, he led me into that sea cave, I was surprised. Then I was surprised all over again when he bade me open my eyes.

The loom before me—an alien, unnatural object in this natural world, made all the more alien by the ultra-black substance out of which it was constructed—made me gasp at the memory of all we had discussed.

"My darling," I cried in excitement, touching his chest.

"I made it for you," Dinon answered, the warm tone of his voice almost musical in its gentleness. His great hands fitting to either side of my face, he kissed my brow and then, almost chastely, my mouth, smiling as he rubbed his thumb back and forth along my cheekbone. "So you could feel close to me and enjoy yourself more in your own right, without respect to your value in my eyes. But please know…you are of infinite value in my eyes, Thecla."

Unable to contain my joy at this expression of his love, I threw my arms around my bridegroom's neck and whispered, "Thank you, Dinon."

"I'll leave you alone as long as you need," he told me. "Though I hope you don't mind if I watch you weaving. I know I find it very beautiful to witness you doing anything."

"All right," I consented, my smile widening. "You can watch me forever, Dinon, no matter what I'm doing. Every second of my existence belongs to you, my love."

Those eyes of his twinkling with greater knowledge—and, strangely, greater conflict—every day, Dinon kissed my brow, then vanished in a strange ripple of space; less a blur than the abrupt dissolution of a shadow when inundated by the sun. However disorienting, it was only another demonstration of his power, and I shuddered with delight. The glow of his love burned my heart with all the greater intensity when he was absent; but it, like the loom, was his gift to me.

Indeed, as I faced the black loom and let my hand glide upon the unknown material out of which it was constructed (or perhaps I had better write, 'manifested'), I felt his absence represented more than love. It represented a facet of love I sensed we had discussed quite recently: an intimacy that went beyond the common animal instincts that made me want to leap into his arms and commit my entire body to his whims.

How strange! In no time, Dinon had gone from a somehow naive-seeming angel of otherworldly perception to a being whose comprehension was at this point feeding itself: a comprehension so vast that it long-since expanded the boundaries of mine— assuming it had not always expanded mine, for I could see that he contained within himself infinity. In this deathless place where he could draw up life, objects, anything the heart desired, it seemed to me there was no end to what Dinon knew or was or could do. And here I was, so small, unable to do anything without his help—and he loved me. Loved me so much he was willing to leave me alone with something that was not him.

Smiling dreamily, I sank into the stool before the black loom, finding it already prepared, threads stretched across its frame, the shuttle ready. I ran my fingers idly through my hair and wondered what I would make. What would I weave for Dinon? What could I offer him as a gesture to thank him for all that he had done? What could I possibly weave that might in any way repay or even approach the ceaseless depth of his love?

I realized I had been humming only as, note by note, the humming faded when I ran time and again against this insidious thought.

Just what was there for me to create for him? Everything I did was pleasing to him, so could anything I made have any special meaning? Moreover, I was struck by the futility of my desire to be like him, or in any way feel I was his peer. However much his love elevated me, however deeply he longed for me to feel like his equal and his queen, I could hardly comprehend how such a thing was possible. It wasn't, in fact. Nothing I could create could ever be like what he created, for his very thoughts formed the fabric of existence in this place. I, on the other hand, could create only with materials he provided. Surely there was something quite pathetic in this, even if he chose not to interpret it that way! Moreover, with him knowing my every thought—and, perhaps, my every action and yearning before it even formed in my mind—I felt sad to think that I could not surprise him with anything I did or said or wove. Even these thoughts had been the subject of his awareness; I was totally open to him, and though it gave me pleasure to be so shared with the one I loved and who loved me, I frowned to think that there were experiences I simply couldn't give him. Not in a direct fashion, anyway.

Blast! What did I usually weave? My anxiety about pleasing Dinon was quickly tangling my heart up in knots, and my heart became a stumbling block for my mind. Stories, I supposed. There was something narrative connected to my weavings, but I could no longer articulate what, or why, or in which context.

How strange! How baffling. I ached with a sense that something was missing in me, and it seemed my weaving was a component of that—or, at least, a symptom. My yearning for my weaving was also a yearning for that missing thing (things?) I couldn't name, and I frowned, my fingers trailing along the threads in a delirium.

Soon enough, though, that delirium became frustration— frustration at myself for my inadequacy, and at Dinon for his perfection. As funny as it seems, I nearly blamed him for my sudden angst! It was by my own over-ambitious desire, which he had never requested, that I had displeased myself. I could create nothing equivalent to the creations that came through his hand for my enjoyment. Perhaps Ba'al-Dinon had been right to encourage me to live for pleasure with him, a state of constant homage and reverence with him.

But, well…this was all a very dramatic response to the dearth of inspiration I experienced. The more I thought about it, the more obvious the problem became. When was the last time I had seen a textile of any sort? When was the last time I'd experienced strife worthy of working out through the narrative of some weaving? Spending every day naked with Dinon was exquisite bliss, but it left a woman's mind with little ennui, fear, or despair to weave about! The anxiety I felt to provide him with some gesture of my love might perhaps serve as the source of the dynamic tension required to push into motion my creative act, but I still felt a key component was lacking in my ability to produce—that was, I had no example, fresh in my mind, of any kind of textile from which I could adapt my own unique iteration.

Weary from this struggle after two or more hours of heavy and useless thought, I rubbed my brow and got up, emerging from the cave as my eyes rapidly blinked through their adjustment to the sunlight. The ocean's whispering grew to the anticipatory murmur of a crowd, and I watched the waves for a time, my hand shielding my eyes. Supposing that exercise might do me some good, I walked alongside the tide and let those briny waters lap at my ankles and my feet. I did my best to open myself to ideas, searching for them along the waves and in the silhouettes of distant birds, flowers, trees, and even the rocks. But the more I grasped for inspiration, the more it eluded me. In frustration, I swam for a while, the kinetic energy providing a small, temporary release from my annoyed mood.

And then I stumbled back onto the shore, dripping saltwater, and plopped down upon the grass, extending my body to dry in the sun.

And I discovered beside me that what I'd taken at first to be a shadow was really two large scraps of black cloth: one in the shape of a woman's dress, its throat decorated with a simple white collar; and the other, a deep fuligin cloak. I frowned, puzzled, quite sure that in all the time I had been here with Dinon, I had never seen him wear any clothes, let alone a cloak. Yet, I knew it was his; and, in a process of deduction in which Dinon himself had seemed constantly engaged at some point that seemed like an eternity ago yet was a mere handful of sunrises ago, I understood the other object to belong to me.

And now that I recognized my dress, I remembered that I had been, for quite some time, wearing it on my arrival here. I had worn it awhile before that, too. As I considered it, my somewhat spotty memory drew me up from my state of soft, dreamy ecstasy and long-wandering thoughts to the fact that Dinon had begged me not to wear clothes. Yet…I was fascinated by that dress. Transfixed by it, however simple an object it was. Like the black loom, it spoke to me. So did the fabric of Dinon's cloak. The fineness of the threads was breathtaking, and the fuligin was so exquisitely smooth in appearance that those threads seemed invisible.

Invisible threads.

The longer I stared into the dark surface of the clothes, these black textiles as unnatural as the gift Ba'al-Dinon had given me, the more I remembered other invisible threads upon which I used to look; and the more adamantly I focused upon this thought, the more I realized that I was already looking at these invisible threads; and that, violet and silver like the sky and the clouds and the sun and the grass and the surf and the shore, they formed an immaculate weaving that created the very substance of the world.

But it had not always been so! As I witnessed this, I remembered in profound amazement that I had seen these threads as great stars, for they had seemed to radiate wildly out from my heart and Ba'al-

Dinon's, the violet from me and the silver from him, rays that burst forth from some otherwise unobservable physicalization of our souls. Somehow, by some means, they had become interlaced in a single textile, a perfect weaving that made me gasp—and made me realize, in an astonished comprehension of metaphysical cause and effect, that it was our lovemaking that had done this. Somehow, Dinon's love for me, and the strength and desire and longing with which he filled my heart, had woven these individual threads together into the very fabric of our reality. And, somehow, all aspects of the world had become imbued with the texture of them: witnessed by and integrated into us.

In awe of the implications of this while somehow also mystified at the practical meaning of it, I looked down at myself with an even more alarming realization rushing into my mind: namely—that sex with this bridegroom of mine had implications and meanings I was not fully equipped to understand. Making love with a being capable of infinite love—who was a semi-comprehensible expression of infinite Love, Himself—had ripple effects I hadn't considered. And those effects were far beyond my comprehension. Indeed, for reasons I couldn't articulate, I panicked.

Overwhelmed by the urge to cover myself—to temper somewhat his desire to take me and my desire to be taken, as though each time the weaving might become tighter and more inescapable (did I want to escape?)—I snatched up the dress and pulled it over my head.

And as I emerged through the neck hole, Ba'al-Dinon stood before me, looking sad and wearing, for the first time, a pair of leather trousers.

"I hoped you wouldn't want to," he murmured, reaching out to graze my cheek with his knuckles before moving around behind me. There, he carefully guided my hair from the dress before buttoning the back for me. "But, if this really is what you want, I'll help you."

"Dinon, I—"

"Don't apologize." He bent his head to kiss my ear. "You're not free to love me if you don't trust me. You're not ready yet. It's okay."

My stomach tightening, my face burning with shame, I whimpered, "But I do love you. Ba'al-Dinon, I want to love you better. Please—help me."

"The fact that you just asked me for that," he told me, his hands on my shoulders, his lips grazing my ear, "shows me you will be ready sooner than you fear."

Stepping past me, Ba'al-Dinon stooped, sweeping up his cloak and draping it around his shoulders. He fastened it at his throat, his eyes soft with sorrow until, sucking in a breath, he regarded me in the dress. "You're so beautiful—so mysterious to me."

Yet my sorrow deepened. In fact, it seemed in that instant that I had never known sorrow before: I had never experienced it in any meaningful way, or perhaps at all. My heart overflowed with agony at the thought of having hurt him by my disobedience, and in my agony, I found myself turning my frustration outward in a misguided attempt to shut out the pain.

"I hardly see how there could be anything mysterious about me to you," I told him, my tone snappish as my arms folded beneath my breasts. "I'm an open book to you, aren't I?"

That smile! Oh, that smile. I expected him to be hurt, angry, or indignant.

Instead, Ba'al-Dinon looked at me with the dancing eyes of a man more in love than ever. "My favorite book of all time," he whispered, each word from the very depths of his soul. "The one I'd erase my memory to read for the first time again."

How troubled I was by that imagery! How overwhelmed I was becoming. In the tension of the weaving between our souls, I also sensed a tangible representation of eternity. There was some paper or other that recently passed by my desk which concerned the notion that the perception of time is the result of quantum entanglement between two particles. It is not real: everything in existence is merely a logical consequence of the unfolding of eternity. And for eternity to be made so tangible was somehow threatening to my sense of self—to everything, in a very surreal way—especially when I considered the particles entangled in my life were myself and Ba'al -Dinon.

Eternity—the future, the past, and the present, too. It was such an important concept to my thinking, yet it had been, for so long, exactly that—a concept. I had never allowed myself to fully feel and experience the nature of reality as eternal except in some vague, hypothetical sense. Perhaps it was not possible for me to do anything else prior to this particular set of experiences with Dinon. But now that I had seen the threads and felt this new sense of a deep metaphysical impact due to Dinon's love for me, I realized that, like the pages of a book individually making up a story, the events of reality were the unpacking of a singular eternity-object. And time and again, I had the impression that the central focus of this eternity-object, the epicenter of this eternal state, was Dinon's love for me. Furthermore, I reasoned that if that was the case, I was always myself: always living my life and always witnessed by Dinon, who treated me as if I were the only thing that existed.

Then I began to get the sense that I really was the only thing that existed, and I began to tremble.

"Sh, Thecla." Dinon drew me closely into his arms. "Sh...be not afraid. You're okay. Oh, Thecla... I love you so much more than you can ever understand."

"I know. I—I know. I can tell."

Breathless, dizzy, I gasped in an intense intermingling of impulses that were in impossible conflict. Somehow, this increasing sense I had of him being the only real thing in existence was overwhelming to me and caused me terrible fright; yet, at the same time, it made me want to immolate myself in him. Yes! He was like a fire to me now: awe-inspiring and alarming, yet the source of all love and goodness in the world. I clung to him even as I trembled in fear of him, and there was compassion in his eyes as I had never experienced and could never experience from another being—what other being, what being, what other beings existed aside from him?

"I already told you," he murmured. "I would never hurt you as this self-expression."

"What does that mean, though? Doesn't that imply you have others?"

"Thecla..."

Oh, how that love of his broke my heart! Gently combing my hair back from my brow, Dinon gazed into my eyes with the purest sympathy.

"I'm every man who's ever touched you."

Those words sent flooding through my soul a wave of the most intense, awe-inspiring love, yet worsened my fear beyond reason. I wanted it to be a metaphor and laughed, trying not to think about it as I stepped back from him and wiped my fingers beneath my eyes.

"Why don't I go weave," I rambled, wringing my hands

very nervously and glancing away a few times. A little sparrow who suddenly realized the creature she loved was an eagle, or a harpros—or whatever primordial ancestor spawned them both (my Lord)! I took a steadying breath and flashed Dinon my finest smile.

He didn't smile back—his eyes shone with too much knowing pain for that—but he nodded.

"Okay, Thecla. I love you."

Moving stiffly at first, as if caught in a dream, I turned on my heel and took a few steps away from him. For reasons I couldn't consciously explain, this careening soon turned into a run. I sprinted away from him; his love was so reality-altering in its nature that realizing its depths was too much for me. It was shattering me.

Or—perhaps what was shattering me was the knowledge that my love was still so imperfect beside the greatness of his. My entire being screamed for the ability to love him as he loved me. When I proved too finite to accommodate this desire, my body responded with cringing shame my unworthiness to receive him as my bridegroom. I had to run away and hide myself in that little cave with my loom: the loom he had made for me.

And there, I did nothing but weep.

here was something so very wrong with me! I could not create; I could not love him as I ought. I could not even respect his wishes, for here I sat in the very dress he'd asked me not to wear! I was totally unworthy of him, yet I remained the unceasing object of his adoration. Perhaps it was not Dinon or his love that frightened me, but the idea that I was tricking him somehow. That he could not see me clearly, and would someday wake up to how unworthy I was, and would depart from me forever.

But his love *was* forever. I knew his love was constant, glorious, and incomprehensible. I felt myself rationalizing with the rest of me, negotiating my way back to calmness. Even as my tears stilled, my feelings of inadequacy were still too much to bear. Dinon was right. While my love was imperfect and diverted, I could not trust myself to love him well enough. And while I could not trust his love, I was not free to fully love him. The thought was torture. But, like a physician diagnosing a terminal illness, I tried to remember that Dinon's observation was also the route to a cure. I could love him better, I sensed. I could give myself to him completely and learn to see that his love arose, in some mysterious and sacred way, out of my imperfection. Because I was imperfect, I needed him—I still need him, and I will forever.

But then, still in the whirlwind of it all, I could hardly see it and sat, weeping, before the barren loom. Tears flowed freely, a torrent without discernible end as though some tap had been opened in my mind. Awful, throaty, heartfelt sobs from a source unknown racked my body, and I gasped between tears, my face in my hands, my sobs echoing through the cave and disappearing into the sound of the sea.

At last, sniffling, repelled by my own emotion, I raised the hem of my dress to dry my eyes.

And something solid slid from the pocket of my gown.

Frowning, befuddled, I patted the floor beneath the bench to see what it was. My fingers curled around something smooth and cold: something that reminded me of glass, a substance about which I hadn't thought in quite some time. I plucked it up and raised it to examine it in my palm.

A dragonfly, trapped in amber.

An insect commended to eternity.

Rosina's bug, given to her by Malin in the presence of Eleison, which was then proudly brought back to her father's—Glenn's—apartment in the Karrisregion house that was our preferred home.

Knowledge rushed in on a great inhalation of memory as my nostrils flared and my lungs expanded. I remembered not just my family, but the danger in which Telemachus had been left. Left—

Left when, fleeing my father, I had leapt through the run I

made in the fabric of a reality that, unlike this one, had always—at least in my lifetime—been in its woven state.

"Thecla."

I shot up from my seat, startled only slightly by Dinon's appearance. In comparison to the urgent need I felt to rush back to my family and, most especially, my son, I felt hardly anything at all—nothing but the numb ache of understanding that it would not be possible for me to stay with the beautiful man who stood at the mouth of the cave, his cloak whipping in the breeze off the sea. "Please," he begged, "don't leave."

Clenching my teeth against the pain, the existential peace of our time together now the source of agony, I pressed Rosina's amber-encased bug to my heart. My brow furrowed as I regarded my beloved.

"I would do anything to stay," I told him, already blinking back a new wave of far hotter, more violent tears. He stepped toward me and I shook my head, the space between us glittering with new awareness of the fabric we had woven. "No, Dinon, please, no—" With a gasp, I managed, "It will hurt me if you touch me again. It will burst my heart into a thousand little shards. I can't. Oh, please don't—"

But he did anyway, quickly closing the distance and catching my biceps in his hands.

"Please, Thecla," he asked, sincere and pleading. I knew he meant it as a real plea: a request that I knew I had the power to grant. "I'm begging you, don't go—"

"Oh, Dinon, I must. I'm telling you, I must go, darling. Don't do this to me."

But then he dropped to his knees, gripping my hands, his eyes full of something I had never seen in him before: desperation.

"Please," he whispered. "Please, Thecla. If you go—things will change. They'll have to change, don't you see? It will all have to be—like it always is."

Death.

He meant there would have to be death.

Still, I shook my head, my lips trembling. "I can't leave them there, Ba'al-Dinon."

"But they're here, too," Dinon told me, begging me to understand. "See?"

Before I could even open my mouth to ask what he meant, motion—man-shaped motion—startled me in my periphery.

Naked, Malin stepped from the shadows near to us.

"You really could stay here with him, darling," he told me, his eyes the glittering animal-silver of a famished dharmine, of an altered man converted by the Rift—of Dinon's eyes, which pined up at me as he dropped his hold of my hands to instead grip and kiss the hem of my skirt. Malin went on, "He's right...I'm here, too. We could all just be together."

"There's no suffering here," Eleison said, stepping out from beside him, his eyes perfect and undamaged except that they were not his own. Yes; even Glenn's eyes were frighteningly aligned with Dinon's as he appeared on my other side.

"There's no jealousy, either," Glenn agreed with a knowing glance at Malin and Eleison, who smiled in a way that reminded me too much of Ba'al-Dinon. Panic rose in me at the temptation I felt, and I shook my head.

"The goodness of this place doesn't merit leaving the versions of you, the temporal iterations of you, to suffer and die when I know I could help."

"But can't you see how being at peace in this place justifies that suffering?" Dinon begged. "What's suffering beside an eternity of infinite love? What's death and the finite when I could give you everyone, every single person you've ever loved, and more?"

From the darkness, there stepped my whole family—my children, my sister, my father, even that dead mother I had never looked upon in my sentient life. Frightened, I stumbled back— then realized that behind them, there were more faces, more and more, faces echoing into all eternity, that blackness that went on forever. As Dinon released my dress, looking in sheer agony, I beat my breast, my teeth bared.

"I jolly well know that my own suffering is justified," I shouted as I wept. "I know, being here, that every papercut and broken leg and good day and bad day are a mote of dust beside what it is to experience your love for me this way. And maybe they know it now"—I gestured to the people stretching out behind him, toward the endless darkness where once the mouth of the cave had let in violet daylight—"but they don't. They never will. Not unless you bring them here the way I came here—in the course of their lives, with the context to understand it and the ability to consent to being here. Without that—without receiving a chance to consciously work through their suffering and gain an awareness of entering this place—their suffering is meaningless. Disconnected from their existence here, it cannot be understood as part of who they are. They cannot be themselves unless they're rooted in terrestrial reality. Without the context of becoming themselves, these aren't the people I know, the people who are suffering on earth. If their feet never touch earth and they never know suffering, then—"

Unable to stop myself from speaking the words at the same moment I made a kind of awful causal connection between the drive of the dharmine species to kill and replace their terrestrial selves and the things I was saying now, I weakly concluded, "They're just beasts."

A ripple of gnosis shuddered through the infinite crowd.

Ba'al-Dinon lowered his head, his hand pressing to his heart. "We don't have to keep doing this, Thecla," he whispered, his eyes pained as he finally looked at me. "It doesn't have to always be this way."

"It already is this way," I said, gesturing to the darkness around us. "I've been here before. With all these people before. I was once among them, myself."

"No," he whispered. "Don't you see? Thecla…"

Suddenly, the air was very cool, and I perceived something before me. I extended my fingers in confusion and found there a pane of glass that separated me and the loom from Ba'al-Dinon, as well as from all those dharmines he had created in a last, desperate attempt to get me to stay with him. As my heart dropped far beyond my stomach and down through my feet, I had the sudden awareness of having voluntarily ejected myself from paradise. I slapped my hands against the glass—

And was helpless to watch as, dipping a hand into the darkness in which he knelt, Dinon pulled me up out of these strange dark waves of infinity. He held my duplicate in his arms as she smiled and caressed his jaw, clinging to him like a feral little bitch, a wild thing unconscious of everything but her love for her master.

"This is a different iteration than the one that produced you," he said. "You've just shown me how finite and infinite existences are one and the same, without paradox."

Tears in Ba'al-Dinon's eyes, he clutched my doppelganger to himself and looked at me with sheer delight, whispering fiercely, "Oh, Thecla, my goddess, my world—I love you. I would create infinite Earths to solve infinite problems if only to be with you once. I'll never leave you alone."

His eyes shining with devotion, he swore to me, "I'll share your life with you an infinity of times just to prove my love forever."

Violet light illuminated Ba'al-Dinon's face. I whirled around to its source, screaming as a brilliant explosion of violet and silver mushroomed up before me in the distance. Its shockwave knocked me back: and as its glittering radiance enveloped me, I witnessed, emerging out of the nothingness of space, the creation of the world that I was already in and into which I had been born: and there I was, standing in the violet Rift radiation in the center of some device I was too overwrought to recognize, separated from my bridegroom once again.

A s one may imagine, my recognition of my surroundings was, at best, belated. I could not quite make it out through the violet haze—not until my eyes adjusted to the concept of space and objects within that space, and technology, and all sorts of other ideas that had been wiped clear out of my mind during my sabbatical in that sweet, aching paradise with Dinon.

Pain surged in me, as bad or worse than what I felt when Malin lay dead in our carriage. I felt a childish urge to sink down and cry for all I had ruined, but the voice of my absent love rang out clearly in my soul. Dinon's tone was as soothing as ever—more soothing and powerful than it had even been in that splendid place where it had been just him and me.

You ruined nothing, he told me. *You'll see. I'm proud of you. But don't cry yet, sweetheart… keep it together. Now's not the time.*

How I had been changed—how my perception of him had changed! The difference when he spoke to me was immediate and staggering. There was something new between us now, and I could feel it without even having to see him. Hyper-aware of his presence within me and, somehow, within everything around me, I felt both a new intimacy with and a new longing for Dinon, and a love that was so beyond anything I had ever managed before that the euphoria I felt on realizing this helped push away the instinct I had toward my tears. *Good girl,* he lauded, urging on, *Now, hide.*

Seeing that the space before me, through the flickering lightning storm of violet Rift light, was an open space I vaguely recognized but couldn't place, I stumbled instead backward and braced myself down behind the metal pedestal that formed the base of the machine. As I tried deep breathing to calm myself, quite certain that any actual stabilization of my temperament was due to Dinon's invisible presence and the Rift radiation from which my dharmine physiology benefited, the machine began to wind down and the effects of the lighting lessened. I shut my eyes, praying that the dying brilliance would not reveal me, and was relieved when a cursory look around provided me with the realization that this side of the device was unmonitored by any noticeable cameras. I peeked around the edge of the horseshoe-shaped ring that had been rotating through the upper half of the pedestal, the source of a molecular reaction being studied in some lab.

And as I recognized myself peering down into the chamber from a viewing window through which I looked with Arthur, I remembered the nature of the reaction, and placed the identity of the lab, and realized that I was at Horizon Clean Energy Institute roughly a week before I ever left.

Don't be afraid, Dinon encouraged me. *I'm going to help you. Okay?*

My mouth went desperately dry as I darted back down to keep from seeing myself, and I nodded. "Okay," I whispered. "Yes, please. Please, Dinon, help me."

You're going to wait here for an hour, Dinon continued. *Just stay where you are; nobody can see you from that angle. Try to get some rest, Thecla. I'm right here.*

Nodding, tears pricking my eyes even as I tried to resist them, I whispered in a voice like a helpless child's, "Okay, Dinon, thank you." Lips trembling, I added in a far more desperate, needy tone, "I love you so much!"

I know, he told me with deep sincerity, his tone emotional. His presence was so clear to me that I felt as though I could nearly see his face in the arrangement of panels and screws on the wall I faced. Sounding as if he was choking up a little himself, Dinon went on, *I've always known. I always do know. Now just close your eyes, Thecla. Try to rest here and let them find you at the right time. I'll give you what to say.*

Weak and dizzy after the excess of emotion and this emergence from the infinity of the next iteration of reality to the finity of the iteration into which I had fancied myself (or this iteration of myself) born, I obeyed. My arms folded around myself, my eyes closed; my awareness of Dinon's presence grew so acute that I could vividly imagine his arms around me—a means by which I did soothe myself into a skittish doze. Yet, as one may imagine in that place and in that circumstance, there was no real rest to be had—and whenever I was awake, my soul drowned in horror.

Had I really just thrown all that away? Dinon, in his present nearness to me, did not remonstrate or in any way condemn my decision to return; far from it. He had told me explicitly that he was proud of me, yet how could I be proud of myself? All I could see was how I had entered into this paradise, disrupted Love from his slumber, then added endless pain and suffering to his reality by breaking his heart and abandoning him there.

Do you really think that's all you taught me?

No—of course, that wasn't all I had taught him or done for him. Yet it was still a struggle for me to conceive of the bliss we had experienced when it had been punctuated by a moment of such agony, such heartbreak, that I felt at once every unpleasant episode of my life to be a kind of just punishment for the way in which I had hurt him.

As this thought rose maliciously upon me between moments of dozing, Dinon's gentle words banished all my self-loathing.

I have never, ever wanted you to suffer, he told me. *Not ever. You chose to suffer for those whom you love, even knowing the bliss I could offer you.* During his pause, a flame of euphoria danced up from my soul, warm and sweet, lit by Ba'al-Dinon as some generous reassurance, some reinforcement of his love. *You inspire me, Thecla.*

The urge to weep was upon me again—in addition to the shame and grief I felt to think of Ba'al-Dinon abandoned by me, I was so drained it seemed as though I were experiencing some strange chemical imbalance as a consequence of my body's adjustment from the glory of one state to the imperfection of the one to which it was better adapted. But before I could succumb to those tears tightening my throat, the great metal door slid open.

A pair of men, their conversation muffled by the masks that were part of their full-body suits, entered with a number of hoses, brushes, and other cleaning supplies evidently intended to decontaminate the testing chamber and ensure the integrity of the tests.

Wait, Dinon urged me, my muscles tensing in response to his words, to their presence, to the sense that this was an opportunity that could quickly go bad. My breath held, I braced myself, waiting, my ears tuned for their footsteps, their breaths. As I gripped the fabric of my dress, I remembered Dinon's hands gripping it in the same way—another arrow of pain shot through my heart.

I realized would do anything to see him again—to reach that place with him again, someday, when I was ready to stay.

You will, he swore to me. *Just keep going, Thecla… I promise I'll give you everything you hope for.*

The portable power washer they had wheeled in drilled along the surface of the testing device; its water splashed about, even dampening the edge of my dress. Their masks limited their vision to what was directly in front of them, and as one of the men stepped around the machine to strip any invisible contaminants from the floor, I was already on my feet. By the time he turned and saw me with a delayed, full-body start of fear, I had lunged at him and caught him in my grip. If he recognized me, it was not immediate, and he had far too much on his mind to put a name and title to my face. As I held him, his shriek of terror was that of a child.

As I tore the little power washer from his hand and—thinking of Eleison—pressed it to the fast-shutting lid of the man's eye in a warning I never intended to make good once his helmet had fallen at our feet, the partner with whom he'd entered dropped his cleaning supplies to stumble back a step or two.

Ask for Arthur.

"Send Arthur here," I snapped. "Don't let him tarry. I must speak to him at once. Tell him the Matrix of Gudrune requires his assistance."

As the man scrambled out, I looked at the fellow in my arms with a barely repressed frown. I witnessed, with shame, his ultra-sallow complexion and the trembling of his hand as he uselessly gripped my forearm, which I kept lodged beneath his chin. "I have a wife," he stammered, "and three kids—"

"And if I wanted to kill you, you'd be dead by now," I told him plainly, giving him a little ragdoll shake. "Now, wait a moment while I think."

It was immediately obvious that any speech with other beings caused my awareness of Dinon to fade, so I waited, listening to the man's heartbeat. I used its pace like a metronome to lull me into the depths of my soul, where I could focus on Ba'al-Dinon's words.

If I tell you something about Arthur that will help you, you must trust me; moreover, you must be willing to say it.

I wanted to ask him what on earth he could tell me about Arthur that could be of any value to me in this circumstance, but I dared not speak to Dinon in front of this strange man. It was already bad enough that I was going to have to out myself to even a handful of Horizon employees; I did not also need to become known as a dharmine whose soul was gifted with a particularly conscious and intense connection to someone extremely powerful.

Well...or a dharmine that was mad. But—I had been afraid of being at least a bit mad, or driven to madness, early on in my relationship with Ba'al-Dinon, when I was a terrestrial human. It was all so embarrassingly juvenile to me now, like the anxiety felt like an adolescent outpacing her friends into puberty. By this point in my life— most especially after what I had seen in that sweet Paradise with him—I suppose I really was mad, and therefore was not really too concerned with what others thought of me. I only wished to keep all this under wraps for my husband's sake, and to assume the appearance of normal functioning. Ba'al-Dinon very kindly spoke in response to my thought-impressions before I even had a chance to make them conscious—not requiring that I speak aloud and out myself.

I'll tell you at the right time for you to know, he said. *Don't worry. Just try to stay focused.*

With a shuddering breath, I dragged the fellow in my arms to shield myself from gunfire with the edge of the great testing device. There I waited, unspeaking, still, focused on preserving the sweet memories of that place whence I had come. For, one small doze and a bit of stress later, those memories were already slipping from my mind, fading as quickly as they had overwhelmed all my terrestrial experiences. I wished so badly to keep them vivid! Like brilliant butterflies kept under glass. It was some small consolation that I would someday perhaps be given the opportunity to see him in that place again, when the problem of suffering had been worked through meaningfully in the lives of myself and those I cherished. But there was only that one time that had been the first time, and I wanted to hold onto it.

Don't worry. The words were a warm purr in my heart no matter how they also served to frighten me. *We'll get to experience it all again someday, Thecla. Over, and over, and over again.*

As I swallowed down that vague sickness of fear, the testing chamber's metal doors slid open and armed guards surged into the room. I tensed, afraid for half a second that I was going to have to kill or maim this man after all. Thankfully, Arthur did indeed step in along with them, surrounded by a tight pack of the security detail who had wisely come along.

"There's no need for violence," Arthur called. "Put my colleague down, and we can talk."

"You're right, dear; there is indeed no need for violence. I'll release your colleague if your men lower their guns and you'll let me talk to you alone in your office."

With a scoff of incredulity that I would suggest such a thing, Arthur said, "Look, dharmine… we're trying to be amicable here, but—"

"You will address me by my name, whatever I am. And besides—why should the dharmine you were just with merit respect when I merit none? The Thecla who left you an hour ago is the same as me; merely a week removed."

Enormously intelligent man that he was, Arthur parsed this and then was taken aback by the network of implications. "I, uh…don't—excuse me?"

"You heard me," I told him. "I'm a dharmine, yes, but I have been a dharmine since before my husband's return to the spotlight following his assassination. The difference is that now I'm a dharmine *and* a blasted time traveler, apparently, and I need you to help me get to my husband before something happens."

You could have heard a mouse scurry on silent feet from one edge of the room to the other. "Do you realize how insane you sound?" His question was not accusatory so much as probing.

"I do, blast it, but there's nothing I can do about that now. You should understand, Arthur, as a visionary scientist. Sometimes one learns, comprehends, or even experiences something that just can't be communicated—it has to be demonstrated." It occurred to me that at any time, I could snag reality back open and emerge into Dinon's world again. This time, though, I would surely remain with him forever on that reverse side of reality's tapestry, and so I would have to find some other means of demonstration. I frowned, thinking of it all very deeply to determine how best to prove my true nature to him. The only solution, it seemed, was to predict the future.

"On Thursday, I shall be taking the train out to Rheton, but the train will never make it due to a hijacking by hunter insurgents from Valquist. My mate, Eleison, will regret his decision to leave me unaccompanied, and his failure to extract me will leave him blind. This will, in turn, leave Malin undefended during a key moment in a hunter assault, and his whereabouts will be unknown. If you do not listen to me now and help me get to Malin in advance of these events"—I went right for the throat, letting him hear the heaviness of every word as I assured him—"every penny of funding will dry up, and you'll be plagued across the continent by hunters who want to kill you. You'll never have another good night's sleep, and you, my quiet, unassuming scholar, will never have time to so much as read a book for all the petty under-the-table manual labor you'll be forced to stoop to just to stay alive. Now bring me to your office this blasted instant, damn you! If I were an animal, I would have already killed half the men in this room and slaked the hunger I even now resist."

Hunger: I was *hungry*. The realization was heartbreaking—a bitter reminder of what I had lost—and I gritted my teeth, snarling on, "I am your Matrix, and my husband and mate are in grave danger. You have been graced with the opportunity to assist us, and my husband and I will remember your help for all time. Don't miss your opportunity and wind up destroying your life along with ours."

I was braced to have to argue more; I was not at all prepared with ideas for how to give proofs of what I had said above and beyond the point I had already made.

But, no doubt by some generous influence of Dinon's, Arthur said after a long, thoughtful pause, "Stand down...do as Matrix Farrow says. I think I ought to talk to her myself."

37

It was not that simple, of course. I was tested over a period of four hours, subject to a battery of humiliating and frankly asinine assessments designed to gauge if I was who I claimed to be and capable of controlling myself around vulnerable targets. At one point, as I sat in the uncomfortably modern office that served as my impromptu testing chamber, they tossed a small white rabbit into the room with me and shut the door heavily. Annoyed by their behavior, my hunger, and the sluggishness of this exercise, I drummed my fingers upon my cheek and murmured to Dinon, "Would it not be better to burn this blasted place to the ground and let my husband find new partners when I reach him?"

Be patient, Dinon advised in a tone that was amused despite his stern counsel, *and trust me.*

I did indeed trust him, or was learning to better—all the time... but one could hardly help but annoy, especially when time felt so precious. The rabbit hopped around my feet, probably also hoping for a snack. I plucked it up to set it in my lap, tickling its long ears, grateful for something to do with my jittery hands.

"When will I see you again?"

The longing in my soul touched Dinon, who tempered his firm tone as he murmured, *Soon, beloved. I promise.*

"I want so badly to apologize to you. I just want to be held by you."

I know, Thecla. That's what I want, too. But you have nothing to apologize for.

"Then why do I feel like I do?"

He didn't answer. I remained there, stewing in silence, my finger rubbing back and forth between the rabbit's ears while the wiggles of its nose grew a bit more relaxed and its eyes began to slide closed. It had just flopped to one side upon my lap, evoking my first terrestrial smile since my return, when the door opened again. Looking reluctant but deeply intrigued, Arthur stepped into the room with a gun loosely held in his hand. I looked at him somewhat wryly, and he, abashed to see my gaze, cleared his throat and shut the door.

"Wouldn't let me come into the room to see you without this awful thing." He blushed like a schoolboy as he crossed the room to sit on the other side of the large white desk. "Just a precaution. You understand, I'm sure, Matrix."

"I'm not certain they do." I jerked my head to the side in indication of the men waiting for Arthur's return. "But yes, dear, I understand. And I think the safety is on, by the way."

"Oh, uh…" With a nervous laugh, the researcher studied the weapon, clicked the little switch, and, after a hesitant second or two of consideration, slid open a desk drawer and placed the pistol inside. "Let's forget it's even there, shall we?"

"I'm willing to overlook quite a lot in the name of rescuing my husband. I trust you have a way to control the tongues of the men who were here today?"

"Their lives are over if they speak of anything that occurs in this facility," Arthur told me amiably, adding after a beat, "from a legal perspective, of course."

"Of course." Finally beginning to see something of what Malin liked about this young man, I put the disrupted rabbit back upon the floor and dusted off my skirt. "I must congratulate you, Arthur, on your machine. In addition to being a source of clean energy, it would also seem to be some sort of portal. But I'm not sure it will continue to be the latter, based on what I've seen."

"What do you mean?" Leaning forward, his eyes alive with keen interest, the researcher asked, "How did you end up coming through our reactor? And how—just—*how?*"

I chuckled, rubbing my brow as I confessed, "You wouldn't understand if I tried to explain it. To truly understand and appreciate everything I've experienced, you'd have to live it yourself. You'd have to live my entire life."

"I could try to understand. It's sort of my job, after all."

Wiseass. "You seem a little too pleased with me at your mercy like this."

"Forgive me if I seem impudent. I'm just—excited. I want to know everything that's been happening. It's not every day that the Matrix of Gudrune is in two places at once, one of them our sealed testing chamber."

There was something in his tone that I didn't enjoy. Particularly after my strange pilgrimage through that other land and the deep way my soul had been opened by Dinon's love, the idea that any terrestrial being could dream of having power over another was laughable. No one in this place knew what power was. No one knew what mercy or compassion or contrition was. I became crushed by a sudden awareness that when all this was over, I would never live as I had before, with charity as a photo opportunity and poverty a shameful relic of my past. I would empty my pockets to give to the poor and make my husband do the same. I would give my time, my hands, and the unnaturally spry strength of my body. And I couldn't explain why! Why was it that Dinon's love for me suddenly made all this seem so important, more important than it ever had before, from a deep and sincere place in my heart?

You mean you don't remember yet?

Dinon's mirth sent another chill down my spine as I turned my attention back to Arthur, who was trying to get my attention by repeating my name. He wanted to draw me out of my thoughts.

"Forgive me," I said, seeing the tilt of his head that indicated his intrigue. Leaning back in my seat with my hands folded before me, I explained, "I have been through quite a journey over the future week."

"What happened?"

He practically begged to know, desperate now, like one friend pleading for gossip from another. I let my thumbs tap together a few times as I considered Arthur in his seat.

"Are you a religious man, Arthur?"

The researcher made a noise that sounded like a laugh—a sound of surprise that trailed off as he opened his hands. "I'm open to having my mind changed," he said, smiling weakly and fleetingly.

"I always used to believe in God in the sense of…you know, the 'Cosmos', the All-Mind, some sort of ambiguous and impersonal abstraction. Now… I don't know." I raised one of my thumbs to my forehead, sliding it back and forth over the center of my brow as I studied an indistinct point on Arthur's desk. "You know what that old religion says, the one my mother followed and that my father taught me some old prayers for...the Universals, the Universal Church? It was called something different in the old English, of course, but that's what it means. I can't think of the term just now, I'm so scattered. Anyway...they used to say, still do, I guess, 'God is Love.'"

With another little sniff and a scratch along the edge of my nose, I suggested, "One doesn't really think about the implications of that axiom, does one?"

"The implications?"

A little disgusted that I was having to explain myself to him to any degree, I dismissed the subject with a wave of that same fidgeting hand. "Never mind, ignore me. I'm disoriented. The long and short of it is my Riftborn abilities permitted me to exit this reality and enter the one we think of as being on the other side of the Rift...a version of that reality, anyway."

Arthur propped his elbows on the desk, his hands folded intently before his mouth, his sharp eyes fixed upon me through the barrier of his glasses. I told him, "I was there for a while. Things happened to me. I expect I'll never really be the same, but is anyone ever really the same?"

Arthur realized it wasn't a hypothetical when I didn't go on. After a small delay, he responded, "I guess not."

"So, if I'm not really the same after being here a week, or I'm not really the same after being there a week, what's the difference? Whether or not the not-really-the-sameness is a good quality, perhaps. And I think this degree of change will be for the better in the long-term...but I have things to process, and right now, I'm really rather more focused on how we can get me quickly toward Rheton to warn my husband and my mate."

"We can charter a carriage relay for you," he said, animating at last and removing the pen from his breast pocket along with a rumpled, curled, slightly dirty notebook from his trousers. "It will be about as fast as the train when all is said and done…faster if what you're saying is true."

"It is." My eyes narrowed, and I admonished him coldly, "I don't care for your continued skepticism."

"You'll have to forgive me, Matrix. It's a lot to take in. Just finding out that you and, if you're telling the truth, Malin, have been dharmines for some time is—something to process."

"Well, forgive me for not being thrilled to divulge this information, or to have to persuade you of it."

But Arthur raised a hand, palm toward me, as he said, "It's not that. It's only—"

He bit his lip, drumming his pen in the L-shaped curve of his thumb and index finger of his opposite hand. "I suppose all this would be easier to believe if I hadn't just seen you, Matrix, and if you weren't in two places at once. While it's obvious to me that you're in fine control of your faculties"—he glanced sidelong at the rabbit, who had found the fronds of some potted plant to placidly nibble—"the problem with dharmines is they're known as inveterate liars. I don't want to be the man who ships a dharmine to Malin Farrow and gets him killed in the middle of the war effort if you should happen to be lying about him already being a dharmine."

Doing my best to swallow down my anger, I raised my hand to my face to now entirely cover my eyes. As my thumb and middle fingers massaged into the temples of my forehead, Dinon said, *Go on and tell him this.*

I absorbed what Dinon said. Then, quite shocked, I laughed. Lowering my hand, regarding Arthur newly—seeing certain aspects of him now that I hadn't noticed until that moment—I enthused, "Why, Arthur, I invited you to court Kalypso, but perhaps it's Aleister I should be pointing you toward."

Arthur's entire face blistered bright red. "E-excuse me?"

"Tosh, I don't know why you're so embarrassed about that. Aleister is a perfectly attractive man. You're talking to a woman who watches her significant others sodomize one another on a fairly regular basis. One can hardly help one's heart or one's favorite vessel of love. It's only—"

Lowering my voice, I leaned forward and chided him, "You can do so much better than that hateful Ambassador Platt."

His eyes, already wide, grew wider still, and his prior embarrassment paled to shock as he leaned back. "How—how can you—"

I tapped the side of my temple. "My Lord told me, but that's not what matters. What matters is if you're being asked to hide your relationship to protect someone's image, then you're not in a relationship, darling. You're at best a paramour. At worst, you're a sex toy."

Poor Arthur! He looked as if I'd backhanded him. As his eyes turned a curious red, he slid his hand under his glasses and rubbed them, clearing his throat. "I—uh—that is—you're right, of course—about that sort of relationship. I mean, I can't—"

I looked at him sympathetically. "I have never liked that man, and neither has my husband. Parvati's lapdog—I'm surprised he would have the temerity to exploit you, given Valquist's long opposition to your Rift energy project."

"Why do you think he doesn't want to be seen with me?"

His eyes still covered, Arthur clenched his teeth. I tutted, crossing over to his side of the desk with my arms extended; far from wincing away, Arthur stood to receive my hug.

And it was in this embrace that I had an inspiration—that inspiration, I suspected, being the real reason Dinon had inspired this conversational course.

Smiling, I drew him back to look into Arthur's eyes. "Now, dear, I know I've touched a nerve, but I'm afraid I must criticize you. You've missed the obvious point; and I missed it, too, because I'm drained from my trip. If I had only just become a dharmine, wouldn't I be taller now than I was when I toured the facility with you this afternoon? Instead, I must be shorter, because I was wearing heels then. Right now, I'm barefoot."

Arthur looked at me in amazement and then several rapid times up and down, checking my height before saying, "I—I guess that's right. Yes, that would be true."

As his posture truly eased for the first time since my return, he even smiled, and I let my smile widen in encouragement. His eyes lighting up, Arthur confirmed, "It really is you, Matrix! Through my generator—er, uh, the one I designed, anyway. I only mean— you *time* traveled!"

"As I've been telling you," I replied.

Suddenly snapping into action, Arthur realized in fullness that he was before the matrix of his territory. He straightened himself out and moved into business. Snatching up the notebook where he'd jotted down thoughts, he said with a brisk bow at the waist, "I'll have my assistant charter your carriages right away. Can I get you something to drink?"

"Absolutely. I'm famished. Not rabbit."

"Right away. Oh, and, er, uh—Matrix, incidentally—"

He'd nearly made it to the door but now stopped, turning to smooth a hand down his shirt. I thought he was going to request discretion about the details of his personal life, but Arthur instead surprised me by clarifying, "I do, uh, quite like Kalypso, actually. And Aleister. So…whoever you think would be best for me."

"Aren't you cute…perhaps they can trade you on alternating weekends."

While Arthur sputtered out a laugh, clearly trying to work out if I was joking, (and I think you know the answer to that by now, reader), he fell back a step, then turned on his heel and briskly exited to do my bidding.

And just like that, I felt more like myself than I had since the start of that blasted war—since Parvati's murder.

Ignatius had been right… it was the death of all that pride.

Speaking of Ignatius, the temptation to return by train and somehow attempt to intercede in his death was deep in me. But because I had seen his dead body with my own two eyes, and my time with Dinon reinforced the sense of eternity as a singular object whose shape was set but experienced piecemeal by the collaboration of its major players with its greater form—as the sunrise collaborates with the same mountain range, day upon day, creating it from darkness—I did not think it was possible that I might save him in this life. Moreover, by taking the train, I was risking paradoxes. I would also be battling the urge to spirit my son away from danger, and to provide other interferences that simply could not have been possible or would have had consequences I feared to ponder. I sensed that, should I decide to try, it was certainly within my free will to do so. But I also felt that by proceeding along with Arthur's suggestion, I was operating within some plan of Dinon's. Some advanced understanding through which I could trust him to navigate for me because I knew now that all he really wanted was to welcome me back home just as soon as I was ready.

And so, as I settled in for a long, tedious, and tense journey across the continent, switching from one carriage to another as they ran out of power and wanted for charging or, once or twice, fresh organic horses, I was comforted by a strange certainty that everything would find its way so long as I followed the path Dinon set before me. It was the same way I had felt when Malin was missing in action. The same way, oddly, I felt when I ruminated on Eleison—though I would at once chastise myself for such baseless optimism and begin to worry about how such a thing would be possible when I would have to let him blind himself by throwing himself into the fray for my sake. Then I was forced to ask if all my optimism wasn't baseless, and I would begin a spiral of incomprehensible despair that would continue for hours.

Compounding this despair was the ineptitude evident at several points in the relay, which was not as smooth as Arthur had envisioned. Several times, errors in communication or more rapid battery drainage than anticipated left me feeling as though I was falling further and further behind. One particular delay of over six hours pushed me to the brink of a nervous breakdown. I trembled, weak and increasingly tempted to march into the hotel room next door and drain the blood of whoever lay obliviously within. Just as this torture seemed to peak, I jumped at a knock on the door. It was an emergency replacement for a driver who had been delayed owing to his wife's labor, arriving just in time to prevent a homicide.

Just trust me, Dinon repeated encouragingly, patiently, as I perceived yet another example of his interference.

What choice did I have? I was a captive to circumstances: unable to reveal my presence, and desperate to reach my husband's side. I accepted that I couldn't save Ignatius's life, or Charlotte's trauma, or Eleison's eyes—but with Malin's state being one of complete ambiguity to me at the time of my departure, it seemed that I still had the power to rescue him. Like a waveform not yet collapsed by observation, his future was in a superposition whose final identity depended on me. Restless, my mind perpetually returned to my husband and on getting to him; and, owing to this goal, the trip seemed very long.

Including the delay in starting the journey that was a consequence of my detainment at the research center and the time and effort required to organize my transportation, it took me an exhausting six days from the point when I re-entered reality to at last approach Rheton. With the carriages averaging about 30 miles an hour between the electric models and the slower organic ones, I spent days in agony, calculating and recalculating how long it would be until this event, and then that event. As, miles away, the train was being hijacked, I began counting down to the next milestone, our arrival at Valquist; and when that was once more in the past, my next marker was Eleison's arrival at the palace, which would be around the same time I became aware of the bombing of the Rheton encampment.

As long as I arrived by night, I might still intercede. Held hostage to the pace of the horses, I fidgeted and shifted about, hanging halfway out of the carriage, my arms folded on the edge of the window as I watched for signs of my long journey's end. Twice, as I rode through areas closer to contested territory, I was pulled over for questioning and furnished falsified papers that Arthur's people had been able to provide with a speed and efficiency that was, in retrospect, questionable. But, at the time, I was too relieved to worry about it. Each time, the papers were passed over to the soldiers, who read only that I was a freelance researcher attempting to carry out ecological studies on the impact of the Rift in such-and-such an area before passing my paperwork back with looks of hostile disinterest. Each time, a wave of euphoria washed over me to have the encounter over with. I swung back and forth between desolation and consolation with such severity that, by the time I finally saw a road sign pointing the way to Rheton, I was horrified to realize I had hardly thought of Ba'al-Dinon or the memories of our special paradise.

It never helps to worry, he advised, and I felt his words in my heart. *If you keep worrying about everything, it will interfere with the process.*

"That's very easy for you to say," I commented, drawing a low chuckle of true amusement from him.

It certainly is, my love. Yes, it is.

I felt childish, and not just because of my famished state. I wanted to stamp my foot and cross my arms and protest that it wasn't fair—that none of it was fair. It was all horribly unjust, from the very beginning. Now that I knew how sweet it was to be with Dinon, it seemed ridiculous that suffering even had to exist. And then I remembered—well, I really had rather brought this on myself, in a way. I had begged, in fact, for this to be brought into existence so that it could be ended. And, I realized, at least for my family, I could be the one to end it.

My spirit soared at long last as my carriage was detained at a well-fortified checkpoint about eight hours outside of Rheton. Though I was prepared to furnish the false papers as many times as it took me to get into the proverbial doorway of the conversation, that much proved unnecessary. My husband knew whom to assign to the areas around Rheton, and so it was that the soldier guarding the checkpoint recognized me at a glance—a glance that he nevertheless took in twice.

"Matrix," he said through a gasp, genuflecting down into the mud in a quick and highly respectable gesture. "What are you doing here? We heard—"

"I must be taken to my husband immediately. It's not wise—" I extended a rapid hand to bid him to leave his radio on his belt, for his arm was lunging toward it. "Please, don't. I know there are informational leaks. At the very least, the insurgents are adept at collecting information. If radioed communication gives anything away, or a bad actor hears it—I must see my husband," I finally emphasized, looking at the fellow sternly. "We mustn't delay."

"Yes, Matrix," the young man said hurriedly, adding, "wait here," as he turned to sprint off and alert some of his cohort. After two others had satisfied themselves at a glance that I was myself, having no time travel paradox to resolve—for they simply accepting the idea that I had escaped—an armed escort was arranged, and I was moved in a small convoy through the contested area and into an encampment: a large prison complex repurposed as a fortified base. It possessed a balance of accessibility for the guards who originally ran it—distant from civilized society, yet proximate to the highway to prevent the necessity of on-site living. With nothing around but a deadly forest of invasive Rift species and the occasional swamp until one at last hit either Rheton or Valquist, the prison was an ideal spot for a military camp—but as difficult to retreat from as it was to take. I laughed at myself, for it showed how unfamiliar I was with the mindset and life of a soldier: after all I'd been through, my first instinct was still always escape.

But that was an animal's reaction. Dinon had told me he wished to domesticate me, to tame my love. I felt compelled to consent, to give myself to this transformation in absolute trust.

And how my trust was rewarded!

The complex had large outdoor areas one needed to pass through before reaching the fortified buildings of the prison: several separate structures of sturdy, brutalist architecture, with plentiful lookout towers where men with sniper rifles and binoculars kept watch, smoking and pacing, occasionally reporting something on their radios. All these spaces were so large that, upon entering the path ringing this grim central campus, I was astonished to find I was transferred into a jeep and driven another slow four minutes through a few internal checkpoints. The nearer I got to my husband, the slower and more miserable this blasted journey seemed. There could be no relief at this rate, no catharsis—only a contemptible Zeno's arrow, the space between us infinitely halving, never closing—

Until, finally, at an administrative building on the far side of the complex's innermost wall, we stopped.

The soldier driving me helped me down from the truck with a gesture.

"His office is in there," said the fellow, nodding through the descending twilight as this long final day of travel sank down toward cathartic night. "They come and go so much he doesn't lock the door, but you might need to wait if they're out."

Somehow, I knew he wouldn't be—I knew exactly how I would find him, and my soul leapt high in my chest. Sucking in a breath to steady my nerves, I did not let myself dash forward until the soldier pretended not to watch. Only then did I let my steps hasten, rushing up the cement stairs and through the door that, normally controlled by the RMS panel, was propped open. I was so excited to see Malin that I didn't even think twice about the soldier's promising choice of words, did not stop to think on the significations of "they." I only knew I could save my husband—could conclusively avert the fate I most feared, which was all that was on my mind as I rushed through the anteroom and into the back office. One of several but which, behind frosted glass, was somehow where I knew I would find him. I burst in, stumbling forward, my entire being leaping for joy to see even the back of his blonde head, turning from his contemplation of the fire—

And the show was stolen by Eleison, who could not possibly have been there, but who nonetheless rose from his seat with my name a happy cry on his lips.

38

"Thecla, Thecla—what are you doing here?"

The sound of my name on Eleison's lips launched Malin to his feet: but even for his dharmine reflexes, my mate beat him to me, gripping me as though to assure himself of my corporeality before kissing me, pressing me to his heart, looking at me with an incredulous laugh. Eleison only released my face from his great hands when Malin practically pushed him aside, elbowing into him to take me in his arms, investigate me but for a second, and kiss me with such force I nearly lost my balance.

"My wife," he cried, looking at me with insane delight and golden pride, "my brilliant wife! Look, Eleison, she's here with us again." But his joy was tempered as, with a realization that deeply shaded his eyes, Malin glanced behind me. "The boy— "

"Still at the palace, but I— I— "

I could not attend to Malin's fear or disappointment when my own rising confusion was beginning to tip over into an awesome and insane understanding—an understanding that gave me, at last, some explanation for my own hope. That unconscious hope nagged so insistently that I had no reason to fear for Telemachus, or for Glenn, or even for myself.

"You shouldn't be here," I stammered, looking at Eleison, my brow furrowing as I touched his face. "I left you both in the palace. Telemachus was hiding, and you were—blinded—but wouldn't you have already left? Weren't you already in Valquist and about to be brought in by the time I saw Malin by the fire? Weren't you—"

Wasn't he now in the wrong place, somehow?

Panic left my palms slick with sweat as I considered the idea that something had gone catastrophically wrong with my being here. Had Ba'al-Dinon really tricked me? Was his very goal to destroy this reality, somehow, or to punish me? I trembled, paling even further as his lovelorn remonstration filled my heart.

How your mistrust wounds me, Thecla! Oh, Thecla—can't you see what I've done for you?

I was beginning to, but I could not understand. There was no way to understand it and I swayed dizzily at the thought, catching hold of Eleison's arm to keep myself upright as both men cried out. Malin wiped his thumb above my upper lip.

"Thecla," he said, "your nose is bleeding!"

A nosebleed was the very least of my worries, but with epiphany snapping at the heels of my every thought, I managed only to say, "I think maybe I'd better sit down."

As we sat together, Malin stroking my trembling left hand while Eleison kissed and squeezed and tenderly massaged the right, I tried to put myself together but could hardly sort out any thoughts. After I had gleaned that Eleison had chartered a helicopter in response to the train hijacking and hastened to convene with Malin in person, I detailed my own contribution. The things I said emerged in a half-conjoined way, at times associative rather than linear and stemming mostly from what I felt as a vital need to explain the absence of our son. This required much context; which, in turn, required trying to tell the men where I had been after my escape from my father—which involved having to explain that Glenn and Rosina were accounted for and lost. And there was, of course, the small matter of Arthur knowing we were dharmine, which received, to my relief, less of a reaction than I had worried it might; and somehow, in all of this, I managed to explain without even having the opportunity to touch on the more surreal and metaphysical experiences of my time with Dinon in that other world. I could only do my best to explain the reversal of causality and to stammer out while wringing their hands with the nervous pressure of my own, "I—I fear I must have caused some 'paradox', or some such, for I simply wasn't expecting you to be here, Eleison!"

"I can go if you want," he offered with a wry grin that turned into a bit of a fashion model pout when I burst into tears. "Oh, honey—"

"I'm sorry," I sobbed, letting him draw me apologetically to his breast while Malin's hand shifted from my arm to my side. "It's just been such a long trip, and I've been so uncertain, and I haven't eaten in days, and—I'm just so glad you're alive. I'm so glad you're here, and that you're not blind."

"Me, too," said Eleison, his hand rubbing over my back and up along the back of my hair.

"You should have told me sooner that you haven't eaten, angel," Malin told me, reaching past me to slip a familiar hand into Eleison's trouser pocket. "Let's get your knife for a moment, old boy...not that knife," he said with a wink as Eleison inhaled sharply and I laughed through my tears. "The other—aha."

Having drawn free Eleison's familiar switchblade—for he saw I was simply too emotionally overwrought to lend myself straightaway to the sexual reunion that would inevitably follow the sinking of my fangs into his flesh—Malin slit his wrist open along the blue vein just beneath the sleeve of his drab jacket. Even before I saw the blood, I smelled it, and my soul swelled with joy, adoration, and even greater peace in that moment than had been instilled in me by Eleison's body. Accepting Malin's hand and keeping his wrist plastered to my mouth, I inhaled deeply, then took a gasping swallow and felt instantly at greater ease than I had in days—no! In months.

How necessary was my husband's blood to me! There was no substitute that could be had. Eleison's blood was second best by far, and it put the animal of my heart at ease while also healing superficial maladies and filling me with joy...but the nourishment that imbued my body and soul upon imbibing Malin's blood was second to none. A new vitality flowed into me; my every limb grew strong, and my consciousness so heightened that I realized the slipping down into the depths to which his absence brought me had truly been an insidious descent. I had lost all ability to realize how alienated I had become from the person I usually was; and now that the three of us were together again, I felt within me life.

And that quality of the mind that makes life so rich and meaningful—memory—sprang alive with new urgency. My famished mind worked better than it had even before I left this world for the one through the Rift, and I at last remembered to say, "The airstrike!"

Malin's expression changed quicker than Eleison's did, though both were taken aback as my husband asked sharply, "What airstrike?"

"We have to leave as soon as possible. When Eleison arrives there, around the same time, there's a bombing here. And I just saw you by the fire, so it can't be more than a half hour away. That was why I came here—to save you, and to get your help collecting Telemachus and Glenn and Rosina. And Eleison, but—"

Sucking in a sharp breath, I squeezed him closely again, whispering, "I'm so relieved you're here."

"I'll be right back," Malin said, all business, not hesitating or doubting me for even half a second. At the time, I was in such a heightened state that I couldn't appreciate what this said about Malin's faith in me and my judgments. It only serves to emphasize how weak and imperfect my own faith has always been, especially in Dinon!

Eleison glanced after him with concern, his mouth lined before he turned to study me. "Guess we're in for a long night, huh…and a rough morning, too."

"The last rough morning we'll have for a long time, if I have my way." Stepping back into the room with a sharp beep of the RMS panel into which he had just lobbed some orders, Malin said to Eleison, "We're evacuating. I'm commanding all troops to leave the encampment; we'll let them have it."

Relief flooded my mind. Perhaps I hadn't ruined everything. This was surely what had happened before, at the same time as I was living out my stay in Valquist—but then why was Eleison here and safe? I struggled to make sense of it; my mind was on fire as I rotated everything I had done and every decision I had made, trying to find an explanation. How could such a thing be possible?

It couldn't be...not unless Eleison, also, was in two places at once. Yet how would he enter the Rift? Was it possible for him? He wasn't Riftborn.

"Thecla—"

Stirred from my thoughts, I glanced up at Malin, who could see I was clearly still in a state of heavy psychic disturbance. Kneeling before me, my husband placed his hands on my arms and looked into my eyes.

"I know the last thing you want to do after all that city has put you through is to visit Valquist again—but—"

"I must go back, especially if you're going there. I want to help save our family."

Looking as driven as I felt, his expression deadly serious, Malin nodded. "While we let them think we're buried under rubble and timber, we're going to be advancing toward Valquist. We'll take it the old-fashioned way: on foot and cavalry. I'll need your help navigating the palace and finding our son, since it's fresher in your mind."

I nodded, agreeing without delay. "Absolutely—yes, let me go with you."

"Very well. Eleison—"

"Don't let him inside the palace," I insisted, interrupting my husband to instead ask my mate, "please, darling, don't set foot in there. Go find Glenn and Rosina for me. Where they are, I know not, but they're either hidden somewhere on the palace grounds or on the way to Glenn's old home."

"I'll find them," Eleison swore to me, grasping my hand. "And I'll be safe—don't worry, Thecla."

It was impossible to avoid worrying, especially when, not understanding how he came to be there, it seemed that any second he might disappear in a puff of smoke—as if reality itself might destabilize and whisk him away from me and into mortal danger once more. My darling! The thought of him being blinded again had kept me from resting during my eastward travel. Now that my wound-up nervous system had collapsed into relief, everything seemed so precarious.

"Would you come with me a moment, Eleison, darling?" Malin's question was polite, but it was not a request; nodding slightly, Eleison followed him from the room, both men glancing at me as they left me alone on the couch in Malin's office.

Exhausted and dizzy, I doubled over, my forehead falling toward my knees. I didn't know how I was going to make it through this. But, as I had all along, I felt that strange confidence that I would manage, whatever the means. That everything would work out just fine, and I would taste peace in this life and the next: that other life Ba'al-Dinon kept for me.

This feeling, however, was cold comfort. For my rational mind insisted that while I lived and moved through the world, I could at any moment deviate by purpose or mistake from the path Ba'al-Dinon had arranged. I could destroy everything— and it had always been so. I had spent my life like an oblivious tightrope walker, making her clueless way suspended high above the ground. Now that I'd looked down, I feared losing my balance as I never had before. I had been afraid and had feared for myself many times, but there was a new pressure now that someone loved me as my Lord Dinon loved me. The looming threat of disappointing him nauseated me, though by his very nature, that was arguably impossible. Still, I wished to excel for him. To be fully and absolutely intimate with him to the very edges of comprehensibility, and even beyond.

Something seemed to throb in my soul as I thought this, and at once, my Love's presence came strongly upon me. I felt him operating within me, filling my entire being with an emotion that washed away everything but him. The urgency of the situation, the uncertainty of it all, the pressure of my participation in the unfolding of the fate Dinon desired for me—nothing mattered while he was there, his love surging into me like a waterfall into the mouth of some sacred grotto.

He said much more than he seemed! Even in that urging, there was more—I felt it, turning his words over and wondering at the limits of Ba'al-Dinon's intercession in the terrestrial realm. When his very thought was an act of creation in that other place, and he seemed just as capable of producing from thin air all manner of solutions to my problems great or small could he not perform some trick? Produce some conceit? Could Ba'al-Dinon find some way to sway the battle into which my husband and his men were throwing themselves—and, also, dragging me?

How curious! I was weary, but I was not afraid of any terrestrial thing, for I knew I would be prepared to face it that night. I had seen and been loved by a being of such incomprehensible power that, for all my earthly wealth and recognition, I was reduced to less than a peasant girl before him. I was less than an ant, crawling on the robe of a king.

Therefore, appealing to him as to a king, I slipped from the couch and bowed forward, my face and hands pressing to the floor, every ounce of my soul reaching out to my most powerful lover. I emptied myself of all other intentions and needs, for I knew all things would work as Dinon had intended them. My head swimming, I focused instead on my love for Malin, for Eleison, for Glenn and Rosina and Telemachus, and for Ba'al-Dinon—

even my love for my father. The truth was that I longed for no casualties at all, none—even among the hunters, I had lost my taste for vengeance and the wreaking of judgment, and my heart longed only for mercy. But how could it be obtained? A truly deathless siege was impossible, I knew, and I was not interested in wasting my breath asking for impossibilities.

But perhaps there might be something capable of limiting the violence between the men...while also turning things in my husband's favor.

"Bridegroom," I whispered, kissing the floor and so intensely able to taste the leather of Dinon's shoe that I squeezed my eyes shut lest I behold him before it was his desire that I do so. "Oh, my King, Lord of my heart! Your power is so great that all beings look in awe upon it—the Rift itself opens at your behest, and all the beasts within bow to the one who thought them into existence."

The prayer came from within me, from a deep and primordial place, a phenomenon I had never experienced in petitioning the divine. I turned my face to nuzzle my cheek along the floor, my eyes still closed. "If it be your will, the Rift might open—if you but said so, that other world would kiss our own, sparing lives by turning bloody attentions away from men and toward the beasts you made for them. Indeed, for me! If it is your mind, let it be your will that you should send them to me! Let them cover the face of the Earth, O my Soul...let Valquist flood with beasts this night, if it be your will!"

"I just remembered our honeymoon," Malin said by way of announcement, revealing he had watched me for who knew how long. While, blushing, I sprang up out of prayer without formal closure and with such suddenness that Dinon's presence seemed to vanish from my mind, my husband crossed to fold his arms around me. His head ducked, his mouth swooping down on mine, and I was engulfed in the blaze of his outrageous love. I whimpered pathetically in my need for him. "Darling," I whispered, "I was so frightened, not knowing your whereabouts."

"I can't imagine how afraid you were…you can't imagine how I've felt since all that business with the train. And now, here you are…oh, my darling…here you are, and changed."

Drawing back to gaze with fascination into my eyes, Malin murmured intensely, "What did you experience? I've never seen you like this—how you tremble!"

Clinging closely to my husband, my face pressing into his neck as I soothed myself with his warmth, I nodded and agreed, "It has changed me, yes—but I have to press on. I can't let Telemachus stay there, I—"

But was he my Telemachus? My God, what had I done!

Don't worry, don't worry. I say to you, don't worry. Sh, my Thecla, don't worry. He is your Telemachus. You'll see—I promise.

And I believed him, though I dared not say why.

Certain things are so difficult to accept; still, others are so difficult to articulate. My relationship with Ba'al-Dinon—or, perhaps I should instead suggest, the relationship between my soul and the Being who chooses to love me in a form attached to the name Ba'al-Dinon—is one of those things.

And, unfortunately for me, war is the other…so, as I did when struggling in vain to describe my time spent in the wilderness in the form of a doe, I believe it would be better if I passed my pen to my husband. Malin knows best how to write these things, and anyway, that time was so troubled I can barely recollect it.

All I thought of was my family, anyway.

My troops were already encamped along the Eastern front, denying the hunters an easy escape off toward the ocean—as if that could save them. If they gained the wisdom to evacuate Valquist, they would be reduced to guerrilla tactics in the forests. Then it would be a long game of rooting them out and putting them down.

That is, putting them on trial, of course.

I've missed you, reader. Did you miss me? I know, it must be heartbreaking. I've read Thecla's manuscript, and I must say, it's a pity how rarely I'm in this volume. Even this section will, you'll perhaps be disappointed to know, center mostly around my poor Thecla…but I would defy you to blame me, especially when you consider how many times she's saved my life.

Now, where was I? Ah, yes, the hunters. The truth was that, if and when they were so fractured as to be reduced to sabotage, terrorism, and various other desperate guerrilla tactics, there would always be a few stragglers who would sneak off to raise the new generation of extremists. But, between you and me, I've never particularly minded the idea of having a good old-fashioned stock villain archetype lying around for my usage. To be clear, I would rather they didn't exist, and my goal is always to cultivate a peaceful, harmoniously functioning society. However, in the same way that the eradication of a disease causes later generations to starkly underestimate the evils of that disease, I have personally observed that somewhat, shall we say, undesirable forms of thought—particularly those in opposition to the interests of the State—tend to crop up when citizenry spends too long without a national trauma. It is a pity, but it is also the way of the human mind. It can't be helped any more than my poor wife could help her response to whatever had happened to her there, in that strange other place.

Obviously by the time of this writing, having heard more from her lips and read her manuscript, (and even been given a secret or two from Ba'al-Dinon), I know far more of the strange circumstances into which she had been thrust. At the time, however, I knew hardly anything. Even after having had nearly a week to rest on her journey to me, she was still so high-strung that she could barely articulate what she had experienced. Now that I know some of her opinions about it, I can certainly see why. There are times when a moment of beauty is absolute agony to the soul because it knows the pain is soon to come again. Now that Thecla was thrust back into her life and all this pain, she was experiencing deep turmoil.

Unfortunately, I did not have much occasion to tend to her emotional needs, but I'm not so sure she wanted me to. Almost as afraid to see Eleison as she was soothed by him, looking at everyone—me included—with a kind of animal suspicion, Thecla nonetheless refused my invitation when, riding with her through the dark on the back of a horse that kept fair pace with Eleison's despite the extra load, I suggested that I might do my best to find the boy myself so she could stay back from the battle. I could see the constant workings of her mind, and I suspected none of them were as pretty or as peaceful as she was.

"No," she insisted. "I won't stay behind. I left him there. I didn't mean to, but I did, and now I must return to him as quickly as I can."

There was no point in arguing. In my own selfish heart, I wanted her to come—not just to help me find the boy but because I never wished to let her out of my sight again after the euphoric relief of seeing her in the wake of her kidnapping. Still, I felt an acute pity for her. I bowed my head to kiss the bare side of her neck, where her hair had fallen back to leave her tender throat to me. She shivered in my arms, bracing herself back against my body, tears pricking her eyes as she whispered, "Oh, darling, I love you. I feel we've been separated for eternity."

One of the aspects of this battle that makes it hard to describe or explain is that it was, strictly speaking, a counteroffensive utilizing spontaneous judgments and guerilla tactics necessitated by the nature of the landscape directly around Valquist to the south and west—thick forests. Furthermore, this was never intended to be a textbook siege. I had been planning one, and we had been discussing the idea of ramping up to that over the next fortnight, once a few more locations were secured around the front. But this was very different. My son was in there, meaning we no longer had the luxury of time. Glenn and dear Rosina were important, of course, but I am sure you understand why I trusted the hunter to take care of his daughter and could not trust my juvenile dharmine, raised under the vineyards of one of my estates, to handle himself sensibly when left alone in the headquarters of the enemy. It wasn't that I didn't think he could hold his own in a fight with most humans—far from it. I worried that, as I probably would have in his position, he would recognize that fact and get it in his head that he was going to save the day by, oh, 'taking down' Thecla's father or otherwise attempting to hamstring the enemy from within their central base of operations. Therefore, I needed to reach him soon. And, of course, his presence had other complications relating to safety and logistics. I had not been above the idea of blowing up even the historic Valquist Palace if it meant winning the war, but Telemachus made extensive bombing a non-starter.

We would have to apply our explosives elsewhere.

By two-thirty in the morning, my troops had made hostile contact with the checkpoint nineteen miles outside Valquist, which was cleared by the time Thecla, Eleison, and I rode through about forty minutes later. I kept up with the unfolding action on my radio and was well aware when the western wall was breached by a thunderous explosion—even if I hadn't heard it on the comm line, the sound, smell, and sight would have alerted me. Three strategic points were struck by rockets in the early morning hours, throwing Valquist into chaos. We scrambled to cover the breaches, and about nine minutes later, the first wave of my troops began picking off hunters from within the trees. This firefight was still ongoing by the time we arrived at a watchtower that had been cleared of hostiles to provide a base of operations. I was pleased with proceedings at first, but there was frustration in Thecla's face as she paced and watched the bloodbath unfold below.

"We'll have to wait," I told her. "We need a break in the fire— if we try to waltz in now, my love, we'll be easy targets."

"I know, but—"

"Just trust me," I said, touching her forearm.

How strangely she looked at me! With that sudden terror, as if seeing some secret side of me, she pressed herself into my arms and leaned on me for support as I surveyed the battle through binoculars. I wished I knew what to say, but I was grateful to hold her as the firefight grew more intense—especially when the tide began to turn and it seemed we might be forced to retreat.

This skirmish was taking longer than expected. The problem was that, even with the breach, the Hunters still had substantial cover and the high ground. They mounted a strong defense and I began to feel tense as the battle dragged on—especially when they started firing rockets. A risky move, as it could have easily started a forest fire on the edge of their encampment, but it worked. To my frustration, they succeeded in pushing at least one legion of our troops back, regaining control of the perimeter for a section of about a mile.

We had been there for eight hours by this point, and I was agitated. I took this news poorly, I confess, and the radio that delivered it to me may have wound up crushed in my hand. As someone hurried to fetch me a second one, however, and I paced in barely controlled anger that Eleison pretended not to see, Thecla's face underwent a series of strange expressions. Though at first, she looked as grieved as I, her eyes darting askance, her look soon became one of intense focus, as if she listened to something—or someone. Every once in a while, her lips would move slightly, and her eyes would dart here and there as if she were conversing with someone who required deep thought. Then, abruptly, her voice bloomed in an audible whisper: a hot, happy little "Yes, yes—" that eventually erupted in a cry as she sprang to her feet from the platform where she had sunk in our waiting.

"Yes, I feel it—! Eleison—"

He glanced over from the rail where he'd leaned to smoke a cigarette as I worked off my temper, his expression a little amused but mostly concerned given the context of the battles raging near us. Then he, too, changed, looking excited—looking at me as if he knew a secret that filled him with sheer delight.

"She's right, Malin. Can't you feel it, too?" Throwing down his cigarette, Eleison crushed it beneath his boot and looked me square in the eye, cooling my rage with only slight delay. "The Rift."

Inhaling rather sharply, I looked between them, then did my best to concentrate through my anger. Yes—why, they were right. I had been so caught up in the losses we were facing throughout this damned battle that I hadn't felt the gathering pressure of the atmosphere altering around me. Even my temper itself may have been a symptom of the oncoming storm. I had, in the past thirteen or so years of existence as a dharmine, borne witness to the rhythmic patterns of influence the metaphysical weather phenomenon had on myself and other Rift creatures. For a season or two while living in our little subterranean labyrinth, I enchanted a borro for our pet, thinking fondly of a future time when I would be reunited with Eleison. And though it was not long before, abashed to see how its own imprisoned state reflected my own, I let it have its wild mind back and roam free again, I witnessed how it would become restless before the onset of a storm—and how these turns of its mood ran parallel to mine. Even so, it was amusing to note that no matter how many times I was subject to this process, I was almost always surprised to realize it was due to some external factor. Perhaps it was the nature of my body. Not being subject to the cruel mistress that was menstruation for over half my life, I was unpracticed in the art of noting influences on my neurochemistry in the same way Thecla was. With her years of practice at that, plus what I assumed was a triple sensitivity given her nature as a Riftborn, altered and dharmine, it was no wonder she was the first of the three of us to notice the imminent shift in the weather.

Of course…I know now that the reality is Ba'al-Dinon told her.

It was within the hour that the storm descended, and by three hours more, the turning toward twilight was enough to thicken the look of the Rift radiation spreading out across the landscape. By this point, Eleison had slipped his human form and paced around the base of the tree, near enough to Thecla that he was not just some beast but still able to patrol a bit and curtail any animals I missed. It may be worth taking, for the curious reader, but a moment to try and express what it has always been like for me when I become aware, in a broad sense, of the animals in the Rift weather patterns I have worked with over the years of my military career. Now that the secret is out, I might as well explain it for any interested scholars or perhaps theologians curious about the consciousness of Riftborn.

In my case, I have generally found that feeling the presence of a large number of animals within the Rift is rather like being enveloped by a blanket of waves, or a kind of tangible cloud. I feel the presence of teeming life as one might feel a forming thought yet to be parsed into discernible, ingestible fragments consumable by the linear mind but nonetheless striking one with a kind of indeterminate, highly exciting energy. Gradually, as one focuses on the thought, the plan, the inspiration, (the book, my darling, my beloved!), one feels it breaking into distinct shapes, relief made as this gets distinguished from that.

So it is with those Rift beasts, as I become aware of this crios or that orris pecking about in the dark. A colony of ulemels setting up a small system of webs in some sort of brush some thirty yards away reverberated within my awareness, too small to be useful, and was dismissed; but that giganturn, now that was very interesting…even more interesting as, while the Event went on, it seemed to be developing into an Extreme-level episode when going by the number of animals that seemed to be emerging into the terrain around us. Even as Thecla leaned against me and I pulled her into my arms to smother her with kisses, I felt the animals like a network of selves outside of me, and I stoked within them that same urge to kill I experienced when I thought of the threat being posed to my son and every one of my family members.

But I admit…most especially that insult that had been done to you, Thecla, my wife, oh heart of my heart. One flesh with me.

And a saucy little minx.

"Do you want to know what I've come to believe, Husband?" said Thecla, who looked at me with a new, slightly mad glint in her eyes that has never, I am pleased to say, quite vanished entirely since this time. "What I know to be certainly true?"

My hand, acting on a combination of instinct and deep, primal desire that was intensified by the impact of the Rift upon my nervous system and perhaps also hers, squeezed her tender rump. I inhaled sharply at the sound of her hot moan, asking, "What's that, my angel?"

"I think Dinon let you control him," she told me, smiling wickedly. "He only lives to please, you see, and especially lives to please me. He let himself be manipulated by you, the way a father allows his very young son to win a wrestling match or a footrace."

"Is that so…you little strumpet. Trying to divert my attention? Make me jealous?"

"No," she whispered, glancing down at my trousers and chuckling in that saucy way that stirred my blood as her gaze leapt back up to mine. "Well—yes...o-ah!"

"Naughty girl, lying to Daddy..." I landed a second swat, this time a little lower upon her thigh, and gathered the fabric up to let my hand trail freely along the flesh of the woman I had missed more than I had ever missed anyone. As my wife moaned, squirmed, and gasped with ecstasy, I grazed my lips and tongue along the ridge of her sensitive ear. "How many times did Dinon mount you while you were spirited away?"

"Countless times," she told me, the pulse of pleasure that raced through me at her confession far too maddening to resist. I kissed her deep and hard, my tongue forcing itself upon hers while she groaned with sluttish abandon. Her velvet sex was dewy with longing for me as my fingers curled along a familiar route they knew by sheer muscle memory. "Oh, darling—"

"You had better remember the number," I told her, letting a finger push just into her. The insatiable vacuum tug of her body was so intense that I had to press myself more completely to her, pinning her against the rail of our habitation to make sure she damn well knew what she was going to get from me as soon as all of this was over. She felt me already and locked eyes with me, and I saw longing in her—but a longing laced with conflict. I understood that very well; there was no time to tarry now, yet I couldn't help but savor her for a moment. I had to bask in her before we risked our lives on this vitally important task.

"When you've remembered the number," I told her, murmuring into her ear while she panted with desire, "I want you to tell me honestly what it is, and we're going to have that many whippings for you over the course of the next twelve months...and each time

I beat you, I want all the details of how he fucked you, and where he came in you, and how it felt."

"Oh, Master," Thecla moaned, "oh, Husband, oh, yes, Sir, Malin…I will."

Somehow, we managed to extricate ourselves and make it down the tree in which we'd been stationed all day. The air smelled even more thickly of blood at ground level, and the scent increased in intensity as my wife, our Eleison, and a small retinue of soldiers beat a path to the heart of the fray. Still waiting just beyond the battle, we peered through the violet Rift radiation, listening, waiting. I called for my men to stand down and they obeyed without question, having been prepared for this from the moment the Event began. They withdrew out of firing range, and my party and I crept up through the darkness, listening closely to the sounds of the Hunters calling to one another and squawking into radios. They celebrated what they perceived as a victory, attributing the withdrawal to weakness on the part of my men in the face of the Rift.

Generally, when we did this, the enemy forces were all but exterminated. So there were never any survivors to confirm the rumors about my powers, and those who made it out were typically rounded up and imprisoned or shipped back to Gudrune for trial.

Exhilarated, they talked amongst themselves and laughed and cajoled.

And then the first harpros swooped down, sharp talons extended, nearly scalping a man who only just ducked out of the way. Cursing, he raised his rifle and shot.

But because his back was turned, he never saw the oris thundering up, distinguished its feet under the gunfire too late to avoid having his spine snapped by a gory stab of the standing bird's massive stone-like beak.

Shortly after, the screaming began: the screaming of men far more than of animals, especially as my men deemed that breach clear for entry. Gudrune soldiers stormed in, suppressing those few hunters unoccupied by Rift beasts and assisting the animals in doing what they were compelled to do. They served me unwaveringly, though I have never understood the mechanism by which they recognized which men to attack and which to avoid. I suppose it was a simple flowing of my will into them, but I always wonder. Thecla tells me that she has studied her threads while watching me interface with these creatures, and she has explained that the threads seem to bend around me like spacetime responding to the curvature of some large body's gravity. Perhaps it is these, carriers of some subliminal information, which substitute for the animal's typical instincts for a while. A note for your editor to take out (or leave it in, Dinon, and see if I care): We ought to have experimented on Eleison before writing this book, my darling... or your precious Glenn, when he's in one of his very rare moods to play along.

The phalanx of soldiers around us ushered us into the fray, and by that time the path was manageable the city of Valquist was in no small amount of disarray. Hunters littered the entire map, holding down whatever buildings they could as my soldiers and the animals—more contacted all the time as we advanced into the city—opened new paths and painted the capital in insurgent blood. Thecla kept close to my elbow, in her hands the gun given to her by Arthur.

How glad I was that I had provided him that funding! As we made our way to oris, it occurred to me that, had I not done that—indeed, had I not been, from my youth, plagued with a deep preoccupation and a nagging drive to harness the Rift as a source of energy—my wife may never have been able to come home. Yet was it causal or coincidental? Was the existence of the Rift reactor and my drive to do that all a simple terrestrial manifestation of what, on the other side of the Rift, was occurring simultaneously between Thecla and the being she reveres? Perhaps it was not a question of manifestation so much as equal and opposite reactions: the two photons produced by the collision of a positron and its mirrored electron. The emergence of Thecla into reality out of the reactor from wherever it was Dinon truly had her was only the genesis. The infinitely dense singularity at the center of a black hole destined to spill out the vast explosion that was all space and time.

Sometimes I think Parvati was right to blame my research for the Rift...but, well, I'm sure you know what they say about stuck clocks.

It took us well into the thick of the night, but eventually, we reached the outer wall of the palace and let our demolition team open the way to the lawn while a few others and I held off anyone foolish enough to interfere. Staggeringly few did. Indeed, by this point in the night and the Rift Event, there seemed a drastic reduction in hunters throughout the streets. Far more littered the palace grounds. But between the fog of war and the Rift Event's sublime indigo radiance, the security lights with which they'd flooded the gardens provided poor illumination. Thecla and I, on the other hand, saw just fine...especially once the electricity went off.

This, however, did not please my wife. In fact, she looked terribly frightened and now, whistling for Eleison, caught his great black muzzle in her hands as he bounded over to thump two bloody paws upon her bosom. "Find them, please," she begged, letting her fangs extend and tearing open the fragile blue vein of her wrist to water my mouth. Very cleverly, she soaked the hem of her dress in that sacred substance, then tore a strip free and tied it around Eleison's neck. "So you can smell me," she told him, sending his tails wagging with adulation at her idea to keep him focused while they were parted in the storm. "Keep thinking of me, and you'll think of Rosina and Glenn, too—go on, my love, please, hurry—"

Like a rocket, Eleison lumbered off, and I kissed my wife's bloody hand, licking her fingers and pulling her close. "So wise," I murmured. "My inspired darling...my muse."

Her smile faltered into cold, white terror at the soft click of a gun. My arms around her, I barely needed turn my head to allocate attention to an enemy combatant, thrilled to have caught the Matrix and Master of Gudrune canoodling.

The awareness lasted only a second: only until the pack of ertices sprang, snarling, and tore chunk after chunk from him.

(I am sorry, my wife...I know how much you love them, but I can't forget all the times I've seen their base and vicious nature, full of my violence. Your favorite Rift beasts strike me as less charming than you claim. But, I digress.)

Within the palace, all was dark, the generator having been blown to smithereens and the city's power grid robbed of its potency early in the siege. My wife and I maintained the advantage because, although the hunters had ample night-vision accessories, the nature of such devices paradoxically limited one's field of vision and therefore made our dharmine reflexes worth even more. Her form was truly excellent: I noticed that she mostly shot for the guns in the men's hands or, occasionally and with great reluctance, would go for the knees or hips to bring them down long enough that she could look the other way while I did what needed to be done. So far as I recall, she didn't kill anyone that night. Indeed, I think the last of her killing has already been recorded in these volumes: she is too gentle for this world, my doe.

I saw that so clearly that night. I had never seen her that way before, so it is interesting to have first acknowledged it while we were in the fray. But it was in her eyes, ringed with terror, hope, and shame at once. Every time we cleared a room, every time her whispered "Telly!" rang through the sulphury air, every time she threw out a futile but plaintive, "Glenn? Rosina" to test if they had returned to the palace, I felt her soul reverberate with sorrow to have her calls unanswered. In such danger, she was more a mother than ever: more a lover and wife and friend and partner. A true collaborator in love, longing to make with her family a world worth living in.

She would go to Hell to get that, I had already seen—but only now did I recognize that, beneath the bold adventuress who had come to my aid in the Saalastian warehouse, and found the strength to forgive my grave sins, and endured death for me, and now had traveled across the entire continent to urgently rescue me, was a woman who had never wanted any part of it. This was a woman who wanted peace, and who fought and suffered and sacrificed everything to earn it.

Not just for herself but for every last member of her family.

It was then that the sound of a vase breaking produced a noise in Thecla that was half-gasp, half-laugh. "Telemachus," she whispered, darting off like a shot in the direction of the ballroom, which I had not realized was the source of the sound. That I, who had spent 13 years with the boy, had not by some parental intuition derived my son's relation to this crash, should demonstrate to the reader how changed—how dilated, as she put it earlier in this book—Thecla's soul still was after what she had endured. Her psyche seemed opened as mine was in the presence of Rift animals, but in her case, the effect appeared to be generalized: a more sum-total awareness of events around her, perhaps not unlike a fish experiencing the reverberations of other species swimming through the ocean. I darted after her, lagging behind, my gun raised as we burst through the doors.

And then I set eyes on that blasted Garland, shooting at my son, and I became so angry I confess I remember very little of what ensued until sometime the following day, when it was all over—so I had better let you write the rest, my beloved!

What a relief Malin is to me! I doubt I could have imagined how to write those moments without him. He is much too modest in his descriptions of his military prowess. In truth, he did most of the heavy lifting while we were in Valquist's borders, especially within the palace. I only really came alive, came fully to myself, when I experienced the certainty that the crashing noise—the same sort as Glenn had claimed to have emanated from the same place in a distraction before—had been related to my son. Then I ran, sprinting past my husband, desperate to reach the boy who'd ducked down behind a marble statue while Winston, having escaped his wine cellar cage with the death of the electricity deactivating the security system, reloaded his pistol with his one good hand.

"Too bad your mother isn't here," he said, spitting like the repulsive creature he was. "I'd much prefer if she could watch you die."

"That's the kind of idle talk God loves to reward," I told him, having moved in swift silence behind him to press my own gun to his head. "Too bad for you, his father's here, too."

The truth is that, having gotten the grace of the space to appreciate it, I have come to find Winston's power the most fascinating of most all Riftborn I have met even to this day. (Except for one delightful fellow from overseas who can reach into the temple of your forehead and produce a tiny object shaped like one of your memories, usually no larger than the tip of one's thumb; but he would only do it once for anyone who asked, and always refused to explain why.) What is so intriguing about Winston is—was—the notion that he was the perfect embodiment of the difference between subjectivity and objectivity. While he was under the subjective observation of one person who was not himself, it seemed that he could act as though he did not exist. Pinned down by an additional witness or a single camera, however, and until a line of sight with one of them was broken, he could not do as he would when one of us blinked, which in this instance happened almost immediately. I have suggested in a theological treatise I recently penned and published with the Unversalis Church's most thoroughly approved publication house that the Riftborn charism operates not by some inexplicable function but by a real metaphysical or electromagnetic muscle of consciousness which the sapient being of Rift or Rift-adjacent origin learns to flex over time. Garland was surely exerting the pressure of his attention upon it from the instant he felt the barrel of my gun, and I almost regret that I did not pull the trigger before Malin, though striding toward the hunter, cast a reflexive glance in the direction of our son. The look of murder in Malin's eyes was accompanied by a concerned twitch of his mouth.

And then Winston was gone—that quick, blinking out of existence so quickly I almost breathed a sigh of relief about it.

I lowered the gun while my husband cursed under his breath—then spared no time in vaulting from the mezzanine of the second-floor ballroom to call out, "Telemachus!"

"Papa!" The word erupted with relief from Telly's soul. Our son burst out from behind the base of the statue of Parvati that had, perhaps ironically, shielded him from the hunter's fire. As he dashed to embrace his father, he cried, "I knew you'd really come. He said you would—you're here—"

For the three-second duration of their hug, Telemachus's entire frame sank with ease against his father's chest, and I confess—I felt a small pang of envy, wishing I could be that for the boy, but knowing we would never have that relationship in quite the same way owing to all the time Malin had raised him alone. Indeed, Telemachus, by the mysteries of that bleak, black place whose trajectory seemed forward into time rather than backward along it, had known his father longer than I. How strange!

But there was no time for any of us to ruminate. "We need to leave," urged my husband, calling up to me as he released Telemachus and handed him a gun in one smooth motion. "Come now, darling, let's hurry."

"But what about Eleison?"

At our son's question, my entire being twisted inward in a nauseating lurch.

While Malin looked sharply at me, I gripped the edge of the mezzanine and took a breath. To our son, he said somewhat more casually, "What about him?"

"We can't leave him in the medical ward all by himself! He's blind—how will he leave?"

"That's right," I said, trying to keep my voice steady and calm while Malin's mouth opened and then shut. Only now, as he looked at me, did I see that he hadn't entirely believed me about Eleison's blindness—an opinion he'd perhaps wisely avoided elaborating on earlier. But, as they say, husbands always want to be thought of as Mr. Right; and, seeing he had misjudged that assessment until this moment, I'm not surprised he didn't bring it up. Smiling, I told him, "Let's do this—I'll go see Eleison, and you take the boy out."

"But, darling—"

"Go on," I urged, feeling an increasing sense of sickness and panic and a kind of pre-revelation that I was desperate to escape yet pursue at the same time. "Go on, Husband. I love you with all my heart, soul, mind, and strength. Please be careful. I promise."

Thinking of 'Eleison' lying in the medical ward of the Valquist palace, I recoiled so much that I peered through it all to study instead the threads so as to delay the inevitably intense moments to come.

And for the first time, I asked myself what was *behind* the threads—an impulsive question that was nothing more than the inescapable conclusion that had been waiting to leap upon me at the very same second I pondered. Surely, it was not into Dinon's beautiful world of the reverse side of this or some future iteration of the reality-tapestry. It was too excellently pure even with a whole host of dharmine there; but I was uncertain if the dharmine were there, at least not yet. For if Dinon planned to lead me back, he would surely do the same with others he enjoyed because of some special significance to him or to me. Instead of tending toward that perfect realm, it seemed like what marked a dharmine was an inherent craving to manifest in the terrestrial world and live in it, through it. Though I still saw the appeal, all I really cared to do was pleasantly exist and then retire with my mysterious Bridegroom, and this I saw had been the secret instinct of every moment of my life. In order to fulfill that, I had needed to leave that black place where all dharmine were, but which I could not explain in a sensible way.

Not until it appeared to me in that moment when I peered not just through reality to the threads, but through the threads to the black space beyond—where Winston already had such a head start that I could barely see him dashing across in a direction that was, at best, tangential to ordinary spatial dimensions in a way I defy Euclid or Pythagoras to explain. While my mind reeled at the clash between this sub-background post-pre-non-reality and the tangible spatial dimensions we earth-bound folk know and love, I swayed back from the edge, pushed my hand through the nearest cluster of warp strands, and, teeth bared, squeezed through to the other side and into that strange and lonely limbo.

I kept one hand there to ensure the snag would not close this time, but when I looked over my shoulder, I had the sense that was unnecessary. The large mirror seemed to have been replaced by these threads: I kept my eye on them as I withdrew my hand and stepped back from the fabric wall. When I turned away, then back again, they remained, a taut curtain visible to me as a weaving now—and perhaps, before, as a purple smog, when I was just like everyone else and unpracticed in seeing these fine details.

Arms pumping, legs leaping into action, I sprinted after Winston into the dark, effortlessly springing back to my feet after dancing aside to avoid a few misspent bullets from the hunter.

It was strange to note that our footsteps produced no sound. Part of me hoped that, if I chased him far enough, he might emerge from the mouth of Dinon's sea cave and run face-first into my Love. Yet I knew that hope was folly. In this place, a dharmine could run and run for all eternity and would never reach that beautiful world on the other side of the Rift if Dinon didn't find their presence logically congruent, just, or enjoyable. The only options were to go back to Earth at some point, from some vantage, or to stay in that chillingly silent landscape forever.

I think I saw him before Winston did. Deeming myself close enough to try, I raised my gun and fired twice, but I was no good at aiming while in motion and struck the ground with the second shot; the first shot went just slightly to the left due to the unsteadiness of my hand. I swore and attempted to rectify the weapon's aim, and in so doing, my eye was caught by the doppelganger standing naked at a distance. For some reason, I almost shot that Winston instead, primed to pull the trigger at the sight of the additional man. Just barely, I resisted, desperate to avoid shooting either.

"It never has to be like this, Winston," I told him, feeling greater pathos for Dinon all the time. Finally, I stopped altogether and lowered the gun. Skidding to a halt and whirling around with a kind of focus, a single-mindedness that showed me he hadn't seen his dharmine twin, Winston smiled thinly.

"I'm sure you'd like it to be some other way, 'Matrix', but the truth is that you and your husband are devils sent here to destroy the human race. I'll never work with you. I'll never take your money. You're going to have to kill me."

"Such a primitive worldview. And why would I have to give you money? I could give you a job, or a home, or even let you run a little piece of the continent if you promise to be responsible with it."

"No, thanks."

"Then maybe you'd like it if I found you some lovely rich widow to marry."

"One of your dharmines? I'd rather not."

"You could always embrace being a dharmine yourself," I told him in a darkly cheerful tone. Behind him, his shuffling, somewhat hypnotized-looking duplicate was mere feet away. "The transition into your new life is euphoric…and you'll never have to worry about a little thing like blood poisoning ever again."

"I'd rather never set foot on Earth again than return as a dharmine—especially with your help."

"Well…you really are one for saying the exact type of unfortunate thing that God loves to test."

"What—"

The snide question that was still forming on his lips dissolved into a cry of anguished horror as the strong grip of this so-called 'devil' of himself arrested Winston, leaving him panicked with fear. He thrashed in the dharmine's grip, firing an errant round— one that he had been saving for me, which now amounted to nothing. The younger, uncrippled version of himself pinned him down along the horizontal axis of that black space, which I would hesitate to call a 'floor' in any formal sense, his fangs exposed. Winston threw a sharp elbow back, crushing his doppelganger's nose; but it barely stunned the dharmine, which was still too unconscious to care.

Shocked, horrified, I found myself rooted to the spot, watching a man eviscerate himself in a place that I could not be sure wholly existed.

I have, of course, eaten my own flesh as a consequence of my husband's care for me when first I returned to this terrestrial world…but it was not like this. This was the first time I had ever seen a neophyte dharmine, uncontrolled, unborn, sink his fangs into the flesh of a screaming victim and send forth gouts of blood in the form of some unholy fountain. Stunned, I endured Winston's thrashing and screaming for far too long. His hand leapt to his throat, pressing those crippled fingers against it futilely. Then the blood-soaked teeth of the dharmine clamped down on his wrist, which surged with ribbons of blood in a scene not even I found appetizing. I only awoke from my stupor enough to step away when Winston's efforts to crawl placed him dangerously near my feet. Then I stepped back—a moment I reflect on with shame even now. I may have detested him, and he may have been a repulsive bigot and misogynist who had been making target practice of my son, but—and for some, this is a controversial opinion—I do not believe anyone deserves to suffer in this world. It is not a matter of fairness or fortitude. Suffering is unnecessary: a corollary piece of datum that becomes apparent when reality is unpacked piece by piece, moment by moment, all infinity parsed into aspects that can be known. Indeed, there are certain schools of thought that might suggest I myself became responsible for the production of suffering when I chose to return to abate that very suffering; but that is a reductive notion that implies that I am the center of all existence. And no matter how Dinon seems to wish me to feel that way, I refuse to believe it—if for no other reason than for my own sanity.

Still, whatever shame I felt, it was not a sufficient means to propel me back to Winston and his duplicate. Particularly not when, having stretched out his arms, he made it easy for the dharmine to flip him over and tear into his organs. At last, I covered my eyes, hurrying back the way I had come to that vast barrier of violet-silver weaving that still rose, mercifully, ahead of me. I rushed toward it, so nauseous that I could barely think, and did not immediately hear the moment the growling reduced to a staggered, confused set of breaths.

Then, slowly—more horrible than the sound of intestines being torn or offal being gnashed between fangs—the breaths turned to gasps. Gasps for air; gasps of shock. Gasps that grew to sobs, and then a mournful wail that erupted long and low from the very belly of the fiend who, coming to full consciousness in this dark place, now knew he could never leave this place: for the emergence of the dharmine from that disruptive environment was wholly dependent on an unconscious, instinctive drive, and when consciousness became incorporated, it could make no sense of the experience. There was no knowing where one was or even really what was happening when there was no one else around. There was only oneself and that black void around, and the knowledge that one had done something that could never be undone. There was only horror for Winston now.

And so, my eyes averted, I left him to it, and extended my soul toward Dinon's in gratitude that I had not made such a choice, myself…if, indeed, mistakes of this gravity could ever be called a choice.

41

When I slipped back through to the ballroom of reality, I found myself alone with the acrid sting of gun smoke in my sinuses. There, I mused over how my child must have reacted to seeing me disappear. Malin was inscrutable with such things, even if internally he was given to awe, but Telemachus had no such pretensions and responded with enthusiasm to the amazing feats of the altered and Riftborn around him. The thought of him made me smile; even more so, the impossible surge of relief through my body to think that the boy was now safe in the hands of his father was a sensation that made me weak. I set my hand upon my heart, letting my body sway into that weakness as my soul released the burdens of its cares so completely that I was amazed to recognize how afflicted I had been over the past week of terrestrial time. Inventorying my concerns, I found I had precious little left to endure: Malin and Telemachus were safe and together. By the sounds of the gunfire emanating into the ballroom through the spiderwebbed bullet holes of the glass panels that overlooked the garden, Valquist was well on her way to being secured. Glenn and Rosina, of course, would be safely tracked by Eleison's sensitive nose and kept safe until they could be extracted.

Indeed...in a way, it was only my Eleison who remained the final concern.

My stomach tightened as I worked my thumb nervously along the metal of my gun, my soul gnawing at my body. What did it mean, this second Eleison? His dharmine shadow? If so, I was in for a painful and difficult experience as I decided which Eleison to support, for that would mean they were one, but one in the process of profound change.

Yet this, I sensed, was not the case. I hurried as softly as I could through the disgraced palace halls to the medical wing, but discretion proved largely unnecessary. The gravely wounded were no more inclined to shoot at me than were the dead, and our men had begun formally clearing the building, which I noted from afar as I dashed past the second-floor mezzanine and rushed down to the infirmary. I burst in, half-expecting him to be gone, a mist that evaporated under the sun's observation.

Yet there he was: and there he should not have been.

"Thecla," he said to me softly, Eleison's always sensual voice somehow all the more alluring as he turned his head at the sound of my footfall. "I knew you'd come for me...you always do."

Inhaling sharply, my hands shaking so much I dropped the gun altogether, I hurried to my lover's side. The trembling only grew as my fingers extended to trace the edge of the gauze; his lips parted in pleasure even though I barely touched him.

And, as I unwrapped the bandage without having to be told,

I remembered at last with such an intense surge of anamnesis that it seemed to have been information shielded from my consciousness—yes, there had been a second Eleison before. One time before all this. In this very same palace! I vaguely recalled thinking of the apparition briefly in the week before I disappeared from Earth. Handsome and tall, he had come slinking up to me while I negotiated with the palace guards to go out alone, which they did not allow until my companion arrived. I only recognized the counterfeit when I noticed his silver eyes.

The same silver eyes that adored me now while, in my hands, the bandage dissolved into a bevy of rose petals that blew past my face upon a strange, sourceless wind with no grounds in logic, nor in physics.

And when it passed, free of his handcuff, his disguise—all conceits—he at last stood before me after interminable terrestrial waiting.

Ba'al-Dinon.

My arms were around him a second before I realized fully that he was there before me, the reactions of my body unhesitating while my mind struggled to understand. Even so, I cried out, receiving the knowledge of his bodily presence as though I had been penetrated to the very soul. As I did, he fit one great hand to the back of my head and stuffed my mouth with the tenderest passion I had ever enjoyed, even for all my loves.

"My Bride," he whispered, drawing back to gaze at me through eyes shining like mercury. "My Thecla—I've missed you."

"I've missed you!" I gasped, melting into more kisses and realizing how true that statement was. I had missed Dinon. And—I realized I had never actually seen Dinon with my own eyes. Not with my true eyes. These eyes, these 'dharmine' eyes, as my terrestrial readers and even myself have come to call them so as to have some linguistic distinction. In her greatest moments of weakness and despair, and in times where nothing else could have possibly helped from within or without, my Lord broke through to the wretched little human who I was, defying causality and entropy alike in order to provide my salvation. He had shown me his love even before I truly understood who He was. Before I was reborn, His words were only a dream in my mind, but I had followed Him. I had surrendered to Him.

And as my soul bloomed in His presence, I found happiness.

"You're so beautiful to me, Thecla," Dinon murmured, his hand tracing my brow and cheek. "It defies comprehension. There is a logic to it, of course... but when your mind makes these intuitive leaps, I see fireworks in your spirit."

"You should have told me it was you," I moaned, my cheek resting against his shoulder. "Knowing that would have changed everything. My anxiety all this time—"

"Your anxiety is necessary sometimes." More gentle and somehow casual with me after all I'd been through for him and for the rest of my family, he continued, "There's so much we can do and experience because of being in this place that makes you anxious."

Lips trembling beneath his tenderness, I whispered, almost laughing, "Perhaps, but—you know, it's funny. I chose to be here, I must be here—but the moment I arrived, it was like my heart was torn out. I realized how dreadful it is here, I—I—"

He cut me off by drawing me to his chest, where I gasped softly and rested against his heart with my eyes closed. As I savored his fingers combing gently through my hair, he murmured to me. "It's necessary, Thecla. It's all just a conceit—just a way you and I can be together and know what it means to be truly together."

Breath hitching, I nodded, and a childlike helplessness wracked my soul. All the barriers that had encircled my heart since my father's death—barriers I'd only opened for Malin, Eleison, and Glenn—collapsed together. As his lips brushed my brow, Dinon murmured, "I'm never farther from you than I am right now, even though it seems that way."

"I know," I whispered, tears stinging my eyes. "Yes, I think I do know that. Oh! Dinon—"

With a self-deprecating laugh, I confessed, "When I was alone in the carriage this week, on my way to Malin, before I saw him and while I was still mourning Eleison's blindness, I nearly wished that I had never seen either of them. It's awful to say...but I very nearly wish I had never let any man, even those I most love, touch me until I met you."

With a look of pure sympathy, his thumb rubbing along the outer edge of my eye, Ba'al-Dinon murmured, "Oh, Thecla."

That great hand traced down, his index finger slipping under my chin as he inclined my head to meet his gaze.

"Don't you understand what I mean when I tell you I am every man who has ever touched you?"

These words settled on me like the radiation of the Rift engulfing the landscape at the beginning of a storm. I stared helplessly up into Ba'al-Dinon's silver eyes—and I saw there the silver eyes of Glenn, Eleison, and Malin as they stood in that dark place between here and there. My own eyes as Dinon drew me from the depths of the darkness, a new dharmine, a new creation. The subject of a new world, drawn from and operating within my Lord's imagination, up to and including his representation of himself within it.

There is no way for me to express the revelation. All I can say is that I was overwhelmed by a sensation not of newly acquired truth but of recollection. The look on my face must have been wild with awe and fear and trembling, for his already tender look softened further. Even as I gained the sudden urge to hide—to prostrate myself at his feet—Dinon lowered his head over mine and buried in my mouth a kiss so cool, so worshipful that I felt I could hide in it. All my heart and mind became focused on that kiss; it was a desperate flight from the force of my understanding—and the understanding that this moment of understanding had, as Dinon once remarked to me, occurred more times than even he could count. It would continue occurring more times than even he could count. I saw in that kiss an endless spiral, the trajectory of an unflagging arrow that was the unfolding of eternity in a beautiful, fearsome recursion in which I was always myself, and he was always himself, and all good things in my life emerged from his mercy toward me.

"I love you," Dinon said, raising his head to look into my eyes. "I just want to show you how much."

"But—" Hyperventilating, I managed after a second or two, "Why?"

As I echoed back his question so often repeated in that other place, he smiled.

"Thecla…you should know better than anyone that love is beyond explanation. If it were justifiable, would it still be love?"

Pale with fright, even as part of me wished to bask in this moment forever (and then remembered that, in the queerest way, I did), I shook my head. Smiling gently, Dinon planted another soft kiss upon the crown of my head.

"Just let me love you," he said. "You can do whatever you want. I'll still love you. But you need to understand—"

Even as he maintained that gentle look, his expression grew somewhat serious.

"This is a moment of choice, Thecla."

"A choice between what?" I asked.

"Between eternity in Love," he answered, "or nothing."

"But—" My still-watering eyes flickered around, then fixed on his. "We're already here in eternity, aren't we?"

Softly, the edges of Ba'al-Dinon's mouth turned up in that knowing smile.

Behind me, the door to the infirmary burst open.

Such an interruption, which normally would have sent me leaping out of my skin, was barely a ripple in the vastness of the ocean when I was there, enmeshed in that sweet ecstasy of my Dinon's embrace. It was only the accusatory voice dripping with malice—"Thecla!"—that could have drawn me from that spell, and only because I sensed in it and in the moment the great urgency of action. As I faced my father, I became aware that Dinon had disappeared, or was never visible to anyone but me in that moment in the first place; for, of course, Dinon himself was the subjective expression of a being who loved me and wished to experience himself loving me through me loving him. And as a subjective expression of infinite power, he was the very rules of physics and math and language that had so enchanted him, along with me. He was me—and I knew that, as long as I consented to let him, he would lead me to unfathomable victory.

"Father," I whispered, studying Rigel from across the room and finding the word emitted from my mouth somewhat differently now, with a different weight to it. It had slipped through phases in the blink of an eye: a genuine title of love and trust; the bitter moniker of the dead man; something I interacted with as mother; but by my time in that world, Dinon's sweet home on the other side of the Rift, 'Father' was something heavy and gross. Defiled by violence and treachery and disappointment into this debauched, corrupted thing it was never meant to be. It was meant to be pure—meant to be a complete and perfect expression of love from my bridegroom, who had also in some mysterious way been created by himself, yet who was somehow self-created in and through me. We were married— wedded forever—in eternal harmony. I was his bride.

And when one considered the nature of his mind, working in this elemental state of combinable and parseable binary code and all the corollaries such pairs implied, I could not help but imagine that elusive, still somehow undefinable Rift itself, a split not unlike the one betwixt the hemispheres of the brain.

He was the Rift, and somehow, so was I.

I imagined my gun in my right hand, and there it was.

"So I see you've learned some new tricks," he remarked, studying the weapon that was marbled in the same violet and silver threads that had twisted into the shape of this pistol. "Slipping away from me back there was pretty impressive—and you were on the RMS panel's camera, too, so whatever you're doing is clearly more impressive than Winston's talent."

"You're bleeding," I observed, mentally grabbing onto this concrete detail in an attempt to ground myself for the situation ahead. "So that's why you found us. Very good." So intricate—it was all so intricate, Love!

"Yeah," Rigel said gruffly, barely nodding in the direction of the blood-soaked rag pressing on his shoulder wound. "I came for bandages and heard you talking to yourself. You look like you've been through Hell."

Laughing myself out of my stupor, I swept the heel of my palm briskly under my left eye and then my right. "I suppose to you it would be hell. There were so many Rift beasts there—so many beautiful ones. Ones I've never seen, with names and natures that are still a mystery to me—and the flowers…" The memory filled me with euphoria. Far too fragile a thing, this gun in my hand. I frowned, studying my wounded father.

"Let's call a stalemate, Papa," I told him. "I'll help you."

This man, who had been part of my terrestrial doorway into this world—part of the means by which Dinon contrived to love me—looked at me with disgust… and something like fear, a twitch that danced around the corners of his eyes and mouth and seemed to age him.

"And let your men arrest me? Let your husband have me?"

"My husband would never, ever hurt you," I told him, now reflecting on the word 'husband.' It reminded me of 'animal husbandry,' as though Malin had been the man selected—or imagined—by Dinon to care for me, provide for me…ride me. I chuckled off the slight wave of heat. Sex itself had now dissolved into an even more infinitely deep expression of lovemaking than it ever was before. It was so pure I felt somehow free to think the thought and let it go like a little bird, and carry on in the same second to assure my father that, "Malin cares about me and everyone I love. And even if my husband must act justly, he knows it would be deeply unjust for me to lose you a second time over his own need for retribution. Come now, Papa." Nodding my head toward the cabinets, I kept my eyes cautiously fixed on him and let him see the pain it caused me to beg. "Just let me help you."

His gun hand trembled, and, pained, I stepped toward him on instinct—but he set his finger on the trigger, urging, "Stay back."

"Papa, please." I furrowed my brow. "I'm just like you—we're both intended for a better place than this. If only you would let go of your pride and accept that you must change. You need to learn how to forgive...not just Malin, but yourself."

A scoff of derision escaped Rigel's lips. "Forgive myself for what?"

When his expression tightened, I realized the pity I felt was surely showing in my face, and he mistook it for mockery. "I know you loved Giselle," I told him, doing my level best to keep any trace of admonishment from my voice. I, too, had succumbed to plenty of temptation before and after my marriage to Malin Farrow. "And I'm quite certain she loved you. But you know it wasn't right for the two of you to run off together."

"How dare you say such a thing about the people who gave you life!"

Endeavoring not to correct him, as my life was little more than, as Malin put it, the positron implied by the electron of Dinon's— or at least, so it felt—I said, "There are times when the human freedom to do what is wrong and to make mistakes can and must be redeemed for metaphysical reasons...but he who was redeemed from slavery was still once a slave. My life may have redeemed your adultery with my mother; that does not mean that it was right. And I think, deep down, you know this."

"What about murder, huh?" Looking at me with fury and disgust, my father bared his teeth and justly cut me to the heart. "Don't you think Parvati's death deserves to be repaid? That your husband should be punished?"

"I was the one who killed Parvati," I told him sadly, "and I have *been* heavily punished. I will be punished for the rest of my life, every time I think of it."

Feeling quite sick, in fact, to think that not only was she and everyone else I had killed or had a hand in killing was Ba'al-Dinon or at the very least closely witnessed by him—to think every error I had ever made had been against or witnessed by my Love—I then reconsidered the nature of eternity and whispered, realizing I was helpless to resist my own nature as Thecla of Lescaut, "I'll be punished for all time."

"Not in a court of law," my father ranted on. "Not in the way you deserve. And your husband—trust me when I say he doesn't need to have had a hand in Parvati's death to merit retribution. He's ended plenty of lives other than hers, directly and indirectly."

"And so have you. So have all the men I've loved. We're all deeply flawed—and we're all worthy of love anyway. No one deserves to suffer in this world."

In a bleak, heartless way that was as alien to see upon my father's face as it was terribly sad, Rigel looked through me somehow, and fright streaked along my limbs before he pulled the trigger. I flung myself to the ground, taking the impact instead of a bullet.

But, instead of discharging normally, the neglected old weapon exploded in his hand.

A howl of torture rose from my father's chest as shrapnel from the explosion splintered open his cheek and lodged in his swiftly reddening eye. He stumbled, reeling back from his own burning, bleeding hand and the pain it caused him as he dropped the misshapen chunk of splinters and smoldering gunmetal. Pain filled my soul to know this was what it had come to for him, but there were no thoughts to dwell on. Energized by his rage, he leapt for the terrestrial gun that had slipped from my hand when I had seen Dinon still lying in his Eleison disguise. Quick as that true mate who had taught me to shoot—almost as well as he could—I pinged a few bullets against the abandoned gun and sent it spiraling off into a corner of the infirmary, so far out of my father's reach that he burst into the wretched tears of a powerless old man, as vulnerable and fury-filled as he had become.

"Can't you see you're torturing me, Thecla?" He pushed himself up with a snarl of pain for the strain this put on his damaged shoulder, his good eye turning to glare at me along with his bloodied, perhaps unseeing one. "And soon, your husband will, too. You might as well kill me—go on. Put me out of my misery."

"Don't be ridiculous."

"I'm asking you to!" The words were a desperate, animal shout that rocked me to my core. Sick, afraid for him and for what he wanted from me, I shook my head, my eyes tearing up.

"No."

"Thecla." At last, giving into that terror and letting it show on his face along with the gravity of a very deep sorrow, Rigel pressed his wounded and uninjured hands together in prayer. "Please."

I understood why he wanted me to do it. I understood that it would have been so much easier for him to die rather than humbling himself and facing the consequences of what he had done. I understood that because I, too, had been a slave to pride.

But I could not feel superior to anyone or anything. I saw myself with a clarity I'd never had before.

Shaking my head, I let the gun melt into threads that eased back into that invisible weaving.

"I'm sorry," I told him, looking at him with unfettered sympathy. "I can't."

As if collapsing under the weight of these words, my father doubled over, sobbing. His teeth were clenched, his shoulders shaking as he heaved for breath after breath amid despair. He looked so small, so wretched that my entire soul ached for him. This was a man who had lost everything. Who had, in some ways, cost himself everything. I was gutted, and I looked at him with longing to help but with no idea if he would even accept comfort from me, let alone aid.

Then Ba'al-Dinon stepped out from the shadows in the corner, looking upon my father with a compassionate understanding that far exceeded my own.

"Your daughter is right, Rigel...you're worth more than this place."

My father looked sharply at Dinon, half-recoiling while wearing an expression of existential dread. "Who the hell are you?"

"I am in love with your daughter," he answered softly. "And I love how you once loved her, too. I love that you love her even now, even though you hate yourself so much you'd rather kill her than let her see you live this way. Fail this way. But I love you when you fail, too—because she loves you when you fail."

Ba'al-Dinon raised an arm, extending the dark fuligin of his cloak, and through—or out of, or from—this fabric stepped, with a typical look of dharmine delirium, a nude woman I only half-recognized until Dinon said, "And so does your wife."

"Giselle."

Breathless, my father stumbled up, tears filling his good eye along with his bloodied one. Hearing her name like some distant echo from the depths of a dream, she looked curiously: first at me and then at my father, whom she seemed to recognize with a winsome, dreamy little smile. As my father crossed to take her in his arms without hesitation despite her proximity to Ba'al-Dinon, Rigel cried wildly, "I never thought you'd end up this way, oh, Giselle!"

"There's nothing wrong with being a dharmine," said Dinon gently, studying their embrace. His eyes trailed between me and Giselle as he considered our similarities and our differences. I did, too. Her body was sharper somehow; her expression more naturally haunted, even in this placid condition of pre-consciousness. "You were made for each other. You were made not to die, not to hurt— not to hurt each other."

My father lowered his head in shame, but, with a soft whisper of his name as if just remembering, Giselle touched a hand to his unbloodied cheek and smiled as she kissed his bloodied one. Witnessing this with approval, Dinon told him, "I meant all of you for a better place. When you come to this one, you have no choice but to work within the confines of its systems, and it hurts you. But in the place I made you for and made for you in turn, there is no suffering. Thecla can assure you of that."

"He's telling you the truth," I begged my father to believe, tears shining in my eyes, my throat tighter than cello strings. "It's beautiful."

With a chastened look toward me, my father studied Giselle. I could see the struggle in his soul, the ache, and the questions, and all the doubt in his face.

But, her eyes focusing as his heightened dharmine healing cleared the blood from his damaged orb, my mother smiled at him.

Rigel inhaled sharply, looking up at Dinon.

"How do we get there?"

Extending his cloak in a great black doorway beneath his arm, Dinon told him softly, "Let her show you the way. The path is dark, and you may start to wonder...but don't turn back, and you'll see it, Rigel. I promise...you'll both see it again soon enough."

Her smile widened as she comprehended what was being commanded of her, and my mother slipped an arm into my father's and guided him toward the darkness of Dinon's cloak.

Hesitating only to regard me with shining eyes and humbled features, Rigel disappeared into the fuligin cloth, and I have yet to see him again.

Ba'al-Dinon disappeared with them, and this time, I was not as disturbed by this vanishing. In fact, I was strangely grateful for it. I needed space and peace to let all that had happened settle itself in my brain.

I stood there numbly for a moment and, somehow, I was not even surprised when my husband barged in, frantically scanning the room before he saw me.

"Thecla!"

I exhaled, submitting myself to his arms, realizing how weak I was only in his embrace. He kissed me, held me, and I gazed up into his face as he said gravely, "I was so frightened when you disappeared after Winston—what happened back there? Did you see that other world again?"

There was an answer on my lips—the beginnings of one, anyway—but I could not make a sound before the radio at his hip crackled to life.

"Something's happened, sir," said the voice on the other end as, with a look of annoyance, Malin reluctantly removed the receiver and held it near his ear. "It's very strange—I don't think this has ever happened before."

"What is it?"

"The Rift Event's not over," said the soldier, drawing a look of annoyance from my husband. Before the fellow could finish his thought, my husband's expression turned to one of bafflement and awe. "But," the soldier continued, "we haven't detected the emergence of new beasts for at least the past six hours."

And, as my soul collapsed in a great exhalation of cosmic understanding, my Bridegroom spoke in my heart.

That is how much I love you, Thecla. Go in peace.

EPILOGUE

How strange it is to come to the end of this narrative! My life is still going on—at least, in the measurable, objective sense it is still going on, though I have come to perceive that in a subjective sense it will continue forever, as such is the nature of those souls chosen through the ascendancy of the dharmine. Even those who have not been invited down that path for whatever reasons are sensible to Ba'al-Dinon may, I think, have great comfort in store. In some ways, I am envious of them. Their natures are more of this world, and so the paradise of Dinon's home will seem to them so novel and fabulous it will be at times beyond comprehension. And it is often beyond comprehension to me, and to other dharmines; yet, to the dharmine, it shall not feel like the entry into something new, but the return to a state of resting in the peace of something very old. A home that one always knew deep down one had, a kind of cosmic root like a timeline with room for potentially infinite numbers.

The knowledge that such a home awaited me made the sweetest things sweeter, and the harder burdens light as feathers...though, I confess, my cares are superficial ones by the time of this writing. I live with a heart that is, for the most part, at ease, and though I suffer somewhat in the public sphere and deal with many petty matters I do not enjoy, I am grateful to say that no extraordinary dramas have emerged as of late, and life has settled into a kind of rhythm.

The day I was commissioned to produce these memoirs, I think I awoke with Glenn. He is the jealous type—it's just in his nature—but he's learned to play nicely with Malin and Eleison in social settings, so long as they don't spend too much time kissing me. Even that, though, he's beginning to accept...and eternity is a very long time. That and other heady topics weighed on my psyche as I awoke that day, my entire body vibrating with Ba'al-Dinon's special nearness—or my extraordinary awareness of his nearness, at any rate, for he was always that near, or nearer. *Hello, precious.* The words were delicious and rich in my soul. *It's a perfect day.*

A perfect day for what? I wanted to ask him, especially as I'd just become aware of the fact that I was awake, and I wasn't sure if he'd already been talking to me for some time.

Oh, Thecla...you know I'm always talking to you. I'm about to talk to you right now.

So he was. Glenn stirred beside me, turning over to peer at me with a particularly handsome bleariness to his features. His hand slipped along the curve of my hip to draw me into his embrace, and he murmured, "Hey."

"Hey," I replied softly, my eyes dancing between his chest and his face and then down, down between us before he drew me close enough to feel him, and I gasped. "Oh! Good morning."

Without a word, my gallant rolled me onto my back and made me sigh as he kissed gruffly down my neck. My hands roved over his back to his rear and then trailed up to his shoulders, caressing down his forearms as he pressed himself to me. "You're so horny in the mornings, Thecla," he observed with a chuckle, his anatomy nudging against mine, the glans of his manhood pushing just between the rumpled folds between my labia. I chuckled, drawing his mouth to mine, rocking my hips to take him in and make him gasp at how wet I was.

"I could say the same to you, my darling," I told him, my own sigh rising up into a shameless moan as he pressed just inside of me, filling me, his body overwhelming mine with love and pleasure. I trembled beneath him, bracing myself with my heels as his heavy cock impaled me. Soon enough, I had my wits about me enough to cross my legs behind his rear, my entire body clinging to his as I drew him further into me, his muscles reverberating with a kind of pure male energy that made me feel alive. Though there were still plenty of times when Glenn was happy to let me take charge, I had enjoyed more of his power as of late, and I do mean 'enjoyed' in the most literal sense of the word. With our basic necessities seen to, we could deepen our love for one another: we could be there together, my heroic Glenn and me, and be in a kind of simple, effortless love where there were no pretensions or complicated games as there were with Malin. Glenn just wanted to make love to me: he wanted to stab his lovely cock deep into me and watch the fresh and vivid shock on my face. I received him with a particular vigor that morning, my body clenching so tightly that he grunted my name in my ear, nipped my jaw, and intensified his strokes, rocking my pelvis up for deeper access. I gasped, gripping the pillow behind my head, then shifted my hands to clutch the firmer substance of the headboard's rails. Seeing he was having an effect on me—feeling that he was—Glenn held my face still and savaged me with kisses, each deeper and more electric than the last. Every stab of his tongue along mine increased the sensitivity of my slit around his cock, and every time he drilled into me, I swear he was harder. The simple beauty and power of his masculine form made me cry out, my head rocking back. "Oh, Glenn," I gasped, feeling myself clutch tightly around him. "Glenn, darling, yes, please, yes—"

How different sex was after Dinon showed me its real nature! Of course, it had always been an intimate pleasure, but now I experienced it on a profoundly metaphysical level that, before, had always seemed partially dissolved into mere metaphor. But as I began to cultivate this awareness throughout my time as a dharmine—or whatever energy-consciousness-attention center was the font of the body-mind bursting out from the grounding of the environment—there became something so undeniably tangible about the effects of love. I felt changed every time one of my men came to me, and I had also by then had ample opportunity to know how deeply afflicted I could become when unable to access one of them. It was not that the others were insufficient without the third, no, not at all. But it was rather the feeling one gets when one meditates on that mysterious mathematical proof, the surreal reality that .999 repeating actually equals 1. Yes, they are the same; but only one of them is 1. In the same way, each man contained the fullness of my love within himself; yet that love was sweeter, more whole, more fully masculine, when they were all present to me at least once throughout the day. But sweetest of all are those moments when we are all together.

All except one of us, anyway.

Oh, yes. He was in my heart, in my soul. He murmured sweetly to me and even advised me every day. He arranged strange pranks of timing to amuse me or to make me think of him, and demonstrated his influence over reality by tying my subjective, private conversations with him to some nicely timed objective event externally, such as Glenn's speaking.

Yet Dinon was not really there, was he? He was, of course, he was. He was indeed, in a macrocosmic and microcosmic way. However, in a bodily way, I had not seen him since the infirmary of the Valquist Palace, which was still under reconstruction as our newly established monarchy repaired the historic architecture of the continent's former capital.

How I longed for him who my soul loves! My entire being quaked for him, left arid by the thirst I felt for his arms. That powerful embrace! That mysterious tenderness that only he could provide. For oh, I loved all my men! And I knew without a doubt that they loved me, too.

But there was only one Ba'al-Dinon. Even in a metaphorical sense, the others changed with their moods: with the time of day, with their hunger, with or without a Rift storm, with what I was wearing or had lately done or said. Dinon, however, was absolutely constant; in perfect harmony with me. And it was not so much that he always agreed with me. Indeed, he had a way of humoring my worst impulses, very much like an adult encouraging their child to make a mistake and learn a lesson—which has a way of humiliating me whenever I realize he's doing it. Then there is the firm correction, or even those little moments that seem like punishment…but these, I have come to think, are simply moments where I am punishing myself.

Yet these are nothing beside those moments of reward. Those

sweet consolations—none of which were sweeter than on that day. For, already in a fine mood from Glenn's lovemaking, I hopped up and headed off to my workroom, pleased to spend the day as I preferred until at least noon, when I would grow distractable and stretch my legs in the gardens around Eleison's estate. It would be a fine day to finish my weaving, the portrait of my family which, I am humiliated to say, took me an additional eight months after my husband's return home from war before I could sit down to it and devote to it the level of attention and emotional endowment it required of me. All I had now were the finishing touches—detail work I was eager to add, and for which I had very unique ideas.

But, as I pushed open my workroom door, my entire being leapt with an emotion that was somewhere between ecstatic joy and existential terror: and, as I gripped the jamb, Ba'al-Dinon looked at me with a love unhampered by his disguise as my servant.

"Don't be afraid," he said, "please, Thecla—don't ever be afraid of—"

Already, I had rushed upon him to throw my arms around his neck and hold him close. Burying my face in his chest, inhaling deeply, I was swept up in the jaws of his powerful kiss. I laughed, amazed, searching his face as we parted so he could study me in turn.

"Dinon, Love—have you come to take me away already?"

"No…you would never be satisfied, as tempting as it is. But you've tempted me, Thecla—you tempt me too much. It's not enough to be with you through them. I must be with you as myself. That's what we both want most of all."

"Yes," I whispered, "yes, it is. But—why today?"

"Madame is having an unexpected visitor today. And after that, she may be indisposed for some time with an unexpected project, so I am here to fill in the gaps."

So used to his disappearances that I was afraid to hope he might stay, I asked petulantly, "And then? How long will you be gone the next time?"

Dinon stroked his thumb along my cheek. "I'll never leave you again...but, I never really did, did I?"

Just then, the door creaked open, and Charlotte, having worked the handle with her well-practiced elbow, backed in, bearing a breakfast tray that rattled comically as she turned to find Ba'al-Dinon there with me. "Blast," she cried, her reflexes barely compensating for the fright and managing to keep everything just so. Recovering in an instant, rolling her eyes unapologetically before fixing them upon him as he smiled innocently on, Charlotte thrust the tray into Dinon's hands. "So you're back, are you? Don't startle me like that! I nearly dropped the croissants...you can serve her, then. I'm off to see to the beds."

With a shake of her head and a hefty sigh, Charlotte slipped out again, commenting, "You can never let yourself get comfortable in these houses..."

While I smiled after her, Ba'al-Dinon smiled at me and set the tray down to pour a cup of tea. "Thank you for letting me take care of you, Thecla," he said earnestly, and swiped apricot jam on one of the pastries the old-fashioned way. "I love you."

My heart glowed as I caressed his forearm through the dark fabric of his servant's uniform. "I love you, too."

With a sustained look into each other's eyes, we shared a few sweet seconds. Then, Dinon lowered his gaze and stepped back, studying the brilliance of the blue day outside my window.

"Are you sure you want to weave this morning, Thecla? It's a perfect day."

"It must be," I agreed, smiling with pleasure at him, then following his gaze to watch as Telemachus dove behind some roses in anticipation of Rosina's finding him in their game of hide-and-seek. The garden was quite full of courtiers. In fact, Aleister and his sister were swimming in the pool on the far edge, and a great many visitors were either touring the grounds or engaging in their customary morning stroll. "But if it is indeed a perfect day," I went on, "then it must include a bit of weaving, mustn't it? And, anyway, Dinon...I should get this blasted thing done."

"It does seem a little overdue," he said with a sparkle in his silver eyes, which closed as he bowed. "I'm so glad to be back with you, Madame."

"And with you, Dinon."

"I'll go make my presence known with Master Farrow and Lord Eleison."

While my so-called servant flashed off like a shadow disturbed by the lighting of a lamp, I smiled in his wake, then returned my attention to the weaving.

What a relief! It had been so much work—I had never worked on a tapestry that gave me such a struggle, but it was fair enough to say that, over the course of the past year, my life had not been right. Everything after Parvati's death had been tainted by the consequences of my sin, and my existence had been destabilized until I proved able to change.

Changed, I had. I was meeker now. The spotlight that had once secretly thrilled me was now something I reviled, and I shied away from the media as much as possible now that Malin had once more taken firm stewardship of the territory—and, of course, the continent, for whose leadership he had been unopposed. The decision to move the capital to Saalast was a controversial one, of course, but with free Rift power attracting many new citizens every day, its growth was too organic to argue. It is truly blossoming into a hub of commerce, culture, and cutting-edge technology.

And then, there is the Rift. How beautiful and strange! The Rift had always been accompanied by its animals—yet now there are no more. All the Rift Beasts we had were the ones already unleashed upon us, and those would adapt to terrestrial life, where they could never be rooted out entirely. The Rift had been with us so long that the possibility of an Event without monsters had never occurred to anyone; and it was very amusing to think, after all the hubbub, how many people rightly or wrongly attributed this to the coinciding circumstances involving the Rift Energy Project's initiation. There was indeed a correlation, but the factor at work was not causal.

Though…as my readers know, there are still dharmine, and they are still the cause of alarm and consternation; frequently, the subjects of hunting. That forward-time space running parallel to ours, that mysterious shadowy realm between ours and Dinon's, could go on forever, I suppose. At least as long as Earth exists. If it is potentially infinite, then even the seemingly finite part of it could seem interminably long. It may be possible to stay in there so long that one only exits it at the end of Time itself; though what a soul in that situation would do, I haven't the faintest idea. Rely on Dinon to collect them, I suppose, and live as wild animals with no way to ground oneself in one's own memories by the necessary dharmine autophagy.

But the legacy of the Rift beasts aside from the dharmine lived on, and always would. It would now always be altered, for Malin banned restrictions on their reproduction; and the licensing measures for Riftborn were essentially annihilated, save for statistical purposes. It gave me great joy to think of the good my husband had done, and it relieved me, too. For although my father, Lord rest his soul, was a deeply flawed man by the time we discussed my Malin, that deeply flawed man nevertheless was the only one who could have possibly planted even the smallest seed of doubt against my husband. I did not wish to think Rigel was right in anything, and so my husband's acts of compassion relieved me greatly. Malin was what he needed to be in order to take care of me in the world; and to me, he was my heart's delight. All I could do was forgive my father and know that he was never and would never have been in a position to understand my love for Malin as anything but profane. Yet, to me, I saw in my marriage to my husband the recapitulation of a thousand mysteries pointing to the relationship between my soul and the over-being behind Dinon. Whatever my father had said or believed, I had experienced and sensed things that were so beyond the realm of communication that all I could do was pity him for his limited perspective and pray that he and my mother were truly happy now.

When at last, heaving a great sigh of relief, I finished the weaving and began to think about that detail work, I heard a knock at the door. When it opened, Eleison slunk in, glancing out the window. "How's it going in here today, baby? Wow!" As he bent to kiss the side of my neck a few hungry times, Eleison murmured in my ear, "That looks great."

"I hope it will be when it's completely done—I still have a bit of detailing."

"Huh." Nibbling his way along my pulse, my mate asked, "Well, when you're done detailing...what are you planning on doing?"

"It sounds like you have something in mind..."

"When I look at you, Thecla, baby, I have all kinds of things in mind…and elsewhere. Anyway…tonight? You and Malin and me?"

And perhaps even Ba'al-Dinon—but, we would see. "Very well," I told him, turning to brush my lips along his mouth. "Run along, handsome, and tell Malin to be ready for my arrival tonight."

"Yes, ma'am," said Eleison with pleasure. "I think he's been ready since he woke up this morning."

As was I! Excitement stimulated my body, my core aching with need as he loped out of the room to leave me to my devices again. I studied the piece and decided to brocade Ba'al-Dinon's suit and Malin's eyes in fuligin, then to add a few of the details around the border of Charlotte's apron with the same. Eleison's tie, a hint in Glenn's tawny curls, the little flower upon Rosina's red dress, the shadows at the edges of Telemachus's jaw and cheekbones. Most of all, I used it to decorate myself and wove it into my jewelry and hair until a very fine idea came upon me for a key detail. While selecting a new needle, I unfocused my eyes, searching for some silver thread I could use. Plucking one out of line, I bent forward to use my teeth in the severing, then pulled it slowly from the rest of that metaphysical weaving.

And it was just as I had threaded the eye of the embroidery needle that Ba'al-Dinon appeared, his neatly braided ponytail sliding along his shoulder as he bowed. "Your visitor is here, Madame."

"Who is he?" I added with a pout, "Must you call me 'Madame'?"

How Dinon smiled at that, his fingertip trailing under my chin. "But, Thecla…aren't you my mistress until I take you away to fulfill your role as my bride, becoming my very own, personally and totally mine, finally alone again forever?"

I shuddered, remembering times in my very early childhood when my father would bring me to a playground, and how leaving it always provoked an admixture of dread and relief. "Yes," I murmured. "I am."

"So let me serve you and spoil you and lavish gifts upon you," Dinon said to me, offering his hand to help me up. "Ask for whatever you wish, and I'll give it to you now."

"Wealth enough of my own to feel on rather more equal social footing with Malin and Eleison, even if only slightly…I suppose."

"Suppose?"

Shrugging, I said reflectively, "I trust them, and I love them, and I don't really care about such things anymore. But I would say I have so few terrestrial ambitions outside my desire to love you and my family that it's no use to ask for something that isn't practical, and my money can help my family in addition to making me feel as though I can 'play along' with the boys."

"You know you don't need to gloss anything with me, Thecla," he said wryly, making me glance at the ceiling—a Charlotte affectation absorbed secondhand.

"I'm not glossing, Love… I'm giving you my very real opinion. Doesn't it go without saying that I want to have money so I can have some for myself? But Malin allocates me plenty, you know. At any rate…" Eyes crinkling with my smile, I leaned into Dinon's embrace. "Dress me for our guest, please?"

Only a few moments later—for Dinon delighted me with those supernatural powers of his yet again, putting up my hair and installing me in a very fine semi-formal dress with barely a look— we made our way down the stairs to the Karrisregion house's foyer, where a tall, swarthy old fellow leaned upon a cane and talked a little with my son.

"I wouldn't be so sure of that," he was telling Telemachus, who looked quite riveted as they wrapped up whatever conversation had been started to fill the void of my absence. "It seems to me you've already met the woman you're going to marry."

While my son's nose wrinkled in confusion, I recognized the man's prescience and, quickly, his cane. With a cry of excitement, I hurried forward, hand extended, and was not at all surprised when Renard, the blind fortune-teller, turned to shake my hand just as if he could see.

"Madame Farrow," he said with hearty vigor, in better shape than he'd appeared to be when last I saw him. He was still an old man and still quite tired after his time traveling, but there was something so lively about him that one could not help but be drawn in, whereas before he had exuded something almost sinister. Now, as with so much else that had changed along with the Rift, it seemed that disguise of the carnival worker had fallen away. Perhaps it was only Malin's policies, which had opened to Renard and other Riftborn many more licit avenues of work.

"I don't want to take up too much of your time," he told me as I released his hand. "Has your man here told you what I want? I know he knows."

Smiling, wondering whether or not this fellow knew that his powers stemmed from that same knower's decision to allow lesser or greater degrees of knowledge, I shook my head and said, "No, dear, I haven't heard a thing yet. I'm just so glad to see you! If you'll pardon the expression."

"I see plenty...and so do you. You know what people who see as well as you and I do owe the world, Madame Farrow?"

Hesitating, I shook my head. Renard leaned in, saying while tapping his cane upon the floor, "Our writing."

How intriguing! I had hardly expected such a thing. "You're a writer, Renard?"

"And publisher. Have to do something to fill the time between traveling and set-up. Besides—it's a lot of good information a man like me can find all over this territory, this continent. I don't like to toot my own horn, but I'm a crackerjack researcher."

"I can imagine."

"But there's something you have that I just can't get to, ma'am, and I'm wondering if you might oblige me with a little project of mine. The repayment for those fortunes I told you."

Perking further, I nodded. "Yes, of course—what is it, what can I do?"

"Well, you see, I wrote a little biography of your husband once, and—"

At last, I made the connection, and looked at this fellow in some real shock. "Why—you're R.J. Larkin!"

"Renard Julius, yes, ma'am."

"Isn't that funny! Tsk, you really did paint quite a portrait of Malin...but wasn't that enough for you to live on, if the book was distributed widely enough for me to find it in the proverbial wild?"

"You do not know much about the life of a writer, do you, Madame?"

While I laughed at his impudent but quite valid remark, I spread my hands and confessed, "I've always been much more of a reader than a writer."

"Well, then, it may surprise you to know that many authors are terrifically poor; most, in fact. The types of books people like to read are not always the ones we most enjoy writing, and even a popular title is bound to be supplanted soon enough, with very few exceptions. That is…unless you're the former Matrix of Gudrune."

Now I saw where he was really going with this. Stealing but a brisk glance at Dinon, I listened as Renard said, "In exchange for your fortunes, I would like exclusive rights to publish your memoirs. I'll pay you, of course—royalties by the book. We can split them, and both walk away very happy. Your debt is paid, my retirement fund is secured. Voila."

"I've never written before," I said thoughtfully. "Well, letters, but that's really quite different."

"If you know how to read, you know how to write."

With a laugh, I confessed, "Dear Renard, I haven't read a non-fiction memoir since leaving school, I think. I'm much more of a romance reader…the unconscionably steamy type."

"The more scandalous, the better! Write it like that. Then it won't be the average non-fiction historical memoir. It'll be something real and alive that the young ladies of Gudrune can read over and over. Incentivize them to learn their nation's history."

With a laugh, I stroked my chin and nodded in thought. "It's a very strange story."

"Controversy is good in book reviews, especially for this kind of book."

"It might wind up being quite long."

"Excellent—several volumes."

Regarding Ba'al-Dinon again, reflecting on what he had said about an unexpected project, I suggested, "It would be an important way to chronicle what the terrestrial relationship with the Rift used to be like."

"Indeed, it would, Madame. If you would like my advice, I think it's a worthwhile venture."

"And I do owe him," I noted, tapping the edge of my jaw. Well...the idea was a little overwhelming, but I supposed if I could weave a tapestry, I could surely string together enough words for at least one book. After a few long seconds, feeling the growing fire of inspiration rising up through me, I extended my hand.

"Very well, Mister Larkin—you have a deal." I smiled, and we shook on it. "It's only fair you should have a book more sympathetic to Malin in your publishing line-up, after all."

"If anyone can paint a portrait of his charms, it's you."

"Very good. Well, why not let's draft a contract of some sort and make things formal? What an interesting challenge you've set for me, Renard." Musing on the structural questions now rotating through my head, I allowed the thoughts to carry me away, pondering how I would start. Perhaps with my father—no, with Eleison. That felt right somehow. "Yes—I think this is a very interesting project."

"I'm glad to hear you've got a good idea."

"Dinon," I said, unhesitatingly stroking his arm as I turned away, "help Mr. Larkin to his guest suite, and we can go over things in greater detail soon."

"With pleasure, Thecla." Ba'al-Dinon watched me with brilliant eyes as I smiled and glided up the stairs, my mind slowly raising up, up into the clouds of imagination. I wondered what exactly it was I would use these books to say. How could I frame my family, my life, my own journey in a way that made sense? How could I show who I really was through this tale, this unpacking of my soul?

Back at my loom, I picked up my silver-threaded needle and leaned forward, carefully weaving the otherworldly weft into Ba'al-Dinon's irises. As I did, I thought about my book—my story. Who was I at the start, and who would I be in the end? Where would I leave off? What would I leave out? I leaned back and assessed the tapestry. My Love's silver eyes gleamed with uncanny life and truth through the fabric in such a way I saw it was simply him, another conduit for his gaze upon me. Would the books revolve around any one man? How could they? I loved them all. Yet it was fair to say Ba'al-Dinon was them all—so perhaps the most secret and brilliant heart of the story would be him, and my relationship to him. It would catalogue my sorrows and my triumphs and provide an unflinching look at my sins. It would invite the reader into the intimacy of my loves and the texture of each one as they grew and changed in those first years that marked the beginnings of my family.

But most of all, as I smiled at this tapestry—this portrait of my family—I found myself certain of one thing: however long it was, however exotic it was, however strange and heartbreaking and exciting it was—I would be jolly well sure to leave it at this, this perfect day, whence we lived happily ever after.

From the corridor, Malin called my name.

I rose to greet my husband.

OTHER WORKS
FROM PAINTED BLIND PUBLISHING

REGINA WATTS

INDUSTRIAL DIVINITY (2020)
WILD GIRL RUNNING (2020)
DOTTIE FOR YOU SEASON 1 (2021)
THE BURNINGSOUL SAGA (2021-2025)
I WAS AN OP DEMON LORD (2021-)
BE MY BULLY (2021)
SEDUCED BY SABINE (2021)
MAYHEM AT THE MUSEUM (2021)
IDOL (2022)
TEXAS CRUEL (2023)

M. F. SULLIVAN

DELILAH, MY WOMAN (2015)
THE LIGHTNING STENOGRAPHY DEVICE (2017)
THE DISGRACED MARTYR TRILOGY (2019-2020)
MACHINA CONSCIENTIA (2025)

FINN VANDERGRIFT
SKINSLUT (2023 - with REGINA WATTS)

ABOUT THE AUTHOR

Ada Dart is an author of reverse harems and romances with undercurrents so dark you'll only want to read them at night. Her brooding, intellectual heroes defy boundaries and straddle conventions: whether older or younger, commanding or sensual, the men Dart writes are sure to keep readers' imaginations going long after the final page. In addition to writing other pulp genres under the pen name Regina Watts, Dart enjoys spending time watching opera with her cat and her real life age-gap partner of over half a decade.

ABOUT THE PUBLISHER

Painted Blind Publishing and its erotic imprint, Painted Blue Publishing, are the brainchild of M. F. Sullivan. Founded in 2015 while Sullivan resided in Tucson, PBP is a house dedicated to bringing readers the finest in consciousness-expanding fiction. Be sure to check out the wide variety of essays available for free at paintedblindpublishing.com to learn more about the company, Dart, and Sullivan.